His for Christmas

CARA COLTER
MICHELLE DOUGLAS
JANICE LYNN

D1627914

LM 1511850   9

Published in Great Britain 2014
by Mills & Boon, an imprint of Harlequin (UK) Limited,
Eton House, 18-24 Paradise Road, Richmond, Surrey, TW9 1SR

HIS FOR CHRISTMAS © 2014 Harlequin Books S.A.

Rescued by his Christmas Angel, Christmas at Candlebark Farm and *The Nurse Who Saved Christmas* were first published in Great Britain by Harlequin (UK) Limited.

Rescued by his Christmas Angel © 2010 Cara Colter
Christmas at Candlebark Farm © 2010 Michelle Douglas
The Nurse Who Saved Christmas © 2010 Janice Lynn

ISBN: 978-0-263-91212-8
eBook ISBN: 978-1-472-04507-2

05-1214

Harlequin (UK) Limited's policy is to use papers that are natural, renewable and recyclable products and made from wood grown in sustainable forests. The logging and manufacturing processes conform to the legal environmental regulations of the country of origin.

Printed and bound in Spain
by CPI, Barcelona

RESCUED BY HIS CHRISTMAS ANGEL

BY
CARA COLTER

Cara Colter lives on an acreage in British Columbia with her partner, Rob, and eleven horses. She has three grown children and a grandson. She is a recent recipient of the *RT Book Reviews* Career Achievement Award in the 'Love and Laughter' category. Cara loves to hear from readers, and you can contact her or learn more about her through her website: www.cara-colter.com.

To Lynne and Larry Cormack
with heartfelt gratitude
for twenty-five years of friendship

CHAPTER ONE

TEARS. BOOKS THROWN. And pencils. Breakage. Name-calling. Screaming. Hair-pulling. It was like a scene from a bad marriage or the kind of drama that a reality television show *adored,* rife with mayhem, conflicts, conspiracies.

But it wasn't a bad marriage, or bad TV.

It was Morgan McGuire's life, and it didn't help one bit that each of the perpetrators in today's drama had been under four feet tall. The day had culminated with a twenty-one-child "dog pile on the rabbit."

It was the kind of day they had failed to prepare her for at teacher's college, Morgan, first-year first-grade teacher, thought mournfully.

And somehow, fair or not, in her mind, it was all *his* fault.

Nate Hathoway, father of Cecilia Hathoway, the child who had been at the very center of every single kerfuffle today, including being the rabbit in that unfortunate dog pile.

Now, Morgan McGuire paused and stared at the sign in front of her. Hathoway's Forge. Her heart was beating hard, and it wasn't just from the walk from school, either.

Don't do it, her fellow teacher Mary Beth Adams had said when Morgan had asked her at lunch if she thought she should go beard the lion in his den.

Or the devil at his fire, as the case might be.

"But he's ignoring my notes. He hasn't signed the permission slip for Cecilia—"

"Cecilia?"

Morgan sighed. "Ace. Her real name's Cecilia. I think she needs something feminine in her life, including her name. That was what the first fight this morning was about. Her hairstyle."

Not that the haircut was that new, but today there had been a very unusual new styling for the haircut. How could *he* have let her out of the house looking like that?

"And then," Morgan continued, "one of the kids overheard me ask her about the permission slip to be in *The Christmas Angel*. She didn't have it."

The production of *The Christmas Angel* was descending on Canterbury, Connecticut.

The town had been chosen by the reclusive, aging troubadour Wesley Wellhaven for his second annual Christmas extravaganza.

The fact that Mr. Wellhaven would be using local children—the first graders would be his backup choir if Cecilia managed to get her permission slip signed—had whipped the children into a frenzy of excitement and dramatic ambition.

"Morgan, rehearsals are starting next week! Mrs. Wellhaven is arriving to supervise the choir!" Mary Beth said this urgently, as if the fact could have somehow bypassed her fellow teacher.

"I know. And I already told the class that we are all doing it, or none of us is doing it."

"That was foolish," Mary Beth said. "Can't Ace Hathoway just sit in the hall and read a book while the rest of the children rehearse?"

"No!" Morgan was aghast at the suggestion. But meanwhile, poor Cecilia was being seen as the class villain because she was the only one with no permission slip. "If I don't talk to him, Cecilia is going to continue to suffer."

Mary Beth shook her head. "Just let her sit in the hall."

"It's not just the permission slip. I have to address some other issues."

"You know that expression about going where angels fear to tread? That would be particularly true of Hathoway's Forge. Nate wasn't Mr. Sunshine and Light before his wife died. Now…" Mary Beth's voice trailed away and then she continued. "It's not entirely Nate's fault, anyway. Kids always get high-strung around Christmas. It's hitting early because of all the hoopla around the whole *Christmas Angel* thing."

Naturally, Morgan had chosen to ignore Mary Beth's well-meaning advice about going to visit Nate Hathoway.

Now, taking a deep breath, she turned off the pavement and up the winding gravel driveway, lined by trees, now nearly naked of leaves. The leaves, yellow and orange, crunched under her feet, sending up clouds of tart aroma.

Morgan came to a white house, cozy and cottage-like, amongst a grove of trees. It was evident to her that while once it had been well loved, now it looked faintly neglected. The flower beds had not grown flowers this year, but weeds, now depressingly dead. Indigo paint, that once must have looked lively and lovely against the white, was peeling from the shutters, the window trim and the front door that was set deep under a curved arch.

Despite the fact light was leeching from the late-afternoon autumn air, there were no lights on in the house.

Morgan knew Cecilia was at the after-school program.

The road continued on to a building beyond the house. It dwarfed the house, a turn-of-the-century stone barn, but a chimney belched smoke, and light poured out the high upper windows. Morgan realized it was the forge.

She drew nearer to it. A deep, solid door, under a curved arch that mirrored the one on the house, had a sign on it.

Go Away.

That was the kind of unfriendly message, when posted on a door, that one should probably pay strict attention to.

But Morgan hadn't come this far to go away. She drew a deep breath, stepped forward and knocked on the door. And was ignored.

She was absolutely determined she was not going to be ignored by this man anymore! She knocked again, and then, when there was no answer, turned the handle and stepped in.

She was not sure what she expected: smoke, darkness, fire, but the cavernous room was large and bright. What was left of the day's natural light was flowing in windows high up the walls, supplemented by huge shop lights.

In a glance she saw whiskey-barrel bins close to the door full of black wrought iron fireplace pokers and ash shovels, an army of coat holders, stacks of pot racks. Under different circumstances, she would have looked at the wares with great interest.

Nate Hathoway, she had learned since coming to Canterbury, had a reputation as one of the finest artistic blacksmiths in the world.

But today, her gaze went across the heated room to where a fire burned in a great hearth, a man in front of it.

His back was to her, and even though Morgan suspected he had heard her knock, and even heard her enter, he did not turn.

From the back, he was a breathtaking specimen. Dark brown hair, thick and shiny, scraped where a leather apron was looped around his neck over a denim shirt. His shoulders were huge and wide, tapering perfectly down to a narrow waist, where the apron was tied. Faded jeans rode low on nonexistent hips, hugged the slight swell of a perfect masculine butt.

Even though his name was whispered with a kind of reverence by every single female Morgan had encountered in Canterbury, she felt unprepared for the pure *presence* of him, for that masculine *something* that filled the air around him.

She felt as if the air was being sucked from her lungs and she debated just leaving quietly before he turned.

Then she chided herself for such a weak thought. She was here for the good of a six-year-old child who needed her intervention.

And she was *so* over being swayed by the attractions of men. A bitter breakup with her own fiancé after she'd had the audacity to consider the job—her own career—in Canterbury still stung. Karl had been astonished that she would consider the low-paid teaching position in the tiny town, then openly annoyed that his own high-powered career didn't come first. For both of them.

Morgan was making a new start here. No more stars in her eyes, no more romantic notions.

Her mother, whom Morgan had thought liked Karl, had actually breathed a sigh of relief at Morgan's breakup news.

Darling, I do wish you'd quit looking for a father figure. It makes me feel so guilty.

Not guilty enough, however, to postpone her vacation to Thailand so they could spend Christmas together. In lieu of sympathy over her daughter's failed engagement her mother had given her a book.

It was called *Bliss: The Extraordinary Joy of Being a Single Woman.*

Surprisingly, given that she had initially resented the book being given to her in the place of some parental direction about how to handle a breakup, Morgan found she was thoroughly enjoying *Bliss.*

It confirmed for Morgan the absolute rightness of her making the break, learning to rely only on herself to feel good. Not her boyfriend. And not her mother, either.

Two and a half months into her teaching career and her new location in Canterbury, Morgan loved making her own decisions, living in her own home, even buying the groceries she liked without living in the shadow of a nose wrinkling in disapproval—*Do you know how many grams of sugar this has in it?*

Just as *Bliss* had promised, every day of being an independent woman who answered to no one but herself felt like a new adventure.

But now, as the man at the forge turned to her, Morgan was stunned to find she had no idea at all what the word *adventure* meant.

Though something in the buccaneer blackness of his eyes promised he knew all about adventures so dark and mysterious they could make a woman quiver.

One who wasn't newly dedicated to independent living.

Morgan fervently reminded herself of her most recent joy—the absolute freedom of picking out the funky purple sofa that Karl, and possibly her mother, too, would have hated. Amelia Ainsworthy, author of *Bliss,* had dedicated a whole chapter of the book to furniture selection and Morgan felt she had done her proud.

But now that moment seemed far less magical as this man, Nate Hathoway, stood regarding her, his eyes made blacker by the flicker of the firelight, his brows drawn down in a fierce lack of welcome that echoed the sign on the door, his stance the stance of a warrior. Hard. Cynical. Unwavering.

One hand, sinewy with strength, held a pair of tongs, metal glowed orange-hot at the end of them.

Morgan felt her breath catch in her throat.

Cecilia's father, Nate Hathoway, with his classic features, strong cheekbones, flawless nose, chiseled jaw, sensuously full lips, was easily the most handsome man she had ever set eyes on.

"Can't you read?" he growled at her. "I'm not open to the public."

His voice was rough, impatient and impossibly sexy.

It shivered across the back of Morgan's neck like a touch.

Ignoring her, he placed the hot iron on an anvil, took a hammer and plied his strength to it. She watched, dazed, at the ripple of disciplined muscle as he forced the iron to his will. His will won, with ease.

"Um, Mr. Hathoway, I can read, and I'm not the public. I'm Cecilia's teacher."

The silence was long. Finally, his sigh audible, he said, "Ah. Mrs. McGuire." He shot her a look that seemed uncomfortably hostile and returned his attention to the metal. He doused it in a bath. It sizzled and hissed as it hit, and he turned his eyes back to her, assessing.

Maybe it was just because they were so dark that they seemed wicked, eyes that would belong to a highwayman, or a pirate, or an outlaw, not to the father of a fragile six-year-old girl.

Morgan drew in a deep breath. It was imperative that she remember the errand that had brought her here. The permission slip for Cecilia to participate in *The Christmas Angel* was in her coat pocket.

"It's Miss, actually. The kids insist on Mrs. I corrected them for the first few days, but I'm afraid I've given up. Everybody over the age of twenty-one is Mrs. to a six-year-old. Particularly if she's a teacher."

She felt as if she was babbling. She realized, embarrassed, that it sounded as if she *needed* him to know she was single. Which she didn't, Amelia forgive her!

"*Miss* McGuire, then," he said, not a flicker in that stern face showing the slightest interest in her marital status.

He folded those muscular, extremely enticing arms over the massiveness of his chest, rocked back on his heels, regarded her coolly, *waiting,* the impatience not even thinly veiled.

"Morgan," she said. Why was she inviting him to call her by her first name? She told herself it was to see if she could get the barrier down in his eyes. Her mission here was already doomed if she could not get past that.

But part of her knew that wasn't the total truth. The total truth was that she did not want to be seen *only* as the new first-grade teacher, and all that implied, such as boring and prim. Part of her, weak as that part was, was clamoring for this man to see her as a woman.

There was an Amelia Ainsworthy in her head frowning at her with at least as much disapproval as Karl ever had!

But that's what the devil did. Tempted. And looking at his lips, stern, unyielding, but somehow as sensual as his voice, she felt the most horrible shiver of temptation.

"It's obvious to me Cecilia is a child who is loved," Morgan said. It sounded rehearsed. It *was* rehearsed, and thank goodness she'd had the foresight to rehearse something, or despite her disciplined nightly reading of *Bliss,* Morgan would be standing here struck dumb by his gorgeousness and the fact he *exuded* male power.

Now, she wished she had rehearsed something without the word *love* in it.

Because isn't that what fallen angels like the man in front of her did? Tempted naive women to believe maybe love could soften something in that hard face, that maybe love could heal something that had broken?

He said nothing, but if she had hoped to soften him by telling him she knew he loved his daughter, it had not succeeded. The lines around his mouth deepened in an expression of impenetrable cynicism.

"Cecilia has the confidence and quickness of a child sure of her place in the world." Originally, Morgan had planned on saying something about that quickness being channeled somewhere other than Cecilia's fists, but now she decided to save that for a later meeting.

Which assumed there would be a later meeting, not that anything in his face encouraged such an assumption.

She had also planned on saying something like in light of the fact her mother had died, Cecilia's confidence and brightness spoke volumes of the parent left behind. But somehow, her instinct warned her not to speak of the death of his wife.

Though nothing in his body language, in the shuttered eyes, invited her to continue, Morgan pressed on, shocked that what she said next had nothing to do with the permission slip for *The Christmas Angel*.

"It's the *mechanics* of raising a child, and probably particularly a girl child, that might be the problem for you, Mr. Hathoway."

It's none of your business, Mary Beth had warned her dourly when Morgan had admitted she might broach the subject while she was there about the permission slip. *You're here to teach, not set up family counseling services.*

Morgan did not think sending the odd note home qualified as family counseling services. Though Nate Hathoway's failure to respond to the notes should have acted as warning to back off, rather than invitation to step in.

Obviously, he was a man who did not take kindly to having his failings pointed out to him, because his voice was colder than the Connecticut wind that picked that moment to shriek under the eaves of the barn.

"Maybe you'd better be specific about the *problem*, Miss McGuire."

Cecilia needed her, and that made Morgan brave when it felt as if courage would fail her. "There have been some incidents of the other children making fun of Cecilia."

In half a dozen long strides he was across the floor of his workshop, and staring down at her with those mesmerizing, devil-dark eyes.

She could smell him, and the smell was as potent as a potion: the tangy smell of heat and hard work, molten iron, soft leather. *Man.*

"What kids?" he asked dangerously.

Morgan had to tilt her chin to look at him. She did not like it that his eyes had narrowed to menacing slits, that the muscle was jerking in the line of his jaw, or that his fist was unconsciously clenching and unclenching at his side.

This close to Nate Hathoway, she could see the beginning of dark whiskers shadowing the hollows of impossibly high cheekbones, hugging the cleft of his chin. It made him look even more roguish and untamable than he had looked from across the room.

His lips were so full and finely shaped that just looking at them could steal a woman's voice, her tongue could freeze to the roof of her mouth.

"It's not about the kids," she managed to stammer, ordering her eyes to move away from the pure sensual art of his mouth.

"The hell it isn't."

"You can't seriously expect me to name names."

"You tell me who is making fun of Ace, and I'll look after it. Since you haven't."

Morgan shivered at his accusing tone, but felt her own strength shimmer back to life, her backbone straightening. She was as protective as a mother bear with cubs. All of those children were her cubs. Sometimes, looking out at the tiny sea of eager faces in the morning, it still stunned her how tiny and vulnerable six-year-olds could be.

And, after a day like today, it stunned her how quickly all that innocence could turn to terror on wheels. Still, she was not going to sic him on *her* kids!

She took a deep breath, tried not to let her inner quiver at the expression on his face show. "We are talking about six-year-olds. How would you propose to look after that, Mr. Hathoway?"

"I wasn't going to hunt them down," he said, reading her trepidation, disdain that she would conclude such a thing in the husky, controlled tone of his voice. Still, he flexed one of the naked muscles of his biceps with leashed anger.

Morgan's eyes caught there. A bead of sweat was slipping down the ridge of a perfectly cut muscle. She had that tongue-frozen-against-the-roof-of-her-mouth feeling again. Thank goodness. Otherwise she might have involuntarily licked her lips at how damnably *tantalizing* every single thing about him was.

"I wouldn't deal with the children," he continued softly, "but I grew up with their parents. I could go have a little talking-to with certain people."

The threat was unmistakable. But so was the love and pure need to protect his daughter. It felt as if that love Nate Hathoway had for his daughter could melt

Morgan as surely as that fire blazing in the background melted iron.

"Mr. Hathoway, you just need to take a few small steps at home to help her."

"Since you are unable to help her at school?"

The sensation of melting disappeared! So did the tongue-stuck-to-the-roof-of-her-mouth feeling. She was not going to be attacked!

"That's unfair!" She was pleased with how calm she sounded, so she continued. "I have twenty-two children in my class. I can't be with every single one of them every single second, monitoring what they are saying among themselves, or to Cecilia."

"What are they saying?"

There were old incidents she could bring up: the fun they had made of Cecilia's hair before he had cut it, how someone had cruelly noticed how attached she was to a certain dress. Though it was always clean it was faded from her wearing it again and again. With boys' hiking boots, instead of shoes. They were situations that had caused teasing. Cecilia was no doormat. She came out fighting, and looking at the man before her, Morgan was pretty sure where she'd learned that!

Still, Morgan had prided herself on creatively finding a remedy for each situation. Only it was becoming disheartening how quickly it was replaced with a new situation.

Morgan had to get to the heart of the problem.

"Just for an example, this morning Cecilia arrived with a very, er, odd, hairstyle. I'm afraid it left her open to some teasing even before she revealed her secret holding ingredient."

"She told me it was hair gel."

"It was gel, but not hair gel."

He looked askance at her.

"She didn't know gel wasn't gel. She used gel toothpaste."

He said a word people generally avoided using in front of the first-grade teacher. And then he ran a hand through the thick darkness of his own hair. Her eyes followed that motion helplessly.

"Didn't you say anything to her about her hair before she left for school?" she managed to choke out.

"Yeah," he said ruefully, the faintest chink appearing in that armor. "I told her it looked sharp."

It had looked *sharp*. Literally. But if she planned to be taken seriously, Morgan knew now was not the time to smile.

"Mr. Hathoway, you cannot send your daughter to school with a shark fin on top of her head and expect she will not be teased!"

"How do I know what's fashionable in the six-year-old set?" he asked, and a second chink appeared in the armor. A truly bewildered look slipped by the remoteness in his dark eyes. "To be honest, her hair this morning seemed like an improvement on the raised-by-wolves look she was sporting before she finally let me talk her into cutting her hair."

Remembered hair battles flashed through his eyes, and Morgan found her gaze on those hands. It was too easy to imagine him trying to gentle his strength to deal with his daughter's unruly hair.

But the last thing Morgan needed to do was couple a feeling of tenderness with the animal pull of his male magnetism!

"It was not an improvement," she said firmly, snippily,

trying desperately to stay on track. "The children were merciless, even after I made it clear I wanted no comments made. The recess monitor told me Cecilia got called Captain Colgate, Toothpaste Princess and Miss Froggy Fluoride."

"I'll bet the froggy one was Bradley Campbell's boy," he said darkly. "Ace told me he's called her Miss Froggy before, because of her voice."

"Her voice is adorable. She'll outgrow that little croakiness," Morgan said firmly. "I've already spoken to Freddy about teasing her about it."

Nate glowered, unconvinced.

Morgan pressed on. "To make matters worse, today at lunch break someone noticed her overalls. They said she had stolen them, that they belonged to an older sister and they were missing."

"Somebody accused Ace of *stealing?*"

Morgan thought he was going to have problems with the joint in his jaw if he didn't find a different way to deal with tension.

"Cecilia said she had taken the overalls from the lost-and-found box."

"But why?" he asked, genuinely baffled.

"When's the last time you bought her clothes?" Morgan was aware of something gentling in her voice. "Mr. Hathoway, I sent you a note suggesting a shopping trip might be in order."

"I don't read your notes."

"Why not?"

"Because I don't need a little fresh-out-of-college snip like you telling me how to raise my daughter. Oh, and I also don't do shopping."

"Obviously! And your daughter has suffered as a consequence!"

He glared at her. A lesser woman might have just touched her forelock and bowed out the door.

But blessed—or cursed—with the newfound strength of a woman who was working her way through *Bliss* and making careful notations in the margins, and who had purchased a sofa in a rather adventurous shade of purple, she plunged on.

"Cecilia told me that's why she took the overalls from the lost-and-found box…to spare you a shopping trip. She doesn't have anything that fits properly. She wears the same favorites over and over. She wears hiking boots with skirts, Mr. Hathoway! Haven't you noticed that?"

He said that word again, and something besides hardness flickered in those eyes again. It was worse than the hardness. Pain so deep it was like a bottomless pool.

"I guess I didn't notice," he said, the warrior stance shifting ever so slightly, something defeated in his voice. "Ace could have said something."

"She seems to think if she asks nothing of you, she's protecting you in some way."

The smallest hint of a smile tickled across lips that had the potential to be so sexy they could make a woman's heart stop.

"She *is* protecting me in some way. Grocery shopping is tough enough. I have to go out of town for groceries to avoid recipe exchanges with well-meaning neighbors."

Whom, Morgan was willing to guess, were mostly female. And available. She could easily imagine him being swarmed at a market in a small town where everyone would know his history. Wife killed, nearly two years ago, Christmas Eve car accident. *Widower. Single dad.*

"The girl's department is impossible," he went on grimly. "A sea of pink. Women everywhere. Frills." He said that word again, softly, with pained remembrance shadowing his eyes. He shook his head. "I don't do shopping," he said again, firmly, resolutely.

"I'd be happy to take her shopping."

It was the type of offer that would have Mary Beth rolling her eyes. It was the type of offer that probably made Morgan's insanity certifiable. Could she tangle her life with those of the Hathoways without dancing with something very powerful and possibly not tamable?

But whatever brief humanity had touched Nate's features it was doused as carelessly as he had plunged that red-hot metal into water.

"I don't do pity, either."

Good, Morgan congratulated herself. She had done her best. She should leave now, while her dignity was somewhat in tact. Mary Beth would approve if she left without saying another single word.

Naturally, she didn't.

"It's not pity. I happen to love shopping. I can't think of anything I would consider more fun than taking Cecilia on a shopping excursion."

CHAPTER TWO

I CAN'T THINK of anything I would consider more fun than taking Cecilia on a shopping excursion.

Mary Beth is going to think I'm crazy, Morgan thought.

Plus, standing here in such close proximity to his lips, she could think of *one* thing that would be quite a bit more fun than taking Cecilia on a shopping excursion. Or maybe *two*.

"I'll look after it," Nate Hathoway said, coolly adding with formal politeness, "thanks for dropping in, Miss McGuire."

And then he dismissed her, strode back across his workshop and turned his back to her, faced the fire. He was instantly engrossed in whatever he was doing.

Morgan stared at him, but instead of leaving, she marched over to one of the bins just inside the front door. It contained coat hooks, in black wrought iron.

She picked up a pair, loved the substance of them in her hands. In a world where everything was transient, everything was meant to be enjoyed for a short while and then replaced—like her purple sofa—the coat hooks felt as if they were made to last forever.

Not a word a newly independent woman wanted

to be thinking of anywhere in the vicinity of Nate Hathoway.

Still, his work with the black iron was incredible, flawless. The metal was so smooth it might have been silk. The curve of the hanger seemed impossibly delicate. How had he wrought this from something as inflexible as iron?

"I'll trade you," Morgan said on an impulse.

He turned and looked at her.

"My time with your daughter for some of your workmanship." She held up the pair of coat hooks.

She could already picture them hanging inside her front door, she already felt as if she *had* to have them. Even if he didn't agree to the trade, she would have to try and buy them from him.

But she saw she had found precisely the right way to get to him: a trade in no way injured his pride, which looked substantial. Plus, it got him out of the dreaded shopping trip to the girls' department.

He nodded, once, curtly. "Okay. Done."

She went to put the coat hooks back, until they worked out the details of their arrangement, but he growled at her.

"Take them."

"Saturday morning? I can pick Cecilia up around ten."

"Fine." He turned away from her again. She saw he was heating a rod of iron, and she wished she had the nerve to go watch how he worked his magic on it. But she didn't.

She turned and let herself quietly out the door. Only as she walked away did she consider that by taking the coat hangers, she had taken a piece of him with her.

Morgan was aware she would never be able to look at her new acquisition without picturing him, hammer in hand, and feeling the potent pull of the incredible energy he had poured, molten, into manufacturing the coat hangers.

"I wonder what I've gotten myself into?" she asked out loud, walking away from the old barn, the last of the leaves floated from the trees around her. And then she realized just how much Nate Hathoway had managed to rattle her when she touched a piece of paper in her coat pocket.

And realized it was the permission slip for *The Christmas Angel*, still unsigned.

"Ah, Ace," Nate said uneasily, "you know how I promised I'd take you to the antique-car show this morning?"

His daughter was busy coloring at the kitchen table, enjoying a Saturday morning in her jammies. They were faded cotton-candy pink. They had feet in them, which made her seem like a baby. His baby.

He felt a fresh wave of anger at the kids teasing her. And fresh frustration at the snippy young teacher for thinking she knew everything.

He had tried to think about that visit from the teacher as little as possible, and not just because it made him acutely aware of his failings as a single parent.

No, the teacher had been pretty. Annoying, but pretty.

And when he thought of her, it seemed to be the *pretty* part he thought of—the lush auburn hair, the sparkling green eyes, the wholesome features, the delicate curves—rather than the annoying part.

Ace glanced up at him. Her shortened red hair was sticking up every which way this morning, still an improvement over the toothpaste fin of last week, and the long tangled mop he had tried to tame—unsuccessfully—before that.

"We're not going to the car show?" she asked.

Nate hated disappointing her. He had been mulling over how to break this to her. Which is probably why he hadn't told her earlier that her plans for Saturday were changed. Sometimes with Ace, it was better not to let her think things over for too long.

"We're not going to the car show?" she asked again, something faintly strident in her voice.

Just as he had thought. She was clearly devastated.

"Uh, no. Your teacher is coming over." He had an envelope full of cash ready to hand Morgan McGuire for any purchases she made for Ace. His guilt over changing the car-show plans was being balanced, somewhat, by the incredibly wonderful fact he didn't have to go shopping.

The devastation dissolved from her face. "Mrs. McGuire?" Ace whispered with reverence. "She's coming here?"

"It's not like it's a visit from the pope," he said, vaguely irritated, realizing he may have overestimated the attractions of the car show by just a little.

"What's a pope?"

"Okay, the queen, then."

"The queen's coming here?" Ace said, clearly baffled.

"No. Miss McGuire's coming here. She's going to take you shopping. Instead of me taking you to the car show."

The crayon fell out of Ace's fingers. "I'm going shopping with Mrs. McGuire? *Me?*" Her brown eyes got huge. She gave a little squeal of delight, got up and did a little dance around the kitchen, hugging herself. He doubted a million-dollar lottery winner could have outdone her show of exuberance.

Okay, he admitted wryly, so he had overestimated the appeal of the car show by quite a bit.

Nate felt a little smile tickle his own lips at his daughter's delight, and then chastised himself for the fact there had not been nearly enough moments like this since his wife had died. Slippery roads. A single vehicle accident on Christmas Eve, Cindy had succumbed to her horrific injuries on Christmas day. There was no one to blame.

No one to direct the helpless rage at.

Ace stopped dancing abruptly. Her face clouded and her shoulders caved in. It was like watching the air go out of a balloon, buoyancy dissolving into soggy, limp latex.

"No," Ace said, her voice brave, her chin quivering. "I'm not going to go shopping with Mrs. McGuire. I can't."

"Huh? Why?"

"Because Saturday is *our* day. Yours and mine, Daddy. Always. And forever."

"Well, just this once it would be okay—"

"No," she said firmly. "I'm not leaving you alone."

"I'll be okay, Ace. I can go to the car show by myself."

"Nope," she said, and then furiously insisted, "it's *our* day." She tried to smile, but wavered, and after struggling valiantly for a few seconds to hide the true cost of her sacrifice, she burst into tears and ran and locked herself in the bathroom.

"Come on, Ace," he said, knocking softly on the bathroom door. "We can have *our* day tomorrow. I'll take you over to Aunt Molly's and you can ride Happy."

Happy was a chunky Shetland pony, born and bred in hell. Her Aunt Molly had given the pony to Ace for Christmas last year, a stroke of genius that had provided some distraction from the bitter memories of the day. Ace loved the evil dwarf equine completely.

But Happy was not providing the necessary distraction today. There was no answer from the other side of the bathroom door. Except sobbing. Nate realized it was truly serious when even the pony promise didn't work.

Nate knew what he had to do, though it probably spoke volumes to his character just how reluctant he was to do it.

"Maybe," he said slowly, hoping some miracle— furnace exploding, earthquake—could save him from finishing this sentence, "since it's our day, I could tag along on your shopping trip with Miss McGuire."

No explosion. No earthquake. The desperate suggestion of a cornered man was uttered without intervention from a universe he already suspected was not exactly on his side.

Silence. And then the door opened a crack. Ace regarded him with those big moist brown eyes. Tears were beaded on her lashes, and her cheeks were wet.

"Would you, Daddy?" she whispered.

The truth was he would rather be staked out on an anthill covered in maple syrup than go shopping with Ace and her startlingly delectable teacher.

But he sucked it up and did what had to be done, wishing the little snip who was so quick to send the notes criticizing his parenting could see him manning up now.

"Sure," he said, his voice deliberately casual. "I'll go, too." Feeling like a man who had escaped certain torture, only to be recaptured, Nate slipped the envelope of shopping cash he had prepared for the teacher into his own pocket.

"Are you sure, Daddy?" Ace looked faintly skeptical. She knew how he hated shopping.

Enough to steal overalls to try and save him, he reminded himself. "I don't want to miss *our* day, either," he assured her.

Inwardly, he was plotting. This could be quick. A trip down to Canterbury's one-and-only department store, Finnegan's Mercantile, a beeline to girls' wear, a few sweat suits—Miss McGuire approved, probably in various shades of pink—stuffed into a carry basket and back out the door.

He hoped the store would be relatively empty. He didn't want rumors starting about him and the teacher.

It occurred to Nate, with any luck, they were still going to make the car show. His happiness must have shown on his face, because Ace shot out of the bathroom and wrapped sturdy arms around his waist.

"Daddy," she said, in that little frog croak of hers, staring up at him with adoration he was so aware of not deserving, "I love you."

Ace saved him from the awkwardness of his having to break it to Miss Morgan McGuire that he was accompanying them on their trip, by answering the doorbell on its first ring.

Freshly dressed in what she had announced was her *best* outfit—worn pink denims and a shirt that Hannah Montana had long since faded off—Ace threw open the front door.

"Mrs. McGuire," she crowed, "my daddy's coming, too! He's coming shopping with me and you."

And then Ace hugged herself and hopped around on one foot, while Morgan McGuire slipped in the door.

Nate was suddenly aware his housekeeping was not that good, and *annoyed* by his awareness of it. He resisted the temptation to shove a pair of his work socks, abandoned on the floor, under the couch with his foot.

It must be the fact she was a teacher that made him feel as if everything was being graded: newspapers out on the coffee table; a thin layer of dust on everything, unfolded laundry leaning out of a hamper balanced perilously on the arm of the couch.

At Ace's favorite play station, the raised fireplace hearth, there was an entire orphanage of naked dolls, Play-Doh formations long since cracked and hardened, a forlorn-looking green plush dog that had once had stuffing.

So instead of looking like he cared how Morgan McGuire felt about his house and his housekeeping—or lack thereof—Nate did his best to look casual, braced his shoulder against the door frame of the living room, and shoved his hands into the front of his jeans pockets.

Morgan actually seemed stunned enough by Ace's announcement that he would be joining them that she didn't appear to notice one thing about the controlled chaos of his housekeeping methods.

She was blushing.

He found himself surprised and reluctantly charmed that anyone blushed anymore, at least over something as benign as a shopping trip with a six-year-old and her fashion handicapped father.

The first-grade teacher was as pretty as he remembered her, maybe prettier, especially with that high color in her cheeks.

"I'm surprised you'll be joining us," Morgan said to him, tilting her chin in defiance of the blush, "I thought you made your feelings about shopping eminently clear."

He shrugged, enjoying her discomfort over his addition to the party enough that it almost made up for his aversion to shopping.

Almost.

"I thought we'd go to the mall in Greenville," Morgan said, jingling her car keys in her hand and glancing away from him.

Why did it please him that he made her nervous? And how could he be pleased and annoyed at the same time? A trip to Greenville was a full-day excursion!

"I thought we were going to Finnegan's," he said. Why couldn't Ace have just been bribed with Happy time, same as always?

Why did he have an ugly feeling Morgan McGuire was the type of woman who changed *same as always?*

"Finnegan's?" Morgan said. "Oh." In the same tone one might use if a fishmonger was trying to talk them into buying a particularly smelly piece of fish. "There's not much in the way of selection there."

"But Greenville is over an hour and a half away!" he protested. By the time they got there, they'd have to have lunch. Even before they started shopping. He could see the car show slip a little further from his grasp.

And lunch with the first-grade teacher? His life, deliberately *same as always* since Cindy's death, was being hijacked, and getting more complicated by the minute.

"It's the closest mall," Morgan said, and he could see she had a stubborn bent to her that might match his own, if tested.

As if the careful script on the handwritten notes sent home hadn't been fair enough warning of that.

"And the best shopping."

"The best shopping," Ace breathed. "Could we go to The Snow Cave? That's where Brenda Weston got her winter coat. It has white fur."

Nate shot his daughter an astonished look. This was the first time she'd ever indicated she knew the name of a store in Greenville, or that she coveted a coat that had white fur.

"Surrender to the day," he muttered sternly to himself, not that the word *surrender* had appeared in a Hathoway's vocabulary for at least two hundred years.

"Pardon?" Morgan asked.

"I said lead the way."

But when she did, he wasn't happy about that, either. She drove one of those teeny tiny cars that got three zillion miles per every gallon of gas.

There was no way he could sit in the sardine-can-size backseat, and if he got in the front seat, his shoulder was going to be touching hers.

All the way to Greenville.

And even if he was determined to surrender to the

day, he was not about to *invite* additional assaults on his defenses.

"I've seen Tinkertoys bigger than this car," he muttered. "We'd better take my vehicle."

And there was something about Miss Morgan McGuire that already attacked his defenses. That made a part of him he thought was broken beyond repair wonder if there was even the slimmest chance it could be fixed.

Why would anyone in their right mind want to fix something that hurt so bad when it broke?

He realized he was thinking of his heart.

Stupid thoughts for a man about to spend an hour and a half in a vehicle—any vehicle—with someone as cute as Morgan McGuire. He was pretty sure it was going to be the longest hour and a half of his life.

Stupid thoughts for a man who had vowed when his wife died—and Hathoways took their vows seriously—that his heart was going to be made of the same iron he made his livelihood shaping.

Out of nowhere, a memory blasted him.

I wish you could know what it is to fall in love, Nate.

Stop it, Cin, I love you.

No. Head over heels, I can't breathe, think, function. That kind of fall-in-love.

Cindy had been his best friend's girl. David had joined the services and been killed overseas. For a while, it had looked like the grief would take her, too. But Nate had done what best friends do, what he had promised David. He had stepped in to look after her.

Can't breathe? Think? Function? That doesn't even sound fun to me.

She'd laughed. But sadly. *Hath, you don't know squat.*

There was a problem with vowing your heart was going to be made of iron, and Nate was aware of it as he settled in the driver's seat beside Morgan, and her delicate perfume surrounded him.

Iron had a secret. It was only strong until it was tested by fire. Heated hot enough it was as pliable as butter.

And someone like Morgan McGuire probably had a whole lot more fire than her prim exterior was letting on.

But as long as he didn't have to touch her shoulder all the way to Greenville he didn't have to find out. He could make himself immune to her, despite the delicacy of her scent.

It should be easy. After all, Nate had made himself immune to every other woman who had come calling, thinking he and Ace needed sympathy and help, loving and saving.

He didn't need anything. From anyone. And in that, he took pride.

And some days it felt like pride—and Ace—were all he had left.

But even once they were all loaded into his spacious SUV, even though his shoulder was not touching Morgan's, Nate was totally aware of her in the passenger seat, turning around to talk to Ace.

And he was aware the trip to Greenville had never gone by more quickly.

Because Morgan had switched cars, but not intent. And Nate saw she was intent on making the day fun for Ace, and her genuine caring for his daughter softened him toward her in a way he did not want to be softened.

For as much as he resisted her attempts to involve him, it made Nate mildly ashamed that on a long car trip with Ace he had a tendency to plug a movie into the portable DVD player.

Nate glanced over at Morgan. Her eyes had a shine to them, a clearness, a trueness.

He was aware that since the death of Cindy he had lived in the darkness of sorrow, in the grip of how helpless he had been to change anything at a moment when it had really counted.

Morgan's light was not going to pierce that. He wasn't going to allow it.

"With an oink, oink here, and an oink, oink there," Morgan McGuire sang with enthusiasm that made up for a surprisingly horrible voice.

It was written all over her that she was young and innocent and completely naive. That she had never known hardship like his own hardscrabble upbringing at a forge that was going broke, that she had been untouched by true tragedy.

"Oink," she invited him, and then teased, "you look like you would make a terrific pig."

He hoped that wasn't a dig at his housekeeping, but again he was taken by the transparency in her face. Morgan McGuire appeared to be the woman least likely to make digs.

"—here an oink, there an oink, everywhere an oink, oink—"

He shook his head, refusing to be drawn into her world. No good could come from it. When soft met hard, soft lost.

The best thing he could ever do for this teacher who cared about his daughter with a genuineness he could not deny, was to make sure he didn't repay her caring by hurting her.

And following the thin thread of attraction he could feel leaping in him as her voice and her scent and her enthusiasm for oinking filled his vehicle, could only end in that one place.

And he was cynical enough to know that.

Even if she wasn't.

Morgan glanced across the restaurant table at Nate Hathoway. Nothing in the time they had spent in the truck lessened her first impression of him standing alone bending iron to his will.

He was a warrior. Battle-scarred, self-reliant, his emotions contained behind walls so high it would be nearly impossible to scale them.

So, being Morgan, naturally she tried to scale them anyway.

She had been aware that she was trying to make him smile as they had traveled, deliberately using her worst singing voice, trying to get him to participate. She told herself it was so Ace could see a softer side of her father, but she knew that wasn't the entire truth.

She had seen a tickle of a smile at his forge on their first meeting. She wanted to see if she could tempt it out again.

But she had failed. The more she tried, the more he had tightened his cloak of remoteness around himself.

Though Morgan had not missed how his eyes found Ace in the rearview mirror, had not missed he was indulging her antics because his daughter was enjoying them.

Really, Nate Hathoway was the man least likely to ever be seen at a Cheesie Charlie's franchise, but here he was, tolerating a noise level that was nothing less than astonishing, his eyes unreadable when the menus were delivered by a guy in a somewhat the worse-for-wear chicken suit.

He ate the atrocious food without comment, slipped the waiter-chicken a tip when he came to their table and serenaded them with a song with Ace's name liberally sprinkled throughout.

"Well, wasn't that fun?" Morgan asked as they left Cheesie Charlie's.

"Yes!" Ace crowed. Even she seemed to notice that nothing was penetrating the hard armor around her father. "Daddy," she demanded, "didn't you think that was fun?"

"Fun as pounding nails with my forehead," he muttered.

"That doesn't sound fun," Ace pointed out.

"You're right," he said, and then sternly warned, "don't try it at home."

Morgan sighed as Ace skipped ahead to where they had parked. "How did you allow yourself to get talked into coming? I'm beginning to see you did not volunteer for this excursion."

He hesitated, and then he nodded at Cecilia. "We always spend Saturday together. It's our tradition. Since her mom passed. I was willing to forgo it, just this once. She wasn't."

"Somewhere under that hard exterior is there a heart of pure gold, Nate Hathoway?"

She finally got the smile, only it wasn't the one she'd been trying for. Cynical. Something tight around the edges of it. His eyes shielded.

"Don't kid yourself."

Instead of scaling his wall, she'd managed to get him to put it up higher! And for some reason it made her mad. If she couldn't make him laugh, then she might as well torment him.

"If you thought Cheesie Charlie's was fun, you're going to love The Snow Cave," Morgan promised him.

He gave her a dark, lingering look that sent shivers from her ears to her toes.

The Snow Cave proudly proclaimed itself as haute tot.

If he had looked out of place at Cheesie's, Nate Hathoway now looked acutely out of place in the exclusive girls' store. He was big and rugged amongst the racks and displays of pint-size *frilly* clothing in more shades of pink than Morgan was certain the male mind could imagine.

Ignoring his discomfort, at the same time as enjoying it immensely, Morgan sorted through the racks until she had both her and Cecilia's arms heaped up with selections: blouses and T-shirts, socks, slacks, dresses, skirts.

"Great," he said when it was obvious they could not carry one more thing. "Are you done? Can we go?"

"She has to try everything on."

"What?" He looked like a wolf caught in a trap. "What for? Just buy it all so we can leave."

Not even a little ashamed for enjoying his misery so thoroughly, Morgan leaned close to him and whispered,

"This store is very expensive. You should allow her to pick one or two items from here and we'll get the rest elsewhere."

"Elsewhere?" He closed his eyes and bit back a groan. "Just buy the damn stuff. I don't care what it costs. I don't want to go *elsewhere*."

She waited to feel guilty, but given how easily he had resisted her efforts to charm, she didn't.

Not in the least. This was a show of spunky liberation from needing his approval that even Amelia would have approved of!

"That's not how it works," Morgan said firmly. "We've been shopping for all of ten minutes. Don't be such a baby."

His mouth dropped open in shock, closed again. Morgan was sure she could hear him grinding his teeth before he finally said, "A *baby?* Me?"

"And could you try not to curse? Cecilia tends to bring some of your words to school."

"You consider *damn* a curse?" he said, clearly as astonished by that as by the fact that she'd had the audacity to call him a baby.

"I do," she said bravely.

He stared at her as if she was freshly minted from a far-off planet. He scowled. He shoved his hands in the pockets of his jeans. He looked longingly at the door. And then Ace danced up, with one more *find*.

"Look! Sparkle skinny jeans that will fit me!"

He sighed with long suffering, shot Morgan a dark look that she answered with a bland, uncaring smile, and then allowed Ace to take his hand and tug him toward the change area.

Which, like everything at The Snow Cave, was designed to delight little girls. The waiting area, newly decorated for Christmas, was like the throne room in a winter palace fantasy.

And so there sat Nate Hathoway front row and center, in a pink satin chair which looked as if it could snap into kindling under his weight. But as Cecilia danced out in each of her new outfits, the scowl dissolved from his face, and even if he didn't smile, his expression was at least less menacing.

It was hours later that they finally drove through the darkness toward Canterbury and home. Ace fell asleep in her booster seat in the back instantly, nearly lost amongst the clothing bags and shoe boxes that surrounded her. They could have gone in the back of Nate's huge SUV, but she had insisted she had to have each of her purchases close to her.

Ace wore her new coat: an impractical pure-white curly fur creation that was going to make her the absolute envy of the grade-one girls. She had on a hair band with a somewhat wilted bow, and little red patent-leather shoes on her leotarded feet.

"She's worn right out," Nate said with a glance in the rearview mirror. "And no wonder. Is the female of the species born with an ability to power shop?"

"I think so."

"So how come you didn't get anything for yourself?"

"Because today wasn't about me."

He glanced at her, and she saw a warmth had crept past his guard and into his eyes. But he looked quickly away, before she could bask in it for too long.

Looking straight ahead, as snow was beginning to fall gently, Nate turned on the radio. It was apparently preset to a rock station, but he glanced at the sleeping girl, and then at Morgan, and fiddled with the dial until he found a soft country ballad.

"Why do you call Cecilia 'Ace'?" Morgan asked.

He hesitated, as if he did not want to reveal one single thing about himself or his family to her.

But then he said, "Her mom had started calling her Sissy, short for Cecilia, I guess. There are no sissies in the Hathoway family. Nobody was calling my kid Sissy."

And then he sighed. "I regret making an issue over it, now."

Morgan heard lots of regret in his voice. She had heard about the accident, and knew one minute he'd had a wife, and a life, and the next that everything had changed forever. What were his regrets? Had he called, *I love you,* as his wife had headed out the door for the last time?

His face was closed now, as if he already had said way more than he wanted to. Which meant he was the strong one who talked to no one about his pain.

She wanted to reach across the darkness of the cab, and invite him to tell her things he had told no one else, but she knew he would not appreciate the gesture.

Silence fell over them. Despite the quiet, there was something good about driving through the night with him, the soft music, the snow falling outside, his scent tickling at her nose.

Normally, particularly if she was driving by herself, the snow would have made Morgan nervous, but tonight she had a feeling of being with a man who would keep those he had been charged with guarding safe no matter what it took, no matter what it cost him.

But he hadn't, and he wore that failure to protect his wife around him like a cloak of pure pain.

Even though Morgan knew he had not been there at the accident that killed his wife, she was certain he would in some way hold himself responsible. Did he think he should have driven her that night? Not let her go into the storm?

She could not ask him that. Not yet. Which meant she thought someday maybe she could. Why was she hoping this shopping trip was not the end of it?

Because she felt so safe driving with him through the snow-filled night?

Amelia wouldn't have approved, but it was nice to rely on someone else's competence. Even though it might be weak, Morgan felt herself savoring the feeling of being looked after.

She glanced at his strong features, illuminated by the dash lights. He looked calm, despite the snowfall growing heavier outside, the windshield wipers slapping along trying to keep up.

Nate Hathoway might not smile much, but Morgan suddenly knew if your back was against the wall and barbarians were coming at you with knives in their teeth, he was the one you would want standing right beside you.

It was weariness that had allowed an independent woman such as herself to entertain such a traitorous thought, Morgan defended herself. And then, as if to prove it, the warmth inside the vehicle, the radio, the mesmerizing fall of snow—and the sense of being safe and taken care of—made it impossible for her to think of clever things to say. Or even to keep her eyes open.

When she woke up, it was to absolute stillness. The

sound of the radio was gone, the vehicle had stopped moving, the dashboard lights were off, and the vehicle was empty.

She realized there was a weight on her shoulder, and that it was his hand, not shaking her, just touching her.

Even through the puffiness of her parka, she could feel his warmth, and his strength. It made her want to go back to sleep.

"Morgan, we're home."

For home to be a place shared, instead of a place of aloneness, felt like the most alluring dream of all.

Recognizing her groggy vulnerability, Morgan shook herself awake. He was standing at her side of the SUV, the door open.

A quick glance showed the back was empty of every parcel and package. Ace was gone.

"Put her in bed," he said before Morgan asked. "Thought you might wake up as I moved stuff and the vehicle cooled off, but you were sleeping hard."

Morgan felt herself blushing. She'd obviously slept like a rock. She hoped she hadn't drooled and muttered his name in her sleep. Had she dreamed of the smile she had tried so hard—and failed—to produce?

And then suddenly, when she least expected it, it was there.

He was actually smiling at her. A small smile, but so genuine it was like the sun coming out on a dreary day. He reached out and touched her cheek.

"You've got the print of the seat cover across your cheek."

And then his hand dropped away, and he looked away.

"Miss McGuire?"

"Morgan."

He looked right at her. The smile was gone. "You gave my daughter a gift today. I haven't seen her so happy for a long, long time. I thank you for that."

And then, he bent toward her, brushed the print on her cheek again, and kissed the place on her cheek where his fingers had been. His lips were gloriously soft, a tenderness in them that belied every single thing she thought she had ever seen in his eyes.

And then Nate turned away from her, went up the walk to his house and into it, shut the door without once looking back.

She sat in his truck stunned, wondering if she had dreamed that moment, but finally managed to stir herself, shut the door of his vehicle and get into her own.

The night was so bright and cold and star-filled. Was she shivering from the cold, or from the absence of the warmth she had felt when he had touched his lips to her cheek?

It wasn't until she was nearly home that she realized that while she slept he had done more than empty his vehicle of parcels, and carry a sleeping Ace to her bedroom. Morgan saw he had put two more of the coat hangers on her front seat.

And she remembered she still had not gotten the permission slip for *The Christmas Angel* signed.

And she knew it was weak, and possibly stupid, and she knew it went against every single thing she had decided for herself when she had moved to Canterbury. It challenged every vow she had made as she devoured chapter after chapter of *Bliss: The Extraordinary Joy of Being a Single Woman.*

But Morgan still knew that she would use that unsigned permission slip as an excuse to see him again.

CHAPTER THREE

HE NEVER WANTED TO see her again.

Morgan McGuire was stirring things up in Nate Hathoway that did not need stirring.

That impulse to kiss her cheek was the last impulse he intended to follow. It had been like kissing the petals of a rose, so soft, so yielding. Touching the exquisite softness of her with his lips had made him acutely aware of a vast empty spot in his life.

As had spending a day with her, her laughter, her enthusiasm, contagious.

So, it was an easy decision. No more Morgan McGuire.

Nate, alone in his workshop, vowed it out loud. "I won't see her again. Won't have anything to do with her."

There. His and Ace's lives felt complicated enough without adding the potential messiness of a relationship with the teacher.

Relationship? That was exactly why he wasn't seeing her again. A day—shopping of all things—made him think of the sassy schoolteacher in terms of a relationship?

No. He was setting his mind against it, and that was that.

One thing every single person in this town knew about Nate Hathoway: his discipline was legendary. When he said something, it happened.

It was that kind of discipline that had allowed him to take a forge—a relic from a past age that had not provided a decent living for the past two generations of Hathoway blacksmiths—and bend it to his vision for its future.

His own father had been skeptical, but then he was a Hathoway, and skepticism ran deep through the men in this family. So did hard work and hell-raising.

Cindy and David had been raised in the same kind of families as his. Solidly blue-collar, poor, proud. The three of them had been the musketeers, their friendship shielding them from the scorn of their wealthier classmates.

While his solution to the grinding poverty of his childhood had been the forge, David's had been the army. He felt the military would be his ticket to an education, to being able to provide for Cindy after he married her.

Instead, he'd come home in a flag-draped box.

You look after her if anything happens to me.

And so Nate had.

She'd never been quite the same, some laughter gone from her forever, but the baby had helped. Still, they had had a good relationship, a strong partnership, loyalty to each other and commitment to family.

Her loss had plunged him into an abyss that he had been able to avoid when David had died. Now he walked with an ever present and terrifying awareness that all a man's strength could not protect those he loved entirely. A man's certainty in his ability to control his world was an illusion. A man could no more hold back tragedy than he could hold back waves crashing onto a shore.

Nate felt Cindy's loss sharply. But at the same time he felt some loss of himself.

Still, thinking of her now, Nate was aware Cindy would never have flinched from such a mild curse as *damn*.

And he was almost guiltily aware Cindy's scent permeating the interior of a vehicle had never filled him with such an intense sense of longing. For things he couldn't have.

Someone like Morgan McGuire could never fit into his world. His was a world without delicacy, since Cindy's death it had become even more a man's world.

"So, no more."

What about Ace in this world that was so without soft edges?

Well, he told himself, it *had* changed from the world of his childhood. It wasn't hardscrabble anymore. It wasn't the grinding poverty he had grown up with. The merciless teasing from his childhood—about his worn shoes, faded shirts, near-empty lunchbox—sat with him still. And made him proud.

And mean if need be.

Not that there had been even a hint of anyone looking down their noses at him for a long, long time.

Partly in respect for his fists.

Mostly because within two years of Nate taking over the forge—pouring his blood and his grit and his pure will into it—it had turned around.

The success of the forge was beyond anything he could have imagined for himself. He did commissions. He had custom orders well into next year. He sold his stock items as fast as he could make them.

Nate's success had paid off the mortgages on this property, financed his parents' retirement to Florida, allowed him things that a few years ago he would have considered unattainable luxuries. He could have any one of those antique cars he liked when he decided which one he wanted. He even had a college fund for Ace.

Still, there was no room for a woman like Morgan McGuire in his world.

Because he had success. And stuff.

And those things could satisfy without threatening, without coming close to that place inside of him he did not want touched.

But she could touch it. Morgan McGuire could not only touch it, but fill it. Make him aware of empty spaces he had been just as happy not knowing about.

He was suddenly aware she was there, in the forge, as if thinking about her alone could conjure her.

How did he know it was her?

A scent on the air, a feeling on the back of his neck as the door had opened almost silently and then closed again?

No. She was the only one who had ever ignored that Go Away sign.

Now, based on the strength of their shared shopping trip—and probably on that kiss he so regretted—she came right up to the hearth, stood beside him, watching intently as he worked.

Her perfume filled his space, filled him with that same intense longing he had become aware of in the truck. What was it, exactly? A promise of softness? He steeled himself against it, squinted into the fire, used the bellows to raise the heat and the flames yet higher.

Only then did he steal a glance at her. Nate willed himself to tell her to go away, and was astonished that his legendary discipline failed him. Completely.

Morgan's luscious auburn hair was scooped back in a ponytail that was falling out. The light from the flame made the strands of red shine with a life of their own.

The schoolteacher had on no makeup, but even without it her eyes shimmered a shade of green so pure that it put emeralds to shame. She did have something on her lips that gave them the most enticing little shine. She watched what he was doing without interrupting, and somehow his space did not feel compromised at all by her being here.

"Hi," he heard himself saying. Not exactly friendly, but not *go away,* either.

"Hi. What are you making?"

"It's part of a wrought iron gate for the entrance of a historic estate in Savannah, Georgia. A commission."

"It's fantastic." She had moved over to parts he had laid out on his worktable, piecing it together like a puzzle before assembling it.

He glanced at her again, saw she must have walked here. She was bundled up against the cold in a pink jacket and mittens that one of her students could have worn. Her cheeks glowed from being outside.

Nate saw how deeply she meant it about his work. His work had been praised by both artists and smithies around the world.

It grated that her praise meant so much. No wonder

she had all those first graders eating out of the palm of her hand.

"I just wanted to drop by and let you know what a good week it's been for Cecilia."

"Because of the clothes?" he asked, and then snorted with disdain. "We live in a superficial world when six-year-olds are being judged by their fashion statements, Miss Morgan."

He was aware, since he hadn't just told her out and out to go away, of wanting to bicker with her, to get her out that door one way or another.

Because despite his legendary discipline, being around her made that yearning nip at him, like a small aggravating dog that wouldn't be quiet.

But she didn't look any more perturbed by his deliberate cynicism than she had when she told him not to cuss. "It's not just because of the clothes, but because she feels different. Like she fits in. It's given her confidence."

"I have confidence. I never had nice clothes growing up."

Now why had he gone and said that? He glanced at her. Her eyes were on him, soft, inviting him to say more.

Which he wasn't going to!

"Thanks for dropping by. And the Ace update. You could have sent a note."

She still looked unoffended. In fact, she smiled. He wished she wouldn't do that. Smile.

It made him want to lay every hurt he had ever felt at her feet.

"We both know you don't read my notes."

If he promised he would read them from now on would she go away? He doubted it.

"I actually needed to see you. I need you to sign this permission slip for Cecilia to participate in *The Christmas Angel*. Rehearsals will be starting next week."

"I'm sick of hearing about *The Christmas Angel*," he said gruffly. "The whole town has gone nuts. I don't like Christmas. I don't like Wesley Wellhaven. And I really don't like *The Christmas Angel*."

She was silent for a moment. A sane person would have backed out the door and away from his show of ire. She didn't.

"Perhaps you should post a Grinch Lives Here sign above your Go Away sign."

"My wife was in an accident on Christmas Eve. She died on Christmas Day. It will be two years this year. Somehow that takes the ho-ho-ho out of the season."

He said it flatly, but he knew, somehow, despite his resolve to be indifferent to Morgan, he wasn't.

He didn't want her sympathy. He hated sympathy.

It was something else he wanted from her. When he put his finger on it, it astonished him. To not be so alone with it anymore.

To be able to tell someone that he had not been able to stop Cindy's excruciating pain. That he had been relieved when she died because she didn't have to be in pain anymore.

That through all that pain, she had looked *pleased* somehow, going to be with the one she truly loved. And through all that pain, she had looked at him and said finally, seconds before she died, with absolute calm and absolute certainty, *You've been my angel, Hath. Now I'll be yours.*

And he hated that he wanted to tell Morgan McGuire

that, as if it was any of her business. He hated that he wanted to tell her if Cindy was his angel, he'd seen no evidence of it, as if she, the know-it-all teacher, should be able to explain that to him. Wanting to tell her felt like a terrible weakness in a world built on pure strength.

Morgan moved back over to him until she stood way too close, gazing up at him with solemn green eyes that looked as if she could explain the impossible to him.

"I'm so sorry about your wife."

If she added a *but* as in *but it's time to get over it,* or for *Ace's sake* he would have the excuse he needed to really, really dislike her. He waited, aware he was hoping.

She said nothing.

Instead, without taking her eyes from him, she laid her hand on his wrist, something in that touch so tender it felt as if it would melt him, as surely as his fire-tempered steel.

She seemed to realize she was touching him, and that it might not be appropriate at the same time he jerked his arm away from her.

Brusquely, Nate said, "We won't be here for Christmas. So there's no sense Ace getting involved in the Christmas-production thing. I'm taking her to Disneyland."

He made it sound as if he had been planning it forever, not as if he had just pulled it from the air, right this very moment, a plot to thwart her.

She didn't seem fooled.

"You know," she said softly, after a time, "this town is really suffering as a result of the downturn in the economy. Last year's concert, *The Christmas Miracle*, in Mountain Ridge, Vermont? The production alone pumped a lot of money into the town. But they couldn't have bought that kind of publicity. The filming of some of the winter scenery around that gorgeous little town sent people there in droves at a time of year when they don't usually get tourists."

"And that has what to do with me? And Ace?"

"The same could happen for Canterbury."

"So what?" he asked.

"It seems to me," she said softly, and if she was intimidated by his show of ill temper, she was not backing away from it, "that people need something to hope for. At Christmas more than any other time. They need to believe everything is going to be all right."

"Do they now?" How could she be that earnest? How could she be so sure of what people needed? Why did he think, given a chance, she could show him what he needed, too?

The fire was fine. He picked up the bellows anyway, focused on it, made the bellows huff and the fire roar, but not enough to shut out her voice.

"Ace needs to believe," Morgan continued softly. "She needs to believe that everything is going to be all right. And somehow I don't think that belief will be nurtured by an escape to Disneyland, as pleasant a distraction as that may be."

He put down the bellows. This had gone far enough, really. He turned to her, head-on, folded his arms over his chest. "This is beginning to sound depressingly like one of your notes. How did you get to know what the whole world needs? How do you get to be so smart for someone so wet behind the ears, fresh out of college?"

She blushed, but it was an angry blush.

Finally, he'd accomplished what he wanted. He was pushing her away. Straight out the door. Never to return, with any luck. Nate was aware that accomplishing his goal didn't feel nearly as satisfying as he thought it would.

"Somehow," she said, surprising him by matching his battle stance, folding her arms over her chest and facing him instead of backing away, "even though you have suffered tragedy, Nate, I would have never pegged you as the kind of man who would be indifferent to the woes of your neighbors. And their hopes."

His mouth opened.

And then closed.

How had a discussion about a damned permission slip turned into this? A soul search? A desire to be a better man.

And not just for his daughter.

Oh, no, it would be easy if it was just for his daughter. No, it was for her, too. Miss Snippy Know-It-All.

"I'll think about it," he said.

The famous line was always used, by everyone including him, as a convenient form of dismissal. What it really meant was *No, and I don't ever intend to think about this again.*

This time he knew he wasn't going to be so lucky.

"It means a lot to Ace to be in that production," Morgan said. "I already told the kids in my class we were all doing it, or none of us were."

"Nothing like a little pressure," he replied, turning away from her now, picking up his tongs, taking the red-hot rod of iron from the fire. "Are you telling me the Christmas joy of a dozen and a half six-year-olds relies on me?"

He glanced at her, and she nodded solemnly, ignoring his deliberately skeptical tone.

"That's a scary thing," he told her quietly, his voice deliberately loaded with cynicism. "Nearly as scary as the hope of the whole town resting on my shoulders."

She didn't have the sense to flinch from his sarcasm. He was going to have to lay it out nice and plain for her. "I'm the wrong man to trust with such things, Miss McGuire."

She looked at him for a long time as he began to hammer out the rod, and then just as he glanced at her, eyebrows raised, looking askance as if *Oh, are you still here?* she nodded once, as if she knew something about him he did not know himself.

"I don't think you are the wrong man to trust," she said softly. "I think you just wish you were."

And having looked right into his soul, Little Miss Snip removed the permission slip from her pink coat pocket, set it on his worktable, smoothed it carefully with her hand, and then turned on her heel and left him there to brood over his fire.

A little while later, in the house, getting dinner ready—hot dogs and a salad—he said to Ace, in his I-just-had-this-great-idea voice, "Ace, what would you think of a trip to Disneyland over Christmas?"

The truth was, he expected at least the exuberant dance that the shopping trip with Morgan McGuire had elicited. Instead there was silence.

He turned from the pot on the stove after prodding a frozen hot dog with a fork, as if that would get it to cook quicker, and looked at his daughter.

Ace was getting her hot-dog bun ready, lots of ketchup and relish, not dancing around at all. Today she was wearing her new skirt, the red one with the white pom-poms on the hem. She looked adorable. He hoped that didn't mean boys would start coming by here. No, surely that worry was years away.

"Disneyland?" he said, wondering if she was day-dreaming and hadn't heard him.

"Oh, Daddy," she said with a sigh of long suffering, in her *you're so silly* voice. "We can't go to Disneyland over Christmas. I *have* to be in *The Christmas Angel*. It's on Christmas Eve. It's on TV, *live*. I should phone Grandma and Grandpa and tell them I'm going to be on TV."

Then in case he was getting any other bright ideas, she told him firmly, "And I don't want to go after, either. Brenda is having a skating party on Boxing Day. I hope I get new skates for Christmas. When am I going to see Santa?"

He was pretty sure Ace and Brenda had been mortal enemies a week ago. So, Morgan had been right. Superficial or not, the clothes helped. His daughter was having a good week.

That was worth something. So was the light in her eyes when she talked about being on television.

Nate made a promise as soon as Santa set up at Finnegan's they would go, and then he made a mental note about the skates. Then once she was in bed, he took the permission slip, signed it and shoved it into Ace's backpack.

It didn't feel like nearly the concession it should have. He told himself it had nothing to do with Morgan McGuire and everything to do with Ace.

An hour after Ace was in bed, his phone rang. It was Canterbury's mayor, who also owned the local gas station. *The Christmas Angel* needed skilled crafts-people to volunteer to work on the set. Would he consider doing it?

Before Morgan had arrived this afternoon his answer would have been curt and brief.

Now he was aware he did not want to be a man indifferent to the hopes and dreams of his neighbors.

What had she said? *I don't think you are the wrong man to trust, I think you just wish you were.*

It irked him that she was right. He should say no to this request just to spite her. But he didn't.

Small towns were strange places. Centuries-old feuds were put aside if tragedy struck.

Four generations of Hathoways had owned this forge and as far as Nate could tell they'd always been renegades and rebels. They didn't go to church, or belong to the PTA or the numerous Canterbury service clubs. Hardworking but hell-raising, they were always on the fringe of the community. His family, David's and Cindy's.

And yet, when David had died, the town had given him the hero's send-off that he deserved.

And their support had been even more pronounced after Cindy had died. Nate's neighbors had gathered around him in ways he would have never expected. A minister at a church he had never been to had offered to do the service; there had not been enough seats for everyone who came to his wife's funeral.

People who he would have thought did not know of his existence—like the man who had just phoned him—had been there for him and for Ace unconditionally, wanting nothing in return, not holding his bad temper or his need to deal with his grief alone against him.

Sometimes, still, he came to the house from the forge to find an anonymous casserole at the door, or fresh-baked cookies, or a brand-new toy or outfit for Ace.

At first it had been hard for him to accept, but at some time Nate had realized it wasn't charity. It was something deeper than that. It was why people chose to live in small communities. To know they were cared about, that whether you wanted it or not, your neighbors had your back.

And you didn't just keep taking that. In time, when you were ready, you offered it back.

Nate wasn't really sure if he was ready, but somehow it felt as if it was time to find out. And so that awareness of "something deeper" was how he found himself saying yes to the volunteer job of helping to build sets.

Since the school auditorium was the only venue big enough to host *The Christmas Angel,* Nate knew it was going to put him together again with Morgan McGuire. He knew it was inevitable that their lives were becoming intertwined. Whether he liked it or not.

And for a man who had pretty established opinions on what he liked and what he didn't, Nate Hathoway was a little distressed to find he simply didn't know if he liked it or not.

Morgan marched her twenty-two charges into the gymnasium. The truth was, after being so stern with Nate about the benefits of *The Christmas Angel* coming to Canterbury, she was beginning to feel a little sick of the whole thing herself.

The children talked of nothing else. They all thought their few minutes on television, singing backup to Wesley Wellhaven, meant they were going to be famous.

They all tried to sing louder than the person next to them. Some of them were getting quite theatrical in their delivery of the songs.

The rehearsal time for the three original songs her class would sing was eating into valuable class time that Morgan felt would be better used for teaching fundamental skills, reading, writing and arithmetic.

Today was the first day her kids would be showing *The Christmas Angel* production team what they had learned. Much of the team had arrived last week, filling up the local hotel. Now *The Christmas Angel*'s own choir director, Mrs. Wesley Wellhaven herself, had arrived in town last night and would be taking over rehearsing the children.

As soon as Morgan entered the auditorium—which was also the school gymnasium, not that it could be used for that because of all the work going on getting the only stage in town ready for Wesley—Morgan *knew* he was here.

Something happened to her neck. It wasn't so sinister as the hackles rising, it was more as if someone sexy had breathed on her.

She looked around, and sure enough, there Nate was, helping another man lift a plywood cutout of a Christmas cottage up on stage.

At the same time as herding her small charges forward Morgan unabashedly took advantage of the fact Nate had no idea she was watching him, to study him, which was no mean feat given that Freddy Campbell kept poking Brenda Weston in the back, and Damien Dorchester was deliberately treading on Benjamin Chin's heels.

"Freddy, Damien, stop it." The correction was absent at best.

Because it seemed as if everything but *him* had faded as Morgan looked to the stage. Nate had looked sexy at his forge, and he looked just as sexy here, with his tool belt slung low on the hips his jeans rode over, a plain T-shirt showing off the ripple of unconscious muscle as he lifted.

Let's face it, Morgan told herself, he'd look sexy no matter where he was, no matter what he was wearing, no matter what he was doing.

He was just a blastedly sexy man.

And yet there was more than sexiness to him.

No, there was a quiet and deep strength evident in Nate Hathoway. It had been there at Cheesie Charlie's, it had been there when he sat in the pink satin chair at The Snow Cave. And it was there now as he worked, a self-certainty that really was more sexy than his startling good looks.

Mrs. Wellhaven, a pinch-faced woman of an indeterminate age well above sixty, called the children up onto the stage, and the workers had to stop to let the kids file onto the triple-decker stand that had been built for them.

"Hi, Daddy!" Ace called.

"Yes," Mrs. Wellhaven said, lips pursed, "let's deal with that first off, shall we? Please do not call out the names of people you know as you come on the stage. Not during rehearsal, and God knows, not during the live production."

Ace scowled. Morgan glanced at Nate. Father's and child's expressions were identically mutinous.

Morgan shivered. In the final analysis could there be

anything more sexy than a man who would protect his own, no matter what?

Still, the choir director had her job to do, and since Nate looked as if maybe he was going to go have a word with her, Morgan intercepted him.

"Hi. How are you?"

Though maybe it was just an excuse.

In all likelihood Nate was not going to berate the choir director.

"Who does she think she is telling my kid she can't say hi to me?" he muttered, mutiny still written all over his handsome face.

Or maybe he had been.

"You have to admit it might be a little chaotic if all the kids started calling greetings to their parents, grand-parents and younger siblings on national live television," Morgan pointed out diplomatically.

He looked at her as if he had just noticed her. When Nate gave a woman his full attention, she didn't have a chance. That probably included the crotchety choir director.

"Ah, Miss McGuire, don't you ever get tired of being right all the time?" he asked her, folding his arms over the massiveness of his chest.

She had rather hoped they were past the *Miss McGuire* stage. "Morgan," she corrected him.

Mrs. Wellhaven cleared her throat, tipped her glasses and leveled a look at them. "Excuse me. We are trying to concentrate here." She turned back to the children. "I am Mrs. Wellhaven." Then she muttered, tapping her baton sternly, "The brains of the outfit."

Nate guffawed. Morgan giggled, at least in part

because she had enjoyed his genuine snort of laughter so much.

Mrs. Wellhaven sent them a look, raised her baton and swung it down. The children watched her in silent awe. "That means begin!"

"She's a dragon," Nate whispered.

The children launched, a little unsteadily, into the opening number, "Angel Lost."

"What are you doing here?" Morgan whispered to Nate. "I thought you made it clear you weren't in favor of *The Christmas Angel*."

"Or shopping," he reminded her sourly. "I keep finding myself in these situations that I really don't want to be in."

"Don't say that like it's my fault!"

"Isn't it?"

She felt ruffled by the accusation, until she looked at him more closely and realized he was teasing her.

Something warm unfolded in her.

"I didn't know you were a carpenter, too," she said, trying to fight the desire to know everything about him. And losing.

He snorted. "I'm no carpenter, but I know my way around tools. I was raised with self-sufficiency. We never bought anything we could make ourselves when I was a kid. And we never hired anybody to do anything, either. What we needed we figured out how to make or we did without."

Though Morgan thought he had been talking very quietly, and she *loved* how much he had revealed about himself, Mrs. Wellhaven turned and gave them a quelling look.

Ace's voice rose, more croaky than usual, loudly

enthusiastic, above her peers. "Lost annngelll, who will find you? Where arrrrrre you—"

Mrs. Wellhaven's head swung back around. "You! Little redheaded girl! Could you sing just a little more quietly?"

"Is she insinuating Ace sounds bad?"

"I think she just wants all the kids to sing at approximately the same volume," Morgan offered.

"You're just being diplomatic," Nate whispered, listening. "Ace's singing is awful. Almost as bad as yours."

"Hers is not that bad, and neither is mine," Morgan protested.

"Hey, take it from a guy who spent an hour and a half with you oinking and braying, it is."

He was teasing her again. The warmth flooding her grew. "At least I gave you a break by sleeping all the way home."

"You snore, too."

Morgan's mouth fell open. "I don't!"

"How would you know?" he asked reasonably. "Snoring is one of those things you don't know about yourself. Other people have to tell you."

That seemed way too intimate—and embarrassing— a detail for him to know about her.

But when he grinned at her expression, she knew he was probably pulling her leg, and that he was enjoying teasing her as much as she was reluctantly enjoying being teased.

"Little redheaded girl—"

"Still, I'm going to have to go bean that shrew if she yells at Ace again."

"You." Mrs. Wellhaven rounded on him, and pointed her baton. "Who are you?"

"Little redheaded girl's father," he said evenly, dangerously, having gone from teasing Morgan to a warrior ready to defend his family in the blink of an eye.

Amazingly Mrs. Wellhaven was not intimidated. "No parents. Out. You, too, little redheaded girl's mother."

Morgan should point out she was the teacher, not a parent, certainly not a parent who had slept with this parent and produced a child, though the very thought made her go so weak in the knees, she had to reach out and balance herself by taking his arm.

Luckily, thanks to the darkening expression on Nate's face, she made it look as if she had just taken hold of him to lead him firmly out the door.

Touching him—her fingertips practically vibrating with awareness of how his skin felt—was probably not the best way to banish thoughts of how people produced children together.

Morgan let go as soon as they were safely out the auditorium door.

"She's a dragon," Nate proclaimed when the door slapped shut behind him. "I'm not sure I should leave Ace in there. Did you actually talk me out of taking my daughter to Disneyland to expose her to that?"

Morgan knew it would be a mistake to preen under his unconscious admission that she had somehow influenced him. Then again, she probably hadn't. He hadn't even noticed her hand on his arm, and her fingertips were still tingling! With the look on his face right now, he looked like the man least likely to be talked into anything.

Besides, between the look on his face—knight about

to do battle with the dragon—and the attitude of Mrs. Wellhaven, she was getting a case of the giggles.

Nate eyed her narrowly.

"I don't get what's funny."

"If Mrs. Wellhaven is the brains of the outfit—" *and she couldn't even see that Nate was not a man to be messed with* "—the whole town is in big trouble."

Nate regarded her silently for a moment, and then he actually laughed.

It was the second time in a few short minutes that Morgan had heard him laugh. This time he made no attempt to stifle it, and it was a good sound, rich, deep and true. It was a sound that made her redefine, instantly, what sexy really was.

"It's not too late for me to go and bean her," he said finally.

"I'm afraid I don't even know what it means to 'bean' somebody."

He laughed again. "Morgan McGuire, I think you've led a sheltered life. Let's go grab a coffee. I can't listen to that." He cocked his head at the cacophony of sound coming out the door, and shook his head. Ace's voice rose louder than ever above all others. "Maybe I can still talk Ace into going to Disneyland."

"Maybe Mrs. Wellhaven will pay for you to go."

And then he laughed again, and so did she. And she could feel that shared laughter building a tenuous bridge between them.

And so Morgan found herself in the tiny, mostly empty school cafeteria drinking stale coffee and realizing she was alone across the table from Nate Hathoway.

Without a forge as a distraction. Or Ace. Or even Old MacDonald.

They were not strangers. For heaven's sake, they had spent an entire day together! And yet Morgan felt awkwardly as if she didn't have one single thing to say to him. She felt like a sixteen-year-old on her first date. Nervous. Self-conscious. Worried about what to say. Or what not to say.

Be a teacher, she ordered herself. *Talk about Cecilia.*

But somehow she didn't want to. Not right this second. She didn't want to be a teacher, or talk about Cecilia. There was something about the pure *rush* of feeling sixteen again, tongue-tied in the presence of a gorgeous guy, that she wanted to relish even as she was guiltily aware it was the antithesis of everything she had tried to absorb while reading *Bliss.*

"So," he said, eyeing her over the top of the cup, "you get the coat hangers put up?"

"Thanks for the other pair. Two was plenty, but thanks. No, I didn't put them up. Not yet."

"Really? You don't like them?"

Oh, she liked them. Way too much. Liked caressing that smooth metal in her hands, liked the way something of him, his absolute strength and even his maddening rigidity, was represented in the work that he did.

"It's not that. I mean I tried to put them up. They keep falling down again. The first time it happened I thought I had a burglar. They're too heavy. I'm afraid they've made a mess of the wall."

He squinted at her. "You knew they had to be mounted on a stud, right?"

She willed herself not to blush, and not to choke on her coffee. He had not just said something dirty in the elementary-school cafeteria. She was pretty sure of it. Still, she couldn't trust herself to answer. She took a sudden interest in mopping a nonexistent dribble of coffee off the table.

"How long are the kids going to be singing?" he asked.

Thankfully, he'd left the topic of the stud behind him! "I was told the first rehearsal would be about an hour. I think that's a little long for six-year-olds, but—"

"The coffee's bad, anyway. You want to play hooky for a few minutes, Miss Schoolmarm?"

"Excuse me?"

He leaned across the table and looked at her so intently she thought she might faint.

"I'll show you what a stud is," he promised, his voice as sultry as a hot summer night.

"Pardon?" She gulped.

"You shouldn't go through life without knowing."

She felt as if she was strangling.

When she had nearly worn through the table scrubbing at the nonexistent spot, he said, "I'll hang up the coat hangers for you."

"You want to come to *my* house?"

He raised his eyebrows at her. "Unless you want the coat hangers hung somewhere else?"

"You want to come to my house now?"

His eyes had the most devilish little twinkle in them. "It's not as if you're entertaining a gentleman caller, Miss McGuire."

It was true. He was offering to do a chore for her. That involved *studs*.

She was not going to let him see how rattled she was! Well, he already had, but she intended to curb his enjoyment.

"Yes," she said, "that would be fine. A very gentlemanly offer from someone who is not a gentleman caller. Though I'm sure you are. A gentleman. Most of the time. When you aren't talking about beaning the choir director. Or hunting down the parents of children who have teased your daughter."

She was babbling. She clamped her mouth shut.

"Nobody's ever called me a gentleman before," he told her with wicked enjoyment.

But underneath the banter she heard something else. And so she said primly, "Well, it's about time they did."

Ten minutes later, she was so aware of how life could take unexpected turns. Just this morning it would have never occurred to her that Nate Hathoway would be in her house by this afternoon. In fact, Santa coming down the chimney would have seemed a more likely scenario.

And really, having Nate's handiwork in her house was a bad enough distraction. Now having him here, it seemed somehow her space was never going to be quite the same.

As if it would be missing *something*.

Stop it, Morgan ordered herself. She was *devoted* to independence. Nate showing her how to hang something without it falling back off the wall could only forward that cause!

That's why she had given in so easily to his suggestion to come over here.

Wasn't it?

No, said the little part of her that watched him filling her tiny space with his essence. There was an illusion of intimacy from having him in this space.

Now his presence was large as he loomed in her living room waiting for her to find a hammer.

When she came back from the basement with one, she found him eyeing her purple couch with a look that was a cross between amusement and bewilderment.

"Do you like it?" she asked, feeling ridiculously as if it was a *test*. Of course he wouldn't like it, proving to her the wisdom of living on her own, not having to consult with anyone else about her choices, proving the *bliss* of the single life.

"Yeah, I like it," he said slowly. "What I don't get is how a woman can make something like this work. If I bought a sofa this color it would look like I killed that purple dinosaur. You know the one? He dances. And sings. But it looks good in here. It suits you."

She tried not to show how pleased she was, his words so different from what she expected. "I call my decorating style Bohemian chic."

"You don't strike me as Bohemian," he said, looking at her thoughtfully. "I would think of that as kind of gypsylike. You seem, er, enormously conventional."

"Perhaps I have a hidden side," she said, a bit irked. Enormously conventional? That sounded boring!

"Perhaps you have. Perhaps you even have a hidden sheik," he said, "which, come to think of it, would be just as good as a hidden stud. Maybe better. What do I know?"

"C-h-i-c," she spelled out. "Not sheik!"

And then he laughed with such enjoyment at his own humor that she couldn't help but join in. It was a treat to hear him laugh. She suspected he had not for a long time.

She handed him her hammer.

He frowned, the laughter gone. "The couch is good. This? Are you kidding me? What is this? A toy?"

It occurred to her that a woman that linked her life with his would have to like a traditional setup. She would choose the furniture, he would choose the tools. She would cook the meals, he would mow the lawn.

Considering she had left her fiancé because he had taken what she considered to be a sexist view of her career aspirations, considering her devotion to the principles of *Bliss: The Extraordinary Joy of Being a Single Woman*, Morgan was amazed by how easily something in her capitulated to this new vision. How lovely would it be having someone to share responsibilities with?

Shared, maybe certain things would not feel like such onerous, unachievable chores. Could there be unexpected pleasures in little things like hanging a few coat hangers? Is that what a good marriage was about?

She didn't know. Her own parents had separated when she was young, her father had remarried and she had always felt outside the circle of his *new* family.

Her mother's assessment of the situation—that she was looking for her father—seemed way too harsh. But Morgan knew her childhood experiences had made her long for love.

Not just love, but for a traditional relationship, like the one her best friend's parents had enjoyed. How she had envied the stability of that home, the harmony there, the feeling of absolute security.

But after her relationship with Karl, its bitter ending, Morgan had decided the love she longed for was unrealistic, belonged in the fairy tales she so enjoyed reading to the children.

Now, with Nate Hathoway in her front entry, tapping

her wall with her toy hammer, the choice Morgan had made to go it alone didn't feel the least bit blissful. It felt achingly empty. Achingly.

CHAPTER FOUR

NATE HADN'T REALLY expected Morgan's house to have this effect on him. It was cozy and cute, like a little nest. The enjoyment he had taken in her discomfort over agreeing to invite him over to help her find a "stud" was dissipating rapidly.

And who had pushed the envelope, who had suggested this foolishness? He wished he could blame her, but oh, no, it had been all him, lured by her blushing at the word *stud*.

Feeling the need to be a man, to do for her what she didn't have the skill to do herself.

But now, in her house, with her purple sofa and her toy hammer in his hand? It was his lack he was aware of, not hers.

This house made him feel lonely for soft things. Feminine touches, Cindy's warmth, seemed to be fading from his own house. The couch throw pillows she had chosen were worn out, the rag rug at the front door a little more rag than rug these days, the plaid blanket she had bought when Ace was a baby and that Ace still pulled over herself to watch television, was pathetically threadbare.

It reminded Nate, unhappily, how desperately inadequate he was to be raising a girl on his own.

What was it about Morgan that made him look at a life that he had felt he made full and satisfying despite the loss of his wife, to thinking maybe he wasn't doing nearly as well as he'd imagined? Around Morgan his life suddenly seemed to have glaringly empty spaces in it.

"Wow," he said, forcing himself to focus on her wall, to not give her even an inkling of the craving for softness that was going on inside of him, "for a little bit of a thing, you know how to destroy a wall."

"It wasn't intentional."

"Destruction rarely is."

He needed to remember that around Morgan McGuire. His life and Ace's had had enough unintentional destruction wrought on it. They could not bear more loss, either of them. He needed to do what he had come here to do, and get out, plain and simple.

Not that anything seemed simple with Morgan sharing the same room with him as it did when he brooded on it alone over the forge.

Nate brought himself back, shook his head again at the large holes where she had tried to hang his coat hooks and the weight of them had pulled chunks of drywall off the walls.

He tapped lightly on her entrance wall with a hammer.

"See? There's a stud." He glanced at her. She was refusing to blush this time, probably because of his explanation, so he went on explaining, as if his voice going on and on was an amulet against the spell of her. "You can hear the solid sound behind the wall. They're placed every sixteen inches. So you could put a coat hanger here, and—" he tapped the wall gently "—here. Here. Here."

"But that's not where I want the coat hangers," she said mutinously. "It's not centered properly. I want them in a row like this."

She went and took a pair of hangers from where he had set them on the floor, inserted herself between him and the wall and showed him.

"Here and here. And the other two in a straight line down from them."

He went very still. She was so close to him. He had no protection against this kind of spell. His craving for all things soft intensified. Her scent, clean, soap and shampoo, filled him. She was not quite touching him, but he could feel a delicate warmth radiating off her.

It seemed, dangerously, as if she could fill the *something missing* place in his life.

Nate knew he should back away from her a careful step but he didn't. He tried to hold up the amulet of words again. "Hmm. Guys don't think like that. For most men, it's all about function, not form."

But all the words did this time was make him more sharply aware of their differences, male and female, soft and hard, emotionally open and emotionally closed.

"Tell that to someone who hasn't seen your work," she said.

"I do try and marry form and function in my work."

Now his amulet, words, had come back to bite him. He contemplated his use of the word *marry* in such close proximity to her, hoped it was completely coincidental and not a subliminal longing.

He could not help but feel he was being drugged by her closeness, the spell of her winding its way around him, stronger than all that physical toughness he possessed.

Because Nate still had not moved. He could smell that good, good smell that was all hers. Wholesome. Unpretentious. But alluringly soft, feminine, just like this space.

She seemed to realize suddenly that she had placed herself in very close proximity to him. She went as still as him, caught, too, in the unexpected bond of awareness that leaped sizzling in the air between them.

Then, stronger than him, after all, Morgan tried to slip away, back out under his arm, but he dropped it marginally, and they were locked together in the small space of the hallway.

He looked at her for a moment, the intensity between them as tangible as a static shock off a cat, or clothes out of the dryer. He was weakened enough. It was absolutely the wrong time to remember how soft her cheek had felt under his fingertips, and then his lips.

Nate was not seeing her as his daughter's teacher right now. Unless he was mistaken, her eyes were smoky with a longing that mirrored his own.

But he had already buried a wife. And his best friend. To believe in good things again felt as if it would challenge even his legendary strength.

Even this situation should be showing him something important. He had vowed he did not want to tangle any further with the young schoolteacher.

And yet, here he stood in her front hallway.

Nate knew, the hard way, that life could be wrested

out of his control. His young wife had gone out the door, Christmas Eve, for *one more thing.*

One more thing for Ace's sock. He could even remember what it was, because she had told him as she went out the door laughing. *Reindeer poop.* Chocolate-covered raisins that one of the stores had bagged and labeled in tiny ziplock bags.

He'd been so glad to see her laughing, so happy to see her engrossed in getting ready for Christmas that he hadn't really paid any attention to the snow outside.

Why had he let her go? Why hadn't he offered to drive her?

And then, instead of Cindy coming back with reindeer poop, there had been that awful knock on the door, and a terrible descent into hell.

So, he knew, firsthand and the hard way, life could be snatched from your control.

It only made him more determined to control the things he could.

And he could still exercise some control over this. And he was aware that he needed to do it. The last thing he needed to do was give in to the insane desire to kiss Morgan again… And not on the cheek this time, either.

Congratulating himself on the return of his strength, feeling as Sampson must have done when his hair grew back and he pulled that building down, Nate dropped his arm, backed away. He needed to go *now.*

"Look, I'll make you a mounting board for the coat hangers. I've got some really nice barn wood at home that I'd been planning to reclaim. I'll fasten the board to the studs, so it's nice and solid, and then put the coat hangers on that." He looked at his watch. "Rehearsal is nearly over, Miss McGuire."

And he was aware as he said it that it could be taken a number of ways. That *their* rehearsal was nearly over. And what would that mean? The *real* thing to follow?

He hoped not, but now that he had promised her the barn board, he knew his escape was temporary. He was going to have to come back and put it up.

Hopefully he would have time to gird his loins against her before he did that!

They got back to the auditorium just as Mrs. Wellhaven was wrapping up. Ace flew off the stage and into his arms, seeming remarkably unscathed by her hour in the clutches of the dragon.

He lifted her up easily, and he felt the weight and responsibility of loving her, of protecting her from hurt, from more loss.

He glanced at Morgan over his daughter's head. His tangling with her teacher had the potential to hurt her. Bad.

"Guess what, Daddy?"

"What, sweetheart?"

"Mrs. Wellhaven says one of us, somebody from our class, is going to be the Christmas Angel! They get to stand on a special platform so it looks like they are on the top of the tree. They sing a song all by themselves!"

He knew this latest development had the potential to hurt Ace bad, too. His love for his daughter might blind him to her—like every father he thought his little girl was the most beautiful in the world—but he knew Ace's was not a traditional beauty. With her croaky voice and funny carrottop, she was hardly Christmas-angel material.

"She's letting all twenty-two of you think you have a chance of being the Christmas Angel?" He could hear annoyance in his voice, but Ace missed it.

"Not the boys, silly." She beamed at him. "Just the girls can be Christmas angels. It could be me!"

Ace's voice was even more croaky than ever, excitement and hope dancing across her very un-angel-like features.

Hope. Wasn't that the most dangerous thing of all?

Nate's eyes met Morgan's over the top of Ace's head. She didn't even have the decency to look distressed, to clearly see how unrealistic his daughter's hopes were.

He felt the weight of wanting to protect his daughter from all of life's disappointments, felt the weight of his inability to do so.

"I should have beaned Mrs. Wellhaven while I had the chance," he said darkly. And he felt that even more strongly the next morning at breakfast.

"Daddy, I dreamed about Mommy last night."

Nate flinched, and then deliberately relaxed his shoulders. He was standing at the kitchen counter, making a packed lunch, his back to Ace, who was floating battle formations with the remains of the breakfast cereal in her bowl.

He knew his own dreams about his wife were never good. *Cindy swept away by a raging river, him reaching out but not being able to get to her. Cindy falling from an airplane, him reaching out the door, trying desperately to reach a hand that fell farther and farther away...*

He often woke himself up screaming Cindy's name.

Nate hadn't heard Ace scream last night. He tried not

to let his dread show in his voice, but didn't turn around to look at her.

"Uh-huh?" He scowled at the lunch ingredients. If he sent peanut butter *again* was Morgan going to say something? When had he started to care what Morgan had to say?

Probably about the same time he'd been dumb enough to plant that impromptu kiss on her cheek.

It was ridiculous that a full-grown man, renowned for his toughness, legend even, was shirking from the judgments, plentiful as those were, of a grade-one teacher.

"It was a good dream," his daughter announced, and Nate felt relief shiver across his shoulder blades. Maybe finally, they had reached a turning point. Ace had had a good dream.

He recognized that he, too, seemed to be getting back into the flow of a life. If going shopping and volunteering to help with a town project counted. He suspected it did.

And did it all relate back to Morgan? Again, Nate suspected it did.

In defiance of that fact, and the fact that some part of him leaned toward *liking* Miss McGuire's approval, he slathered peanut butter on bread. Ace liked peanut butter. And she liked nonnutritiously *white* bread, too.

"You rebel, you," Nate chided himself drily, out loud.

"Do you want to hear about my dream?"

He turned from the counter, glanced at his daughter, frowned faintly. Ace was *glowing* in her new sparkle skinny jeans and Christmas sweater with a white, fluffy reindeer on it. Even her hair was tamed, carefully combed, flattened down with water.

He turned back to the counter. "Sure. Raspberry or strawberry?"

"Raspberry. In my dream, Mommy was an angel."

Something shivered along his spine. *You've been my angel, Hath, now I'll be yours.*

"She had on a long white dress, and she had big white wings made out of feathers. She took me on her lap, and she said she was sorry she had to leave me and that she loved me."

"That's nice, Ace. It really is."

"Mommy told me that she had to leave me right at Christmas because people have forgotten what Christmas is about, and that she was going to teach them. She said she's going to save Christmas. Do you think that's true, Daddy?"

After David had died, Cindy had found respite from her grief in that time of year. By the time Ace had come along, she *loved* every single thing about Christmas. Every single thing. Turkey. Trees. Carols. Gifts. *Reindeer poop.*

After David's death, she'd developed a simple faith that she had not had when they were children. Cindy believed God was looking after things, that there were reasons she could not understand, that He could make good come from bad.

While not quite sharing her beliefs, to Nate it had been a nice counterpoint toward his own tendency toward cynicism.

After she had died, his cynicism had hardened in him. In fact, he felt as if he shook his fist at the heavens. This was how her faith was rewarded? How could this have happened if things were really being looked after?

Show me the reason. Show me something good coming from this.

And the answer? Yawning emptiness.

He had buried her in the gravesite in an empty plot that was right beside David. Nate had gone to that gravesite a few times, hoping to feel something there. A presence, a sense of something watching over him, but no, more yawning emptiness.

So his cynicism hardened like concrete setting up on a hot day, and he didn't go to the graveyard anymore, not even when Cindy's sister, Molly, went to mark special occasions, birthdays, Christmas.

And now listening to Ace chatter about angels, it felt as if his cynicism had just ramped up another gear.

Why did he have an ugly feeling he knew exactly where this was going?

"I hope so, honey." Because, despite the cynicism, he was aware nobody needed Christmas saved more than him and his daughter.

Unfortunately, he was pretty damned sure Ace's dream had a whole lot more to do with Mrs. Wellhaven's ill-conceived announcement about one of Ace's class being chosen the Christmas Angel than with her mother.

Ace confirmed his ugly feeling by announcing, sunnily, "In the dream, Mommy told me I'm going to be the Christmas Angel!"

Nate struggled not to let the cynicism show in his face. Still, he shot a worried look at his daughter.

Even with the new clothes and better hair, Ace looked least likely to be the Christmas Angel, at least not in the typical sense he thought of Christmas angels: blond ringlets, china-blue eyes, porcelain skin.

Ace looked more like a leprechaun, or a yard gnome, than an angel.

"Poor Brenda," Ace continued. "She thinks it's going to be her. I wonder if she'll still be my friend if it's me."

Brenda Weston, naturally, took after her mother, Ashley, and looked like everyone's vision of the Christmas Angel. Chances were she didn't sing flat, either.

"You know it was just a dream, don't you, Ace?"

"Mrs. McGuire says dreams come true."

Thank you, Miss McGuire. There she was again, somehow front and center in his life.

"Miss McGuire," he said, choosing his words with great care, "doesn't mean dreams you have while you're sleeping come true. She means dreams you think of while you're awake. Like you might dream of being a doctor someday. Or a teacher. Or a pilot. And that can come true."

"Oh, like stupid Freddy Campbell thinks he's going to be a hockey player?"

"Exactly like that."

"Can he?"

"I don't know. I guess if he works hard enough and has some natural talent, maybe he could."

Ace snorted. "If Freddy Campbell can be a hockey player, I can be the Christmas Angel. See? I'm dreaming it while I'm awake, too."

There was no gentle way to put this.

"Ace, don't get your hopes up." He said it sternly.

She smiled at him, easily forgiving of the fact he was doing his best to dash her dreams. "Don't worry, Daddy, I won't."

"You know what?" he said gruffly. "You're the smart-est kid I ever met." Six going on thirty. Maybe that wasn't such a good thing, but Ace beamed at him as if he'd presented her with a new puppy.

"The Christmas Angel probably has to be smart," she decided happily.

He sighed. Over the next few days, he'd try and get it through to her. She wasn't going to be the Christmas Angel. And he'd better let Morgan know he didn't want this particular brand of hopeless optimism encour-aged.

An excuse to talk to Morgan, a little voice inside him, disturbingly gleeful, pointed out.

He had to deliver her the board he'd made for her coat hangers anyway. So, maybe he'd kill two birds with one stone. And then he'd be out of excuses for seeing her.

And *then* he'd get back on track in terms of dis-tancing himself from her, protecting his daughter and himself from the loss of coming to care too deeply for someone.

Which meant he knew the potential was there. That Morgan McGuire was a person you could come to care too deeply about if you weren't really, really careful.

"Come on, squirt, I'll drive you to school." He shoved Ace's lunch into a bag, and went to the table. He roughed her hair, and she got up and threw her arms around his waist, hugged hard.

"I love you, Daddy."

And for one split second, everything in his world seemed okay, and Ace, the one who had given him a reason to live, seemed like the most likely angel of all.

* * *

Morgan's doorbell rang just as the Christmas tree fell over. Thankfully it made a whooshing sound, probably because it was so large, so she heard it and leaped out of the way, narrowly missing being hit by it.

"Hell and damnation!" she said, regarding the tree lying in a pool of bent branches and dead needles on her floor.

Her bell rang again, and Morgan climbed over the tree that blocked her entrance hallway and went and flung open the front door.

Nate Hathoway stood there, looking like damnation itself. Despite the cold out, he wore a black leather jacket and jeans. Whiskers darkened his cheeks. His eyes sparked with a light that would have put the devil himself to shame.

"I thought you were opposed to cussing," he said mildly, white puffs of vapor forming as his hot breath hit the cold air.

Silently, she *cussed* the lack of insulation in her old house that had allowed her voice to carry right through the door. She also cussed the fact that she was wearing a horrible pair of gray sweatpants and a sweatshirt that said Teachers Spell It Out.

While she was on an inward cussing spree, Morgan also cursed the fact that she could imagine, all too well, what the slide of that warm breath across her neck would feel like.

"I am opposed to cursing in front of children!" she defended herself. "In cases of duress, amongst consenting adults, it's fine."

His eyes narrowed with fiendish delight. She wished she would have chosen a term different from consenting adults. It was a mark of how flustered his unexpected appearance had made her feel that she had said that!

And it was obvious he was thinking that phrase usually referred to something quite a bit more exciting than cussing.

"What was the crashing noise?" he asked, peering over her shoulder.

"Nothing!" she said stubbornly. It was her first Christmas by herself. She had never set up a tree before. Frankly, it was one of the loneliest and most frustrating experiences of her single life. And she wasn't pretending otherwise because Amelia Ainsworthy, someone she did not know, and was not likely to meet, thought such efforts at aloneness were character building!

He glanced behind her. The tree was lying there, blocking the door.

"Did your tree fall down?"

He did *not* sound gentle. Did he? Maybe he did, a little bit. But it didn't matter!

"I set it there," she lied, hoping to hide both her loneliness and her frustration from him. "It's too tall. I'm going to put the lights on before I stand it up."

"Don't take up poker," he advised her solemnly. "You made that decision after it fell, didn't you?"

She shrugged, trying not to let on how his appearance had made her aware of a dreadful weakness in her character. Morgan *wanted* a big, strong guy just to come in and take over.

She wanted a man to figure out the blasted stand, saw off those bottom branches, muscle the huge, unwieldy tree into place, put the star on top and figure out lights that looked as if they required a degree in engineering to sort out.

Nate truly was the devil, arriving here at a horrible moment, when she felt vulnerable and lonely. He was tempting her to rely on something—or *someone*—other than herself. She was sending him back into the night.

"Do you want help with the tree?"

"No," she spat out quickly before the *yes, yes, yes* clawing its way up her throat could jump out and betray her.

He nodded, but he could clearly see the horrible truth. She was the kind of helpless female the new her was determined not to have any use for!

"I brought over the board to put the coat hangers on. I could put it up for you if you want."

Her eyes went to what he was holding. A helpless female might weep at the beauty of the board he had reclaimed for her. It was honey-colored, the grains of the wood glorious, the surface and edges sanded to buttery smoothness.

Well, right after he put it up for her, she was sending him back into the night. She would draw the line at allowing him to help with the tree.

Despite wanting to rebel against the teachings of the blissfully single Amelia, Morgan knew she would be a better person, in the long run, if she put that tree up herself. She stepped back from the door, and he stepped in.

She touched the board. "That's not what I was expecting," she said. "Something worn and weathered. When you said it was barn wood, I thought gray."

"It was, before I ran it through the plainer. Some of this old wood is amazing. This piece came from a barn they pulled down last year that was a hundred and ten years old." His fingers caressed the wood, too. "Solid oak, as strong and as beautiful as the day they first milled it."

Morgan was struck again by something about Nate. His work always seemed to be about things that *lasted*. There was something ruggedly appealing about that in a world devoted to disposable everything.

Including relationships.

There was a tingle on the back of her neck. A relationship with this man would be as solid as he was, a forever thing, or nothing at all.

Don't you dare think of him in terms of a relationship, the devoted-to-independence woman inside her cried. But it was too late. That particular horse was already out of the barn.

"Where's Ace?" she said, glancing behind him.

"The Westons took her to the Santa Claus parade and then she's sleeping over at their place. Ace is thrilled."

As she closed the door, she read a moment of unguarded doubt on his face. "You, not so much?"

"I don't know. I don't quite get the purpose of it. I get going tobogganing, or to a movie. I don't get sleeping at someone else's house."

Don't blush, she ordered herself. They were not talking about *adult* sleepovers.

"Sleeping is not an activity," he muttered.

"Believe me, they won't be doing much sleeping. Probably movies and popcorn. Maybe some makeup."

"Makeup?" He ran a hand through his hair and looked distressed. "I hoped I was years away from makeup. And don't even mention the word *bra* to me."

Believe me, that was the last word I was going to mention to you.

He could fluster her in a hair, damn him. She tried

not to let it show. "Not serious makeup. Not yet. You know, dress-up stuff. Big hats, an old string of pearls, some high heels."

"Oh."

"Is there something deeper going on with you?" she asked. "Something that needs to be addressed?"

Morgan saw she could fluster him in a hair, too.

"Such as?" he asked defensively.

"Any chance you don't like losing control, Nate?"

He scowled, and for a moment she thought she was going to get the lecture about knowing everything again. But then she realized he wasn't scowling *at* her. After a long silence, he finally answered.

"I don't know what I'm supposed to do," he admitted reluctantly. "I felt like I wanted to call the Westons and conduct an interview."

Interrogation, she guessed wryly. "What kind of interview?"

"You know."

She raised her eyebrows at him. He sighed. "Just casually ferret out information about their suitability to have Ace over. Don't you think I should know if anyone in the house has a criminal record? Don't you think I should know if they consume alcoholic beverages? And how many, how often? Don't you think I should know if they have the Playboy channel? And if it's blocked?"

Morgan was trying not to laugh, but he didn't notice.

"Even if I got all the right answers," he continued, "I still would want to invite myself over and just as casually check their house for hazards."

"Hazards? Like what?"

"You know."

"I'm afraid I can't even imagine what kind of hazards might exist at the Westons' house."

His scowl deepened. "Like loaded weapons, dogs that bite, unplugged smoke detectors."

She was biting the inside of her cheek to keep from laughing. She knew it would be the wrong time to laugh. "The Westons are very nice people," she said reassuringly. "Ashley is active in the PTA."

He sighed. "Intellectually, I know that. That's how I stopped myself from phoning or going in. I grew up with Ashley Weston. Moore, back then. She was a goody-goody. I guess if Ace has to sleep somewhere other than her own bed, I want it to be at a house where I know the mom is a goody-goody. Sheesh. The PTA. I should have guessed."

"Don't knock it until you try it," Morgan suggested drily.

"I'm not trying it. Don't even think about sending me a note."

There were quite a few single moms in the PTA, probably the same ones who swarmed him at the supermarket, so, no, she wouldn't send him a note.

"Still—" he moved on from the PTA issue as if it hardly merited discussion "—what about next time? What if Ace gets invited to someone's house where I didn't grow up with their parents? Or worse, what if I did, and I remember the mom was a wild thing who chugged hard lemonade and swam naked at the Old Sawmill Pond? Then what?"

No wonder he had an aversion to doing his grocery shopping locally. That was way too much to know about people!

"I'm not sure," she admitted.

"Oh, great. Thanks a lot, Miss McGuire! When I really want an answer, you don't have one. What good is a know-it-all without an answer?"

Morgan was amazingly unoffended. In fact, she felt she could see this man as clearly as she had ever seen him. She suddenly saw he was *restless*. And irritable. He had needed to do something tonight to offset this loss of control.

"Is this the first night you've been apart since the accident that took her mom?" she asked softly.

He stared at her. For a moment he looked as though he would turn and walk away rather than reveal something so achingly vulnerable about himself.

But then instead of walking away, he nodded, once, curtly.

And she stepped back over the fallen tree, motioning for him to follow her, inviting him in.

Morgan knew it was crazy to be this foolishly happy that he had picked her to come to, crazier yet that she was unable to resist his need.

But how could anyone, even someone totally emancipated, be hard-hearted enough to send a man back into the night who had come shouldering the weight of terrible burdens? Not that he necessarily knew how heavy his burdens were.

He hesitated, like an animal who paused, sensing danger. And what would be more dangerous to him than someone seeing past that hard exterior to his heart?

And then, like that same animal catching the scent of something irresistible, he moved slowly forward. He stepped over her tree, and she wondered if he knew how momentous his decision was.

If he did, he was allowing himself to be distracted. He

surveyed the strings of lights strewn around her living room floor, the boxes of baubles, the unhung socks. For a moment it looked as if he might run from the magnitude of what he had gotten himself into.

But then he crouched and looked at the tree stand, a flying-saucer-type apparatus, that was still attached solidly to the trunk of the tree. It just hadn't kept the tree solidly attached to the floor.

"Is this what you expected to hold your tree?" he asked incredulously.

It was the kind of question that didn't really merit an answer. Though it had been the most expensive tree stand at Finnegan's, a tree nearly crashing down on top of her was ample evidence that the design was somewhat flawed.

"It's worse than your hammer," Nate decided, with a solemn shake of his head. Still, he looked pleased that he had found something in such dire need of his immediate attention.

"I bought a new hammer," she said.

After his last visit, she had decided she wasn't having her hammer choice keep her from the promised bliss of the single woman.

Though somehow, in this moment, Morgan knew she had missed the point because she felt ridiculously eager to show it to him, secretly, weakly wanted his approval of her choice.

"Really?" But he hardly seemed interested in her new acquisition of a hammer. He had already moved on to other things.

With raw strength that made her shiver, he yanked the stand off the trunk of the tree and scowled at it, looked at it from one way and then another.

"I think I can fix it." He began to whistle through his teeth, a song that sounded suspiciously like "Angel Lost" though she decided against pointing that out to him, because he was so obviously pleased to have things to look after since Ace was out of his reach for the evening.

Morgan told herself she was duty bound to resist this beautiful gift of a man coming to help her. Duty bound.

So, naturally she didn't.

"I'll go make cocoa," she said, and then, in case that might be interpreted as far too traditional, she let the independent and blissful woman speak up, too. "And I'll get my new hammer, too."

CHAPTER FIVE

"THIS IS YOUR HAMMER?" he asked. Nate tried not to laugh. Good grief. She was an all-or-nothing kind of girl. She had gone from the toy tapping tool that had looked more like an instrument her first graders would use in a percussion band, to this, a 23-ounce Blue Max framing hammer with a curved handle. It looked like a hatchet.

"What's wrong with it?" Morgan asked.

"Nothing."

"It was very expensive."

"I'm sure it was. I'll bet that tree stand was, too."

"Don't take that 'there's a sucker born every minute' tone with me."

"Yes, ma'am," he answered her schoolmarm tone of voice.

But she wasn't fooled. Not even a little bit. "You think my new hammer is funny. I can tell."

It probably wasn't a good thing that she was getting so good at reading him.

"No, no, it's not funny." Despite saying that a snort of laughter escaped him. And then another. Then he couldn't resist. "When are you building a house?"

"A house?" she asked, flabbergasted.

And he dissolved into laughter. He had not laughed, it seemed, for a very long time. Oh, little chuckles had been taking him by surprise here and there. But it had not been like this. A from the belly, caught in the moment, delight-filled roar of genuine laughter.

It felt good to laugh again. Maybe too good. It almost made him forget he had other worries tonight, like Ace and her new little pal, who could at this moment be gooping on makeup, or eating popcorn in front of an unblocked Playboy channel.

"A big hammer is called a framing hammer. It's used for framing a house."

"I'm sure it can be used for other things."

"Yeah. If you can lift it. And swing it. Have you seen house framers? They have wrists nearly as big as your thighs."

Shoot. Was she going to guess he'd been looking at her thighs? Maybe not, because she suddenly seemed distracted by his wrists. She licked her lips. He decided it might be best to avoid mentioning body parts from now on.

Or looking at them. For a prim little schoolteacher, she had lips that practically begged to be kissed, full and plump.

He wasn't going to be held responsible for what happened next if she licked them again.

"You don't buy a hammer you can barely heft," he said, a little more sharply than he intended. His sharpness had nothing to do with her hammer choice, not that she ever had to know.

She reacted to the tone, which was so much better than lip-licking. Rather than looking educated, she looked annoyed. Annoyance was good!

"I like that hammer," she said stubbornly.

"Really?" he challenged her. "What do you like about it?"

She hesitated. She looked at the hammer. She looked at him. She looked at her toes. And the fallen Christmas tree. It was written all over her that she wanted to lie, and that she was incapable of it.

"The color," she finally admitted, giving him a look that dared him to laugh. It was a look designed to intimidate six-year-old boys and it was effective, too.

Or would have been effective if she hadn't started laughing first. He liked it that she could laugh at herself, and then they were both laughing. Laughing with her, for the second time in just a few minutes, was a worse temptation than sneaking peeks at how those prison-issue sweatpants hugged her thighs.

Because it invited him back toward the Light. Nate was aware he was walking way too close to the fire.

He reined himself in. "I'll just put up the coat hangers now," he said. To himself he added that he would put up the coat hangers—that was what he had come here to do—and go. Immediately.

"Show me how to do it," she said, setting down the cocoa she had brought in. "Next time I need something done, you might not be here."

Not *might not,* he corrected her silently. *Won't.* A week ago, he would have said it out loud… Why not now? Because, despite his vow to stay away, he kept coming back to her, magnet to steel.

Because there was something about her that was funny and sweet and even a hard man such as himself could not bring himself to hurt her by tossing out carelessly cruel words.

"Come on then," he said gruffly. "I'll show you."

It was a surrender. Because putting up a few coat hangers should have been the simplest thing in the world. It should have taken five minutes.

Instead, because of his surrender, half an hour later the reclaimed barn board was finally up. His hand had brushed her hand half a dozen times. Their shoulders had touched. He was aware of her lips and her thighs and her shoulders and her scent.

He was amazed he'd managed to get that board level, the coat hooks spaced out evenly.

Morgan was glowing as if she'd designed a rocket that could go to Mars as she surveyed their handiwork.

"It looks so good."

"Except for the additional hole," he pointed out wryly. She had put the huge hammer through the drywall when she had missed the nail he was trying to teach her to drive.

He had supplies to fix it, since he'd come prepared to fix her previous holes in the wall. He taped the hole, stirred the drywall mud and began to patch.

"I want you to promise you'll return the hammer." Then, he heard himself promising that if she did, he'd help her pick out one that was better for all-around household use and repairs.

Even though he knew darn well Harvey could help her. Harvey had been handling the hardware department at Finnegan's since time began. Nate could even go in and warn him to offer her a little advice on her purchases, before he actually let her buy them.

Whether she wanted it or not.

But she probably wouldn't, and for some reason he

thought she might listen to him a little more than she would listen to Harvey.

Thought that meant something.

She was coming to trust him.

Oh, Nate, he told himself, cut this off, short and sweet. Wouldn't that be best for both of them?

"The cocoa's gone cold," she said, oblivious to his inner war. She took a little sip and wrinkled her nose in the cutest way. A little sliver of foam clung to the fullness of her lip. "I'll go make some more. Let's take a break."

Which meant she thought he was staying, and somehow, probably because of the damn foam on her lip, he could feel short-and-sweet going right out the window.

Well, Nate rationalized, he couldn't very well leave her with her Christmas tree sprawled across the floor, with a stand that was never going to stand up, could he?

Yes.

But he'd said he'd fix it.

He trailed her to the kitchen and watched her make cocoa. Since she was going to the effort, he'd drink that. Then he was leaving, tree or no tree. He had a kid he hired to help him sometimes, he'd send him over tomorrow. He could look after having it fixed without fixing it himself. But then would it be done right?

Her kitchen, like her living room, made him aware of some as yet unnamed lack in himself.

Everything was tidy, there was not a single crumb on the counter, no spills making smoke come off the burners as she heated the milk. She reached for a spice and the spices were in a stainless-steel container that turned, not lined up on top of the stove. The oven mitts weren't stained and didn't have holes burned in them.

He could feel that horrible *longing* welling up in him.

Leave, he told himself. Instead of leaving as completely as he would have liked, he left the kitchen and went and worked on the stand. So it would be done right.

By the time she came back in, he had the stand modified to actually hold up a tree, and had the tree standing back up.

"This is a foolishly large tree," he told her.

She smiled, mistaking it for a compliment. "Isn't it?"

He sighed. "Where do you want it?"

"I should put the lights on while it's on the ground," she told him. "Come have your cocoa before it cools this time. I'll worry about the tree later."

But somehow, he knew now he'd be putting the lights on it for her, too. It was too pathetic to think of her trying to put them on with the tree lying on the floor, creative as that solution might be to her vertical challenges.

It occurred to him, she was proving a hard woman to get away from. And that with every second he stayed it was going to get harder, not easier.

Okay. The lights. That was absolutely it. Then he was leaving.

He went and sat beside her on the couch as she handed him cocoa. He took a sip. It was not powdered hot chocolate out of a tin, like he made for Ace on occasion. It was some kind of ambrosia. There was cinnamon mixed with the chocolate.

Morgan McGuire had witch-green eyes. She was probably casting a spell on him.

"So, do you and Ace have family to spend the holidays with?" she asked.

He wished he would have stuck with the lights. That was definitely a "getting to know you" kind of question.

"We alternate years. Last year we were with my parents, who live in Florida now, so this year we're with Cindy's side of the family, Ace's aunt Molly and uncle Keith. They have a little place outside of town. We'll go out there after the production on Christmas Eve and spend the night."

He didn't say his own house was too painful a place to be on Christmas Eve. He did not think he could be there without hearing the knock on the door, opening it expecting to see Cindy so loaded down she couldn't open the door.

By then, Cindy had been gone so long he suspected she was coming home with a little more than reindeer poop.

"How about you?" he asked, mostly to avoid the way his thoughts were going, to deflect any more questions about his plans for Christmas.

Which were basically *get through it*.

She was the kind of woman you could just spill your guts to. If you were that kind of guy.

Which he wasn't.

"Oh." She suddenly looked uncomfortable. "I'm not sure yet."

"You won't go home?" he asked, suddenly aware it wasn't all about *him,* detecting something in her that was guarded. Or maybe even a little sad.

"No," she said bravely. "With *The Christmas Angel* on Christmas Eve I decided to just stay here."

Again, focused intently on her now, he heard something else. And for whatever reason, he probed it.

"Your family will be disappointed not to have you, won't they?"

She shrugged with elaborate casualness. "I think my mom is having a midlife crises. After twenty-three years of working in an insurance office, she chucked everything, packed a backpack and went to Thailand. She told me she'll be on a beach in Phuket on Christmas day."

"And what about your dad?"

"He and my mom split when I was eleven. He's remarried and has a young family. I'm never quite sure where I fit into all that." And then she added ruefully, "Neither is he."

Nate didn't know what to say.

His family might have been rough around the edges, but not knowing where you fit into the arrangement? He had been alternating where he spent Christmas since he had married Cindy and his mother still cried when it wasn't her year to have him and Ace.

The idea of your own family not wanting you was foreign to him. He felt so shocked and saddened by it, he had to fight back an urge to scoop her up and take her on his lap and rock her, like the lonely child he heard in her voice.

"It's actually been good," she rushed on bravely. "I'm doing all these things for the first time by myself. Before my mom decided to be a world traveler, she always *did* Christmas. And she was elaborate about it. Theme trees.

New recipes for stuffing. Winning the block decorating party. Christmas was always completely done for me. In fact, God forbid you should touch anything. Then it might not look perfect. So, I don't know how to do anything, but I'm happy to learn. You don't want to go through life not knowing how to do things like that. For yourself."

She was not a very good liar. She was not *happy* to learn. But he went along with her.

"No," he said soothingly, without an ounce of conviction, "you don't."

"Of course, I probably won't cook a turkey," she said. "For myself. That would be silly."

"You aren't going to be alone on Christmas." He wasn't quite sure why he said it like that. As if he knew she wasn't going to be alone at Christmas. When he didn't. At all.

She was silent. Too silent.

He shot her a look. Her face was scrunched up, and not in the cute way it had been when the chocolate had gone cold.

"Are you going to cry?" he asked with soft desperation.

"I certainly hope not."

"Me, too."

He fought again that impulse, to pick her up and lift her onto his lap, to pull her head against his shoulder and hold her tight.

Instead, and it was bad enough, he reached out and took her hand in his, and held it. It was a small gesture. Tiny against the magnitude of her pain.

Nothing, really.

And yet something huge at the same time. She clung to his hand as if he had tossed her a life preserver.

That should have been enough to make him let go. But it wasn't. He was leaving his hand there as long as she needed to hold it.

Nate understood instantly that something had shifted in him. He had come out of the cave of his pain just enough to reach out to someone else.

A shaft of light pierced the darkness he had lived in.

And he saw the truth: all evening the dark place had called him to come back. And he almost had obeyed that call.

There was something comforting and familiar about that place of pain where he had been. Save for Ace, it made few demands on him. He did not have to feel anything, he did not have to truly engage with life. It certainly did not ask him to grow or to *give*.

But now, now that that shaft of light had pierced him, he was not sure he could go back to living in darkness. He was not sure at all.

Morgan took a deep shuddering breath.

"Let's put up the lights on the tree," he suggested. If there was one thing personal pain had taught him, it was that sitting around contemplating it was no way to make it go away. Action was the remedy.

"Okay," she said, her voice wobbly with the tears she had not shed. She let go of his hand abruptly and leaped to her feet. "I guess that means I have to find the star."

Nate noted that everything she owned was brand-new, and there was a sadness in that in itself.

His childhood might have been poor, but both sides

of his family had given him Christmas relics that went on his tree every year. He was pretty sure his lights, the color cracked off them in spots, predated his birth by several years. He had antique ornaments that his grand-mother had carried across the ocean with her, acorn ornaments that Cindy had made when she was Ace's age.

Morgan's lack of anything old in her Christmas decoration boxes made him acutely aware of how bad her first Christmas alone could be.

And it was that awareness—of her aloneness, of how close to tears she had been—that made him tease her.

About the size of her tree, and the rather large size of the striped sock she put on the mantel for herself, about her selection of treetop star, a gaudy creation of pink-and-green neon lights.

He teased her until she was breathless with laughter, until the last remnants of sadness had left her face, and the sparkle in her eyes was not from tears. He was heartened when she began teasing him back.

Together, they put up the lights, ornaments way too scanty for such a big tree, tons of tinsel that she demanded, in her schoolteacher voice, get added to the tree a single strand at a time.

By the time they were done, it was close to midnight.

She insisted on making more hot chocolate. She turned off all the other lights in her house, and they sat on her purple couch in darkness made happy by the glow of the Christmas tree lights.

Nate had not realized how on guard he was against life, until now, when his guard came down.

He felt as relaxed as he had felt in years. And

exhausted. Keeping a guard up that high was hard work he realized, it required constant vigilance.

And that was the last thing he thought.

He was still sitting up, but Nate Hathoway had gone to sleep on her couch, Morgan noted. Another woman might have thought it wasn't a very exciting end to what had turned out to be a wonderful evening.

But, staring at him mesmerized, Morgan thought it was perfect.

Sometime during the night—around the time she had made that announcement about spending Christmas alone, intended to solidify in her own mind and his her independence, but somehow turning pathetically maudlin instead—he had let go of some finely held tension in him.

Now, she loved watching him sleep. She could study him to her heart's content without the embarrassment of him knowing.

And so she indulged in the guilty pleasure of just looking at him: the crumple of dark hair against his collar, the lashes so thick they could have been ink-encrusted, and cast soft shadows that contrasted the hard angles of his face, cheekbones, nose, chin.

His jaw was relaxed. And he didn't snore.

Sighing with the oddest contentment, she got up, finally, moved the hot chocolate from where he had set it on the ottoman and unplugged the Christmas lights. She fetched a blanket.

Her intention was to toss it lightly over him and tuck it around him.

But his head was tilted at an odd angle, so she gently

leaned over and put pressure on his shoulder. He sighed, leaned, and she tucked a pillow behind his head.

Better, except that she felt reluctant to remove her hand from his shoulder.

He reached up and took her wrist, yanked gently. "Lie down beside me."

She knew he was sleeping, or in that groggy state between being asleep and being awake where he didn't really even know who she was or what he was asking.

His guard had come way down tonight. Now he was in a really vulnerable state, admitting something he would probably not normally admit.

He did not want to be alone.

Just like her.

She knew she should disengage his fingers one by one from her wrist and tiptoe off to her own room. Probably he would wake sometime in the night, be embarrassed to find himself asleep on her couch and disappear.

So she knew what she *should* do. But it seemed all her life had been about *shoulds*. The one time she'd rebelled and not put her own life on hold because she *should* defer to her fiancé's more lucrative career it had ended rather badly.

So, maybe she'd become even more attached to shoulds than before.

For all its talk of the joy of freedom, wasn't *Bliss: The Extraordinary Joy of Being a Single Woman* just another book of shoulds? It was a desperate need for an instruction manual to guide her through life, to make the rules for her. Hadn't the book just provided another excuse not to rely on herself, *not* to risk following her instincts, *not* to risk taking control of her own life?

This was the truth: there was no instruction manual for life.

No one was going to grade her on what she did next. It was possible no one even cared. Her mother was in Thailand. Her father had long ago replaced his first family.

So why not do what she truly wanted? Why not do what would give her a moment's pleasure, even if that pleasure was stolen?

She didn't have to *stay* tucked into Nate's side. She could just see what it felt like, enjoy it for a few minutes and then go to bed.

With a sigh of pure surrender, Morgan sat on the edge of the couch, leaned tentatively into him. He was so solid it was like leaning against a stone, except the stone was deliciously sun-warmed.

He let go of her wrist, but his arm, freed, circled her waist and pulled her deep into his long leanness. For a moment, she felt as if she couldn't breathe.

What was she going to say if he woke up suddenly and completely?

She held her breath, waiting, but he didn't wake up. If anything his breathing deepened, touched the sensitive skin of her ear, felt on her neck exactly as she had always known it would, heated, as textured as silk.

She willed herself to relax, and as she did, she noticed her awareness of him deepening. Her own heart seemed to rise and fall with his each breath. He was not all hard lines as she had first thought. No, he radiated warmth, and his skin, taut over muscle, bone, sinew, had the faintest seductive give to it.

There, she told herself, she had felt it. She could get

up and go to her own bed now, satisfied that she had followed her own instincts.

Except it was harder than she could have imagined to get up, to leave the warmth and strength of him, to walk to her lonely room and her cold bed.

It was harder than she could have ever imagined to walk away from what was unfolding inside of her. A brand-new experience. A very physical feeling of connection. Closeness. Awareness.

A physical experience that had a mental component...

For as she snuggled more deeply into him, Morgan felt the moment begin to shine as if it had a life of its own.

Her mind struggled to put a label on the level of sensation she was experiencing. And then it succeeded.

Bliss.

Morgan fell asleep in the circle of his arms. And woke in the morning to winter sunshine pouring through her windows.

For a moment, she felt it again, *bliss.*

But then she realized why she had awoken. It was because he was awake. Oh, God. Why hadn't she just enjoyed the sensation for a moment and then gone to bed as she had originally planned?

It would have saved them both the terrible embarrassment of this situation.

Now it felt horribly awkward. He hadn't even been fully awake—maybe not even partially awake—when his hand had encircled her wrist and he had asked her to lie down with him.

What was he going to say now?

What the hell do you think you're doing?

Morgan could feel her whole body stiffening, bracing itself for his rejection.

Instead, his fingertips brushed her cheek.

"Hey," he said softly, something of discovery in his voice, "you have a print on your cheek again."

He didn't kiss it this time, though, just put her away from him, got to his feet and stretched.

The rumpled T-shirt lifted as he stretched his arms over his head, showing her the taut washboard of his stomach.

Her gaze drifted upward to his face. He was smiling. He didn't seem to find the situation awkward or embarrassing at all.

"Hmm," he said thoughtfully, "I guess now I know what's so great about sleepovers."

He was not sorry. It occurred to her that he hadn't been asleep at all when he'd invited her to cuddle with him. It hadn't been an accident. Or a case of groggy mistaken identity.

"Is my hair standing straight up?" she asked him.

He cocked his head. "No. More sideways."

That's what *wasn't* so great about sleepovers. And what now? Did she offer him breakfast? Did she show him the door?

He had his cell phone out of his pocket, scrolling through it. "No calls from Ace," he said with relief.

It was the mark of what kind of man he was that Morgan had not even known he had a cell phone until that moment.

Karl's had been more than a cell phone: it could practically start his car on command, and she realized now that Karl's cell phone had been like a third party in their relationship.

And that it would never be like that with Nate Hathoway.

"But I think I better go get her. Saturday is *our* day. She's pretty fussy about that."

"Okay." Was she being dismissed? That made her feel so bereft she couldn't even tease him about not going shopping this time.

"You want to spend our day with us?"

Her mouth fell open.

"I promised Ace a sleigh ride."

A sleigh ride?

She had to say no. Look at how she had just spilled the beans to him last night about her whole life history! Look how she had reacted when she thought she was not going to be included in his plans for the day!

Bereft.

No, throwing out the rule book did not mean leaving herself wide-open to hurt. And to get involved with this man had the potential to make her redefine *hurt*.

On the other hand, a sleigh ride?

Morgan nearly sighed out loud. It was the kind of family outing her childhood dreams had been full of. Despite her mother creating a picture of a perfect Christmas, there had never been the connection of a perfect Christmas. Christmas activities had involved *entertaining,* not playing.

Morgan had dreamed of tobogganing and skating and sleigh rides. She had dreamed it in such perfect detail that she could picture it already, with startling clarity. The three of them—her, Nate, Ace—nestled in a sleek red sleigh, their legs covered in a soft, plaid blanket.

He would be holding the reins of a spirited white stallion. The horse would snort, throw up clouds of snow with each prancing footfall. The air would be full of diamond ice crystals and the sound of bells.

There was an old-fashioned romance about his invitation that was irresistible.

"I'd love to join you and Ace on a sleigh ride," Morgan said.

Even though it was against her better judgment, this thing was unfurling inside her, like a flag. More than happiness. More than excitement. More than anticipation.

This time it was familiar to her, so Morgan identified it much more quickly.

"Happy," Nate said.

She preened that he had recognized her mood so quickly.

"That's Ace's pony's name. It's kind of like when people name a Great Dane Tiny. He's not that great with a sleigh."

Okay, so he hadn't recognized her mood. And the white steed was out. Still, gliding across snow-covered fields was gliding across snow-covered fields.

"I'll come back for you in an hour or so," he promised.

And he was gone, which was good, because she had been gravely tempted to lean forward, close her eyes and offer her lips as a form of goodbye.

"You're dreaming," she warned herself as she heard his vehicle roar to life outside.

In fact, it would have been too easy to dismiss the whole thing as a dream, except that her coat hangers were hung and her Christmas tree was up. Except lights winked from the branches, and the star, that age-old symbol of hope, shone bright from the very top of that tree, a pinnacle she could not have reached without a ladder.

It would be easy to dismiss the whole thing as a dream, except that when Morgan looked in the mirror, her hair was standing up sideways and her cheek held the perfect imprint of his shirt.

CHAPTER SIX

"MRS. McGUIRE, this is Happy." Ace patted the Shetland pony vigorously, kissed his nose. Ace's lips were stained an unnatural shade of red as if she had smeared them with raspberries.

"You were right about the lipstick," Nate had told Morgan, rolling his eyes, when they had picked her up.

"And you were wrong about—"

"Everything," he admitted. "No hazards of any kind. Don't ask me to admit I was wrong ever again. It unmans me."

He was teasing her, and Morgan was coming to enjoy the growing ease between them so much. But she liked the underlying message, too. That somehow their lives were linked, and *ever again* suggested it might be staying that way.

Even this outing suggested that. By inviting her to this Christmas-card-pretty farm—red barn, snow-covered fields, cows behind white fences—that belonged to his and Ace's family, weren't the links that connected them growing stronger?

Now Nate was trying to get a harness on the uncooperative, chunky brown-and-white pony. So far his hand

had been stepped on twice. He had said something—
both times—quite a bit stronger than "damn," then shot
Morgan looks that dared comment.

But she did not want to be the schoolteacher today.
Just a woman enjoying the extraordinary bliss of not
being alone, of sharing a wonderful winter day with a
glorious man and his adorable little girl.

"This is the meanest horse ever born," Nate grumbled. "Keep your face away from his teeth, for God's
sake, Ace. He might mistake your lips for an apple."

"He loves me," Ace said with certainty. "He won't
bite me."

"I don't know why he doesn't bite her," Nate told
Morgan, apparently not convinced it was love. "He's
bitten me at least six times since our unhappy first meeting. Mostly, now I can manage to outwit him."

"But not the time he bit you on the bum," Ace said.
"Remember, Daddy?"

"Speaking of being unmanned," he muttered with a
sigh. "That's kind of a hard one to forget. I couldn't sit
down for a week."

She shouted with laughter.

The sleigh ride might not be turning out quite as
she'd expected, but Morgan loved the feeling growing
inside her. It was blissful. She didn't just feel as if she
was being included in this little family outing. She felt
as if she belonged.

If she contemplated it, she might find it just a little bit
frightening that she was feeling something right now, in
this very moment, that she had been waiting her whole
life to feel.

But she determined not to contemplate it, not to wreck
these precious moments by trying to look into that foggy

place that was the future. For once, she would just enjoy what she had been given, no worrying, no analyzing, no planning, no plotting.

"He's going to be good today," Ace predicted. "Be good, Happy."

"Ace thinks he's going to pull the sleigh. I think he won't. Unless there's a cliff nearby that he can pull us all off."

"I don't think horses are that…devious, are they?" Morgan asked. The stocky miniature steed trying to sidestep the traces was so different from the stallion of her imagination she laughed out loud again.

Or maybe the laughter had nothing to do with the surprise of the pony. It was the day. And being with him. Them. The very air seemed to be tingling with merriment, with joy.

Snow was beginning to fall gently. The little horse stamped his feet and shook his mane, and a lovely smell drifted up from him. In the background was a redbrick farmhouse, snow drifts in the front yard, a cheery wreath on the front door.

Ace had told her that was her aunt Molly's house, and that she wasn't home right now. Happy had been her Christmas gift from her aunt last year.

Morgan thought it took a pretty special aunt to know what a hard time Christmas would be for this child, and to come up with a gift good enough to make a dent in all that sadness.

In fact mischief and merriment seemed to dance in the air around the pony. Finally, Nate loaded her and Ace into a red sleigh. The pony did have bells on, and as it set off, their music filled the air.

And that was about the only part of Morgan's fantasy

that had been realistic. Nate wasn't even cuddled under a blanket with her and Ace. He walked to one side of the pony, trying to persuade him to keep up a forward motion.

An hour later, Morgan thought she had never laughed so hard in her entire life. She was doubled over she was laughing so hard.

"You have to stop," Morgan gasped. She was begging.

"We are stopped," Nate pointed out, not sharing her amusement. "That's the problem. Unhappy hasn't moved for ten minutes."

It was snowing, but it was no longer big, gentle flakes floating down around them. It was coming down hard now, the wind whipping it up in gusts around the sleigh. But even the freezing cold could not dampen Morgan's enjoyment.

Nate stood in front of Happy, pulling on the pony's obstinate head, trying to get him to move.

The pony had pulled the little sleigh, with Ace and Morgan in it, only in stops and starts, mostly stops. Ace held the reins, and jiggled them and shouted encouragement, while her father walked slightly behind and to the right of the pony.

Forward movement was accomplished sporadically when Nate slapped the pony's ample brown-and-white rump with his gloves.

Now, a mile from the house, Happy was no longer startled by the rather frequent popping across his rump with the gloves. Apparently he had decided against forward motion and was not going to be persuaded with glove smacks.

"I think he likes it," Morgan said, watching the pony

sway his rump happily into the pressure of Nate's hand after every increasingly vigorous smack with the gloves. Happy turned his head just enough that she could see the pony's decidedly beady eyes half shut in an expression that Morgan had to assume was pure pleasure.

Nate had his hands firmly planted on either side of the pony's headstall and was leaning back hard on his heels, pulling with all his might.

"Come on, you dastardly little devil."

Considerable as Nate's might was, the pony outweighed him by several hundred pounds. Happy planted his own feet, and showed Nate he wasn't the only one who could lean back!

"There's a dog-food factory waiting for you!" Nate warned the pony darkly. "One phone call. The meat wagon comes by here on Monday."

"Please stop," Morgan begged again. All this cold, all this jolting and all this laughter was having the most unfortunate effect on her kidneys.

"He's just kidding," Ace whispered. "He says that every time."

The pony stepped back instead of forward, pulling Nate with him.

"On second thought, dog food is too good for you," Nate muttered. "Bear bait. The bear-bait wagon comes by on Wednesday."

The pony cocked his head, as if he was actually considering this, then stepped back again, yanking Nate backward with him.

"Please," Morgan moaned.

"It's time for the apple," Ace yelled. If she was enjoying her sleigh ride any less for its lack of forward movement it didn't show in her shining face.

"I am not bribing him to move. I'm just not. It's a matter of pride with me. Hathoways are renowned for their pride, Morgan."

But after another few minutes of unsuccessfully playing tug-of-war with the four-hundred-pound pony, Nate sighed and produced an apple, apparently kept on hand for just this purpose.

With a sigh of resignation, he held it at arm's length. Happy opened one eye, caught sight of the apple and lurched forward.

A terrible move for a suffering kidney.

"Greedy little pig," Nate muttered, keeping the apple carefully out of the snapping pony's reach and breaking into a jog.

Morgan howled with laughter as the fat pony stirred himself into a trot, stretching his neck hard to get the apple. The sleigh jolted along behind him, as Nate wisely looped back toward the barn while the pony was moving!

They finally got back to the barn, Happy's only true ambition demonstrated when that building came back into view and he broke into a clumsy gallop that had Nate running to keep up.

"Give him the apple, Daddy," Ace insisted when they arrived at the barn door.

Panting, Nate obliged, yanking back his fingers when Happy tried to devour them along with the apple.

Morgan decided then and there you could learn a lot about the true nature of a man from how he bargained with a pony—and from the lengths he was willing to go to make his daughter happy.

Nate helped Morgan out of the sled with a rueful grin. He gave a little bow. "I see I have entertained you." And then more solemnly revealed, looking at her so intently her face burned, "I like it when you laugh, Morgan McGuire."

"I like it, too."

"I'm sure that this was not exactly what you pictured when I promised you a sleigh ride."

"The truth?" she said. "It's not. And it was so much better! Except for one thing." She leaned forward and whispered her urgent need to him.

"Ace? Take Miss McGuire up to the house."

The door of the farmhouse opened just as they arrived. An attractive wholesome-looking woman with dark hair and a Christmas sweater smiled her welcome at them.

"Aunt Molly!" Ace cried.

"You must be frozen," Molly said, as she gave Ace a huge hug.

"Actually," Morgan said awkwardly, "if you could point me in the direction of—"

Thankfully she didn't even have to finish the sentence, because Molly laughed. "Right there. I've jounced around in that sled, too."

When Morgan joined them again, Molly explained she had been out Christmas shopping when they arrived.

"How was Happy today?" she asked her niece.

"Happy was extra bad for Daddy today," Ace declared gleefully.

"Oh, good," Molly said, and they all shared a laugh that made Morgan feel, again, that deepening sense of family, of being part of a sacred circle. She had a sense of ease with Molly that usually she would not have with a person quite so quickly.

"I'm Morgan McGuire, Ace's teacher," Morgan said, extending her hand.

"Oh, the famous Mrs. McGuire."

"It's Miss. I can't get that through to the kids. I've stopped trying."

"Miss. Oh," Molly said, and she turned and looked down to where Nate was taking the harness off the pony. Her eyes went back to Morgan full of soft question.

Questions that Morgan was thankful had not been spoken out loud, because she would have had no idea how to answer them.

There was something happening between her and Nate, there was no question about that. But it was ill-defined and nebulous. Were they becoming friends? Morgan thought it was something more. Possibly a lot more. But did he?

"Ace's mom, Nate's wife, Cindy, was my sister," Molly said, leading Morgan through to the kitchen.

It could have been an awkward moment, but it wasn't.

Molly laid her hand on Morgan's. "We love him very much. We just want him back. Sometimes," she mused, sighing, "I feel as if I lost all three of them."

"Three?" Morgan said.

"Never mind. It's a long story. And maybe it will have a happy ending someday. I could have sworn when I looked out the kitchen window a few minutes ago, I saw Nate smiling. A rare enough occurrence in the last two years, and even rarer after he's had to deal with the pony!

"Oh. Here's Keith, my husband. Keith, this is Morgan. Nate brought her out to have a sleigh ride with Ace."

No mention of her true role in their lives, as Ace's teacher.

"And how was that?" Keith asked her.

"One of the most deliriously delightful experiences of my life."

He watched her for a moment, and like his wife, seemed satisfied.

Silly, to be so pleased that Nate's family by marriage liked her. They hardly knew her.

Though that seemed to be a circumstance they were determined to change, because after Nate came in, stomping the snow off his boots, they were all invited to share the pot of chili that had been heating on the stove.

"Morgan?" Nate asked. "Does that fit with your schedule?"

Schedule? Oh, a woman more clever than her would probably at least pretend to be busy on a Saturday night. But somehow, there was no way you could play games with a man as real as Nate.

Or not mind games. Not flirting games. Other games? He proved to be enormously good at them.

Because after the feed of chili in the warmth of the kitchen, with banter going back and forth between the two men, there was just an expectation they would stay. The kitchen table was cleared of dishes and a worn deck of cards came out.

They taught her to play a game called 99 that she was hopeless at. But two late night's in a row soon proved too much for Ace, and despite her winning streak at 99 she finally went and laid down on the couch and fell asleep.

And then the adults gathered around the fireplace,

and Molly made hot rum toddies, though Nate refused and had hot chocolate instead.

Morgan wished she had refused, too. The drink filled her with a sense of warmth and well-being as the talk flowed around her. About the farm and the forge, the coming production of *The Christmas Angel*.

"Did you hear they were deciding who gets to go by a lottery system?" Molly asked.

Morgan confirmed that. There were only three hundred seats available in the auditorium, so the seats would be given away by a lottery system. But she told them that there would be a live feed to the community center and one of the local churches so that everyone who wanted could see it.

"And have they chosen the Christmas Angel yet?" Molly said, casting a worried look at her sleeping niece. "She's called me several times about it. Tonight's the first night I haven't heard her mention it."

"I understand Mr. Wellhaven will announce the choice at his welcome party. It's a skating party at the pond, a week from tonight. He's been sent video of some of the rehearsals."

"I'd like it to be over with," Molly said.

"Me, too," Nate said. "I hate to think how disappointed she's going to be."

"Who knows?" Morgan said. "Maybe she won't be disappointed. Maybe it will be her."

Molly's and Nate's mouths fell open in equal expressions of shocked disbelief.

"Ace?" they said together.

"I've told all the girls they have an equal chance of being chosen."

"But that's not true," Nate said grimly. "Ace can't

sing a note, and she doesn't look like anyone's idea of an angel."

"Her singing has actually improved quite a lot under Mrs. Wellhaven's tutelage."

"She sings all those songs around the house all the time. I haven't noticed any improvement."

"Well," Morgan said firmly, "there has been. And I think anyone with a little imagination could see she would make a perfectly adorable Christmas Angel."

"I don't want her getting her hopes up for something that doesn't have a snowball's chance in hell of happening."

It was the first grim note in a perfect day, so Molly quickly changed the subject, but the mood had shifted.

A few minutes later, saying goodbye on the doorstep, Nate cradling the sleeping child against his chest, it seemed to Morgan as if she had never had a more perfect day. She realized it was not the toddy alone that allowed her to feel this sense of warmth and well-being. It had only allowed her to relax into the feeling instead of analyzing it.

"Nate," she said, as they drove through the snow, "it's so nice that you still are so connected with them, with Cindy's family."

He shot her a surprised look. "Family is family. They became my family the day I married Cindy."

Morgan shivered. She had always known he was a *forever* kind of man. Not like in her own family, where loyalties shifted with each new liaison. She could feel herself longing for what he represented.

Morgan realized tonight had been the kind of night she had always dreamed of.

A simple night of family. And connection. A feeling of some things not being temporary.

"I still think it's nice," she said.

"We had already lost Cindy. It would have just made everything so much worse if we lost each other. Ace is what remains, she's what Cindy is sending forward into the future. I could never keep her from her aunt, from her mom's sister."

But Morgan thought of all the people—including her own family—that when something happened, like a divorce, that's exactly what they did.

"When my mom and dad divorced," she told him, "it was like my dad's whole side of the family, including him, just faded away."

"You didn't have any contact with your dad?"

"A bit, at first. Then he moved for a job, and then he remarried. So, it was a card and some money on my birthday. He always paid my mother support, though."

"Yippee for him," Nate said darkly. "There's a lot more to being a dad than paying the bills."

"Yes," she said. "I can see that in the way you parent."

"Now you like my parenting?" he teased her. "What about the notes?"

"You haven't gotten one for a while!"

"I kind of miss them."

"You do not."

They were in front of her house now, but he made no move to get out of the truck. "What your dad did? That was wrong," he said, after a long time. "And sad."

She liked that about Nate Hathoway. He had a strong value system. He knew what was right and what was wrong, and he would never compromise that.

"Nate, tell me if it's none of my business, but did someone else die, besides your wife? Molly said something."

For a long moment he didn't answer. Then he said gruffly, "There were three of us who grew up together. Me, Cindy and David. Cindy and David had been in love since they were about twelve. I mean really in love. The head-over-heels kind. Some people outgrow things like that, other people don't. They didn't."

He was silent for a long, long time. "David joined the army. Before he left he made me promise I'd look after her. If anything happened."

"Something happened," Morgan guessed when he was silent for a long time again.

He cast her a look that said it all, that confirmed that strong value system.

"David was killed in Iraq," he said roughly. "And I looked after Cindy, just like I promised."

She wanted to ask if he loved her, but it was so evident from the agony on his face that he had loved her. Loved both his friends.

"You are a good man," she whispered. She wanted to ask, *Did she love you? The really-in-love kind? The head-over-heels kind?* But she could tell by the set of his face he already felt he might have said too much.

He shrugged it off uncomfortably, and they pulled up to her house. He shut off the truck, and leaped out, not wanting to discuss it anymore. Still, he walked her up to her front door, helped her with the key.

"Thank you, Nate," she said softly. "It was such a perfect day."

"You're welcome." He turned to go down off her stoop.

Maybe it was the hot rum toddy.

Or maybe it wasn't. Maybe it was that he was a good, good man, who had made a vow to his best friend and kept it. Maybe it was because she thought he deserved to be *really* in love and suspected that he had sacrificed that feeling in the name of honor.

"Nate?"

He turned back to her.

Something else had been between them all day, too.

Awareness.

She crossed the small distance between them, stood on tiptoes and did what she had wanted to do from the moment she had met him.

She tasted him. She touched her lips to his own.

He tasted exactly as she had known he would.

Of mysterious things that made a woman's heart race, but underneath that, of strength and solidness. Of a man who would do the right thing.

Of things made to last forever.

She stumbled back from him, both frightened and intrigued by the strength of her longing.

He was a man, she knew, who had been tremendously hurt.

She held her breath knowing that everything between them had just shifted with the invitation of her lips.

So far everything had been casual and spontaneous.

Now their kiss changed that.

It asked for more. It demanded some definition, it asked where things were going. It asked if he was ready to *really* fall in love.

The head-over-heels kind.

Because despite it all, despite her determination to be independent, to not give her life away, she felt ready to surrender to the tug inside her.

To love him.

Morgan held her breath, thinking he would walk away, perhaps never to look back.

But he didn't. He regarded her solemnly, and then said, softly, "Wow."

Then he walked away, leaving her feeling as if things were even more up in the air and ill-defined than they had been before.

"Mr. Hathoway?"

Nate glanced at the clock. It was just a little after 7 a.m. Morgan must have assumed he was up getting Ace ready for school. The truth was he had the process down to a science. He could get her ready, including hair, breakfast and bag lunch in under fifteen minutes.

"Yes, Miss McGuire?" he asked. Nate hadn't called her since the sleigh ride, since her unexpected kiss and the clear invitation in it.

He hadn't called her because he had told her things he had not expected to tell her. She was proving she could take chinks out of armor that not a single other person had even dented.

But Morgan McGuire wanted things that Nate could not promise. After that night with Molly and Keith, playing games, laughing, everything easy and light, he was aware of a deep longing in him, too.

To have a life like the one he'd had before. A stable life, where you woke up in the morning and trusted the day would go as you planned.

The truth? He wasn't even sure he could be the man

he had been before, a man naively unaware how quickly things could go wrong in the world, naively believing his strength would be enough to protect those he loved from harm.

He was aware how vulnerable answering a longing like that made a man.

"I'd like to discuss my last note with you."

But here was another truth. Despite his desire to harden himself against Morgan McGuire, her temptations and invitations, he could feel a smile starting somewhere in the vicinity of his chest. He relished it, that he was lying in bed under the warmth of his blanket, the phone to his ear, listening to her.

He relished when she used that snippy, schoolmarm tone of voice on him. He wondered when that had happened, exactly, that he had started enjoying that schoolmarm tone.

"I sent you a request to send cookies for Mr. Wellhaven's welcome party at the skating rink at Old Sawmill Pond."

"I sent the damned cookies."

Silence. "We've discussed cussing."

"Ace is still in bed."

He could tell she was debating asking how he could get her ready for school in time if she was still in bed, but she wisely decided to stick to one topic at a time.

"All right," Morgan said, after a pause. "Let's discuss the damned cookies, then."

The smile was turning to laughter. He bit it back.

"I'm in charge of cookies for the welcome party for Mr. Wellhaven. He'll be arriving Saturday."

"The note said that." Plus, Ace was in excitement overdrive about the skating party to be held at the pond in Mr. Wellhaven's honor. Nate was going to have to give her the gift he had planned to give his daughter from Santa—the new skates—early.

"You said you missed my notes," she pointed out.

"Hmm," he returned, noncommittally. "I did say that." He realized what he missed was her.

"After she received my note, Mrs. Weston sent four dozen sugar cookies decorated individually like gift-wrapped Christmas parcels."

"Good for Ashley."

"Mrs. Campbell sent three dozen chocolate-dipped snowmen. Sharon McKinley sent melt-in-your-mouth shortbread, shaped like Christmas balls, with icing ribbons."

"How did you know they were melt-in-your-mouth? Are you sampling the cookies, Miss McGuire? Tut-tut." He heard her bite back laughter.

Why were the simplest things such a joy with her?

"Mrs. Bonnabell sent—"

"Look, it sounds like you have plenty of cookies. You won't even need the box of Peek Freans I sent over."

"That is hardly the point, Mr. Hathoway."

"What is the point?"

"Everyone else made the effort."

"Fine. I'll ask Molly to whip me up a batch of brown snowmen, with ribbons around their necks, holding Christmas parcels. Individually decorated."

"Your listening skills are very good, Mr. Hathoway."

"Thank you." Ridiculous to feel pleased that she had noticed how closely he listened to her every word. *However,* he guessed.

"However," Morgan continued, "I don't really

think it's fair to ask Molly to contribute to *our* class project."

"I don't know how to make cookies."

"Well, yes, I understand that. It is a situation that can be remedied. I mean, a few short weeks ago, I didn't know how to hang a coat hanger."

"You're not exactly ready to start building furniture."

"No, I suppose not."

Said a bit doubtfully, as if she might actually be considering trying to build some furniture. He reminded himself he'd have to follow up on getting her a new hammer before she wrecked something else trying to use the one she had.

"The point is," Morgan said, "I was willing to learn. If you and Ace would like to come over this afternoon after school, I would be happy to teach you how to make Christmas cookies."

His schedule had become insane because of the volunteer hours he was putting in on the set of *The Christmas Angel*. He still had special orders he had to get out for Christmas, as well as the gate commission.

Plus, he was avoiding Morgan. And her lips. And the clear invitation he had seen in her eyes the other night after the disastrous sleigh ride. Boy, if a sleigh ride like that couldn't scare a girl off, what would?

And there was the other disastrous thing, too. Telling her about Cindy and David had poked a little hole in the dam of feelings walled up within him… He was all too aware that he might be like the little boy hoping his finger poked in that hole was going to be enough to hold it back.

The thing was, her voice on the other end of the

phone was like a lifeline thrown to a man who had been in the water so long he didn't even know he was drowning.

The thing was, he knew it had cost her to make the move, and he could not bear to hurt her. It seemed she had experienced quite enough hurt in her life. Not at the hands of fate, either, but at the hands of the very people who should have loved and protected her.

Though there was probably a far more sensible way of looking at that. Hurt her a little now. Or a lot later.

He didn't feel like being sensible. Or maybe, closer to the truth, he was not as sure as he had been a few weeks ago about what sensible was.

"Sure," he said, as if he grabbed lifelines every single day. "What time would you like us to come make cookies?"

CHAPTER SEVEN

As IT TURNED OUT, after school, Ace had been offered a Christmas shopping outing to Greenville with the Westons. She still had to buy something for her daddy, she informed Nate, and it would be much too hard to keep it a secret if he came with her.

She was so excited about going shopping with her new friend Brenda that he didn't have the heart to tell her she would be missing making cookies with her teacher. Having to make such a momentous choice would have torn her in two.

Nate knew he could phone and cancel, and maybe even *should* phone and cancel, but as he moved up the walkway to Morgan's house, he contemplated the fact that he hadn't.

And knew he was saying yes to the Light.

Even though he knew better. Even though he knew, better than most, life could be hard, and cruel, and made no promises.

When Morgan opened her door, that's what he saw in her face. Light. And he moved toward it like a man who had been away for a long time, a soldier away at the wars, who had spotted the light pouring out the window of home.

An hour later her kitchen was covered in flour and red food coloring. He was pretty sure there were more sprinkles on the floor than on the cookies.

And, despite the fact she was the world's best teacher, calm, patient, clear about each step and the order to do them in, those cookies were extra ugly. Sugar cookies, they were supposed to look like Christmas tree decorations. They didn't.

He held one of the finished cookies up for her. "What does this look like?"

She studied it. "An icicle?"

"Morgan, it looks like something obscene." He bit into it, loving her blush. "But it tastes not bad."

She put her hands on her hips, still very much Miss McGuire, pretending that kiss of a few nights ago wasn't hanging in the air between them like mistletoe, pretending her face wasn't on fire. "Has anyone ever told you you're incorrigible?"

"Of course," he said, picked up a misshapen Santa and bit his head off. "That's part of being a Hathoway."

"Really?" She surveyed the cookies, apparently realized they were not going anywhere near Wesley's welcome party, picked one up and bit into it. "Tell me about growing up a Hathoway."

And oddly enough, he did. In Morgan's kitchen, surrounded by the scent of cookies baking and a feeling of *home,* Nate told her about how it was to grow up poor in a small town.

"But," he said, making sure she knew he was not inviting pity, "we might have been poor, but our family was everything. We were fiercely loyal to each other. My dad couldn't give my mom much materially, but I don't think a man has ever loved a woman the way he loves her. He would fight off tigers for her. For any of us. There was an intense feeling of family.

"And we might have been poor, but we were never bored." He told her about working in the forge since he was just a little boy, starting on small chores, working up to bending the iron.

He told her about making their own fun, since they could never afford anything. In the summer fun was a secondhand bicycle and the swimming hole, or a hose and a pile of dirt.

"You haven't really lived until you've squished mud through your toes," he told her. "And in winter fun was a skate on a frozen pond in skates way too big because they were purchased to last a few seasons. It was tobogganing on a homemade sled, and snowball fights. It was an old deck of worn-out cards in the kitchen."

"Like at Molly and Keith's the other night?" she said, and he heard the wistfulness.

"Yeah, growing up was like that…" Each of his memories held Cindy and David. It was the first time in a long time he felt the richness of that friendship, instead of the loss. It was the first time he understood how much it had become a part of who he was today.

"Tell me about how you grew up," he invited Morgan.

And then Morgan told him about her family, and how fragmented it was, how some of her earliest memories were of tension, of feeling as if she was responsible for holding something together that could not be held.

"It was like trying to stop an avalanche that had already broken free," Morgan said. "My mom and dad eventually split when I was eleven. And it was a blessing, but it made me long for things I couldn't have."

"Such as?"

She smiled sadly. "I used to watch other families on the block, families on television, and long for that. To be together with other people who loved you in a special way. A way that both shut out the rest of the world, and made you able to go into it in a different way."

He was astonished how sad he felt for her. "I'm surprised you don't have it, if you longed for it," he said gruffly.

"I tried to set it up, to manipulate it into happening, to impose my sugarplums-and-fairies vision of family on every single relationship I was in, but I just ended up more disillusioned. At some point, I decided the kids I taught would be my family."

It seemed to him that this was a lesson Morgan would teach him again and again. It wasn't all about him. Maybe that was part of the legacy his two best friends had left him with.

When you cared about people, putting what they needed sometimes came ahead of what you needed.

He knew he wasn't a man who could be counted on to make anyone's life better forever. Certainly he could not be trusted with sugarplum-and-fairy fantasies about family.

But he could probably be trusted with making her feel better for one single day.

And that day was today.

"Eating all these cookies?" he said.

"Yes?"

"Has made me really hungry. Want to go for Chinese?"

Taking somebody for Chinese food was a sign of a

serious relationship in a small town, but she probably didn't know that.

She smiled at him, and he was bathed in the light of that smile.

"Yes," she breathed as if something was settled between them. So, maybe she knew what going for Chinese in small towns meant after all.

And really over the next few hectic days, it felt as if something *was* settled between them. Whatever it had been in Nate that could fight her, and his attraction to her, could fight no more.

The rehearsals were stepped up now in preparation for Wesley Wellhaven's arrival. The children were practicing their parts in earnest, and Mrs. Wellhaven still frowned on an audience, so more and more Nate and Morgan used that as an excuse to slip away.

They were not dates. Or at least Nate told himself they were not dates.

Because mostly they were mere moments stolen from crowded schedules.

A quick walk around the block the school was on. A cup of coffee in the cafeteria. A shared crossword puzzle and biscotti at Bookworms café down the street. Sometimes, they'd sit in his truck, the heater blasting, just talking or sharing a newspaper. Once they had a snowball fight in the parking lot.

There was a time when all this waiting for Ace to finish rehearsals would have grated on Nate. Now he looked forward to every minute he got to spend with his daughter's teacher.

When he was with Morgan, Nate had the strangest sensation that he was discovering the town he had always lived in as if it was brand-new to him.

He had never ridden the horse-drawn wagon that old Pete Smith drove around town for the three weeks before Christmas. Now he did. He had never taken the Light Tour, following a map through the town of the best Christmas decorated properties, but one night, when the kids were in a late rehearsal, he and Morgan did that. He had never been in Canterbury Tails, the pet store, but one time they went in and played on the floor with the new golden-retriever puppies that would be ready to go home for Christmas. Morgan guided him through the foreign land of the antiques stores and the bookstores and the art galleries. He'd lived in Canterbury his whole life, and he saw its museum for the first time with her at his side.

Morgan's sense of wonder, her joy in discovery, was obviously part of what made her a teacher her students adored. But it was also what gave Nate the sensation that it was all brand-new, an adventure that had always been right in front of him all his life but that he had missed completely.

His own sense of wonder, his joy in discovery, seemed to be all about her. More and more her hand found its way to his, and he savored the feeling of it: soft and small within his larger one.

He kissed her. At first lightly, casually, but as time went on, the kisses deepened, and instead of slaking some desire inside of him the taste of her fueled it.

Nate found himself telling Morgan things he had never told another person, and she told him things he suspected she had never told another person.

Nate began to feel things around Morgan that he had never felt. He would never say it was a better relationship than what he had had with his wife.

But it was different.

He and Cindy had grown up together, he had known her forever. He had loved her, and he had loved David, and when the time came he had kept his vow to David gladly.

But now, with Morgan, sometimes Nate would remember Cindy's words to him, a long time ago.

I wish you could know what it is to fall in love, Nate.

Stop it, Cin, I love you.

No. Head over heels, I can't breathe, think, function. That kind of fall-in-love.

At the time, he had thought she was crazy. He hadn't felt he could love anybody any more than he loved her.

But now, with Morgan, he saw that there were different kinds of love. It felt as if Cindy's wish for him was coming true.

You've been my angel, Hath. Now I'll be yours.

For the most pragmatic man in the world to even consider those words and wonder if they could be true was a measure of what was happening to him.

Nate felt as if he was making a choice, saying yes to something that was bigger than him. He had never felt like this: breathless with wanting, on fire with life and longing.

The simplest things: discussing the newspaper, opening a fortune cookie at a Chinese-food restaurant, playing with a puppy on the floor, it all made him feel so intensely alive, almost as if he had sleepwalked his way through life, and now the touch of her lips, her eyes on his, her hand folded into his hand, were making him come fully gloriously awake.

He was aware of feeling like a teenage boy around Morgan, wanting to show off for her. He loved how he could make her eyes catch on his muscles when he flexed, how his breath would stop in his chest when she caught the tip of that little pink tongue between her teeth.

He loved the stolen kisses, the sizzling moments of pure awareness, the desire building to heat that could melt steel. He loved the smoky look that would cloud her green eyes after they kissed.

And he loved it that they didn't give in, as he had with Cindy. That they let the *wanting* become a part of the tantalizing sizzle of being together.

He felt dazzled, as if he was conducting an old-fashioned courtship, as if he had become the gentleman she had promised him she could see, even when no one else ever had.

When Nate was not with Morgan it felt as if the color had leeched from his world, as surely as the color leeched from the autumn leaves, stealing their reds and golds and oranges until they were just brown.

He anticipated seeing her. He found himself thinking of little ways to win that smile. He sent her a single orchid in a candleholder. He made her little trinkets at the forge, a frog, a chunky bracelet, a set of little metal worry beads.

Morgan's relationship with Ace was a marvel. She knew everything there was to know about little girls. She knew about hair bows and pink shoes and underwear with the days of the week embroidered on each pair. She knew about doll's clothes, and Hannah Montana and baking things.

His little girl was blossoming like a cactus that had waited for Christmas.

But through it all, Nate felt as if he was in a love-hate relationship with himself, as if his surrender to all these good things and good feelings was temporary.

He liked the way it felt to be excited about life, to explore the mysteries and gift of another human being. But at the same time he hated the sensation of losing control.

The feeling of *choosing* this was leaving him. Because with every day that Morgan's laughter and her nearness filled his life with light, it felt the choice to walk away was a door that was closing.

What man could choose to go back to darkness after he had been in the Light?

Maybe walking a great distance in darkness was even about this: recognizing the Light when you felt it. Honoring it by knowing it was something not to be taken for granted.

Nate was beginning to see the events of his life in a larger perspective.

How would you even know it *was* light, if you had never known darkness?

He was so accustomed to being a man of action that these thoughts, deep and complex, troubled him.

And it troubled him even more when he realized what was happening.

He could call it whatever he wanted: discovering the Light, learning to play again, having fun, being awake.

But all those names could not really distance him from the truth that it was far deeper than any of the labels he was trying to attach to it.

Nate knew it when he found himself in Greenville, alone, *shopping,* a weekday when both Morgan and Ace were at school.

The thing was, he knew darn well he had not come here to shop for Ace. No, Ace's parcels were spilling out from under their Christmas tree in a pile so high and wide they were taking over the living room.

No, Nate had taken advantage of the fact Morgan and Ace were in school to make the trip to Greenville by himself to find something to give Morgan for Christmas.

He wasn't quite sure what. The hammer in the bag from the building supply store—a nice little 12-ounce curved-claw trim hammer—didn't quite cut it.

He wanted something that would let her know what she had come to mean to him. He wanted something so special. Something spectacular. And yet subtle at the same time.

Something that would make that light come on in her face, the one that he was starting to live for.

Something...but what?

Everything he looked at seemed wrong. Gloves? Ridiculously impersonal. Hat and scarf? Too generic. Books? Too stuffy. Lingerie? Not nearly stuffy enough.

He found himself standing at the window of Orchid Jewelers in the mall he had never once been to before he met Morgan.

Maybe, he found himself thinking, *I should just make her something at the forge.*

Around him was the bustle of shoppers, the tinkle of bells, carolers, the ho-ho-ho of the mall Santa.

All these things—the noises, the colors, the decorations,

the music, the good cheer—all these things a mere year ago would have made him cringe.

He could feel the healing happening in the fact he felt the Christmas excitement, he was enjoying being part of it, instead of apart from it.

And then he realized he was staring at *something* in the window of Orchid Jewelers. It was something that made him understand exactly what was happening to him.

Nate Hathoway realized he was falling in love. The exact kind of love Cindy had once wished for him.

The can't-breathe, can't-think, can't-function kind that he had once thought sounded awful.

And Nate realized that if he didn't make a choice about that soon, if he didn't stop *falling,* and start making some conscious decisions, the ability to choose might be taken away from him completely.

He might become helpless in the face of the enormous power of that thing called love.

If there was a word that had not appeared in a Hathoway vocabulary for several centuries, it was that one.

Helpless.

But that's exactly what he felt as he pushed open the door to the jewelry shop, walked in and went to the counter.

A perky girl in a Santa hat came and smiled at him.

"Can I help you, sir?"

Last chance to break and make a run for it.

Helpless.

"I'd like to see that ring," Nate said, surprised by how

strong his voice was. How absolutely sure. "The one in the window."

He felt a breath on his neck. He whirled and looked around the store. He was the only customer in it.

It must have been the bells in the mall that made him think he had heard Cindy laughing. That made him think he had heard her breathe, *yes*.

Morgan McGuire was not sure she had ever experienced a more perfect or magical night.

The whole town seemed to have gathered at the Old Sawmill Pond for the skating party that welcomed Wesley Wellhaven to Canterbury.

Wesley was the antithesis of his wife. There was no hiding that he was a shy and self-effacing man. His manner was so mild that Morgan wondered if he could really produce the voice he was so famous for.

She voiced that doubt to Nate in a low whisper when they skated off after being introduced to Mr. Wellhaven, who had thanked them both effusively for their hard work on *The Christmas Angel* project.

"It's probably some trickery of the *brains of the outfit*," Nate said. Despite the miraculous progress Mrs. Wellhaven had made with the children's choir, Nate had never quite forgiven her their initial encounter.

And then they laughed, and Morgan marveled at how easily they laughed together, and how often, and at how the hard lines seemed to be melting from Nate's face, one by one.

"What are you looking at?" he teased.

"You. You're a handsome man, Nate."

"Stop. You'll make me blush." And then he bent and

brushed his lips to hers, and threw back his head and laughed.

Morgan knew it was partly Nate's hand in hers, his easy affection, that made the evening so completely magical. A huge bonfire burned beside the pond, vats of hot chocolate were kept warm, and trays and trays of Christmas cookies sat on tables that had been set up beside the pond.

It was a true community event. Everyone was there, from the mayor to the waitresses, from grandmas and grandpas to small babies being pulled around the ice in sleds.

There were cameras filming some of what would be inserted into the moments right before the commercial breaks of the television special, but after a few minutes of self-consciousness everyone seemed to forget they were there.

But all of this was only a backdrop for what was unfolding inside of her. Nate's hand was always in hers, or his arm around her waist. He would tilt his head to listen to her, or to laugh at something she said.

They were a *couple,* Morgan realized. Everybody knew it. He seemed proud of it and of her.

It came on her suddenly, a delicious sensation of belonging. Not just with him, but in this community.

She did not miss the small smiles people exchanged with them, or the liking and enormous respect these people had for Nate.

She did not miss how much they had hoped for him to be what he was tonight: energized and laughter-filled, mischievous and fun-loving. And because they saw her as part of what was bringing Nate back to them, they accepted her.

Maybe it wasn't even going too far to say that they cared deeply for her, their grade-one teacher, Nate Hathoway's girlfriend.

Girlfriend. She savored the word, like a caramel melting on the tip of her tongue.

Morgan glided across the ice with Nate and a single word formed in her mind. *Belonging.* It was a whisper of something she had waited her whole life to feel.

Morgan had not skated very much, but she soon found she loved the sensation of gliding along the ice, especially with Nate, a strong skater, beside her.

The children were racing around on their skates, shouting with exuberance, playing games that Ace seemed to always be at the center of.

Nate followed his daughter for a moment with his eyes, then smiled, satisfied. "You've worked a miracle, there, Morgan McGuire," he said. "She's happy. To be truthful? I did not think we could have a happy Christmas ever again."

In the past days, he had told Morgan all about growing up with the Three Musketeers, about the closeness of their friendship, about David and Cindy loving each other so much. And then David going away and not coming back.

He told her how for the longest time he had thought he would lose Cindy, too. She had pined, not eating properly, not going out, the light gone from her eyes. Every day he had gone to her, made her eat, made her get out of the house.

They had become a habit for each other. It came to a point that he could not imagine life without her.

And he felt they'd had a good marriage. Solid. Based in respect and friendship.

And then Nate told Morgan about the accident that had taken his wife, about that final errand she had gone to run on Christmas Eve and never come back from.

How even in excruciating pain, she had *something* that he could never hope to have. A simple faith. A belief that somehow everything, even this, was unfolding according to a larger plan.

And then Nate told Morgan about his own black days after. There was no one to come rescue him from that feeling of sinking into a mire that he could never get out of. He had told her the worst of it was a sense of having failed.

"A man wants to believe he can protect those he loves from harm. But he can't. Not always. Learning that," Nate had told her, "has been the hardest lesson of my life."

But for a man who had learned hard lessons, he seemed only at ease now as he guided her around the firelit surface of the frozen Old Sawmill Pond. Nate Hathoway seemed only enormously sure of himself and his place in the world.

Morgan wanted the night never to end, but of course, all good things had to end.

As the magical evening drew to a close, Wesley Wellhaven left no doubt about the genuine gift of his magnificent voice.

As far as Morgan knew, what happened next was completely unscripted. Wesley Wellhaven stood by the fire, facing toward all the people skating on the pond, and he began to sing.

No televised concert, no CD could prepare a person for the pureness of his voice in person. It cut through all the chatter, and it soared above the shouts of children. It rose above the skate blades hissing on ice, and climbed above the crackle of the fire.

It inspired silence. The chatter and laughter died. Even a crying baby stopped its caterwauling.

Everyone drifted across the ice to where Wesley stood in front of the fire, his eyes closed, more than his voice pouring out of him.

His spirit. For such a mild man it was so evident his spirit was gigantic.

"His voice must make angels weep," Morgan whispered, and Nate's hand tightened around hers.

It was one of those moments where time stood still, it was a moment that shone with an inner light, that moved with the life force itself.

He sang the oldest of the Christmas songs, but the way he sang it, it was brand-new.

Morgan felt as if she had never heard it before.

Silent night, holy night,
All is calm,
all is bright…

It felt as though Wesley was describing *this* night in its calmness, in its brightness, the hope that was buried in the stillness.

And as he finished, and the people of Canterbury stood in the stillness left by his voice and the winking stars above them, Morgan knew what she felt was more than belonging.

She glanced up at the man who stood beside her, at the strength in the lines of his face, softened only slightly by the flicker of the fire.

And she knew what she felt was *love*.

Love. Terrifying. Electrifying. Comforting. Calming.

It was both breathlessness, and the deepest and most steady breath of all.

Wesley allowed the silence to envelope them, but after a subtle prod in the ribs from his wife's elbow, he cleared his throat, humbly, sweetly uncomfortable being the center of attention.

"And now I have an announcement that many of you have been waiting for," he said. "Mrs. Wellhaven and I have agreed on the child who should sing the final song in the concert, a song called 'Angel of Hope.'"

Morgan knew she was not supposed to hope it was one child above another. And she knew for the one she did hope to be chosen it would take a miracle.

"That child is Brenda Weston."

Though Morgan had known Brenda was likely to be chosen, and though she loved all her children equally, she could not help but feel deflated. Her eyes sought out Cecilia in the crowd.

"Well, I know at least one angel that will be weeping now," Nate said, his voice gruff and hard.

But when Morgan saw Ace, she wasn't weeping. She was hugging her friend with the exuberance of a second-place finalist in a beauty pageant.

"See?" she told Nate. "She's taking it fine."

But Nate was watching his daughter, too, and he said, "If you think she's taking it fine, you don't know the first thing about her."

She looked at his face. Something had hardened in it. She was not sure what, but it made her shiver.

She felt as if he had left something unspoken. *You don't know the first thing about us.*

Morgan was so aware something had shifted ever so

slightly, changed. The car ride home was silent, Cecilia exhausted, nearly asleep in her car seat.

Nate dropped Morgan off at her house first.

"No, don't get out," Morgan said, when she saw him opening his door. "Just take Cecilia home and get her to bed. It's a lot of excitement for a little girl."

And a lot of disappointment.

She opened the back door, leaned in and touched Cecilia's arm.

"I'm sorry you weren't chosen as the Christmas Angel, sweetie," she said. "I thought you would have made a wonderful Christmas Angel."

And she meant it. It was too bad the world could not see outside the box. With just the tiniest bit of imagination a child like Cecilia could have easily been the Christmas Angel.

Not that Mrs. Wellhaven had ever looked as if she was burdened with an abundance of imagination.

Cecilia smiled sleepily at Morgan. "But I am going to be the Christmas Angel," she said.

"No, honey," Morgan said carefully, "you're not. Mr. and Mrs. Wellhaven chose Brenda."

"I know it *seems* like they did. But, Mrs. McGuire, I'm going to be the Christmas Angel. I just know it."

This was announced with such certainty and with such sunny optimism that Morgan was taken aback.

"Stop it," Nate told his daughter sternly. "It's over. And you are not going to be the Christmas Angel."

Cecilia didn't say a word, but she pursed her lips together in a look of stubbornness that at least matched her father's.

And then Nate, not missing the fact Cecilia was not "stopping it" even if she had chosen silence, gave

Morgan a dark look that she interpreted as somehow making this her fault. And maybe it was. Should she have better prepared Ace? The girl obviously had had unrealistic hopes that she was now unwilling to let go of, even in the face of evidence it was time to let go.

And maybe it was her fault.

Because as she watched them drive away, it seemed to Morgan she had developed quite a few unrealistic hopes of her own. What had happened to the woman she had been when she had first arrived here in Canterbury?

A woman absolutely committed to leaving her fantasies and fairy tales behind her?

"What happened to her?" she murmured to herself. "The Purple Couch Club can't hold a candle to what I've felt the last few weeks."

But what if she was guilty of passing a silly desire to hope for things that were never going to happen on to the children she taught? They trusted her and treated every single thing she said as gospel, treated every single thing she did as an example of how to live.

In a split second, because of one dark accusing look from Nate, Morgan's night had gone from magic to misery.

And she felt as if she had failed herself.

Because somehow, somewhere, when she'd let her guard down, when she wasn't looking, she'd let herself be swept off her feet.

Morgan McGuire realized the truth. She had fallen in love with Nate Hathoway.

CHAPTER EIGHT

NATE SCANNED the newspaper. And there it was, one more blow for Ace. His name was not among the three hundred names, listed alphabetically, that had received one of those coveted tickets for the rows and rows of uncomfortable chairs he had helped set up in the auditorium. He would not be part of the live audience that got to watch *The Christmas Angel*.

"Buy the newspaper right away, Daddy," Ace had told him when he had dropped her at school. "The names are coming out today. I just know you're going to get one of the tickets, Daddy. I just know it."

It had meant a lot to her that he be there, at *The Christmas Angel*, in person. After her disappointment about not being chosen the angel, he had hoped to at least be able to give her his presence as she sang along with the rest of the angel choir. Especially since his little girl was being such a good sport. It hardly seemed like a glitch on her radar that she hadn't been chosen.

She had just switched her optimism, now it was all focused on Nate getting one of those tickets.

What had it been about her certainty that had almost convinced him that he would get one of the tickets?

He was becoming a dreamer, that's what. Had he

actually started to feel, like Ace, as if an angel maybe was watching over them?

Nate, you've been my angel. Now I'll be yours.

It was so unrealistic. So fantasy based, instead of fact based. It could not be a good thing.

His phone rang. He hoped it was Morgan, even though he knew she was teaching school. He hoped it was her, even though he had not called her since the skating party. Holding back. *Proving* to himself he did have control. That he wasn't *helpless.*

The caller was the set designer for *The Christmas Angel*. In a panic. Nate had noticed the people who flooded the town, *The Christmas Angel* production team, were always in a panic about one thing or another.

Today, it had been discovered one of the props wasn't working. A window on the cottage was supposed to slide open, and Mr. Wellhaven was to lean out that window to sing his first song. The window was stuck.

For a minute, the Nate who could already feel his daughter's disappointment that he had not received one of the tickets, wanted to tell the set designer to stuff it. To stuff the whole damn *Christmas Angel*. To stuff himself while he was at it.

But he didn't.

Instead he asked himself, *Where is all this anger coming from?*

Was it because he had bought that damned ring? Or was it because ever since that announcement at the skating party he could feel his hopes dissolving, disappointment circling him and Ace, waiting, like vultures, for the inevitable. As if their very optimism had set them up for the kill.

But he thought of Wesley singing that night at the

frozen pond, and he thought of how that voice had eased something in him. Maybe it could do something for the rest of the world when they watched it live.

So, instead of telling the set designer to stuff it, Nate took a deep breath, looked at his watch, said he'd be there as soon as he could to have a look at the window.

He hung up the phone. "Nate saves Christmas," he told himself sarcastically, but even his customary sarcasm felt funny, like a jacket that no longer fit.

No one was on the set or in the auditorium when Nate got there. It was unusual. Usually the whole area bustled with electricians and light people and sound people. But now it was down to the finishing details. Most of the work was done, and Nate had a rare opportunity to stand back and look at what they had accomplished.

It was amazing. The humble school stage had been transformed. It looked like the set for a highly polished and professional production.

The illusion that had been created was nothing short of magical. The cottage, dripping snow, looked amazingly realistic. Suspended snowflakes that actually moved and changed colors dangled from the ceiling. The tiers the grade-one choir would stand on looked like banks of snow.

And the huge Christmas tree, sent from Canada, a Frasier fir, was stage right. It was filling the whole auditorium with its scent, and it was finally magnificently decorated.

Nate went to the cottage, and went behind it, tested the window. It was sticking. He pulled a screwdriver from his belt, did an adjustment, tried it again. It slid a little more easily, but he wanted it to glide.

The door to the backstage opened and shut, but he paid no attention to the sound of footsteps.

A curtain moved and a shaft of light fell across him. Nate looked up from where he was crouched below the window, and frowned.

Ace?

What was she doing here by herself? He almost called out a greeting, but some instinct stopped him.

Her intensity, her single-minded focus on *something*.

So instead of calling out a greeting, Nate pulled back into the shadows behind the cottage and stood frozen and silent, watching his daughter tiptoe across the stage.

She went behind the tree, and with the familiarity of someone who had done this a million times, she climbed the staircase, hidden from the audience, that allowed the angel to get to the top of the tree.

Once there, she stood for a moment, radiant. From her lofty height advantage, she smiled out at the empty auditorium.

And then she began to sing.

It was an awful sound, reminiscent of alley cats meeting and greeting under a full moon. And yet, despite how awful it was, Nate was transfixed.

His daughter looked so beautiful on that perch above the tree, her eyes closed, her arms extended, singing with exuberance that was attractive, even if the tone was not. He recognized the song and realized Ace had been humming and singing that same tune around the house for days.

"Angel of Hope," the number Brenda Weston had been chosen to sing.

As Ace poured her heart into singing now, there was a look on her face that every parent lives to see on the face of their child.

As if she was sure of her place in the world, and was claiming it. And as if she was accepting the world embracing her back.

But for as ethereal as the moment was, Nate realized he could not be transfixed by this! He was her father. And he had to do the responsible thing, even if it hurt. And it was going to hurt, him more than her, not that she ever had to know.

He stepped out from the cottage, stood before the Christmas tree, gazing up at her, his arms folded over his chest.

It took Ace a minute to realize she had an audience. Her eyes opened, her voice faltered and then died. She looked down at him.

"Daddy?"

"Get down from there," he said.

She came down slowly, not demonstrating even half the confidence she had gone up the staircase with. Finally, she stood in front of him, not looking at him, scuffing her toes against the floor.

The backstage door opened again.

"Cecilia?"

The curtain parted again and Morgan stood there, but he held up a hand and focused on his daughter.

"What were you doing?" he asked Ace.

"Just practicing," Ace said in a small voice.

"Practicing what?"

She hesitated. She looked at Morgan for help. Good God, was Morgan in on this?

"Practicing for what?" he said again.

"To be the Christmas Angel," Ace muttered.

"What?"

"I'm going to be the Christmas Angel."

"No, you aren't."

"I am so! I'm going to be the Christmas Angel!" Ace shouted at him.

"Oh, Cecilia," Morgan said, and stepped forward, but he stopped her with a look. It seemed his daughter's ridiculous, impossible, unrealistic hopes only mirrored his own. It felt as if that ring was burning a hole through his shirt pocket.

He didn't need any of what Morgan was bringing to his daughter. Or to him. All that softness and light. And hope.

He'd even started to think, just like his daughter, that an angel was looking after them! It was enough.

False hopes had to be dealt with. And destroyed.

Before they destroyed the one who harbored them.

"You…are…not…going…to…be…the…Christmas… Angel." He enunciated every word carefully. He wanted his daughter to understand how dangerous his mood was.

"I am!" Ace shouted. "I am. My mommy told me I was."

He closed his eyes and asked for the strength to do what needed to be done. "Ace, your mother is dead. She's been dead a long time. She didn't tell you anything."

"She did so! In the dream. She told me! She was an angel."

"There are no angels," he said. He said it firmly, but he could feel something dip inside himself. Who was he to make a statement like that? Still, it felt as though to show his daughter one bit of doubt right now would be the wrong thing. The worst thing.

Tears were coming up in Ace's eyes, furious, hurt, and he knew he couldn't react to them. Or to that funny feeling that he had just said something really, really bad.

For her own good, these hopes had to be dashed.

"Dreams aren't real," he said. "You aren't going to be the Christmas Angel. Not ever. There's no use thinking it. Brenda Weston is the Christmas Angel."

His daughter looked at him mutinously, not backing down.

"You can't sing," he told her, feeling like Simon in *American Idol*. "You sound awful."

Ace's mouth moved, but for a moment, no sound came out. When it did it was a howl of pain so pure it reminded him of when he had told her Cindy was dead.

He made himself go on. "Brenda looks like the Christmas Angel, and she sounds like the Christmas Angel. She's the perfect Christmas Angel."

"I hate you," Ace screamed, and then ran past him and into Morgan's arms. She buried her head against Morgan, who was looking at him as if he was the devil himself.

"How could you?" she asked quietly.

Yeah, that was the question he was asking himself. How could he have done this? Let hope creep in? Allowed himself and his daughter to believe impossible things? How could he have let things go this far?

"It needed to be said." He could hear the grimness in his tone.

"Not like that, it didn't."

"Yeah. It did. Exactly like that."

"You're breaking her heart."

"No," he said quietly. "I'm not. Her heart has already been broken. Unlike you, I'm doing my best to make sure it doesn't happen again."

"Unlike me?" Morgan whispered.

"We don't need dreams, Miss McGuire. We don't need the kind of dreams you represent."

"You're right," she said, her eyes snapping with indignation and anger. "You don't need dreams. You need a miracle."

He could tell she was within an inch of stamping her foot and announcing she hated him, too.

"We don't believe in miracles, either," he said, his tone deliberately flat, even though he felt that same little dip in his chest as he said it.

Morgan didn't stamp her foot, or tell him she hated him. That almost would have been easier to deal with than her look of hurt disdain, of absolute betrayal. She gathered Ace in close to her, and they left the stage.

Only after the door was shut, did Nate allow himself to crumple. He sat on the edge of the stage, and buried his head in his hands.

"Okay," he said. "Okay, if there are angels, or miracles, I could sure use one now."

He felt instantly ridiculous.

And all he felt was that same yawning emptiness he had felt on those pitiful occasions he had gone to Cindy's grave, hoping to feel something. Anything.

It felt as though the darkness was gathering around him, pitch-black, tarlike, so thick and so sticky that nothing, least of all light, would ever penetrate it again.

* * *

Morgan looked around her little house. The tree was down. Most of her dishes and clothing were packed in boxes stacked along her living room wall.

The coat hangers remained in the hall. She could not bear to take those with her.

She had, she acknowledged, had a problem her whole life. She cared about everything way too much, way too deeply.

She had fallen in love with Ace Hathoway.

And even more, she had fallen in love with her father.

Over the past few weeks, she had cherished a dream. That they were all going to be together, that they were going to be a family. With each moment spent with Nate, with each time he had held her hand, teased her, looked at her, kissed her, her dreams had billowed to life. Filled her. Made her feel something she had never really felt.

Complete.

How could she stay here, feeling that way, loving them both so much and knowing her dreams, like Ace's own, were not based in reality?

It was just wishful thinking. It was just dreams.

"We don't need dreams, Miss McGuire. We don't need the kind of dreams you represent."

The words had been hurtful enough. The way he had been so harsh with Ace had been devastating. The memory of the look on his face—angry, closed—still had the power to make Morgan shiver.

She'd made a mistake thinking she saw things in him that weren't there. She'd made a mistake of the heart.

She was always making mistakes of the heart.

But the thought of him *knowing* how deeply he'd hurt

her was unbearable. She had to get out of here with what little was left of her pride intact.

So, as soon as she got her kids through the production of *The Christmas Angel,* she was going.

On Christmas Day, when everyone was busy with their families, cocooned in those circles of love she had longed for, Morgan would and could just slip away unnoticed. She would get in her little car, the tank already filled with gas, and she would go to anywhere. It didn't matter where. She had some savings. She would leave a check here for January's rent. And then, when she found where she wanted to be, she would hire movers to come get her things.

But maybe she'd tell them to leave the purple sofa.

Maybe she'd just leave everything. Maybe she'd join her mother and they could be blissfully single in Thailand together.

No, her mother was not going to make her happy. And neither was being single.

It was only part of the lies she had spun around herself. The lie that independence could be a suitable replacement for her heart's greatest longing. It was a lie he had shattered at the same time he had no intention of replacing it.

She had seen that in his face.

Morgan had seen something so hard and cold in his face, she knew she could not trespass there.

If only she had paid attention to that sign, the first day, that said everything she had needed to know about Nate Hathoway.

Go Away.

Now she would. For her own self-preservation she would go away.

What about my kids? She wailed to herself. *How would they find a replacement at this time of year. Who would teach them?*

But then she pulled herself up. She was not thinking one thought that made her weak instead of strong. Not one.

Nate thought, by deciding to not call Morgan ever again, by deciding not to give her that ring, he could manage to cheat grief.

Instead, he found out his acquaintance with grief thus far had only touched the surface of where that emotion could go.

With Cindy and with David, there had been no second chances, no second-guessing, no going back...

He'd been forced to say goodbye.

But Morgan lived. She breathed. Her presence in his town, just minutes away from him, beckoned and called.

It made him question himself, his decisions, his sanity.

Ace, who normally forgave him everything, was not forgiving him this. Living with her holding a grudge against him was a form of torment he could not have imagined. And yet to back down, what would that mean?

What would it mean in the long run if he encouraged his daughter to believe in impossible dreams?

Gee, Ace, go ahead. Believe you're going to be the Christmas Angel. Believe it right up until the moment it doesn't happen. Go ahead.

It wasn't the responsible thing to do.

Falling for Morgan had not been the responsible thing to do, either.

To add to his sense of grief he was furious at himself. He was in a pit of recrimination and failure.

He thought he had known darkness before. But he had not even touched the surface of that place that was so black it could swallow a man's soul, whole.

Christmas Eve. Ace had been dropped off in her choir angel costume at the school. She had not looked at him, nor kissed him goodbye.

The absence of the words, *I love you, Daddy* made the world he moved in darker.

Molly and Keith had asked him to join them at the community hall to watch the live feed of the concert, but he wasn't going to.

He was going to sit at home, in his darkness, revel in it, relish it.

And that was exactly what he was doing, when his doorbell rang.

And then, when he chose to ignore it, again, and then again.

Finally, when whoever stood out there made it evident they had no intention of giving up, Nate went and answered it ready to let all his bad temper out on an unsuspecting someone.

But he was astonished that it was Wesley Wellhaven standing here.

Wesley was already in the dark tux he would perform in. He looked wildly uncomfortable. And at the same time, as he had shown by ringing the doorbell over and over again, determined.

"Mr. Hathoway, you need to come." His voice carried urgency. "I have a place for you at the concert."

Nate looked down at the way he was dressed, jeans and a T-shirt. He looked at Mr. Wellhaven's tuxedo. His mouth moved. He tried to say no, he was choosing darkness, but the words wouldn't come out.

"Please don't make me late," Wesley pleaded. "We are live tonight. A foolish idea. I can't tell you how I hate live."

It was apparent to Nate that Wesley Wellhaven, for some reason known only to himself, was prepared to keep the whole world waiting while he talked Nate into coming to his production.

He remembered already thinking, once this week, he could not deprive the world of the gift of this man's voice.

With a sigh, he grabbed his jacket out of the coat closet and allowed Wesley to guide him down to where a long stretch limo waited at the end of his walk.

Once in the limo, Wesley ducked his head, fiddled with his bow tie, glanced at Nate. "I have a confession to make."

"To me?" Nate said. This must be some kind of case of mistaken identity.

"Yes, to you, Mr. Hathoway. I was there."

"Excuse me?"

"I was there. When you argued with your daughter. I like to sit in the seats of the empty auditorium before a performance. I like to see the stage as the poorest audience member will see it. And then make changes to try and make their experience more enjoyable.

"And so, I am embarrassed to say, I saw your very private moment with your daughter."

"Oh," Nate said. "I think it's me who should be embarrassed."

The limo pulled up to the school. Wesley pressed a ticket into Nate's hand.

"Yes, indeed you should at least share the embarrassment, Mr. Hathoway. How could you tell your daughter there is no such thing as a miracle? Why, they happen all the time."

"With all due respect, Mr. Wellhaven, no they don't."

"Really? Then see if you can explain how a humble and mild man such as myself was given such a voice," he challenged. He waited. Nate did not have an answer to that. "Enjoy the performance, Mr. Hathoway. And have faith. If you teach your daughter nothing else, teach her to believe in miracles."

And then he was gone.

And Nate looked at the ticket in his hands, and knew he had no choice but to go in. Or walk home.

But that day, sitting on the stage, his head in his hands, he'd asked for a miracle. What if this was it?

Oh, sure, Hath, he chided himself. *Believe one last time.* But the truth was he could not have prevented himself from going into that auditorium.

Of course he was the last one in there, and had to shove his way past all the people already seated to what seemed to be the only remaining chair in the whole place.

And of course, it had to be right beside her.

Morgan McGuire gave him her snippiest look. And when he scraped back his chair, she placed a finger to pursed lips.

"Shh," she said sternly.

He wondered if she could hear the beating of his heart. To be so near to her, the one he had told himself he could never have, was a form of the purest torture he had ever experienced.

Then the lights went down, and the children's choir filed onto the stage. He noticed immediately Ace was not among them.

Morgan turned to him. "Where is she?" she whispered, real concern replacing her snippiness.

Nate's heart began to race in fear. He thought of the cold war at home. And her disappointments.

Where was his daughter?

And then, just when he thought he would get up and tear the building apart to look for Ace, he saw the curtain open a tiny crack, and Ace peered out at the crowd, then at the choir.

"There she is," he whispered to Morgan.

"But what is she doing?"

Ace was looking woefully at the children's choir. She dropped the curtain again.

But not before he had seen the look on her face when she had seen Brenda, who now stood in the choir angel costume with the rest of the choir. He looked at Brenda, too. Her normally lovely face was blotchy from crying.

Oh, God. What had Wesley Wellhaven done? As well-meaning as it was, Nate could sense disaster coming.

His sense of it was so strong he could barely enjoy the production despite how good the children's choir had become, despite how amazingly Wesley blended his voice with those of the children. Despite the fact the evening was an inspiration and a gift to the world, just as Nate had hoped, he could not relax. And he could not enjoy it.

Morgan seemed equally tense beside him.

Finally, they reached the last number. The lights in the whole building went out, and only one came back on.

It was true.

His daughter was the Christmas Angel. There she was on her perch above the Christmas tree, all the lights now turned off except the one brilliantly white spotlight that was on her.

That familiar music started, and he felt himself cringing waiting for her to begin singing.

But Ace didn't start to sing.

On cue, she began to speak the role that had been a singing one. Her voice, despite the croakiness of it, was loud and strong.

Then it wobbled.

She picked up, but then it wobbled again.

And then Nate's little Christmas Angel, on live television, in front of the whole world, started crying.

And then she stopped, and in a voice that had absolutely no croak to it, that was strong and sure and beautiful, Ace Hathoway said, "If for one person to be happy, another has to be sad, that's wrong. And it's not Christmas. Brenda, you come be the Christmas Angel."

And with grave dignity, she turned around and went down the stairs at the back of the tree, pulled back the heavy velvet curtain and slipped through it.

Nate got up out of his seat. And somehow his hand was in Morgan's and he was taking her with him.

As Brenda quickly made her way up the steps to the top of the tree, Nate and Morgan slipped backstage.

"How could you, you little wretch?" Mrs. Wellhaven

had Ace's shoulders in her bony fingers and was snarling at her.

"Take your hands off my daughter before I bean you," Nate said.

Mrs. Wellhaven turned and gave him a look that could have slayed dragons. But he went right by her and scooped up his daughter in his arms.

Ace's tears flowed down his neck.

"I ruined it, didn't I, Daddy? I ruined *The Christmas Angel?*"

He could hear Brenda's sweet voice filling the auditorium.

"No, sweetheart, you didn't. You made me really proud. That was a good, good thing to do. The kind of thing only someone with a good heart would think of."

"I didn't wreck it?"

"No. I think you made it the best Christmas show, ever."

He and Morgan and Ace stood there, in the back of the stage, Ace's tears sliding down his neck as Brenda sang the song, and then Wesley's powerful voice joined hers as they sang the final number together.

In a moment, as the voices faded, thunderous applause filled the auditorium.

And when it died completely, someone out there yelled, "We want the redheaded angel."

It was a small town, and someone else provided her name.

"We want Ace. We want Ace Hathoway," a man called out.

Now it was like thunder, a chant that was picked up

and called out. "We want Ace. We want Ace. We want Ace."

When it could not be ignored a moment longer, when it felt as if the very roof would fall in under the tremendous volume of that demand, Morgan tugged at his sleeve and ducked under the curtain, bringing him with her.

He looked out at the sea of faces. He saw his friends and his neighbors. And he saw they were on their feet, whistling and stamping.

And he got it.

These people saw Ace's spirit, her willingness to give even though it hurt her, her willingness to put another's well-being ahead of her own.

He remembered her words the night after she had had the dream.

Ace had told him her mommy was going to save Christmas. That her mommy was going to show people what it was really all about.

And he could see that's exactly what had happened. He saw the true spirit of Christmas in his daughter's generous spirit. In the people cheering for her. In Wesley Wellhaven's brave, brave choice to choose a less than perfect Christmas Angel.

And he saw it in Morgan, in the way she was looking at them both, with such love, smiling through her tears.

And the Light broke apart the darkness and chased it from him, like the sun chasing away the last of the storm.

His daughter had just taught him something that was not just a lesson for Christmas, but a lesson for life.

Love gave. Love didn't ask what it was getting back.

Love didn't say, *you might hurt me, so I'm not going to try at all.*

Love said, *give everything you've got, every single minute that you've got it.* Love said, *time is short. Don't waste one precious moment of it being afraid, or protecting yourself.*

Love said, *risk all. It's worth it to know Me.*

And in that moment of illumination, Nate knew Wesley was right. And so was Morgan.

Miracles did happen. They came in the form of people, and insights and moments of inspiration. They came on the magnificent voice of a humble man, and the humble voice of a magnificent girl.

Wasn't that what Christmas did? Reminded people, all over again, especially the weary, especially those who had forgotten, especially those who felt downtrodden, especially those who felt beaten, to hope for a miracle. And to believe it would come.

But a person had to be open to that miracle coming. He had to be willing to see.

Or they would slip away if they were not acknowledged. And maybe after a while, if a man turned his back on enough miracles, maybe they wouldn't come back anymore at all.

As if to show how easily things could slip away, Morgan moved away from him and Ace, and over to her first graders. She was instantly surrounded in their clamor. Even from here he could here them calling for her attention.

"Mrs. McGuire. Mrs. McGuire."

She went down on her knees and opened her arms. In a moment he could not see her for all the wriggling bodies trying to get close to her, to hug her, to cuddle with her.

A man could make his own darkness. And he could live in it forever.

But Nate Hathoway wasn't going to. Not anymore.

What seemed to be a long time ago, Morgan had told him she was going to spend Christmas alone.

And he had known she wasn't.

Now he knew she wasn't ever going to again. Not as long as she lived and breathed. Not as long as he lived and breathed.

If she said yes.

Standing there on that stage, with his daughter in his arms and the woman he loved with that head-over-heels kind of love that made it impossible for a man to breathe or think or function, with the whole town on their feet whistling and clapping, he felt a breath on his neck.

And heard her whisper, once, *yes*.

He glanced at Morgan and realized she had not said a word.

And he realized, his heart swelling, that he and his daughter and the woman he loved stood among angels.

Morgan looked around her tiny house sadly. She snapped her tiny suitcase shut, put her book *Bliss: The Extraordinary Joy of Being a Single Woman* on top of it.

She was going to cry. She knew it.

Just thinking of those last moments on stage—not Ace's performance, or Brenda's, either—but the moment those children had surrounded her. She had hugged each and every one, only she knowing the truth.

Goodbye.

When she thought of not seeing her kids again, or her friends at the school, when she thought of not seeing Nate and Ace, the lump in her throat grew so large she could not even swallow.

Of course, she was going to cry for the rest of her life every single time she thought of Ace, *The Christmas Angel,* giving up her dream so that her friend could have hers.

She was going to cry for the rest of her life every single time she thought of these days before Christmas that she had spent with Nate.

They had a shine to them that was imprinted on her soul.

She was exhausted. She should probably wait for morning, but the thought of waking up alone on Christmas morning in this sweet little house was more than she could bear.

Just as she moved toward the door, there was a tap on it. Morgan froze, thinking she might have imagined it, thinking that maybe a branch had tapped the window.

But no, there it came again.

She tiptoed to her front window, craned her neck and could see her doorstep. Nate stood there.

Now what?

She was determined to go, to give this independent life a genuine shot. To make it a success this time. To not be swept from her chosen path.

He had gotten in the way before, a test that she had failed.

Maybe he was still testing her. And she wasn't going to fail this time.

Hoping only she would ever know her boldness was a complete pretext, she went and threw open the door.

"Hi."

"Nate."

His eyes drank her in, like a man who had crossed the desert, and she was a long cool drink of water.

Then his eyes left her, found the suitcase, went back to her. He frowned.

"Did you decide to go spend Christmas with your family after all?"

"Yes," she lied. So much easier than saying, *I am running away from you who wants no part of me or the kind of dreams I offer.*

Something in her voice tipped him off, because his eyes went back to her face, suddenly skeptical. Without being invited, he moved by her and stood in her living room.

"What happened to your tree?"

"I took it down. I didn't want to come home—" her voice caught on the word *home,* but she rushed on "—to find a pile of needles on the floor."

He was looking now at the boxes packed neatly on top of the purple couch. His eyes scanned her living room.

"Where's all the highly breakable bric-a-brac?" he asked.

She said nothing.

"Are you leaving?"

She couldn't look at him. Her shoulders were shaking. She looked down at her feet. She was mortified to see a teardrop on the end of her shoe.

His feet moved into her line of vision. One lean finger came under her chin and lifted it.

"You can't leave," he said huskily. "We've just begun."

But it was him who wasn't leaving. He took off his jacket and hung it on one of *their* coat hangers. He set down a wrapped Christmas package beside it.

"You said you didn't need me or my kind of dreams," she reminded him shakily, as he turned back to her and regarded her with those steady eyes.

We've just begun? That weakness was sweeping her, that *longing* was knocking the legs right out from under her.

She pulled away from him, caught a glance of her book sitting on top of her luggage, a stern reminder of the bliss that awaited her if she could just get through this.

"Did you know," she told him, "whole cultures are dispensing with relationships?"

He folded his arms over the mightiness of his chest, she suspected to keep himself from shaking her, but she bravely went on.

"In some Scandinavian countries, Denmark, Iceland, women are *choosing* not to get married anymore. They still have children, they've just dispensed with the, er, bothersome part."

"You mean men?" he asked grimly.

"Yes," she said, tilting her chin at him, "the bothersome part."

"Ah. The insensitive part."

"Uh-huh."

"The part that tends to run and hide when something like commitment begins to look likely."

"Exactly."

"The part that looks for an excuse to drive people away when they start getting too close."

Was he talking about *him* or about her? Because wasn't that what she was doing? Literally driving away because she had gotten too close. Her relationship with Karl had never asked this much of her, but she had driven away from that one, too.

"Well, dispensing with men is probably all well and good, we are a bothersome lot, but who puts up their coat hangers?"

"I'm sure they hire it out."

"Ditto for Christmas trees?"

"I haven't got to that part of the book, yet."

"And who deals with the stubborn ponies?"

"Not everyone has a stubborn pony to deal with."

"Who do they teach to make cookies?"

"Their children."

"Ah, the children that they dispensed with the bother of giving a father. How do the children feel about that?"

"I don't know," she said, a little querulously. "I don't know any Scandinavian children. Or Scandinavian women for that matter."

He moved closer to her, stared down at her.

"Who holds them in the night, Morgan? Who do they laugh with? Who do they hold hands with? Who do they kiss? Who makes the loneliness go away? Who makes the sun come out when it's raining?"

"You can't make the sun come out when it's raining!" Oh, hell. They weren't even talking about him. They were talking in *general* terms. Why had she said that?

But he moved closer to her. "Try me," he breathed.

"It's not raining."

"It is in my world, Morgan. The thought of you going away is making it rain in my world."

And then he closed the small distance between them, bent, cupped his hand at the back of her neck and drew her lips to his.

She willed herself to pull away in the interests of being the woman she should be.

But it seemed when her lips met his, she discovered, anew, exactly who that was.

"It's working for me," he said softly against her lips. "The sun is coming out for me, Morgan. And I know. Because I've been without it for a long time. Do you have to go there? Do you have to see for yourself what a lonely place the world can be?"

His lips took hers again before she could answer.

"I've been married," he said to her, a whisper. "And I've been single. A good marriage is the best, Morgan. You live with your best friend. You aren't lonely anymore."

She could feel something stilling in her, rising up to meet him.

"And you know what else, Morgan? You don't have to be afraid."

And that said it all. All her life she had thought she was afraid her dreams would not come true.

Now, she could see, she was much more afraid they would. What could ever live up to the expectation she had in her mind, after all? How long before the disillusionment set in? How long before one of them crashed out the door in the middle of the night and never came back?

Stunned, she realized she was repeating the pattern

of her childhood. She was abandoning the ship because of exactly what he had just said.

Morgan was afraid.

He looked at her, and in his eyes, she knew he could see her fear. He took her hand, and guided it gently to his face.

And found what he had said was true.

She did not have to be afraid anymore.

She touched his face with her fingertips, explored it. The word *beloved* came to her mind and stayed.

"Don't go, Morgan. Stay. Stay and marry me. I love you. I have loved you from the first moment you ignored my Go Away sign."

"You didn't. You were annoyed by me."

"Some part of me may have been annoyed. Another part knew that you had come to get me. To pull me out of the darkness. And now, I'm coming to get you, Morgan. I don't care what they do in Iceland. I don't want you to be alone."

She could hardly believe what she had just heard, what he had just offered, but when she saw his face, she knew it was true.

"Look," he said. "I got you a Christmas present."

He handed her the package he had set on the floor.

"This is one of the worst wrapping jobs I've ever seen," she said, tears, this time of joy, sparking in her eyes.

"You have a lifetime to teach me how to wrap parcels. And bake cookies."

The wrapping fell away, and she saw the hammer he had picked for her. And tied to its sturdy handle with a fine piece of gold wire was a ring.

"And I have a lifetime to show you," he continued

softly, "how to hang coat hangers and choose the right hammer. I have all kinds of skills you don't know about, too."

She could feel herself blushing, and he grinned wickedly.

"Well, there is that. But I'm also a champion diaper changer. You don't get that in every man."

And that the miracle she had waited her whole life for had just come. To have someone to lean on. To belong. To love.

"Will you?" he asked softly. "Will you come and spend Christmas Eve out at Molly and Keith's? And spend Christmas Day with us?"

"Yes," she whispered.

"We'll start there, then," he decided. He took the hammer from her, carefully unwound the sparkling diamond ring and slid it onto her finger.

She held up her hand, and the ring twinkled, and diamond sparks of light flew from it.

That matched the sparks of light that flew from his eyes.

"Yes," Morgan whispered again. Not just to Christmas Eve and Christmas Day, but to a life spent beside this man, bathed in the Light.

EPILOGUE

THE GRAVEYARD WAS QUIET and cold, a little daylight lingered in a cobalt-blue sky. The deep snow muffled his footprints. It was not where everyone would spend a Christmas Eve, but Nate had been drawn here tonight.

"I hope not to escape my mother-in-law," he muttered wryly.

But, of course, it was partly to escape her. Morgan's mother, who used to be plain old Anne, but had changed her name to Chosita after her long stay in Thailand. She said she had adopted the new moniker because everyone had called her that there. She said it meant happiness.

Morgan elbowed Nate in the ribs hard, when he said, coincidentally they had a pony by the same name and that he had almost exactly the same disposition. Nate had since found out that Chosita could indeed mean happiness, but it was sort of the American equivalent of "Hey, lady!"

Morgan's mother drove him nuts, wearing her Thai sarongs in downtown Canterbury where she improved stocks in the bookstore by adding to her substantial self-help collection.

But Ace adored her, and Morgan was thrilled that her mother was here to spend Christmas with them. Morgan genuinely hoped the baby, due any day, would put in an appearance while her mom was here.

Nate exacted subtle revenge on Chosita for what he saw as her astoundingly poor parenting throughout Morgan's childhood and adolescence. This afternoon, for instance, he subjected her to the longest sleigh ride in Happy history. He'd made sure to ply her with several buckets of tea first, too.

He smiled, now, just thinking of it, then knelt beside the two stones.

He knew flowers couldn't handle the cold, so he always brought sprigs of holly, and a fir bough with a candle in it that he would light before he left, and that would burn through to Christmas morning.

"I know, I know," he said, as he brushed the snow from the two stones, "I'm being uncharitable for Christmas. It's just her, really."

The wind howled.

"Okay, so I've never warmed to Mrs. Wellhaven, either."

He had just gotten a thank-you note from the Wellhavens for the intricate iron fireplace grate he had sent them. He never forgot Wesley, or the debt he felt he owed to the man who had not left him in the darkness that Christmas Eve two years ago.

As it had turned out, the whole economy of Canterbury had not been saved by the production of *The Christmas Angel,* but it had certainly been helped over the hump.

As it had turned out, the second annual Christmas production had been the last one Wesley gave.

Shortly after *The Christmas Angel,* Wesley had gone back into retirement to lead the quiet reclusive life he enjoyed. There had been no more Christmas productions, and people thought he did not sing at all. Every now and then one of the tabloids would run a story about the tragic loss of his voice.

But of course Nate knew that not to be true, because on the finest day of his life, when he had stood at the altar waiting for the woman who would be his wife to come toward him, *that* voice had filled the cathedral. Between the beauty of that voice and the beauty of his bride, there had not been a dry eye in the house that afternoon, including his own.

And so, every year, he sent the Wellhavens something.

His reputation as a tough guy seemed to have largely gone out the window as he courted Morgan, anyway. The whole town had seen he was smitten. And he didn't care.

He had serenaded her. He'd delivered wagons of flowers pulled by a reluctant Happy. He had taken her on picnics, and sat at home in front of the fire with her.

Cindy would have been proud. He had not wasted one minute, not one, of that glorious falling-in-love feeling that she had wished for him. He still didn't. He didn't think a man should ever take the gifts he had been given for granted.

Ace was eight now. She was in hockey *and* ballet. She also, much to Happy's distress (the pony, not her grandmother) had started taking riding lessons at the stable where Brenda Weston rode.

The instructor had suggested Ace was ready for a better horse, but Ace had said no. In a statement reminiscent of her famous *Christmas Angel* production speech, she said that if being a good rider meant leaving Happy behind, she would just stay where she was, thanks.

Ace's little speech that had gone live all over North America, was played as one of that year's highlights on almost every news station in America. It was still, two years later, one of the most popular hits on the Internet.

Ace was still tickled when a piece of fan mail reached her.

As far as Nate knew, Brenda, the one everyone, including him, had proclaimed to be the perfect Christmas Angel, had never gotten a single piece of fan mail. But then Brenda, nice as she was, just didn't have the heart Ace had. When the riding instructor had suggested she trade up to a better horse, she'd gotten rid of her epileptic Welsh pony, O'Henry, without a backward glance.

"Which means," he finished softly, "I'm now feeding two ponies, and have double trouble when I try to harness them to the sleigh. At least O'Henry doesn't bite. Okay, he falls over now and then, but who asked for a perfect life?"

He realized he had spoken each of his thoughts out loud, and he smiled. Once, all he had felt here was yawning emptiness.

Now when he came, he felt *full*.

He finished dusting the snow off each of the stones, and then he put the holly and the fir bough between them.

He read them, out loud, too.

David Henderson, gone with angels, son, friend, soldier.

Cynthia Dawn Hathoway. Beloved wife and mother.

When he had chosen this plot next to David, he had

known that though Cindy had married him she had really belonged with David. Heart and soul. Forever. That is who she had been crazy in love with since she was fourteen years old.

Still, she had been beloved to Nate. And she had become his Christmas angel. There was not a doubt in his mind that somehow, in some way, in ways that were far too huge for the human mind to grapple with, she had been there that Christmas he had found Morgan.

Bringing meaning out of tragedy. Showing him she had been right all along. Everything had a reason. And good could come from bad.

Somehow Cindy had a hand in bringing him and Ace the woman who would be the best mom for her daughter.

And the best wife for him.

My wish for you is that you could fall in love.

"I did," Nate said out loud. "I have. Crazy in love, just like you always wanted. It's better than anything I could have ever imagined."

Right now, Morgan and Ace and Grandma Happiness were at home making Christmas cookies and decorating the tree he had put the lights on earlier. He had warned Morgan, direly, about getting on the ladder to put up the higher decorations. Naturally, she had stuck out her tongue at him, which meant she was probably on the top rung of the ladder—the one that said "do not use this as a step"—right now.

The baby was due in the first part of the New Year. Ace was more excited about that than she was about Christmas.

They had chosen not to find out the sex. A boy or a girl, either would be a blessing.

Nate lit the candle. It was getting dark and that candle was a small light in that darkness, but a small light could be enough.

He knew Cindy wasn't really here. Nor was David. He knew love didn't go into the ground. It went on and on. It lived in the people left behind.

Still, he needed to come here, even if they were not here. He needed to come here to remind himself to be grateful for things he could not understand. Angels.

Miracles.

Especially Christmas ones.

"Thank you," he said softly.

Yes. He heard it as clearly as though they stood on either side of him. Exuberant. Triumphant.

That word, that simple affirmation of love and of life, was so real that Nate glanced over his left shoulder, and then his right one. The graveyard was empty. He was alone.

But not really. Not ever.

He was not alone. And he was full. To the top. And then to overflowing.

CHRISTMAS AT
CANDLEBARK FARM

BY
MICHELLE DOUGLAS

At the age of eight **Michelle Douglas** was asked what she wanted to be when she grew up. She answered, 'A writer.' Years later she read an article about romance-writing and thought, *Ooh, that'll be fun*. She was right.

When she's not writing she can usually be found with her nose buried in a book. She is currently enrolled in an English Masters programme for the sole purpose of indulging her reading and writing habits further. She lives in a leafy suburb of Newcastle, on Australia's east coast, with her own romantic hero—husband Greg, who is the inspiration behind all her happy endings. Michelle would love you to visit her at her website, www. michelledouglas.com.

To Cate,
and all our memories of the pink flat

CHAPTER ONE

KEIRA KEELY climbed out of her car and pushed her sunglasses up to rest on the top of her head before double-checking the written instructions the estate agency had given her.

Since she'd turned off the highway several kilometres back she'd travelled along this gravel lane for precisely six and a quarter minutes, just as the receptionist at the real estate agency had told her to.

This had to be the place. She hadn't passed a single house on the road so far, and there wasn't another house in sight. This had to be it—Candlebark Farm.

She hoped so. The big old homestead with its wide shady verandas looked inviting in the December sunshine, and after six hours on the road inviting was exactly what she needed. The country township of Gunnedah was a far cry from the hustle and bustle of Sydney, but so far it hadn't lived up to its promise of easygoing country hospitality.

She stretched her arms above her head and shook out her legs, did her best to banish her irritation.

'Some old-fashioned country hospitality is exactly what we need, Munchkin.' She patted her still-flat tummy. 'And, believe me, this place looks like it delivers that in spades.'

She pushed through the front gate. The lawn was a little long and the shrubs a little shrubby, but that only added to the charm of the place. She paused, breathed in the country goodness, and willed some of its peace to enter her soul.

The day had proved a complete shambles so far. Not only had the estate agent not been free to take her through her aunt's house—although when she'd rung him during the week he'd assured her it wouldn't be a problem—but her appointment with her aunt's solicitor had been cancelled too. 'We can reschedule it for Wednesday, Ms Keely.'

Wednesday! It was Saturday. She was only here for a week. With tight lips the secretary had pencilled Keira in for Tuesday morning for a 'short' appointment. Whatever *that* meant. Keira reminded herself the cancellation hadn't been the secretary's fault.

Her platform sandals with their pink, lime and aqua straps—super-comfortable and strangely accommodating of the way her feet had started to swell—clattered against the wood of the veranda. They were so noisy she half expected to find someone waiting for her at the front door by the time she reached it.

But no.

She tried the old-fashioned knocker and waited. Knocked again. And waited some more.

She glanced back at her car. She had groceries that would spoil soon if she didn't get them out of the heat. Had the Hilliers—the family who lived at Candlebark—forgotten she was coming?

She followed the veranda around to the back of the house. 'Hello?'

After a moment the back screen door jerked open. A boy stared out at her—a teenage boy, wearing a scowl. Keira swallowed. 'Um…is this Candlebark Farm?'

'Yeah.'

She pointed back the way she'd come. 'You didn't hear me knocking on the front door?'

The scowl deepened. 'No one uses the front.'

Right. She'd remember that for future reference.

She drew in a breath and had opened her mouth, meaning

to introduce herself, when the boy muttered, 'If you're looking for my dad he's in the barn.' With that he disappeared back inside the house, the screen door clattering shut after him.

Keira blinked. Right. The, um…barn.

Shading her eyes, she surveyed the landscape spread before her. Just beyond the fence line, stretching for as far as the eye could see, waist-high stalks nodded and swayed, making intriguing patterns as the breeze travelled through them, their golden heads bouncing and jostling. Wheat. Unsurprising, she told herself. After all, Gunnedah was smack-bang in the middle of New South Wale's wheat belt. And although it made a fine sight—pretty, even—she hadn't travelled six hours to admire wheat fields.

She turned her attention to the array of outbuildings on her left. Without further ado she set off towards the largest one.

Were all teenagers surly?

'Ooh, Munchkin, we're going to have some serious talks before you hit that age.'

The thought of the baby nestled safely inside her made Keira's chest expand. She flung her arms out, as if to hug the world, and lifted her face skywards to relish the warmth of the sun. A laugh escaped her. So what if there were a few hiccups this week? That was what she was here to sort out.

Just like that, her usual optimism reasserted itself. She chuckled again, and admitted maybe that had more to do with the fact that her nausea had receded. Finally.

The barn's double doors stood wide open. 'Hello?' She stepped inside. It took her eyes a moment to adjust to the sudden dimness. No sound but her own disturbed the quiet. She moved further inside and made her voice louder. 'Hello?'

'There's no need to shout.'

She nearly jumped out of her skin when a man, flat on his back on some kind of trolley, emerged from beneath a tractor almost directly in front of her. She backed up a few steps to give him more room. He had grease on one cheek and both hands. He didn't get up. His scowl, identical to the teenage boy's back at the house, proclaimed their kinship.

'You lost? Look—head back the way you came. When you hit the sealed road turn left and go straight ahead. Gunnedah is about fifteen minutes away.'

He slid back under the tractor again. She swore she heard him add in an undertone, 'Where you can buy a map.'

Ten minutes ago she might well have been tempted to kick him—not literally, of course. Now the misunderstanding only made her laugh. 'This is Candlebark Farm, isn't it? If so, then I'm not lost. Are you Mr Hillier?'

With a long-suffering sigh he emerged again. 'Yeah? So? Who wants to know?'

'I'm Keira Keely.'

He didn't sit up, so she rested her hands on her knees and grinned down at him. 'I'm renting your room for the next week.'

Those dark eyes blinked. The face shuttered closed, but the frown deepened, carving deep grooves either side of his mouth. Keira's renewed optimism wavered. It wasn't the kind of mouth that promised country hospitality.

'You sure you're meant to arrive today?'

'A hundred percent certain.'

'Right.' In one fluid motion he was on his feet and wiping his hands on a rag that hung from the back of his jeans. 'Didn't Jason show you your room?'

The surly teenager?

The man still hadn't cracked a smile. She swallowed. He was tall, lean-hipped and broad-shouldered. She hadn't noticed that when he'd been sprawled at her feet. He was glaring too. And his words sounded like an accusation.

It hit her then how quiet it was out here…how isolated. She took a step back.

'You—uh—' he lifted a hand in her direction and made as if to grab her '—might want to watch—'

She took another hasty step back, her sandal-clad foot landing in an oozing, steaming pile…

'—where you're going.'

…of something disgusting.

She stared down at her foot, and then back at him. 'What am I standing in?'

'Horse manure.'

He didn't offer to help. In fact he didn't do anything at all. Gritting her teeth, she lifted her foot clear of the mess and placed it on firmer ground, closing her eyes when the stuffed squished between her toes like slimy, putrid mud.

To her disbelief, when she opened them again she found the man making as if to lie back down on his trolley and disappear beneath the tractor again.

'I'll finish up here, and then I'll show you your room.'

'No!'

She didn't mean to snap, but the stuff oozing between her toes had started her stomach roiling and churning—again. If she was going to throw up—again—today, she wanted that to happen in the privacy of a bathroom, not on some roadside and certainly not in this man's barn.

Nobody had warned her that being pregnant could make her feel so awful. Surely the very definition of morning sickness was sickness that happened *in the morning*. Not all day!

She'd never stepped in horse manure before so she didn't know what her reaction in an unpregnant state might be. But in her current ten-weeks-gone condition her scalp started to tighten and a film of perspiration clung to her skin, making her oppressively clammy.

She pointed to her foot. She didn't look at it. She didn't trust her stomach to cope with the sight. 'Lead me to a tap. Now!'

She thought he was going to refuse, but with a cut-off oath he strode out of the barn's double doors back towards the house. Keira half-limped, half-squelched after him. Back in the sunlight, she dragged in deep breaths of air—cleansing breaths. The faint breeze cooled her skin, rescuing her from the worst of her clamminess.

Her scowling host slammed to a halt and pointed to a tap situated to one side of the back steps. Keira hobbled over to it, turned it on—hard—and shoved her foot, platform shoe and all, beneath the jet of water, uncaring that it soaked the bottoms of her three-quarter-length jeans. When she was sure she could bend down without falling over, she unbuckled her shoe and left it where it fell, and set to scrubbing her foot clean, ridding herself of the smell that had made her stomach rebel so violently.

When that was done she hobbled across to the back steps, sat, then shoved her head between her knees and concentrated on her breathing.

She was aware of Mr Hillier's stunned surveillance—irritation emanated from him in tidal waves of folded arms and half-muttered imprecations. Thankfully, though, he didn't address anything to her directly. Finally the nausea receded, and she was able to lift her head and meet his gaze.

And then wished she hadn't. His lip had curled. He was staring at her as if she was something unmentionable that had crawled out from beneath a rock.

'Do you threaten to faint every time you step in horse manure?'

She opened her mouth to tell him horse manure wasn't an occupational hazard in the city, but her mind got sidetracked when the actual sight of him finally registered—when her eyes flashed an unforgettable image to her brain. He stood with legs apart and hands on hips. She doubted whether he cared two hoots about how he came across physically, but whether he meant it to or not his current posture showed off the length of his legs, the strength of his thighs, not to mention the breadth of those shoulders, to perfection.

The woman in her heartily approved of all that masculine

muscle and texture. The physiotherapist, however, noted how tension gathered in the muscles of his neck and shoulders, not to mention his back. If this man wasn't careful he'd end up with a frozen shoulder or—

One of those dark eyebrows lifted. In the next instant heat flooded through her as she tore her gaze away.

She hadn't been staring! She hadn't!

Liar.

She dragged herself to her feet. 'I had a touch of car sickness,' she mumbled, as if that could explain everything. 'I, um, I have groceries in the car that I really ought to unpack.'

'Groceries?'

The snapped-out word had her swinging back to him. His gaze had narrowed. 'You do understand that all you're renting from me is a room? This isn't some fancy bed and breakfast or farm stay holiday.'

This was the country hospitality she was to expect? Keira drew herself up to her full height. 'Mr Hillier—' she injected her voice with as much ice as he '—the agency with whom you advertised your room assured me I would have the use of a kitchen to prepare my own meals.'

Since becoming pregnant she rarely ate out. And in the last couple of days it hadn't been just because she was frantically saving her pennies now she had a baby on the way, but because unfamiliar cooking smells assaulted her in a way they never had before, making her sick. It seemed safer to stay away from restaurants.

She glared. 'Are you telling me I've been given the wrong information?'

He stared at her as if appalled at the thought of sharing his kitchen with her. He made no reply. Keira had to blink and swallow and fight hard to keep her shoulders from slumping. 'I understand that it's only two weeks till Christmas, and that this is a busy time of year. I've obviously arrived at an inconvenient time for you and your family. I won't bother you any further. I'll take my obviously outdated assumptions about old-fashioned country hospitality and make other arrangements.'

She spun around and headed for her car. It was only after she turned the corner of the house that she realised she'd left her soiled shoe behind. She didn't break stride. She wasn't going back for it. It was ruined now anyway.

What the—?

She was leaving without even *looking* at the room? She'd dragged him away from his tractor, when there'd only been one more nut to tighten, for *this*?

Luke considered letting her just leave. The truth was he'd rather undergo a root canal than rent out his room to a woman like her. At least at the dentist's he wasn't expected to make polite conversation. Old-fashioned country hospitality? He didn't have time for that kind of nonsense. He had a farm to run.

He shifted his weight. The thing was she'd paid her week's rent up front. And he'd already spent it on a deposit for the hire of next month's combine harvester.

'Wait!' He swept up her shoe and set off after her. 'You've already paid for the room.' And he didn't want to dip into the overdraft to provide her with a refund.

She didn't turn around.

'And you've forgotten your shoe.'

She whirled around at that. 'It's ruined!'

'No, it's not.' Typical city girl. Get a bit of honest dirt on something and it was instantly unsalvageable. No concept of recycling or making do. But then he noticed her sandal still had greenish streaks of horse manure clinging to it. He pulled the rag from the back of his jeans and set to wiping it clean.

It took a major effort of will not to curl his lip at the sandal—two-inch cork platforms with a criss-crossing of colourful straps. This wasn't so much a shoe as a silly piece of confection. A bit like the lady herself.

He glanced at her again and his skin grew tight. She was too young, too fresh and pretty, too…shiny. It hurt his eyes to look at her.

She folded her arms and tapped a foot. 'Well, that's an improvement.'

He snapped to, glanced down, and found that while he'd been busy cataloguing every line of her face he'd streaked her shoe with grease. He cut back something rude and succinct. Black streaks slashed through the green ones, in some spots completely replacing them. There was no way he'd get that grease out.

Nice one, Hillier. How are you going to convince the lady to stay now?

'I'll pay for the damage,' he found himself offering.

'Not necessary. They only cost me five dollars in a sale and, believe me, I've had my five dollars' worth out of them. But…'

She stared at the sandal, lips pursed, and then she glanced up at him. That glance—it hit him square in the chest. Her eyes were grey—a clear, light grey that somehow picked up and reflected the colour of her surroundings. At the moment he could pick out flecks of green from the nearby bottlebrush tree, blue from the sky, and gold from the swaying fields of wheat. He blinked, floundered, and tried to find his centre of gravity.

'Have you wiped all that disgusting stuff off?'

By 'disgusting stuff' he figured she meant the horse manure. He'd never seen anyone react so irrationally to a bit of dung before.

He reminded himself about the overdraft, and the fact she was only staying for one week. If he could calm her down and convince her to stay, that was.

He made a show of checking the shoe carefully. 'There's

a stain here and here—' he showed her '—but the shoe itself is clean.'

'So…it doesn't smell of…?'

God give him strength. 'No, it doesn't smell of…' His voice trailed off in a mocking imitation of hers before he could help himself.

Thankfully, she didn't seem to notice. Instead she took the shoe and surveyed it. 'Do you think I could black the cork somehow? I know they only cost five dollars, but they're so comfortable.'

He tried to hide his surprise. 'You could give it a go.' He doubted if the end result would set the world of fashion on fire, but he was determined to humour her.

And then just like that she bent down and slid the sandal back onto her foot as if it had never touched 'disgusting stuff.' In the process, though, she overbalanced and had to grab his arm for support.

It was not that he wasn't happy to lend that support—it was better than her landing flat on her face—but she let go so quickly, and then she blushed. Like she had at the back steps, when she'd realised she'd been caught out staring at him. And he wasn't happy about that—the reminder of his own reaction to that steady appraisal and the feminine appreciation that had momentarily lit her face. It had flooded him with hormones he'd forgotten all about, filling him with a primitive need he'd done his best to disown.

He took a step back, fighting the urge to rub the imprint of her hand from his skin. She was soft and warm.

He didn't do soft and warm.

She smelt like vanilla.

Trouble. That was the word that flashed through his mind. His every instinct told him this woman was trouble.

She wore a pair of three-quarter-length jeans and a hot pink top that tied at the waist and left her shoulders bare.

He tried to dismiss her as pale and skinny.

It didn't work. She wasn't pale. Her skin gleamed, luminous like ivory. It wasn't the kind of skin that would tan in the sun—if it got burned it would blister and peel—but to call it pale didn't do it justice. And skinny? He swallowed. Those jeans were a snug fit. Too snug. She might be slender, but she had hips that flared, a waist that curved in, and breasts that would fit in the palms of—

He cut that thought dead.

Her gaze speared back to him. 'Give me one good reason why I should stay at Candlebark?'

He forced his mind from the shape of her lips. 'Follow me.' He led her up the front steps and around to the side of the veranda. 'Look at that.' He gestured to the view. 'It can't be beaten.' He stared at the thousands of swaying heads of wheat and some of the tension eased out of him.

She glanced at it, and then back at him. 'Well…it is kind of pretty,' she allowed.

He folded his arms. 'The perfect place for a country holiday.'

'But I'm not here on holiday.'

He unfolded his arms and tried to think of something else that might tempt her. She'd said something about country hospitality. He pointed to a nearby bench. 'That's a great spot to have coffee in the morning. And, um…' He scratched a hand through his hair. 'And for a glass of wine in the evenings.' That sounded hospitality-ish, didn't it?

Her lips twitched. 'So that's your selling point is it—an old bench?'

It wasn't that old! It… Okay, perhaps it was. But—

'And as I'm currently abstaining from both caffeine and alcohol…'

He slammed his hands to his hips. This woman had turned being difficult into an art form!

'Still, if you substitute chamomile tea for coffee…'

He gave up trying to read her expression from the corner of

his eye and turned to face her fully. She met his gaze without blinking. Her hair—red-gold—tumbled around her face and shoulders in a riot of messed up curls and wispy bits, fizzing up around her sunglasses. It made her look wild and full of mischief, like an errant fairy.

Luke swallowed. He needed water. A long, cold glass of water. He was so dry. He couldn't remember the last time thirst had plagued him with such ferocity.

He cleared his throat and stared back out at his wheat. 'Look, I'm sorry about earlier. I thought you were after some kind of hokey family-farm-stay. Candlebark isn't set up for that sort of thing. I usually only rent the room out to temporary mine workers. It's coming up to harvest, and I'm too busy to...'

He trailed off. The words that had sprung to mind were *play host*. He wasn't a host. He was a landlord, and she was a temporary—very temporary—lodger. 'And of course you have full access to the kitchen while you're here. You can use the dining and living rooms too if you want.' No skin off his nose. He didn't care if she took over the entire house. He was hardly ever in it anyhow.

She surveyed him for a minute, and then she grinned. That off-balance thing happened to him again.

'Help me unload the car?'

He shrugged. 'Yeah, sure.'

'Then I guess you have yourself a guest for the next week, Mr Hillier.'

Lodger, not guest. He bit back the correction and reminded himself about the hospitality thing. 'Luke,' he offered from between gritted teeth. 'Why don't you call me Luke?'

He followed her out to her car and tried not to notice how sweetly she filled out those jeans of hers. He'd carry her bags in and then he was getting back to his tractor. Fast.

Luke returned to the barn and the relatively uncomplicated workings of his tractor. Finishing up the repairs—the tightening of that single nut—took roughly forty-five seconds.

He stowed his tools and then glared at the pile of horse dung that had so offended his 'guest'. The look on her face when she'd stood in the stuff! He seized a spade. The last thing he needed was a repeat performance. He mucked out the horse stalls and removed all signs of horse manure from the barn and its immediate surrounds. That took half an hour.

Next he set about cleaning the tack. He rubbed leather conditioner into his saddle, all the while searching his brain for anything else she might find offensive about the farm— anything as earthy as horse manure, that was—but he came up with a blank. Since Jason's border collie had died—hit by a car eight months ago—he, Jason and the horses were the only living, breathing beings on Candlebark. As long as you didn't count snakes, spiders, lizards, the odd kangaroo or ten, possums, bees and hornets.

He let rip with an oath. What if something else spooked her? What if she just upped and left without so much as a by-your-leave after all?

He threw his cloth down. He'd planned to start clearing the western boundary paddock this afternoon. Get it ready for sowing in April. At the moment it was choked with Paterson's Curse. He sighed and admitted defeat. He wouldn't get out there today. He'd best stay close to the homestead in case anything set his 'guest' off again.

He didn't doubt his first instinct about her—that she was trouble with a capital T—but her money was as good as the next person's, and for the next three weeks—until they had the harvest in—every penny counted.

He glanced at his watch. He'd shown her to her room roughly an hour and a half ago. At least she couldn't complain about that! Her room was big and clean. Spotless, in fact. Luke knew because he scrubbed it to within an inch of its life every week.

But if ants had invaded the pantry again or if, heaven forbid, she caught sight of a mouse…

His temples started to pound and an ache stretched behind his eyes. He wanted nothing more than to get into his ute and bolt—lose himself in the wide plains and open skies of his land. He set his mouth and strode outside. With one longing glance at the swaying fields of gold, he turned towards the house.

He found his lodger in the kitchen, waiting for the jug to boil. A box—in fact several boxes—of herbal tea snuggled up against his jar of instant coffee. A loaf of bread nestled next to the already full breadbox—one of those fancy boutique loaves that were more seed than bread. He didn't know why people bothered. If they wanted seeds, why didn't they just buy seeds?

A women's magazine and a local real-estate guide graced the table. He rolled his shoulders, stretched his neck first to the left and then to the right. He was hardly ever in the house—who cared where she put her stuff?

The jug came to the boil and Keira reached for a mug—his mug. He opened his mouth. He shut it again with a snap. What did it matter what mug she used?

She gestured to the teas and coffee, sent him one of those seemingly effortless smiles of hers. 'Would you like one?'

'No, thanks.'

He didn't want her thinking long, lazy afternoon teas or leisurely meals were commonplace around here. He'd stopped work to make sure she had everything she needed, that she was reasonably comfortable. End of story.

'Is everything up to scratch?' His voice came out rusty, as if he hadn't used it in a long time. 'Are you happy with your room?'

'It's more than adequate, thank you.'

Adequate?

'I cleared a shelf in the fridge and another in the pantry for my things. I hope that's okay?'

'Perfectly.' He worked hard at keeping his tone neutral.

She was here for one week—seven days. After today they'd be lucky to spend more than five minutes in each other's company. He just wanted to make sure she hadn't gone and got spooked again.

'Oh.' She swung around from pouring boiling water into his—her—mug. 'You have ants in the pantry. Thought I'd best warn you.'

He rubbed a hand across the back of his neck and steeled himself for outrage.

'My grandmother used to leave a jar of honey open for them in our pantry. They seemed to leave everything else alone after that.'

He stopped rubbing his nape and steeling himself to stare at her. She'd turned back to jiggle her teabag. 'Let me get this straight. Ants don't faze you, but a bit of horse dung has you running for cover?'

Actually, it had frozen her to the spot and had turned her a deathly shade of green.

She stilled, but didn't turn around. She jiggled her teabag with renewed enthusiasm. 'Haven't you ever had an irrational aversion to anything before?'

You bet! Going into town, for one, and having to endure the stares, the speculation in strangers' eyes as they were no doubt trying to assess if what his in-laws said about him was true.

She dropped her teabag into the kitchen tidy, then turned with hands on hips. He answered with a non-committal shrug. Her lips twitched, as if something funny had just occurred to her. 'I bet I could name a few things you'd be averse to—male cologne, skin care products.'

He stiffened. Did he smell? 'Perfume's for girls,' he growled. So was that goop they slathered on their faces. And he didn't smell of anything worse than honest sweat! 'Right?' he demanded of Jason, who had chosen that moment to slouch into the kitchen.

'Whatever,' Jason muttered.

Luke heaved back a sigh. Some time in the last few months Jason had turned into a moody, brooding teenager, with all the communication skills of a bad-tempered bull. 'This is Ms Keely. She's staying here for the next week.'

Another grunt.

'This is my son, Jason.'

Keira beamed one of those smiles at his son, and held her hand out across the table towards him. 'It's nice to meet you, Jason. And, please, call me Keira.'

Jason stared at Keira's outstretched hand without moving. When he finally shuffled forward to shake it, Luke let out a breath he hadn't even known he'd been holding.

'Jason's fourteen.' For the life of him, Luke didn't know why he'd parted with that particular piece of information.

'Nearly fifteen!' Jason glared, and then he shuffled his feet. 'I though you were clearing the boundary paddock?'

'I'm a bit behind schedule.' Luke managed not to glance at Keira as he said it. 'Tractor had an oil leak.'

Jason stared down at his feet. 'Need a hand?'

'Nah, it's all good.' It wasn't his son's responsibility to get the farm back to full running capacity—that responsibility rested on his shoulders alone. Jason should be hanging out with his friends and having fun—doing whatever teenagers did these days.

Jason scowled. 'Yeah, well, whatever.'

Keira glanced from one to the other, a tiny crease forming between her eyes. 'I...um...brought a caramel mud cake.'

She pulled an enormous box from the fridge and set on the table. When she lifted the lid the scent of cake and sweetness filled the air.

'They didn't have anything smaller than this monstrosity, but I'm afraid I couldn't resist. There's not a chance of me getting through all this on my own, so please help yourselves. It'd be a shame to let it go to waste.'

As she was talking, she cut three generous slices from the perfect round. More of that sweetness drenched the air. Luke couldn't remember the last time the kitchen had smelled so good.

'Sweet!' Jason accepted one of the slices before slouching back off in the direction of his room.

Keira glanced up at Luke, a hint of mockery lighting her eyes. 'Relax, it's only a piece of cake, Luke.' With that she gathered up her magazines, her tea, and her slice of cake. 'I'm sure you'll excuse me if I retire to your veranda to admire that view of yours.'

She left—just like that. As if she didn't need looking after, as if she didn't need that country hospitality she'd been so hot about. And without inviting him to join her.

Not that he'd wanted an invitation.

Luke stared around his now strangely colourless kitchen, his gaze coming to rest on the remaining slice of cake. From somewhere deep inside yearning gripped him. For a moment he was tempted to swipe a finger through the rich chocolate frosting.

He reached out.

What the hell…? He snapped back. Then he seized the plate and shoved it into the fridge.

He stormed out through the back door. He had work to do.

CHAPTER TWO

LUKE shot upright—still groggy from sleep—and groped for his bedside clock. Through slitted eyes he read 3:21. With a groan, he dropped it back. Something had woken him from a dead sleep. What?

Closing his eyes, he concentrated on picking out any noise unfamiliar amid the normal night sounds of crickets, cicadas, and a call from the occasional tawny frogmouth.

He relaxed when the low whine of the tap in the bathroom broke through the other night noises. His lodger. It would take him a night or two to get used to someone else's rhythms. *Good, go back to sleep.* He punched his pillow, settled back down, and...

Hold on. He lifted his head again. Sat up. That was no normal nightly visit to the bathroom. Keira was... Was she being sick?

For all of two-tenths of a second he considered burying his head in one pillow, covering it with another, and trying to go back to sleep. But he knew it wouldn't work. He'd never been able to ignore an animal in physical distress. Unfortunately, that included lodgers.

Muttering imprecations under his breath, he hauled himself out of bed, dragged on a pair of tracksuit pants to cover his nakedness and made for the bathroom. *Trouble with a capital T!*

He paused outside the door, hand raised to knock, and

then grimaced at the unmistakable sounds that emerged from behind the door—muffled but unmistakable. 'Keira?' He knocked. 'Can I come in?' He wanted to burst in and make sure she was all right, so he could go back to bed. He held himself back, reminding himself she was a lone woman in a strange place.

Behind the door came movement… The door opened, and all his irritation fled. He'd thought she'd looked pale when he'd first clapped eyes on her, but now she was white. The only colour in her face came from the grey of her eyes, but even they were dim and bloodshot. All that red-gold hair fizzing around her face only made her look paler.

His heart lurched. 'Is there anything I can get for you? Would you like me to take you to the hospital or—?'

She shook her head. 'I'm really sorry I disturbed you, Luke. I—'

She turned from white to green. She spun away to kneel in front of the toilet and was immediately and comprehensively sick. Again. Luke leapt forward to drag her hair back from her face. He didn't try to talk, and he didn't rub her back because he didn't know if that would make her feel better or worse, but with every heaving retch his heart clenched harder and tighter.

When this particular bout of sickness had passed, he flushed the toilet, closed its lid and settled her on top of it. When he was certain she wasn't going to fall, he moistened a facecloth and very gently wiped her face.

She didn't open her eyes until he was finished. 'You're very kind,' she whispered.

No, he wasn't. But he couldn't stand by and do nothing if she was sick. 'What did you eat today?'

She frowned. It turned into a glare. 'I can tell you one thing—I am *never* eating caramel mud cake again. I couldn't resist another piece after dinner, but… Ugh, never again.'

It almost made him smile. Only he couldn't smile when

she remained so pale. 'Keira, I really think you should see a doctor.'

She pulled in a breath. 'It's nothing. I promise.' She closed her eyes and pulled in another breath. 'It's become the norm over the last few days, that's all.' A third breath. 'I'm sure it'll pass.'

His head snapped back. The norm? She was slender, sure, but he hadn't pegged her as anorexic or bulimic. Still, she was young and pretty, and he knew women her age felt an enormous pressure to conform to impossible media images. Not for the first time he was grateful he had a son instead of a daughter. Raising a daughter without the help of her mother could prove tricky. Or at least trickier than a son.

Keira's confession settled it—she was seeing a doctor. Whether she had food poisoning or was bulimic or had some ghastly twenty-four hour virus, he was taking her to the hospital. Illness like this should *never* be the norm.

'C'mon.' He urged her to her feet and handed her a glass of water to rinse out her mouth. 'It's better to be safe than sorry. It'll take us no time at all to drive to the hospital and have someone check you over.' When he saw she was about to refuse he added, 'Look, I'm going to be out in the fields from dawn, and I probably won't return till late. Jason will most likely be out with his mates for most of the day. I can't guarantee there'll be anyone here to help you if you need it tomorrow.'

She smiled. She was pale and woebegone, and yet she managed a smile. He didn't know why, but it made his heart crash about in his chest. 'It's sweet of you to consider my welfare.'

Not sweet. He refused to allow that. He just didn't want another woman's death on his conscience.

'Luke, I'm really not sick.'

He raised an eyebrow at that.

'And I have seen a doctor.'

His shoulders loosened a fraction. The pressure eased from his chest. In the next moment the pressure crashed back. If she was this sick after seeing a doctor then that indicated something serious—something sinister.

'I have nothing worse,' she continued, 'than a bad bout of morning sickness.'

He stared at her, trying to make sense of her words. Morning sickness? But that meant…

'I'm pregnant.'

And then she beamed. His legs gave out, plonking him down to sit on the side of the bathtub.

She sat down again too. 'I'm having a baby.'

Only then did he notice that she wore an oversized sleep-shirt in powder blue. It had a picture of a teddy bear on the front and hung down to her knees. She didn't look old enough to have a baby!

He surged to his feet as an unlooked-for and unwanted wave of protectiveness flooded him. 'Where's your baby's father? Why the hell is he letting you go through this on your own?'

'Oh, Luke…'

She pressed two fingers to her mouth. Luke immediately went on high alert. 'Are you going to be sick again?' He readied himself to hold her hair back from her face if the need arose. He glanced at that hair. For all its curly unruliness, it had felt smooth and soft in his hand.

'No, I don't think so. I think I might risk a cup of tea.'

Her colour had started to return. He shuffled back a step. *Pregnant!* 'Do you need a hand with anything else?'

'No, I'm fine now. Honest.'

With a nod he backed out through the door. 'Right. I'll go put the jug on.'

'Oh, that's not necessary. You can go back to bed and I…'

He didn't turn or stop. He headed straight for the kitchen.

Pregnant and alone in the world—he'd read that fact in her eyes.

Trouble with a capital T!

He couldn't get involved. He couldn't risk it. But the least he could do was make her a cup of tea.

When Keira entered the kitchen she was glad to find Luke had dragged a T-shirt over his bare chest. The breadth of his shoulders, those bulging biceps, had all started to filter into her consciousness towards the end there in the bathroom. It had taken a concerted effort to try and ignore the effect they were having on her.

While it had been beyond kind of him to hold back her hair, to mop her face, it had all started to feel a bit too… intimate. And she wasn't doing intimate. Not until she and the Munchkin were well and truly settled, thank you very much.

Still, there was no denying she'd gained a measure of comfort from Luke's presence, and she hadn't expected that. It had brought those niggling doubts back to the surface, though. Taking great bites out of her confidence, making her question the validity of having a baby on her own.

No!

She pushed the very idea of that thought away. She could and she *would* have this baby on her own. Those doubts—it was just the misery of nausea talking.

She saw Luke turn from surveying her various boxes of tea. Besides peppermint and chamomile, she had a selection of herbal teas made up by the boutique tea shop she walked past every day on her way to work at the hospital. The teas had gorgeous names like Enliven, Autumn Harvest and Tranquillity.

'Where's your…?' He paused, his eyes zeroing in on the way her hands fumbled with the sash of her terry towelling robe.

'Where's my what?' She gave up trying to tie a bow and

settled for a granny knot. It occurred to her that Luke might be as pleased as she that they'd both covered up a bit more. The thought made her stumble.

Stop it! It was somewhere between three and four in the morning. Nobody had rational thoughts at this time of the day. She flipped her hair out from the collar of her robe and raked her hands through it…and remembered the way he'd held it back from her face. She'd felt too sick to be embarrassed then. Strangely, she didn't feel embarrassed now either.

Luke continued to stare at her, his eyes dark and intense, and filled with a primitive hunger. It raised all the hair on her arms. Not in a panicked I'm-alone-in-a-strange-place-with-a-man-I-hardly-know kind of way either. Which would be rational. But then she'd already determined this wasn't a rational time of day.

And it was quickly in danger of becoming less so, because as she stared back at him warmth stole through all her limbs, while languor threatened to rob her of her strength…and of the last shreds of her sanity.

One of them had to be rational. Think of the Munchkin!

'You want to know something amazing?' She didn't wait for his answer. 'All my baby's fingers can be separately identified now, and soon its eyes will be fully formed.'

He jerked, and muttered something she pretended not to hear.

Talking about her baby didn't douse her in cold, rational logic, but at least it had Luke swinging away. She wanted to shake herself, shake the warmth from her limbs, but she didn't trust that her stomach would tolerate that kind of punishment just yet.

She frowned and remembered to ask again, 'Where's my what?'

'Liquorice tea.'

She collapsed at the kitchen table and massaged her temples. Of all the things he might have asked her… 'Why would

I have liquorice tea?' She'd never heard of the stuff before. And, quite frankly, it didn't sound all that inviting.

'It's a morning sickness cure.'

She lifted her head. 'Really?'

'So's eating liquorice.'

She watched, half in disbelief, as he sliced a lemon, dropped the slice into a mug, and then poured boiling water over it. He set the mug in front of her. 'Sip that. It should help settle your stomach.'

He made himself some tea and sat opposite. Keira pulled the pad and pen resting on the table towards her and wrote down 'liquorice, liquorice tea, lemon'—before taking an experimental sip from her mug. 'I'm ten weeks pregnant, but the morning sickness has only hit me in the last few days. I haven't had a chance to research cures yet.'

He shrugged. 'Ginger can be good. Ginger biscuits, dry ginger ale—that sort of thing.'

He blew on his tea before taking a sip, and it was only then, through the mirage of steam, that she realised his eyes weren't black, as she'd originally thought, but a deep, rich brown.

When he kinked a questioning eyebrow, she dragged her gaze away and added 'ginger' to her list. 'I'll pop into town tomorrow.'

'Has it been happening mostly at night?'

'It's been happening all over the place.' Why hadn't anyone warned her about this?

'Having something in your stomach is supposed to help. When you go to bed take a banana or some biscuits with you. When you wake up through the night just have a bite or two. It'll help.'

'How on earth do you know all this?' She took another sip of her lemon and hot water concoction. Her stomach was starting to calm down. 'Don't get me wrong. I'm grateful. I really think this is working.'

He set his mug down with a snap. 'Tammy, my wife, had morning sickness pretty bad with Jason.'

Of course! She glanced around. 'Is she away at the moment?' It would be nice to have another woman to talk to about all this.

'She's dead.'

Keira froze, and then very slowly turned back. She knew exactly how wide her eyes had gone, but for the life of her she couldn't make them go back to their normal size.

'She died three years ago.' The words dropped out of him, curt and emotionless.

Oh! 'Oh, Luke, I'm so sorry.' Idiot! Anyone with eyes in their head could see this place lacked a woman's touch. Perhaps that explained why there were no Christmas decorations, too.

'It was three years ago,' he repeated, his voice flat.

As if three years meant anything!

He might not look heartbroken—she suspected Luke Hillier was not the kind of man to wear his heart on his sleeve—but it explained why he looked so worn out, run down…worn down. She promptly forgave him for all his gruffness and shortness to her earlier in the day.

'I don't think it matters if it's been three years, five years or ten years. My mother died ten years ago and I still miss her.' Especially at this time of year.

'Tammy and I had already separated before she died. A separation I instigated.'

Her heart lurched at the pain that momentarily twisted his features. What? Did he think that meant he wasn't deserving of sympathy? 'You and Tammy had a child together. That's a bond that can never be broken.' And Jason—how he must ache for Jason's loss.

'Says you…' his lips twisted '…who's having a baby on her own.'

Yes, well, there was a good reason for that. But he didn't

give her a chance to explain. He shot to his feet and tipped what was left of his tea down the sink. 'I'm going back to bed.'

He almost made it to the door before spinning back to the pantry. He grabbed a packet of digestives and shoved them at her. 'Take these to bed with you, just in case.'

She stared at them and willed her heart to stop its unaccountable softening.

'Thank you. For everything,' she added, but doubted he heard. He'd already disappeared.

Keira pulled up short the next morning when she found Luke seated at the kitchen table, reading the Sunday paper. She'd expected him to be long gone out into those fields of his. It was one of the reasons she'd allowed herself the luxury of a lie-in—knowing she wouldn't be disturbing anyone. Given the kind of night she'd had, it had seemed a perfectly reasonable proposition. But if Luke had delayed his work to make sure she was okay…

'Good morning.' She tried to keep her voice casual, not sure exactly what tone she should be aiming for after last night.

Luke immediately set the paper aside, leapt to his feet and slotted two slices of her nine-grain bread into the toaster before turning back, hands on hips, to examine her. 'Well?' he demanded. 'How are you feeling?'

She couldn't resist teasing him. 'If I'm going to get waited on like this, then I'm at death's door.'

He frowned.

'Relax, Luke. I'm fine. I slept like a log when I went back to bed—' which wasn't exactly the truth '—and I wasn't sick again.'

That, though, was. Thankfully. And she didn't want him feeling responsible for her. She was more than capable of looking after herself and the Munchkin, thank you.

She *really* didn't want her heart lurching at the mere sight of the man either. There was no future in that.

She sat. 'I mean it, Luke. You need to relax,' she repeated when he retrieved her toast and set it in front of her. He returned from the pantry with his arms laden with spreads.

She opened her mouth to protest some more, but suddenly she was ravenously hungry and allowed herself to be sidetracked long enough to slather butter and strawberry jam over one slice of toast. 'Oh, this is divine,' she groaned, devouring it and repeating the process with the second slice. When she was finished she leant back in her chair with a sigh. 'How on earth is it possible to feel so sick just a few short hours ago and now be so hungry?'

'It's normal.'

That was when she remembered what she had to tell him. She had to set him straight. 'Luke, I'm not some pathetic piece who's accidentally found herself pregnant and then been dumped by some low-down, lying snake in the grass.' She could see that was what he thought.

'It's none of my business.' He shot to his feet. 'Would you like more toast?'

No, she didn't want more toast. She didn't want him making her feel all warm and fuzzy inside either.

'For the last twelve months I've been on an IVF programme.' She waited to see if her words made any impression on him.

He bent down to survey the contents of the fridge. 'What about a piece of fruit or a yoghurt?'

'Did you hear what I just said? I've fallen pregnant deliberately. *And* I've chosen to do it on my own.'

He stopped fussing at the fridge to turn and stare. 'What on earth would you go and do something like that for?'

Now that she had his attention—and, oh my, she certainly had that—she wasn't sure she wanted it. 'You…um…

might like to close the fridge door. It's shaping up to be a warm day.'

'You… But… You're too young!'

She blinked. And then she grinned. 'How old do you think I am? I'm twenty-four—old enough to know my own mind.'

Luke sat, scratched both hands back through his hair while he stared at her. 'But you're still so young. You're attractive…'

Her heart did that stupid leaping around thing again.

'Do you have something against men?'

'No!' She stared at him in horror, but she could suddenly see how he'd come to that conclusion. 'I had an infected ovary removed when I was nineteen. In the last couple of years my remaining ovary has started to develop cysts, and it looks like it will have to go as well. And soon.'

'So medically…?'

'If I want a baby, I have to look at doing it now.'

He sat back, let out a low whistle.

'I mean, in an ideal world I'd have found the man of my dreams and we'd…' She trailed off. She wasn't anti-men, not by any stretch, but she wasn't sure she believed in the man of her dreams either.

'That's a heck of a decision to be faced with—and to do it on your own.' Luke leaned towards her, his hand clenched and his eyebrows drawing down low over his eyes. 'Being a single parent—you have no idea how hard it is. You could've found a man who'd have been happy to help you out.' He shook his head. 'It would've spared you the expense of IVF, and going through your pregnancy alone.'

'And given me a whole new set of problems,' she pointed out. But her heart burned for him. He and his wife might have already been separated, but her death had obviously wounded him. He'd certainly never expected to become a single father. That much was evident.

She'd known Luke Hillier for less than twenty-four hours,

but last night he'd held her hair back from her face while she'd vomited. She figured that gave her a certain insight into the man. She leant across the table towards him. She wanted to reach across and touch his hand—perhaps because his eyes were so dark and his mouth so grim? Perhaps because she sensed that behind the grimness lay genuine concern? 'Would you ever marry a woman just because you wanted a baby?'

'No!'

Tension shot through his shoulders. The physiotherapist in her itched to un-knot all that tightness. The thought made the woman in her turn to putty.

Oh, *puhlease*—pregnancy hormones were addling her brain!

'I…' She swallowed, edged back in her seat. 'I couldn't use someone like that either. In the end I had to make a decision I could live with.'

He gazed at her for a long moment and finally gave a curt nod. She could have sworn she saw admiration flash in those dark eyes of his, and it warmed her all the way down to her toes. She couldn't help smiling at him, and just like that an arc of electricity vibrated between them. Keira's heart, pulse, spirits—all started to race.

She dragged her gaze away and forced herself to stare at the strawberry jam. This…this heat that seemed to spring up between them—she had to ignore it. In one week she'd be leaving here, and she and Luke would never clap eyes on each other again. She was here to secure her and the Munchkin's future. She had no intention of getting sidetracked by a sculpted chest and a pair of dark, smouldering eyes. She had no intention of getting used to someone looking out for her. She was an independent woman of the new millennium. She didn't need any of that nonsense.

She lifted her chin. 'I know common wisdom has it that raising a child on one's own is harder, but I'm not a hundred percent convinced of that.'

He raised an eyebrow. How on earth one eyebrow could contain such a depth of scepticism she would never know. Doubts crowded around her, but she pushed them back. She came from a long line of strong women. She was more than capable of providing a good home and a good life for her baby.

'Tell me that after months of broken sleep, colic, and a bad case of the baby blues,' he drawled.

'My father deserted my mother when she was pregnant with me. She raised me on her own. I don't doubt things were hard for her at times, but she was strong and resourceful and full of life.' Keira refused to let her chin drop. She would not let the picture his words had created spook her. 'I had a wonderful childhood, and I certainly never felt anything was lacking from my life.' And her Munchkin wouldn't either!

'I didn't mean—'

'In fact—' she spoke over the top of him '—I'd say my childhood was better than a lot of my friends who had both parents.' Especially if those parents were either divorced or constantly arguing.

Her two best friends had been cases in point, their loyalties torn between their parents. Keira had always considered herself lucky in comparison. She and her mother—they'd been incredibly close. When her mother had died, her grandmother—another strong female role model—had stepped into the breach, helping Keira through the worst of her grief. Keira was determined to follow in their footsteps, to uphold their examples.

Her mother had always claimed it was foolhardy for a woman to pin all her hopes on a man, that first and foremost a woman should rely on herself. Keira believed that with all her heart. She knew her mother would have applauded her decision to pursue IVF and have a baby on her own. The knowledge that she'd have made her mother proud kept her going when doubts plagued her.

And she wasn't going to let some man who seemed to spend less than ten minutes a day in his own son's company make her doubt herself either!

Tell me that after months of broken sleep.

Her mouth went dry. 'I will love my baby, and I don't need virtual strangers telling me I'm not up to the task!'

She loved her baby already. Her hand curved around her stomach. It wouldn't be flat for too much longer. Soon there would be ample evidence of the baby growing inside her, and she couldn't wait. 'I want this baby with every fibre of my being.' She couldn't wait to hold it in her arms, to count all its fingers and toes, to touch the down on its head. 'That's what will get me through the colic and the sleepless nights and the hormone swings and…and everything!'

She glared at Luke, but couldn't prevent her heart from sinking just a tiny bit when she watched the bond that had started to form between them dissolve utterly.

He stood, his face shuttered and his eyes more black than brown. 'Looks like you have everything under control, then.'

She folded her arms. 'I do.'

She did!

'Good. I don't have time to…waste.' He seized his hat and jammed it on his head. 'There's work to be done.' With that, he strode out through the back door.

Keira stared after him. 'Well, why didn't you just say you don't have time to mollycoddle pregnant women?' she muttered. It was obvious that was what he'd meant. Well, she didn't need mollycoddling. She hadn't asked him to mollycoddle.

Still, she couldn't help feeling she'd just thrown his kindness back in his face with a considerable lack of grace. And now she had a whole day to kill, with nothing to do.

She cleared away the breakfast things and then spied the shopping list she'd made earlier. Much earlier. Right. She shoved it in her pocket. The supermarket in Gunnedah would be open, and she'd do just about anything to avoid a repeat of last night's bout of illness—even if that meant drinking something as odd as liquorice tea.

Keira's natural buoyancy reasserted itself as she negotiated her way down Gunnedah's main street. How could it not? The town overflowed with a festive spirit that was nowhere to be seen at Candlebark.

Christmas carols spilled out from the shops and onto the street. Fake snow and tinsel festooned every shop window. Santa displays abounded—Santa in a sleigh, Santa in his workshop with his elves—so did angels and stars. She stopped by a shop window containing a nativity scene, stared at the baby Jesus in the manger. Her hand crept across her stomach. 'Oh, Munchkin, you just wait till next Christmas. We're going to have so much fun!'

This time of year always reminded Keira of her mother. Carmel Keely had adored Christmas—adorning every room of their apartment with Christmas decorations, baking for weeks beforehand, always grumbling that their ginormous tree was far too big for their apartment, which it was, but never replacing it. And every year she, her mother and her grandmother had sat down to a full Christmas dinner with all the trimmings. It had always been a special day. Her mother had made sure of that. And this year Keira knew she'd miss her mother and her grandmother just that little bit more than normal.

She wondered what Luke and Jason did for Christmas. Then frowned. It was kind of hard, imagining Luke being festive.

She chewed her bottom lip, drawing to a halt as she recalled the expression on his face when he'd told her that his wife was dead. Her heart burned. Poor Jason. She knew from experience how hard this time of year could be. Luke had to try and make Christmas special for his son all on his own now.

Just like you'll be doing.

Yeah, but she'd chosen that path. Luke hadn't.

With a heart that had started to feel heavier with every passing second, she recalled how she'd all but told Luke to butt out and keep his opinions to himself this morning. After he'd held her hair back and had mopped her face…and made her lemon and hot water…and given her morning sickness remedies. He was obviously busy with the farm, but he'd taken a significant portion of the morning off to make sure she was okay…*and to make her breakfast*!

She was a shrew. It wasn't his fault her insecurities had momentarily got the better of her.

She bit her lip and glanced around, as if this country street could provide her with inspiration for how to make amends.

Her eyes lit on the Chinese restaurant across the road. She sucked her bottom lip all the way into her mouth. She could cook dinner tonight, couldn't she? That would at least save Luke some of that precious time of his.

Her spirits started to lift again. Maybe this evening Luke and Jason could eat together. Last night they'd simply seized their plates and shot off to separate parts of the house—Luke to what she guessed was his study, and Jason to watch television in the living room. She'd watched in stunned amazement and sworn that she and her child would never end up like that. But if Luke had more time…

The chicken and hokkien noodle stir-fry she'd prepared was ready to serve at precisely the same moment Luke walked through the back door. Keira took it as a good sign—all the planets magically aligned, or something.

'Hi.' She turned from the stove with a grin she hoped hid the nerves that unaccountably assailed her.

She had absolutely nothing to be nervous about. This dinner—it was nothing more than a friendly gesture.

Luke stared at the table set for three, and then at the food simmering on the stove. There was a lot of it. She'd figured a man of the land and a growing teenage boy would have hearty appetites.

He raised an eyebrow. Keira suddenly hated that eyebrow with a vengeance.

'Expecting company?' he drawled.

'Of course not.' But it was hard to get the words out because her throat had started to close over. 'I… This…' She swallowed. Did he hate chicken, or had he taken an unaccountable dislike to her since this morning?

She cleared her throat and gestured across the hallway to the living room, where Jason lay sprawled on the sofa with the television blaring. 'I thought I'd cook dinner for everyone tonight.'

She couldn't stand the way he was looking at her, so she grabbed a plate and turned away to start dishing out food. Luke moved to stand behind her. Close. Keira stilled, her hand trembling as his heat beat at her. She hadn't even heard him move.

'I don't want you doing this ever again.' His voice was low, but its fury sliced through her. 'You hear me?'

She swallowed and nodded.

'Jason and I don't need your charity, and we sure as hell don't need your pity. You can go practise your home-making skills somewhere else. Got it?'

The unfairness of his accusations had her spine stiffening. 'Loud and clear,' she snapped, shoving the laden plate at him. 'Believe me, I won't make the same mistake again.' She pushed the serving spoon under his nose. 'But while we're on the subject of home-making, from what I can see I'm not the one who needs to brush up on that particular skill set.'

His mouth opened and closed but no sound came out.

'And, for your information, cooking dinner was my oh-so-stupid attempt to try and make up for throwing your routine out this morning. *Nothing* more.'

And then she lifted her voice, so it could be heard over the television in the next room. 'There's food here if you want it, Jason.'

With a cut-off oath, Luke spun and stalked from the room. Jason slouched in. He stared after his father. 'What's up with him?'

She shrugged. 'Beats me.'

'Yeah, well, I wouldn't worry about it,' he mumbled. 'He's an old grump.'

He could say *that* again!

Jason took his laden plate back into the living room. Keira collapsed at the table, her heart thumping.

Right—from now on her and Luke's paths were on completely separate planes, trajectories whatever you wanted to call it. She'd make sure of it.

CHAPTER THREE

LUKE halted in the doorway to the living room, brought up short by the sight of Keira rifling through the sideboard. He automatically opened his mouth to ask her what the hell she was doing, but closed it again.

He had no intention of jumping to conclusions again, like he had last night.

This woman—with all her colour and her big, bright smiles—had waltzed into his neatly structured world and he'd been off balance ever since. He ground his teeth together. He was going to find that balance again if it killed him.

Last night he'd hurled words at her in an effort to stop the image of her, the very idea of what she'd represented, from tearing him apart. She'd stood there in his kitchen as if she'd had every right in the world, mocking him with her very… *perfection*!

Once upon a time he'd dreamed of that kind of life. But it could never be his. Ever.

Last night anger and grief had clawed up through him in an explosion of anguish. He'd lashed out at her before he could help himself. He wasn't losing control like that again. He might not want her rifling through his personal things, but flying off the handle wouldn't help him restore that much-needed equilibrium.

With that in mind, he straightened, shoved his hands into

the pockets of his jeans, and drawled as casually as he could, 'Can I help you?'

She half turned. 'I didn't hear you come in. I thought you'd be out in the fields all day.'

He'd come back to grab some lunch. Not that he needed to explain himself to her. 'What are you looking for?'

'The telephone directory.' She stood, hands on hips, and stared at him expectantly.

She wore white linen trousers and a lime-green shirt. She reminded him of the rainbow lorikeets that dipped through the yard in the early morning to feed in the bottlebrush trees.

'Please tell me you have at least some kind of local business directory!'

Her clothes looked summery and cool, but her cheeks were pink and her hair almost crackled. He pointed to the sideboard. 'Middle drawer.'

She spun back, located said directory, and promptly hugged it to her chest. Which made him notice exactly what a nice chest she had.

He forced his gaze to the floor, but he needn't have bothered. Keira hadn't noticed. She raced passed him to settle herself at the kitchen table. She began rifling through the directory, completely oblivious to him.

He watched her, eyes narrowed. Something was up. It was evident in the way she flicked over the pages, the way she sucked her bottom lip into her mouth.

Walk away. The lady had made it clear at breakfast yesterday that she knew what she was doing.

If he wanted lunch he couldn't walk away. It didn't mean he had to engage her in conversation, though.

He filled the jug. He pulled a loaf of bread towards him. Not speaking suddenly seemed a bit childish. He slathered butter on his bread, located the cheese and started to slice it. 'What are you looking for?' He told himself it was a perfectly harmless question.

'A local builder. A *reputable* one.'

She didn't even glance up as she spoke. Luke abandoned the cheese. 'Why?' She was only here for a week. What on earth did she need with a builder?

'Because a disreputable one won't be of any use at all.'

When she met his gaze he could see that lines of strain fanned out from her eyes. And she'd gone pale. He planted his feet. 'Have you eaten today? You can't—'

He broke off, mentally kicking himself.

She sat back and folded her arms. She didn't say anything. Not one word.

Luke stood it for as long as he could. Then he caved. 'Look, okay... Last night I was...'

'Rude?' she supplied. 'Churlish?'

'Out of order,' he ground out.

He cast another glance at her. She really was turning very pale. His hands clenched. She was having a baby. *On her own.* She didn't deserve attitude from him. 'Rude and churlish,' he admitted.

He pulled out a chair. He'd meant to plant himself in it, apologise like a man, but his spine bowed under the sudden weight that crashed down on him and he found himself slumping instead. 'This kitchen hasn't had a woman in it for a long time. Coming in last night and seeing you so at home, with dinner on and the table set...' He dragged a hand down his face. 'It...' He didn't know how to go on.

'Oh!' The word left her in one soft exhalation. 'Oh, I didn't think of that. I'm sorry, Luke. I didn't mean to rake up ghosts from the past.'

The problem was his past had never been like that—it had never been that inviting, that tempting. Fate was laughing at him, deriding him—showing him with one hand all he could have had, and then taking it away with the other.

Which was as it should be.

'I lost the plot for a moment. I'm sorry.'

Keira reached out and placed her hand over his. 'Why don't we just forget all about last night?'

He eased out a breath. The scent of vanilla rose up all around him. 'I'd like that.' He studied her face. Her colour still hadn't returned. He'd gestured towards his abandoned sandwich. 'Have you eaten?'

For some reason that made her laugh. With a self-conscious glance at her hand on his, she drew back and nodded. 'I ate earlier, thank you.'

Good. He couldn't help noticing how she flicked a glance across to the cheese, though. He reached across and relocated the breadboard from the bench to the table. He cut more cheese—far more than he'd need—and made a show of making sandwiches. 'Want one?'

'No, thank you.' But she flicked another glance at the cheese.

He pushed the breadboard towards her and bit into his sandwich. 'I always cut too much, and then it goes to waste.'

'Waste?'

He nodded. Then nearly grinned when she reached out and seized a slice and popped it into her mouth. She closed her eyes in what looked like ecstasy. Luke stopped chewing to stare. She opened her eyes, registered the expression on his face, and pale cheeks suddenly became pink.

Luke forced himself to start chewing again. He swallowed. 'You want to tell me what you want with a builder?'

She snaffled another piece of cheese. 'I…' Her lips trembled upwards in a smile that made something in his chest tighten. 'I've inherited a house in the town.'

He lowered his sandwich.

She nodded. 'I know—amazing, huh? My Great-Aunt Ada—whom I'd never met, mind—left me her house in her will.' She popped the second piece of cheese into her mouth. 'Yum!' She pointed. 'This is really good!'

'Just regular cheddar.'

She grabbed another piece. 'Apparently my great-aunt had no other living relatives. She died back in September, but it took her solicitor a couple of months to track me down.'

That smile of hers slipped and his heart dipped right along with it.

'I wish she'd tried to contact me.' She stared down at the table, one finger tracing the grain of the wood. '*I* should've contacted *her*.'

'Why?' If the woman had never been a part of her life…

'I was her last living relative. She must've been lonely towards the end.' She lifted one slim shoulder. 'And…well…she was *my* last living relative too. I'd have liked to have known her.'

Luke tried to hide his dawning horror. Not only didn't she have a partner—the father of her baby—to help her out, but she didn't have any other family either. She'd told him her mother was dead and that her father wasn't around, but what about siblings, aunts and uncles…grandparents?

For a moment she looked so forlorn and alone he found himself reaching out to squeeze her hand. To choose to have a baby with virtually no support at all—the very idea stole his breath. This woman—she had courage and strength in spades. His admiration for her grew. Right alongside that pesky protectiveness.

It wasn't his place to be protective. He didn't want to get involved. He didn't want his hormones hitting overdrive every time the scent of vanilla drifted across to him. He didn't want concerns about whether her morning sickness had returned, or if she was eating enough, if she was getting enough rest, plaguing him. His every instinct screamed *Run!*

This woman's life was none of his business.

But she had no one, and she was only here for one measly week—five more days. Helping out where he could wouldn't kill him.

'Keira, soon you'll have your baby. You'll be starting a brand new family.'

She squeezed his hand back, and that spark jumped between them again. He knew she felt it too, from the way she let go of his hand at the same moment he let go of hers, and by the way her glance skittered away.

She covered her stomach with her hand and stared down at it. He found it hard to imagine her rounded and full with child. She'd still be beautiful.

'I can hardly wait,' she said, her eyes shining.

For the first time in a long time Luke's lips stretched into a smile. It didn't hurt, it wasn't forced—merely an uncomplicated sign of pleasure at her simple sincerity and excitement. 'I forgot to say something the other night.'

Her eyes widened. 'What's that?'

A hint of breathlessness rippled through her voice. It made the surface of his skin tingle. 'I didn't congratulate you on your pregnancy. Congratulations, Keira. I wish you and your baby all the very best.'

To his astonishment, he found he wasn't merely going through the motions—he meant it. She looked as if she might actually melt, so he sat back and made his voice deliberately businesslike. 'So you've inherited this house…?'

'Which really couldn't have come at a better time. The money from the sale means I'll be able set up my own clinic in the city. I'd really love to have all that finalised before my Munchkin makes its appearance.'

'Clinic?' He shouldn't be asking about this clinic of hers. He should be asking about her aunt's house. If she needed a builder, then obviously the house needed repairs. 'What kind of clinic?'

'I'm a physiotherapist. I specialise in post-surgical rehabilitation and sports injuries. At the moment I'm working at a private hospital, but I've always dreamed of opening my own clinic.' She grinned and polished off the last of the cheese. 'And because of my great-aunt now I can.'

'You're a physio?' His jaw dropped. This slip of a girl was a physiotherapist? He didn't know why he found that so hard to believe. If he'd stopped to consider it at all, he'd have pegged her as a preschool teacher or an artist. A job where her bubbliness and enthusiasm could really shine. But a physiotherapist? It sounded so responsible and serious.

She'd look cute in a white coat, though.

Settle!

'What?' she teased. 'You don't think I'm old enough to be a physio?'

If he said yes, would that offend or flatter her? He didn't want to do either.

She threw her head back and laughed, so he settled for saying nothing. But his lips started to lift again.

'How old are *you*?'

It was a friendly challenge. He shrugged. 'Thirty-three.'

He watched her mind whirl and click, and then her eyes went wide. 'But that means you were only...' more whirring and calculating '...nineteen when Jason was born?'

'Yep.'

'And here I am, wondering if I'm truly ready for all the responsibility at twenty-four. Wow! Nineteen? That must've been hard.'

His gut clenched. 'Yep.'

When he didn't add anything else, she said, 'I'm a good physio, and I can see exactly how much tension you hold in your shoulders. If you're not careful you'll do yourself an injury. And you hold it here too.'

She lifted a hand as if to touch it to the side of his jaw. His pulse jumped. She jerked her hand back.

'Sit back in your chair like this. Nice and comfortable.'

He did as she ordered. He figured it would be easier than arguing with her.

'Now, relax the back of your tongue.'

He frowned. How on earth…?

'It's located about here.' She turned her head to the side and indicated the place. 'Concentrate hard on loosening it.'

He did. It took a moment to work out precisely what she meant, but when he finally got the hang of it a deep ripple of relaxation coursed through him. He blinked, stunned at the effect.

'You should try and remember to do that a couple of times a day.'

He nodded, but it all suddenly seemed a little too chummy—too…familiar. He didn't need anyone looking out for him. She was the one who needed help.

'Back to this house of yours.' His voice had gone gruff again, but he couldn't help it. 'I take it repairs are needed before you can sell it?'

'Apparently.'

She pulled a sheet of paper from her pocket, unfolded it, and handed it to him. It was a builder's quote—and the work it itemised was extensive. He grimaced when he read the total. 'This is going to set you back a pretty penny.' Did she have the money? Perhaps she should be looking for a banker instead?

'The real estate agency organised that last week.' She paused. 'Do you think I'm being overcharged?'

'I'm not an expert, but…' He raked his gaze down the list again. 'There's nothing that jumps out at me from this. Why?'

'Well, maybe it's just pregnancy hormones…'

'But?'

'Something seems a bit…fishy.'

'How?'

'Little things that don't seem like much but when they're added together… For example, the estate agent was supposed to take me through the house on Saturday, but something came up and he was out of the office all day… For some unspecified reason no one else could take me through in his stead.'

'Weekends *are* their busiest times.'

'I know, but when the agent took me through the house today he rushed me through it, barely giving me a chance to get a good look at anything.'

He frowned. 'Which agency?'

'The same one your room is listed with. They booked the room for me.'

'And why would they send you nearly twenty minutes out of town if all your business is *in* town?'

'Exactly. Now, admittedly I was feeling a bit queasy when I was viewing the house, so I didn't put up much of a fight, but… Have you heard any complaints about the agency?'

No—but that didn't mean anything. The few occasions when he couldn't avoid going into town he didn't speak to anyone. And no one spoke to him. He'd chosen that particular agency because, unlike the others in town, he didn't know anyone who worked there—no one who knew his parents, no one he'd gone to school with. That had been the main factor in their favour. But…

Were these low-lifes trying to rip her off? A pregnant woman? A *lone* pregnant woman? His hands clenched. All the tension that had eased out of him from her simple exercise shot back now.

He glanced down at the written quote. He didn't know the builder responsible for this either. He shoved his chair back and shot to his feet. 'C'mon.'

She blinked. 'C'mon, what?'

'We're going to see an old friend of mine—I went to school with him—he's a builder.' John might despise Luke now, but he wouldn't rip him off. Of that, Luke was certain. 'And we're going to drop by the agency and collect the key to *your* house.'

She didn't rise from her chair. She folded her arms and

glared. 'I'm more than capable of speaking to a builder and collecting the key to the house myself.' Her glare lost its force. 'I would appreciate the name of a builder you'd recommend, though.'

For a moment he considered leaving her to it. This wasn't his problem. No skin off his nose. He didn't *want* to get involved. But her face that night at the bathroom door rose up in his mind, and he couldn't shake the thought of what would have happened to Tammy if she'd had to face her pregnancy alone.

He planted his feet. 'It'll be easier if I come along.'

'You have a farm to run.'

'It'll survive without me for an afternoon.'

'No way! You told me you're coming up to harvest.'

He'd forgotten that darn independence of hers. He could add stubborn to the mix now too. He set his jaw. 'Keira, you're only here for what—five more days?' Five days! He could count that off on the fingers of one hand. 'Local knowledge is going to be necessary in this situation.'

She bit her lip.

He pressed his advantage. 'And what if you start feeling queasy again?'

She stood too, hands on hips. Her linen trousers were all creased and wrinkled from sitting, but she still looked fresh and cool. 'If I'm to accept your help, and that help takes you away from the farm, then…then we need to come to some arrangement. Either I pay you for your time to act on my behalf—'

'No!' He wasn't taking her money. At least not for something like this. He wasn't accepting anything more from her than her rent money.

'Or I pay you in kind.'

He folded his arms. He could see she wouldn't be easy to budge. 'What did you have in mind?'

She eyed him up and down. 'It doesn't look as if you've any kind of sports injuries I can work on.'

The thought of her fingers moving over his flesh was far too tempting. And disturbing. 'Nope.' He said it quickly, before he could change his mind.

'Well…' She glanced around. 'From now until I leave I'll cook dinner every night and do some light cleaning. I know it won't make up for losing a whole afternoon's work on the farm.' She folded her arms too and lifted her chin. 'But it's something.'

To come home every evening and find her in his kitchen, cooking their meals, for the next five nights… He swallowed. Could he deal with that? If he were ready for it, expecting it, then he wouldn't lose it like he had last night, right?

'Well?'

He hated cooking. He held out his hand. 'Deal.'

She placed hers in it, and sent him the kind of smile that could blindside a man if he wasn't forewarned. Just as well he was forewarned.

He scowled and let go of her hand. Her skin was warm and soft—and so fair!

'Do you have a hat?' he barked at her. 'You shouldn't be walking around outside at this time of year without a hat.'

She blinked. 'I forgot to pack one. I'll…um…get one next time I go shopping.'

'Good. Now, let's make tracks.'

He turned and strode out of the house, not checking to see if she followed. He knew she did—he could smell her, sense her. His hands clenched. It suddenly occurred to him that forewarned didn't necessarily mean forearmed.

Keira couldn't believe how easy it was to get the key from the agency. To her utter shame, it hadn't occurred to her to request it earlier. Although she knew she had every right to the key, some inner instinct had warned her the agent would do his best to block her, find excuses for why she couldn't have it.

Nothing doing—it was a piece of cake! The receptionist took one look at Luke, and Keira swore the poor woman literally started to shake. She'd handed the key over without a murmur.

It had taken a considerable effort not to burst out laughing. So Luke obviously had a reputation for being difficult, huh? If the agency hadn't worked out yet that his bark was worse then his bite then far be it from her to set them straight. And while she was more than capable of standing up for herself—an independent woman, a strong woman following in the tradition of her mother and grandmother—she had to admit that Luke's reassuring bulk was a decided comfort.

Luke's face grew grimmer, however, when they pulled to a halt outside a long metal building. 'This is John's workshop.'

She unclipped her seatbelt. 'You said you went to school with him?'

'Yeah—John Peterson. He's a good guy. Whatever he tells us, we can take it as gospel.'

'Good.' She paused in the act of opening her door. Luke hadn't moved. 'So what are we waiting for?'

He shook himself. 'Nothing.'

She followed him into the small office at the front of the building. The whirr and buzz of machinery, hammering and sawing, sounded from beyond the partitioned wall, but the office itself was empty.

Keira reached around Luke, who stood frozen, to ring the bell. Almost immediately a barrel-chested bear of a man strode in. He stopped short when he saw Luke.

Oh, dear. Keira bit her lip. Obviously someone else who considered Luke difficult.

But then the tanned face broke into a broad grin and he

moved forward with hand outstretched. 'Luke, it's good to see you! Haven't seen your ugly mug around for a while.'

Luke looked as if he wanted to run, but he held his ground and shook the man's hand. 'Notice you haven't got any prettier since the last time I saw you, Peterson.'

The riposte looked as if it had taken John as off guard as it had her. The other man, though, just threw his head back and laughed. He clapped Luke on the back. 'What can I do for you?'

'This is Keira.' Luke ushered her forward. 'She's my... guest at the moment.'

Keira took pity on him. 'Lodger,' she explained, shaking John's hand too.

'Keira's inherited a house in town. She's been given a quote for some work that needs doing, but she'd like a second opinion.'

Luke pulled out her quote from his shirt pocket and handed it across to John. She saw the way John's lips tightened when he glanced at the letterhead. She also noted the look the two men exchanged.

'I thought you might be able to help.'

'I'd be glad to.' John glanced at his watch. 'If you aren't busy, I've half an hour to spare now...'

'That's what I was hoping you'd say.' Luke smiled. That same smile that had almost knocked her sideways off the kitchen chair earlier.

He should do that more often—smile—it made him look younger. Like thirty-three rather than close to forty, where she'd fixed him.

'Will that work for you?'

She blinked and realised he was addressing her. 'Oh, yes! That's perfect.'

She gave John the address, and they arranged to meet there in five minutes.

* * *

John crouched down to peer under the house, the beam of his flashlight stretching to the furthest reaches. He snorted. 'Who is this joker trying to kid?'

Keira knelt down beside him. 'What?'

Luke crouched down on her other side. She was too aware of him—of his heat, of the strength that rippled beneath the denim of his jeans, informing her of the powerful thigh muscles concealed beneath. Jeans that looked worn…thin… as if they might rip at any moment and give her a tantalising glimpse of flesh. She watched, holding her breath, mesmerised by his latent power, by—

'He claims that the whole house needs to be re-piered.'

She snapped to at John's words. She glanced up to find Luke watching her. His eyes darkened. Heat flooded her face, her neck. His gaze dropped to her lips. She started to sway towards him…

She snatched herself back. *Yikes!*

Luke shot to his feet.

Piers! They were talking about piers. 'So…um…they *don't* need replacing?'

'These four here—' John pointed to them with his flashlight '—could do with jacking up, but it's not urgent.'

'Well, that's good news,' she said, rising and risking another glance at Luke. His face had shuttered closed.

'Okay, let's head on inside.'

She handed John the key, and tried not to mind if Luke followed them or not.

Her great-aunt's house was an old colonial-style weatherboard. It had three generous bedrooms, high ceilings and moulded cornices, picture rails and an eat-in kitchen. Keira loved its lack of pretension and its sense of calm.

She didn't say anything, just followed John as he made his way through the house. He spent a long time surveying the kitchen.

'Okay,' he said finally, 'the kitchen and bathroom could

do with modernising, but again that's not urgent. Currently they're both serviceable.'

She digested the news silently.

Beside her, Luke stiffened. He hadn't said much of anything since John had started his inspection. After that moment outside he'd kept an ocean of distance between himself and Keira—always a room behind or a room in front. Now he opened the back door and stalked out into the yard, pacing its length. She watched him from the window above the kitchen sink and tried to pinpoint exactly what it was about the man that sang such a siren's song to her.

She snorted. Well, how about that magnificent physique for a start?

Deep down, though, she sensed it was something more than that. There was something about the way he held his head—a certain look sometimes in those dark eyes of his. And something about the way he'd mopped her face after she'd been sick, in the way he'd thrust that packet of biscuits at her before he'd stormed off to bed. He might be a tad cantankerous—or a lot, she admitted—but beneath all that gruffness he hid a kind heart.

'I don't know what you did,' John said, joining her at the window, 'but I want to thank you. It's good to see Luke out and about again.'

'What do you mean?' She forced her gaze from the man pacing the backyard. 'I haven't done anything. Except be a nuisance.'

'You've taken his mind off his own misery—for a bit at least. These last few years he's buried himself away at Candlebark and hardly ever emerges.'

Really? Luke was a hermit? She frowned. 'That's…um… taking the workaholic thing a bit far.'

John nodded out of the window. 'He's been through a rough time, whatever anyone says. Don't you go paying attention to small town gossip, you hear? People can be vicious. Luke—he's a good guy.'

'Yeah, I know.'

She frowned again. What small-town gossip? What were people saying about Luke? And why?

She turned from locking the front door to her great-aunt's house, and the three of moved towards their cars. 'So,' Keira said, 'everything this builder Mr Selway has recommended is nonsense?'

John nodded.

She sucked her bottom lip into her mouth. 'Is that legal?'

'It'd be hard to prove,' he said carefully, coming to a halt beside his truck. 'There's little doubt that if he did everything he says on your quote it would add value to the house. I'd say it was overcapitalising, but if you tried to challenge him about misleading you he could simply claim that you misunderstood—that he wasn't saying it *had* to be done, only that it would improve the property.'

Right. 'But…you're not convinced he *would* do everything listed on my quote, are you?' she said slowly. 'You think he means to charge me the earth for doing next to nothing?'

'That's my guess. But I can't prove it.'

Beside her, she was aware of Luke opening and closing his fists, as if readying himself to punch something. 'And both of you also think this Mr Selway and Mr Connors, my estate agent, are in this together—don't you?'

John nodded. 'What's more, I'll make an educated guess that your solicitor is Graeme Aldershot.'

Her jaw dropped.

'He and Selway went to school together. When Connors arrived from the city they all became very buddy-buddy.'

The grooves either side of Luke's mouth deepened. 'I'll be having a word with Connors first thing.'

John flexed an arm. *'I'll* be having a word with Selway first thing.'

Keira planted her hands on her hips. 'Excellent. I have an appointment with Mr Aldershot tomorrow. I mean to tell him that I'm considering pressing charges against Selway and Connors. Not that I am—I don't need the hassle—but he doesn't need to know that. I won't let on that I know he's part of it all, and I'll ask him to represent me.' She dusted off her hands.

John threw his head back and laughed. 'Good for you, Keira. That should put the fear of God into him.'

She hoped so.

John held out his hand. 'It was nice meeting you.'

'Likewise—and thank you.' She'd drop around to his workshop tomorrow with a nice bottle of single-malt Scotch. He'd certainly earned it.

'Great to see you, Luke.'

Luke clapped him on the shoulder. 'Thanks for all your help. I appreciate it. Ever need a favour in return…'

John nodded and climbed into his truck. Keira lifted her hand in farewell as it pulled away, before turning back to survey her great-aunt's house. 'It's nice, isn't it?' Homey. She could imagine a family living there—growing into it and loving it.

Luke leant on the ute beside her. 'Yeah, it is. You won't have any trouble selling it. Especially with the park across the road.'

It *was* a pretty location. A child's paradise. It was the kind of house that if she saw it in the city and could afford it she'd snap up in an instant. A muffled weight settled over her shoulders. She didn't know why selling the house should make her feel sad—except perhaps that it was the only link she had to a part of her family she'd never known. The last of her family.

Now that she was pregnant, family had started taking on

a whole new dimension for her, and at odd moments its lack filled her with nameless fears. What if she died as young as her mother? Who would love and care for her child?

She knew it was pointless fretting about such what-ifs. She had friends who'd be more than happy to step into the breach. But it wasn't the same as being able to rely on family.

She turned to the man beside her. 'Do you have a large family, Luke?'

He stared out to the front, his eyes narrowed as if against the glare of the sun—only the sun was behind them. 'Not really.'

She waited. Nothing. 'Parents?'

'Yeah, but they retired to the coast nearly three years ago now.'

She digested that. Then stiffened. Tammy had died three years ago, hadn't she? Luke and Tammy might no longer have lived together, but surely Luke's parents would have stuck around to help Luke and Jason through such a terrible time?

She swallowed. 'Siblings?'

'An older brother—Evan. He married an English girl and emigrated.'

'So...none of you are close, then?'

He glanced down at her. 'We're not at loggerheads or anything.'

She'd never considered herself short, at five feet five inches, but Luke dwarfed her. She didn't want to find that so deliciously appealing, but she did. She didn't want to lean into him and gain strength from his mere presence, his very solidity.

Liar!

Well, okay...yes, she did. She wanted *that* a lot. But she didn't want to want it.

Don't get too used to relying on this man, she warned herself. She couldn't risk relying on anyone too much at present. She had to focus on her pregnancy and creating a wonderful life for her baby. In eighteen months, two years—maybe then she'd be ready to let someone into their lives, but not yet.

'My mother called me her change of life baby.'

Keira swung back in time to see him pass a hand through his hair. He smelt of dirt and grease and fresh-mown grass. Not one of those smells made her stomach churn, or had perspiration emerging as she tried to combat nausea. In fact she found herself kind of liking the way he smelled. It was refreshing after the heavy colognes of some of her friends in the city.

'I came along when she was forty-six and my father fifty-three. Evan was already grown up at twenty-four.'

Wow! 'It must've been hard, being the lone child among all those adults?'

'It was all right.'

And that was when she saw it—as if he'd spoken the words out loud. Luke had felt like an intruder in his own family. She didn't know what sixth sense had suddenly fired to life inside her, making her see him so clearly. She didn't know what part of her could be so finely attuned to that same part of him, but her heart started to ache for the little boy he must once have been.

No wonder he'd searched for love with Tammy when he was only nineteen.

She slipped her arm though his and hugged it. He glanced down in surprise, but didn't detach himself. 'Thank you for helping me out today. You've saved me thousands of dollars and months of delay.'

'You saved yourself. You were the one who sensed something wasn't right.' His hands clenched. 'I'm glad you did! I'm sorry you were almost taken advantage of like that.'

Beneath her hand, the muscles in his arms tightened. She rubbed her hand up and down it to ease the tension, dug her fingers into the muscle to find the knots and loosen them. 'It wasn't your fault.'

He scowled. 'What a great opinion you'll have of our country hospitality now.'

He glanced down at her hands, and she realised she'd started a full-blown massage on his arm. She leapt away. 'Sorry.' She coughed to hide her confusion, shoved her hands into her back pockets. 'Force of habit.'

He didn't move for a moment, but then one corner of his mouth kicked up. He lifted a shoulder. 'There are worse habits to have.'

Her heart jumped and jerked. Her knees wobbled. 'I… um…my opinion of country hospitality could take an upward swing if you wouldn't mind dropping in at the supermarket on our way home.'

His smile faded.

'Don't worry about it,' she rushed on. Of course he had work he wanted to get to. 'I can come back into town later.'

He shrugged again, but his tension belied the studied casualness. 'We're here now. I'm figuring it won't take long?'

'No time at all. I just want to grab some things for dinner.'

When they entered the supermarket, Luke scanned the crowd. Keira watched and waited. After a moment his shoulders unhitched a notch, and he insisted on pushing the shopping trolley for her. She let out a breath she hadn't realised she'd held, and handed the trolley over wordlessly.

She sped through the shop as quickly as she could, aware that Luke probably had a million things to do and not wanting to hold him up longer than she had to.

She dropped the last thing in the trolley. 'There—that's it. Now we can make for the checkouts.' And home.

But when she turned she found her path blocked. 'Oh, I'm sorry.'

She moved to one side, to let the woman pass, but the woman followed her. And then she pushed her face in close to Keira's. 'I hope you know what it is you're doing!' she hissed.

Keira backed up, but the trolley behind brought her up short. The woman was probably in her mid-sixties, and she was grey, drawn, thin. Everything about her was faded except her eyes, which flashed with sparks of bitter green fury.

'That man you're with—you know he's a monster? That he's a heartless murderer!'

CHAPTER FOUR

'GRAN, don't.'

Keira blinked. 'Jason!'

Jason stood beside the woman, his eyes downcast. Keira tried to pick her jaw up. This was…Tammy's mother? And she blamed Luke for Tammy's death? Bile rose in her throat. Luke was no murderer. She knew that as surely as she knew her own name.

'Gran, this is Keira. She's renting our room.'

The pleading in Jason's voice caught at Keira's heart. He might as well have saved himself the bother, though. His grandmother's venom had already moved from Keira to the man standing behind her.

'Hello, Brenda,' Luke said quietly. Those grooves either side of his mouth deepened. His skin had turned grey.

'How on earth can you bear to show your face in this town? I *spit* on you, Luke Hillier!'

Thankfully she didn't literally put the threat into action, but her words made Luke pale even further. His jaw had set so hard Keira feared for it. She remembered what John had told her about the viciousness of small-town gossip and acid burned her stomach.

'C'mon, love…'

A man—Jason's grandfather, Keira guessed—sent Luke a glare of loathing before leading his wife away. Jason stared from them to his father in anguish. Keira's heart broke for him. She touched his arm and tried to smile. 'Would you like a ride home?'

He glanced up at his father. 'Uh…yeah.'

'I'll wait for you both in the car. You'll carry the groceries for Keira?' Luke said.

'Yeah, sure.'

Keira's heart broke for Luke as he strode away too.

She turned back to Jason, took in his school uniform. 'It's a bit early for school to be out, isn't it?'

'Last day of term,' he mumbled. 'There was an assembly.'

'Right.' She didn't need to ask why Luke hadn't attended. That reason had become startlingly and horrifyingly clear.

'I'm sorry…' he shuffled his feet '…'bout all that.'

'Oh, Jason, it's not your fault.'

His face twisted. 'Then whose fault *is* it? Dad's? Gran's and Grandad's?'

'I'm not sure it's anyone's fault.'

She manoeuvred the trolley to a nearby checkout. Jason started unloading the groceries. Keira didn't try to help. She didn't remonstrate at his rough handling of the vegetables or eggs. She sensed he needed something to do with his hands. Though he did his best to hide it his agitation was evident, and she wanted to do whatever she could to soothe it.

'People react in different ways when they lose someone they love. Sometimes in irrational ways.'

'But—'

He broke off, as if he'd been about to say something and then thought better of it. She didn't press him. '*My* mum died when I was fourteen.'

He spun to stare at that. 'Yeah?'

'It was awful—the worst time of my life. You know all about that, though.'

He shrugged and nodded. He didn't back away from her as he had up until now.

'But I can't imagine how awful it would be to lose a child. It's the wrong order, you see. Children are supposed to outlive their parents.'

Jason's brow creased. 'So you think it might be harder for Gran and Grandad to accept that…that Mum's gone than anyone else?'

'Maybe.'

'They hate Dad.'

Keira swallowed. That had been all too evident.

'They say that because they'd separated and weren't living together any more that proves he didn't love Mum.'

How on earth could his grandparents do this to him—tear his loyalties like this? She did her best to keep her voice even. 'I think there must be more than a hundred different kinds of love in the world. Just because your mum and dad weren't living together any more it doesn't mean they'd stopped caring about each other. What do you think?'

Jason scuffed the toe of one sneaker against the floor. 'Dunno.'

'Have you tried talking to your dad about it?'

He glanced away. She recalled how shuttered and closed-off Luke could be, and grimaced. She wasn't sure if she'd be brave enough to broach the subject if she were Jason, either.

She paid for the groceries and went to lift her share of the bags, but Jason beat her to it. 'Dad told me to carry them,' he muttered.

For a moment he so reminded her of Luke that her lips twitched. She straightened, placed her hands on her hips. 'Did your dad tell you that I'm pregnant?' She didn't mind if he had. It wasn't a secret. She'd already spread the news far and wide among her friends.

Jason's jaw dropped. He stared at her stomach. 'Are you?'

'Yep.'

His eyes lit up. 'Sweet!'

'I think so.'

He grinned. It stunned her. She hadn't seen him grin before, and it transformed him completely. It caught the awkwardness of his age perfectly—trapped somewhere between childhood and adulthood. It brought all her maternal urges rushing to the surface, turning her to mush.

'Am I supposed to offer you my arm or something?' he said, mock gallant, but grinning like an idiot.

Laughter spurted out of her. 'Try it and I'll box your ears.'

That was when it occurred to her that what Luke and Jason needed was a bit of fun in their lives.

Luke couldn't believe it. When Keira and Jason emerged from the supermarket they were…*laughing*!

Keira had obviously told Jason she was pregnant, because all the way back to Candlebark they tossed around babies' names, of all things. As if that incident in the supermarket had never happened.

The ute didn't have a back seat, so they all had to ride in the front. Keira sat in the middle. Every now and again the movement of the car had her shoulder brushing his. Each and every time a wave of vanilla would engulf him.

The scent didn't soothe him. It attacked all his nerve-endings, fraying them with a relentless reminder of all he'd turned his back on, of a life he could never have—a life that held softness and sweetness and bone-deep contentment.

He'd turned all those things to dust for Tammy, and every time he saw Brenda and Alf it was like a scab being ripped off an old wound. He deserved their hate and censure, but *they* deserved to find some peace. Every time he saw them guilt swallowed him whole because he knew they hadn't found it.

And seeing him only made it worse for them.

He bit back an oath. It was why he avoided going into town wherever possible—to try and spare them at least that much. And look where his Good Samaritan act had landed him today!

From the corner of his eye he glanced at Keira. No matter how hard he tried, he couldn't find it in him to regret helping her.

'What do you reckon, Dad?'

Luke shook himself. 'Sorry?'

'What's your favourite name for a girl? In case that's what Keira has?'

He didn't know why Jason was so fascinated by Keira's pregnancy. 'I...dunno.' He shrugged. It was nothing to him.

'Well, what if it's a boy, then?' Jason persisted.

Luke wanted out of the cab of the ute—fast. He turned into the driveway at Candlebark, eased his foot off the accelerator when what he really wanted to do was floor it.

'Well?'

'Uh...Jason.' He latched onto that. 'Jason is a good name for a boy.'

He pulled the ute to a halt by the barn.

'What other names did you and Mum have picked out?'

The question froze Luke's blood. 'I can't remember.' He shot out of the car. 'Got work to do!' he fired over his shoulder.

'Need a hand?' Jason called after him.

Luke shook his head and kept walking.

When Luke pushed through the back door that evening he stumbled to a halt, half frozen in the act of hauling off his hat and dragging his forearm across his brow.

Someone had stolen his kitchen.

And replaced it with a picture of domestic bliss. He blinked. The scene didn't waver and disappear. He tried to raise Brenda and Alf's faces to his mind, to temper the gratitude that raced through him—he didn't deserve this—but that didn't work either.

Keira stood by the stove. Jason sat at the table chatting to her. The table was laid with a red and green checked cloth and the cutlery shone. A glass bowl of salad sat in the middle of the table, and Keira now turned to set a bowl of warmed rolls beside it. She sent him one of those trademarks smiles of hers, and the weight of the afternoon lifted from him.

'You're just in time.'

He nodded. He didn't trust himself to speak.

And then she leant down and pulled a lasagne from the oven. It looked great. It smelled even better. His mouth started to water. 'Did you make that?'

'She did.' Jason shook his head in awe. 'From scratch!'

Luke washed his hands and took his seat. He dragged the scents that filled the kitchen into his lungs. He savoured the way his shoulders and arms ached from the afternoon's hard digging.

Keira set a plate of lasagne in front of him, and he wondered if she knew how lovely she looked with damp tendrils clinging to her neck and around her temples. She'd scraped her hair up into some kind of topknot, obviously to keep it out of the way while she'd been preparing the food. Her skin had a healthy rosy glow. She looked good enough to eat.

'What?' She touched a hand to her face. 'Do I have tomato paste on my face or something?'

He yanked himself around. 'No, I…uh…this looks great.'

He couldn't remember the last time he and Jason had sat at the table and had a meal together. He touched his knife, fingered the tablecloth. They'd used to eat together in the lounge room, with the television on, but somewhere along the way Jason had gravitated towards the computer in the evenings and Luke had holed up in his study to keep on top of the farm accounts.

'It's the least I could do after all your help today.'

'Keira told me what you did,' Jason piped up. 'That was pretty cool, Dad.'

Luke couldn't remember the last time Jason had paid him any kind of compliment either. And it felt good.

In fact it felt great.

Keira must have noticed the way he fiddled with the table-cloth, because she said, 'I found it in the linen press. I hope you don't mind?'

'No.'

She took her seat too. 'It seemed kind of Christmassy, and as it *is* the season to be jolly and all…'

Luke didn't answer. In all honesty he'd forgotten it was Christmas.

'Tuck in,' she said. 'Help yourselves to salad and rolls. Eat up while it's still hot.'

Neither he nor Jason needed any further encouragement.

'So,' she said after a bit, 'what do you guys do for Christmas?'

He shrugged. 'Nothing.' Jason usually spent Christmas with Tammy's parents. 'It's just another day around here.'

Her cutlery clattered back to her plate. 'What do you mean? You take the day off, don't you?'

'Nope.'

'But…but don't you have a special meal, and exchange gifts, and play Christmas carols and charades and pull Christmas crackers?'

Luke shook his head. Since Tammy had died they hadn't had the heart for Christmas.

Luke's forkful of lasagne halted halfway to his mouth when he saw Jason staring at Keira with a kind of enthralled fasci-nation. 'What do *you* do?' his son asked.

Keira picked up her knife and fork again. 'There's a group of my friends and we've dubbed ourselves The Orphans. Not that we all are, mind, but those of us who don't have family, or who can't visit them for Christmas, all get together for a big seafood buffet. We eat too much, play silly games, and just generally have a rowdy old time.'

'That sounds…kinda cool.'

Luke stared at him. It did?

'It is.'

He tried to ignore the glare she sent him.

'Keira was sick this afternoon,' Jason suddenly announced.

'Ooh, traitor!' She pointed her fork at him.

'She said it's normal. Is it?'

'Yeah, sometimes,' Luke assured him. He surveyed Keira through narrowed eyes. 'How are you feeling now?'

'Very well, thank you. I had a nice cup of liquorice tea and it settled my stomach nicely.'

'Keira said you were the one who put her onto that?'

Luke ran a finger beneath the collar of his T-shirt. Was the darn woman set on becoming the all-dancing, all-singing president of his fan club or something? He grunted. 'It was nothing.' He shovelled the last of his lasagne down. The domesticity in the kitchen was starting to wrap around him too tightly.

'Did Mum have morning sickness?'

The lasagne threatened to rise again. Luke swallowed hard. 'For a bit.'

'Would you like seconds?' Keira asked, sending him one of those shiny smiles of hers.

She half rose, but he shook his head. His appetite had fled.

Jason suddenly burst out with, 'Were you and Mum as happy about having a baby as Keira is?'

Luke tried to stop his jaw from dropping. Ice streaked from his scalp down to the soles of his feet. He didn't have the energy, the strength…the *heart* for this. 'Keira's carefully planned becoming pregnant. Of course she's happy to find out that that all her hard work hasn't been for nothing.'

Jason scowled, the familiar surly teenager re-emerging. 'And I wasn't planned.' It was a statement, not a question.

What on earth…? Jason already knew all this. Luke pushed out of his chair. 'We were nineteen. We were petrified.'

He couldn't stand remembering that time—the mistakes he'd made…the miscalculations.

Without another word he strode out through the door and into the gathering darkness.

Keira stared in disbelief as the door slammed shut behind Luke. She turned back to the scowling teenager and swallowed. Was Luke deliberately trying to alienate his son?

'You know,' she started, 'if I'd fallen pregnant at nineteen I'd have been petrified too.'

Jason didn't say anything. He shoved away from the table and stalked off. Keira slumped in her chair. To think she'd thought a nice, cosy dinner would be just the thing…

Luke sat bolt upright in bed and listened, staring intently into the dark.

Was Keira was being sick again?

In the next moment his suspicions were confirmed. He hauled himself out of bed and pulled on his trusty tracksuit pants.

The bathroom door opened before he could knock.

'Oh, Luke!' She pulled up short and tried to smile. 'We've got to stop meeting like this.'

His stomach clenched. She looked ghastly—a sickly pale grey, with fine lines fanning out from her eyes and mouth, and a film of perspiration clinging to her forehead and top lip. Her attempt at a joke kicked him in the gut. He didn't know where she found the strength. Or the courage.

'I'm sorry—I didn't mean to disturb you. Go back to bed. I'm fine again now.'

He took one look at the way she leaned against the door-jamb, as if in need of its support. He slipped an arm around her waist. 'C'mon, we'll make you a cup of something hot. Don't argue,' he added, when she lifted a hand as if to remonstrate with him. 'I'm awake now.'

Her soft weight tucked in against his side as if it belonged there, making him want to pull her closer. The scent of vanilla clung to her hair and he wanted to bury his face in it. Hormones long buried, urges long denied, clamoured to the surface, racing through him with a speed and insistence that made his heart pound. When she laid a hand against his bare chest to steady herself, he thought he might lose the plot altogether.

Get a grip! She's ill. Had he sunk so low he'd take advantage of a sick woman?

No!

But this temptation had been building all day. He'd wanted to touch her from the moment he'd found her rifling though his sideboard. At her great-aunt's place he'd nearly kissed her! She'd turned and looked up at him with those big grey eyes of hers and he'd wanted to seize her face in his hands and slant his lips over hers.

He gritted his teeth and helped her into a chair at the kitchen table, then backed away. 'Liquorice tea or lemon?'

'Lemon, please.'

Kissing Keira was out of the question. He couldn't tarnish this lovely woman with his indefensible irresponsibility, his sinister and inexplicable inconstancy. To dim her wide smiles and all her colour, her bright hopes for the future, would be unforgivable.

'Thank you,' she murmured when he set a steaming mug in front of her.

She closed her eyes and took a sip. Luke stared, fascinated at the way her lips shaped themselves to the mug. With an oath, he kicked himself away to pull a packet of plain biscuits from the pantry. 'You should try to eat something.' He hooked out the chair opposite and planted himself in it, gripped his hands together so they wouldn't do anything stupid.

'Maybe in a bit,' she said, with a tiny shake of her head.

He suspected she didn't want to risk any larger, more vigorous movements. He should go back to bed, put himself out of temptation's way. Even as the thought drifted into his mind he knew he wouldn't act on it. He couldn't leave her like this when she was still so unwell. What if she fainted?

His hands clenched. What if she fainted when she returned to the city and there was no one to pick her up from the floor and put her to bed?

'I'd have been petrified if I'd fallen pregnant at nineteen too,' she said, apropos of nothing.

He stiffened.

'Sometimes I get terrified now, and I planned my baby.'

His back unbent again. 'What do you get scared about?'

'The usual stuff, I suppose.' One slender shoulder lifted. 'Will I be a good mum? Can I do it on my own? Will my baby hate growing up without a father and blame me for the decisions I've made?' She paused. 'The worst one, though, is what will happen to my child if I die as young as my mother?'

His gut clenched. Everything inside him rebelled at the thought.

'I worry that the cancer my mother had could be hereditary, and what if I pass that on to my baby?' She shook her head. 'I know it's silly to brood about things outside of my control, but…'

But it didn't make her fears any less real. 'What happened to you after your mother died?'

'My gran looked after me. She'd always lived with us.'

'Your grandmother didn't die young?'

'Well…no.'

'So maybe you and your baby will take after her.'

Keira stared at him. And then she smiled—a bull's-eye of a smile. 'I hadn't thought of that!'

He angled the packet of biscuits towards her. She took one, nibbled a corner. 'So you were scared about becoming a dad?'

'Sure.' He took a biscuit too, to give him something to do with his hands and in the hope it would distract him from the intriguing mobility of her face.

She stared at him for a moment. She put her biscuit down. 'What was it like the first time Jason was placed in your arms?'

He sat back and rewound his memories nearly fifteen years. He remembered the awe and the all-consuming love that had slammed into him. Jason had been so tiny and perfect. 'It was…magic.'

'Then why didn't you tell Jason that at dinnertime?'

Because it would have meant remembering how things had been, and how it had all then gone pear-shaped. And how that was his fault.

He had to live with that knowledge every day. Wasn't that enough?

'Don't you want a better relationship with your son?'

'There's nothing wrong with my relationship with Jason!'

She frowned. 'You can't honestly believe that?'

Her incredulity stung. 'Jason knows he wasn't planned, but he knows Tammy and I loved him.'

'Are you so sure of that?'

'What makes you think I'm wrong?' he shot back.

'The look on Jason's face when you stormed out this evening.'

He swore. His hand clenched to a fist, crushing the half-eaten biscuit.

That cute little furrow of hers etched itself into the centre of her forehead. 'Are you deliberately trying to push him away?'

'What are you talking about?' He was doing no such thing. He tried to concentrate on ridding himself of the crumbs.

'You won't let him help out on the farm whenever he offers. You won't talk to him about his childhood.' She paused and speared him with a glance. 'You won't talk to him about Tammy.'

He flinched at that last. So? What did that prove? What did she know? Nothing! 'He doesn't need to bother about the farm. That's my responsibility. I want him to hang out with his friends after school and on the weekends—relax, have fun.'

'He doesn't, though, Luke. He shuts himself up in his bedroom. On his own. He's becoming as big a hermit as you.'

Her words sucker-punched him. He stared at her, slack-jawed.

'He *wants* to help out with the farm chores.'

'Why?' The word croaked out of him.

Her eyes softened. 'Because he wants to hang out with you.'

All the strength seeped from his spine.

'And, Luke, you might want to save him from responsibility and the demands of the farm for as long as you can, but it's not going to make up for losing his mum. Even if it does make you feel better.'

Was that what he'd been doing? Trying to atone for the unpardonable, the unforgivable? Was he trying to ease his conscience at the expense of his son? The thought appalled him. He thought he'd been protecting Jason. But…was he only hurting him more?

Luke couldn't stand that thought. He'd lay his life down for his son, do anything to protect him from harm.

He'd have laid his life down for Tammy too, if he'd been given the chance, but life rarely allowed you to make those kinds of bargains. He didn't doubt for one moment that Jason would have been a million times better off if his and Tammy's situations had been reversed.

And now here was this woman who'd been at Candlebark for all of three days and it seemed she knew more about his son than he did.

'You forget,' she said softly, 'that I lost my mother when I was young too. I can guess at, relate to, some of the things Jason is feeling.'

If he were a better father, he would have been able to guess at them too.

'Why won't you talk about Tammy with him and tell him about the things you all used to do when he was little?'

'Why does he need me to talk about that stuff?' The very idea made him go cold all over. Brenda and Alf—they talked to Jason about Tammy all the time. It wasn't as if he was missing out.

She didn't say anything for a long moment. 'You want to know one of the things that scared me most after Mum died?'

He ran his hand through his hair. She'd said her mum had died ten years ago. Fourteen was too young to lose your mum. And she hadn't had a dad. He wanted to get up and walk away, but he couldn't. 'What?'

'That I'd start to forget her. That I'd forget what she looked like and smelt like and the sound of her voice. That the memories would fade.'

Jason forget his mum? He stiffened. 'He'll never forget Tammy!'

'I know that, and you know that. But only you and Tammy's parents stand between Jason and that fear. And, forgive me for saying so, but I doubt he's getting much…balance…from his grandparents. He's a smart kid. He'll know that.'

Luke recalled the stoic eleven-year-old who'd watched his mother's coffin lowered into the ground. If their situations had been reversed, Tammy would have known what Jason needed.

Instead Jason was stuck with a father who didn't have a clue. 'What helped you get through that?'

Keira glanced about the kitchen. 'Why aren't there any photographs of Tammy around?'

He closed his eyes. 'Tammy and I had been living in the city. When we moved back to Gunnedah—' because it was what *he'd* wanted '—we never got around to unpacking a lot of our boxes.' Then they'd separated. And then she'd fallen sick. In the end it had been too hard to go through that stuff.

For him. It hit him now. Not for Jason. 'I'll dig some photos out—put them around.' They'd reproach him every single day, but it was no more than he deserved.

'Jason would love to help you.'

He nodded heavily. 'Right.'

Keira stared at him for a moment. 'Talking about my mum with Gran kept her alive for me. Hearing my grandma and my mother's friends talk about her made me...' Her face grew sad, wistful and even more beautiful.

'Made you what?'

'Happy,' she finally said. 'It made me happy to know that people remembered her and still loved her and understood what the world had lost when she died.' She reddened, pulled back and smoothed down her hair. 'If that makes any kind of sense,' she mumbled.

'It makes perfect sense.' And for a moment, when she smiled, the heaviness left him.

It crashed back down a moment later when she said, 'Talking about Tammy—would it be so hard to do?'

He unlocked his jaw. 'Mine and Tammy's marriage...it didn't last. I let her down. How on earth do I explain that to Jason?'

'Oh, Luke! You and Tammy were nineteen when you married?'

He nodded.

'And you married because she was pregnant?'

He nodded again.

'Then tell Jason the truth. That you were too young. That you married for the wrong reasons, but with the best intentions in the world.'

There was so much more to it than that—a whole lot more…

'Did you ever cheat on Tammy, Luke? Were you ever cruel to her?'

'No!'

'And did you ever make her feel guilty for marrying you?'

His head snapped back. 'No!' How could she even *think* that? Tammy had had nothing to feel guilty about. She'd had a heart as big as Keira's. He should have been able to love her the way she'd wanted him to.

'And you still wished her well after you separated?'

'Hell, yes! She…she was my best friend.'

'Then tell Jason *that* too. Luke, you have nothing to reproach yourself for.'

Yes, he did.

That weight settled around him more firmly—making it hard to move, hard to talk…hard to think. He'd caused Tammy so much pain—what if he did that to his son?

Maybe keeping his distance was the smartest thing to do—the best thing for Jason? He knew Brenda and Alf tried to poison Jason against him. And why not? They were probably more right than not. He knew they pressed Jason to live with them. Every day he expected Jason to announce that was exactly what he meant to do. He steeled himself for it. Dreaded it.

'Luke?'

He glanced up.

'Given all that you know now—that you would be left to bring up Jason alone—do you wish you and Tammy had never had him?'

CHAPTER FIVE

'No!' HOW could she think that of him? He loved his son. 'I could never wish Jason away. I cannot regret having him.' He might regret marrying Tammy, but he could never regret his son.

'Even though it's hard?'

Hard? Some days it was hell. His hands curled into fists. 'Yes.'

'And a struggle?'

'Yes.'

She folded her arms. 'So it's hard, and it's a struggle, but you don't regret your son?'

He didn't know where she was going with this. 'That's right.'

'And you like your farm? You think this is a good place to raise Jason?'

Something unhitched in him at that question. 'That's right.' He loved this place. Returning here was the one thing he'd got right. But, heck, the farm needed work, and money—lots of money—spent on it to bring it up to scratch. That thing hitched up inside him again.

She leant towards him. 'Then where's the joy?'

Joy? With Tammy dead? Had she lost her mind?

She reached out and poked him in the shoulder. 'You've forgotten how to have fun.'

He didn't have time for fun.

'You've forgotten to be grateful for the blessings you do have. You have a son who is healthy and…and lovely.'

That almost surprised a laugh out of him. What he wouldn't give to see the look on Jason's face if he heard himself being described as *lovely*.

'And you have a beautiful place to live. You have more than a lot of people yet all you can do is scowl and frown and… and yell at people and swear!'

His jaw dropped.

'Name me three things you've liked about your day today, Luke.'

His mind went blank.

'I'll go first, shall I? One—I finally got to see my great-aunt's house and it's…it's really lovely.'

She was lovely. And off limits.

'Two—I found out that I don't have to spend thousands of dollars on said house.'

Yeah, but that didn't change the fact that someone had tried to take advantage of her.

'And three—I bought a pregnancy magazine today, and do you know my Munchkin is now about the size of a tennis ball?'

Yeah, but it was making her throw up at every available opportunity.

'Oh, and four—I also bought three pairs of the most gorgeous knitted booties at the women's auxiliary stall. They're too cute for words.' She folded her arms. 'Now it's your turn.'

His mind went blank. All he could bring to mind were Jason's burning questions at dinnertime. And the hatred and grief in Brenda and Alf's eyes.

He pushed his chair back. 'It's late. It's time we were both back in bed.' But as soon as he rose the colour that had started to steal back into Keira's face drained out again. Perspiration beaded her upper lip. Her hands trembled.

It happened in the blink of an eye.

She chanced to glance up, and he knew she could tell he'd recognised the impending signs. Somehow through it all, though, she managed a smile. Not one of those big, bright, blind-siding numbers, this one was more muted, but the simple courage behind it touched him more than anything else she could have done.

'You go back to bed, Luke. I will be fine. Thousands before me have lived through this and survived—as no doubt will thousands after me.'

He wasn't leaving her to face this on her own.

'You're not going to go, are you?' she groaned.

'No.'

'Then you'll have to excuse me,' she muttered. 'For what it's worth, as you've already seen me at my worst.'

With that, she promptly moved to the floor, braced her back against one of the kitchen cupboards, and stuck her head between her knees. Luke wanted to reach out and cradle her in his arms until she felt better.

He didn't have the right.

She wouldn't thank him for it.

Do something useful!

He racked his brain, and then retrieved the first aid kit, along with two dried kidney beans from a packet in the pantry. He sat down beside her. 'Hold out your arm.'

She did—straight out in front of her. She didn't ask any questions, and just for a moment his lips twitched. She'd make up for that later. He didn't doubt that for a moment. The reminder that the only reason she wasn't asking questions was because she felt so sick had his smile disappearing before it could form.

He turned her arm over, pressed one bean against the pressure point of her forearm about ten centimetres from her wrist, and wrapped a bandage around it to hold it in place. He repeated the process with her other arm.

She lifted her head and rested it back against the cupboard. Luke moistened a cloth and held it against her forehead. 'I'm sorry,' she whispered.

'There's nothing to apologise for.'

'Nobody warned me I'd feel this awful. I...I mean if somebody burst through the door with an axe and threatened to chop my head off I don't think I could even put up a fight.' All this was said with her eyes still closed.

'Well, for tonight at least I promise to take care of all axe murderers.'

That managed to put a faint smile on her face. It disappeared a moment later. She opened her eyes. 'Luke, what am I going to do if I ever feel this sick after I've had my baby?'

Her lovely eyes filled with tears. It kicked him in the guts. 'You'll manage amazing feats once you have a baby, Keira, I promise. And you'll have friends you can call on, and neighbours, and a babysitter you've trained up—some maternal, middle-aged mother hen—' Gunnedah abounded with those '—who'll love your baby almost as much as you do.'

'Yeah?'

'It'll work out just fine—you'll see. Now, no more talking. Close your eyes and focus on your breathing.'

'You could keep talking,' she murmured.

There was something in the way she said it that caught at him. He glanced down, but she'd obediently closed her eyes. Slowly, he removed the cloth. He'd keep talking if it helped, but...what did he talk about?'

'Tell me those three good things about your day—three things you're grateful for.'

One side of his mouth kicked up. She was irrepressible. Not to mention persistent. 'Three good things...' he said, playing for time. 'Uh...one—I had a great dinner cooked for me.' Until all that talk about Tammy it *had* been great. The food had been spectacular.

'Lasagne is my signature dish,' she whispered. 'You'd better lower your expectations for tonight.'

'I'll be grateful for anything you cook.' He'd definitely received the better part of the deal they'd made. He rushed on, because he wanted her to rest and not talk. 'Two—I got to help you out today a little, and make sure you didn't get ripped off.'

'Help a lot, you mean.'

Her voice had gained in strength, but she still kept her eyes closed. Her lashes were fair—the same red-gold as her hair—but they were long, and they rested against her cheeks in a curling sweep that he wanted to trace with a fingertip. He curled his fingers into his hands and held them in his lap.

'How was it to see John after so long?'

The question took him off-guard. He'd had to brace himself for the meeting, but he and John had fallen into their old pattern as if it the last three years had never happened. 'It was… good.' And he meant it.

'I don't really understand what's going on, but you can't honestly believe the things Tammy's parents accuse you of?'

Not literally, perhaps. But Brenda had sensed his doubt and he deserved her scorn.

'John doesn't believe a word of it.'

She was right, he realised. Today had proved that.

'I bet there are more like him in the town too.'

Could she be right?

'What's your third thing?'

He floundered for a moment, trying to come up with something. Then it hit him. 'Jason paid me a compliment at dinner.'

Her eyes opened. 'That's nice.' And then she smiled. All her colour had returned. She held her arms out to inspect them. 'Of course—pressure points. Thank you.'

'You're welcome.'

'Are you angry with me for the things I said earlier about Jason?'

He had been angry, but he could see now that his anger had been directed at himself, not her. 'I'm not angry with you, Keira.' And with that admission came the realisation he wanted to fight for his son, whatever the cost to himself.

'I thought maybe I ought to apologise.'

He shook his head. 'You've held a mirror up to me, and I can't say I much like what I see.'

'You should smile a bit more, and you shouldn't cut yourself off from your friends, but…I like what I see.'

And, although he knew it wasn't what she meant, he suddenly noticed how her nightshirt had shucked up to reveal a tantalising length of thigh. He dragged his gaze away, clenched his hands tighter, and rested his head against the cupboard behind. 'I don't want Jason becoming a hermit. That means setting him a better example.'

'Luke, you're kind and generous to lone pregnant women in distress. You fight a fair fight, you'd never cheat someone, and you work hard. I think you're the perfect example. With Jason, all you need to do is talk to him—you'll see.'

He turned his head to meet her gaze. Her eyes had gone liquid warm. It filled him with corresponding warmth. He reached out and touched her face. 'So young…so wise,' he murmured.

Her skin was soft, and her breath hitched when he traced the contour of her cheek with his fingertip. Her eyes darkened, desire flaring in their depths. An answering flame flared to life inside him. He turned to cup her cheek more fully, to tip up her chin. Her lips parted, her gaze fastened on his lips, and the pulse at the base of her throat beat like a wild thing.

He started to lower his mouth, his mind blanked of everything except the way she lifted her face to his, how her lips parted, filling him with an anticipation that had the blood roaring in his ears.

'Oh!' She pressed her fingers to his mouth with a groan just seconds before his lips could claim hers. For a brief moment she rested her forehead there. 'Bad idea,' he heard her whisper. 'Very bad idea.'

She was right, of course.

In the ordinary course of events he'd have disentangled himself and stormed off, flaying himself for so completely forgetting his resolutions. But he didn't know if sudden movements would make her nausea return, and although he knew he'd flay himself for his weakness later, he didn't have the energy for anger at that moment either.

She removed her hand from his lips, edged back. 'This really is a most irrational time of day.'

She was doing her best to keep things light. For both their sakes he had to play along. 'Disrupted sleep patterns can play havoc with a person's judgement.' And obviously their sanity. 'Sleep deprivation is a form of torture.'

'Believe me, at the moment so is my breath. It reeks! You've had a lucky escape, Luke Hillier. I best go and brush my teeth.'

He threw his head back and laughed. He had no idea how she could dispel the tension so easily, but he was grateful for it—another one of those things he could add to his list of good things to be grateful for. He helped her to her feet. 'Goodnight, Keira.'

'Goodnight, Luke.'

But after she left Luke couldn't help wishing they'd both been irrational for just a little bit longer.

He knew he'd really flay himself for that thought later.

For dinner the following evening Keira cooked steak and steamed new potatoes, and served them with a salad. As far as Luke was concerned it was as good as the previous night's lasagne.

Jason must have enjoyed it too, because, although subdued,

he ate everything placed in front of him. He even went back for a second serving of potatoes.

Luke followed suit and then, as casually as he could, asked, 'What do you have on for tomorrow? Any plans?'

Jason's fork, heaped with potato, halted halfway to his mouth. He stared at Luke as if he couldn't quite process the question. Luke's gut clenched. Had he cut himself off so completely from his son that a simple question could stupefy him?

Luke sliced a potato in two, although he no longer had the appetite to eat it. 'I really want that boundary paddock sown this autumn, but there's a lot of work to do before then. If you don't have any plans for tomorrow, and could see your way to giving me a hand, I'd be grateful.'

'Yeah? Sweet!' Jason's eyes lit up. But in the next instant he assumed that whole teenage nonchalant slouch again. 'I mean—yeah, no sweat.'

Luke tried to hide his grin. 'Thanks, son.' He tucked in to his potato with renewed enthusiasm.

After dinner Jason didn't immediately leap up from the table, so Luke pulled in a deep breath. 'I was rummaging through one of the sheds the other day, looking for a crowbar, and came across a couple of boxes your mum and I brought back from the city.'

'Some of Mum's things?' Jason stared at him. 'I thought Gran and Grandad had all her stuff.'

Luke rubbed a hand across his nape and forced himself to keep talking. 'This is stuff we bought together. Plus some books and photo albums.'

Jason leaned forward eagerly. 'Can I see? I—'

He broke off and eyed Luke warily, as if he expected Luke to holler no and storm from the room.

Luke had to swallow before he could speak. 'I thought that if you wanted to help me haul them out we could go through them. This place is looking a bit…dull.' All of Keira's colour had brought that home to him. 'From memory, we had some nice stuff.'

No matter how nice Tammy had made their apartment in the city, though, Luke had never stopped longing for home.

'When?' Jason had lost all pretence at nonchalance. 'Now?'

'As soon as we've helped Keira with the dishes.'

The grin she sent him when she turned from the sink made him feel a million dollars.

CHAPTER SIX

'YOU'RE baking?'

Keira swung around from taking the last sheet of cookies from the oven, to find Luke silhouetted in the kitchen doorway, bringing with him the scent of the outdoors and a reminder of her own wayward desires. Her hand shook. She hastily set the tray down on a rack to cool, and wiped suddenly damp palms down the sides of her shorts. 'I'm practising.'

'I like the sound of that.'

Backlit by the sun she sensed rather than saw his grin. He and Jason had spent yesterday working in the fields, and ever since Luke had seemed to find it a whole lot easier to smile. Which was great, she told herself, a definite improvement. Even if those smiles were proving lethal to her pulse.

It would be a bigger improvement if she could forget about kissing him. But all it took was one glimpse of those broad shoulders and strong thighs and yearning would stretch through her, pulling her skin thin and tight across her bones—as it had when they'd sat on the floor together at that ridiculous time the other morning.

Dwelling on that, though, wouldn't help. You're a strong, independent woman, she reminded herself.

She waved a hand at the cooling cookies and tried to banish all thoughts of broad shoulders, strong thighs and kissing from her mind. 'All the best mums bake.'

A chuckle emerged from the strong column of his throat.

Before her thoughts could go all wayward again she added, 'I just know I have a speciality.'

'Speciality?'

'You know—something that will make my kid swoon whenever he or she smells it baking or sees it cooling on the kitchen table.' She gestured to the cookies. 'Like choc-chip cookies or scones or pineapple upside-down cake or pikelets.'

'Or lamingtons or lemon-meringue pie,' he supplied, that grin still stretching through his voice.

'Exactly! So much baking, so little time. You can see why I have to start practising now.'

Christmas and cakes and birthday parties and bedtime stories—they were what childhood memories were made of. She might not be able to give her baby a father, but she was working on the baking and the bedtime stories. She'd bought a stack of children's books the other day in town, and when no one else was in the house she'd taken to reading them out loud. She wanted to get all those funny voices just right. Besides, her pregnancy books told her that her baby would hear her voice while it was in the womb, and would recognise it once it was born. The thought thrilled her.

She couldn't wait to hold her baby in her arms!

'Oh, Luke.' She clasped her hands beneath her chin and recalled what he'd said about the first moment Jason had been laid in his arms. Magic—that was how he'd described it. 'Wouldn't you just love to have another baby?'

'No!'

His vehemence startled her. The choc-chip cookie goodness leached from the air, the wholesome baking scents dissipating in the face of Luke's stark denial. Her mouth went dry. Did he hate single parenthood so much?

She tried to erase the frown from her face, moderate her shock. He and Jason had sorted everything out, hadn't they?

Everything between them was good again, wasn't it? So why…?

He dragged a hand down his face. 'I will never have more children.'

He said it with such quiet finality it made her blood run cold, and she wasn't even sure why. 'Why not?'

His lips twisted, but not a spark of humour lit his eyes. 'Let's just say that marriage and I are a poor pairing.'

There was nothing she could say in answer to that.

He pulled his hand away and shoved his shoulders back. 'Is that what you have planned for the rest of the afternoon?' He gestured towards the oven, the table. 'Baking?'

'Um, no. It seems silly to bake more than we could eat.' She tried to shake off the sombre cloud that threatened to descend over her. How this man chose to live his life, the decisions he made, was none of her business. 'Why?'

'I've finished my work in record time today, and I've just dropped Jason off at his grandparents'…'

'So?' She strove as hard as she could to be casual.

'I wondered if you'd like to take a drive down to the river? I was going to make some sandwiches, grab a nectarine or four and a couple of cans of soda, and head on down there.'

A picnic? His thoughtfulness suddenly touched her. He wanted to make sure she rested up and ate well, didn't he? 'That sounds lovely.' She held her arms out and turned on the spot. 'Will I be okay to go as I am?'

She wore navy cargo shorts and a raspberry singlet top. Luke's eyes darkened as they travelled over her, and her insides expanded while her skin contracted, making her hot and cold all at once.

He glanced away at the same moment she did. 'Do you have a long-sleeved shirt you could put on over that? You're very fair. You look as if you could burn up.'

Oh, she was burning up all right—but it had nothing to do with summer heat.

'You'll need to wear a hat, and slap on plenty of sun-screen too.'

With that he turned and pulled a loaf of bread towards him, his shoulders stiff with tension. She gritted her teeth and reminded herself that kissing him was a seriously bad idea. Why was it that all her common sense flew out of the window whenever she so much as glanced in Luke's direction?

'Friends,' she mumbled under her breath, retreating to her bedroom to find shoes and a shirt. 'Friends,' she intoned, slathering on sunscreen. 'Friends,' she whispered, standing in the hallway.

Pasting on a big smile, she breezed into the kitchen. 'Have you made those sandwiches yet, Hillier?' She *could* do friends.

'Packed and ready, Keely.'

He grinned, and predictably Keira's heart thump-thumped. She clapped her hands. 'Well, let's get this picnic on the road.'

'Hat?' he demanded.

'Oh um... I keep forgetting to buy one.'

He rolled his eyes. He dropped one on her head as she walked past. 'It's an old one of Jason's.'

She touched a hand to its brim and warmth billowed in her chest. *Friends,* she reminded herself.

'Oh, Luke,' Keira breathed as he pulled the ute to a halt by a stand of gums.

'Is this good enough for you, Keely?'

She heard the grin in his voice, but she didn't turn to grin back because somewhere between here and the homestead she'd come to the conclusion it would be a whole lot easier to do the friends thing if she kept her eyes firmly averted from broad shoulders and rich brown eyes.

Unfortunately she'd only gone on to notice how tanned and muscled his forearms were, how sure and strong his hands on the steering wheel. So she'd decided it might be best to avert her gaze from them too.

She hadn't worked out how to prevent his voice from doing that mush thing to her insides yet, though. She supposed she could always stop her ears with her fingers if she didn't care what he thought of her.

But she did care.

Dangerous, a little voice whispered through her.

She ignored it. She'd be leaving here in two days—how dangerous could one little picnic be? Besides, it had been interesting listening to him talk about the farm. He was working on improving the seventy hectares of pasture at the western end of the property. He was clearing weeds by hand because down the track he meant to go organic. It sounded exciting.

The enthusiasm in his voice had caught at her. She admired his dedication. Not to mention the view spread out before her now. *That* stole her breath.

'I… This is…' She couldn't find words to do it justice, so she pushed out of the car and made her way to the top of the bank to gaze down at the river below. Directly beneath her was a strip of sand that glittered gold, bound on either side by boulders and tall grass. The river flowed by smoothly, the water so clean and clear she could see the sand and pebbles in the shallows.

'The Namoi River,' Luke said from beside her.

In the field on the other side of the river something green grew. Its particular deep hue in combination with the shade provided by the trees behind her and all that gold…

'Canola,' he said, gesturing to the field opposite.

She spun to him. She couldn't help it. 'This place is gorgeous!'

'It is today.' He pushed the brim of his hat back. 'You should see it when there's been rain upriver in the ranges. The water roars through here like you wouldn't believe.'

He loved it then too, she could tell. She pointed to the strip of sand. 'Can we have our picnic down there?'

'That's the plan. Head on down while I grab the food.'

'Is it safe to paddle?'

'As safe as houses,' he promised, halfway back to the car already.

The second she hit the sand, she kicked off her sandals and plunged her feet into the water. It was cool and pleasant against her over-heated flesh. She wished Luke had told her to bring a swimsuit.

In the next instant she fanned her face. She and Luke with nothing on between them but thin Lycra and a pair of board shorts? *Not* a good idea.

'It gets colder further out,' Luke said, obviously mis-interpreting her face fanning. He settled himself on a rock. He didn't come any closer.

Keira rolled up her shorts a couple of extra inches and waded out up to her knees. 'It's lovely,' she called back.

He nodded and stayed exactly where he was. So she waded back to shore and sat on the sand nearby. Not too close.

She rested back on her hands and lifted her face to the sun. This was like being on holiday—heavenly—and she was determined to enjoy it while she could. 'C'mon, Hillier, pass out the sandwiches. I'm starving, and I'm eating for two, you know.'

With a low laugh, he tossed her a packet of sandwiches.

They munched them in silence, staring out at the river and taking deep breaths of gold-green goodness. When she glanced up, she found him watching her. 'What?'

'I wanted to thank you for the advice you gave me about Jason the other night. It's made a difference. An enormous difference.'

'So working together yesterday was good?'

He nodded. 'I can't believe how badly I let things slide with him.'

She wanted to tell him he'd had a lot on his mind—being thrust into the role of single parent, trying to work the farm single-handedly, dealing with Tammy's parents' bitterness—but she sensed he wasn't interested in making excuses.

'Have the two of you talked about Tammy?' She'd left him and Jason alone together on Tuesday night. She'd hoped that over those boxes they'd dragged in from the shed that Jason would find the courage to ask Luke the questions he needed to.

'Yeah.'

She grimaced for him. 'Hard?'

'Hell,' he bit out. Then frowned. 'It was hell at first,' he amended. 'It got easier as it went along.'

Her stomach unclenched.

'Tammy's parents have been telling Jason that mine and Tammy's separation is what caused her brain tumour.'

Tammy had died of a brain tumour? Oh, poor Tammy! Keira abandoned her sandwich.

'I told Jason that's not the truth.' His lips twisted. 'I know because I asked her doctor at the time.'

So he'd thought…

Her heart burned. She curled her hands into the sand. She ached to go to him to put her arms around him and offer whatever comfort she could. She suspected, though, that he wouldn't welcome her sympathy, so she stayed where she was.

'Is that why you and Tammy moved back here from the city?'

He shook his head. 'We moved back here six months before she was diagnosed.'

She cocked her head to one side. 'You know, I can't imagine you in the city.'

One corner of his mouth kicked up, but the smile didn't reach his eyes. 'It was Tammy's dream to live there. We moved not long after we were married.' He paused. 'It wasn't my cup of tea.'

She digested that silently. From the expression on his face, he'd loathed it. 'How long did you live there?'

'Nearly eleven years.'

She straightened and gaped at him. 'You…you…lived in the city for nearly eleven years?' To her he seemed as elemental as the gum trees up there on the bank. He seemed an extension of the landscape. Eleven years in the city. Wow! 'What did you *do* there?'

'I was apprenticed to a motor mechanic not long after we arrived. I like tinkering with engines, and it's a handy trade to have when you're living on the land.'

So even in the city he'd always had one eye trained on Candlebark?

His lips tightened. 'Moving to the city seemed the least I could do in the circumstances. As you can imagine, our parents were less than pleased when they found out we were expecting a baby. It felt good to get away. And Tammy and me…we were best friends from our first day in kindergarten. I pulled her plait and made her cry. She kicked my shin and made *me* cry.'

He looked suddenly young, as if this was one memory that couldn't hurt him. Keira smiled. 'Sounds like the basis of a lasting friendship to me.'

One corner of his mouth lifted. 'I can't remember a time when she wasn't a part of my life.' The smile faded. 'So I thought when we married… But I was wrong. We wanted different things from life.'

She wanted to tell him that these things happened, that he and Tammy had been too young, but the sudden darkness in his eyes kept her quiet.

'Dad was having some health issues, and we moved back so I could help him out for a bit. We rented a place in town. There was plenty of room at the homestead, but…'

'You wanted your own place,' she finished for him.

'I couldn't believe what bad shape Candlebark was in, and I knew Tammy would go stir crazy out here with me in the fields from sunrise to sunset. At least living in town she could visit her parents and friends.' He rubbed the back of his neck. 'She went stir crazy anyway. She wanted to return to the city almost immediately. I didn't. Our marriage only lasted another three months.'

'I'm sorry.'

He shrugged and stared down at his hands. 'Not long after that she was diagnosed with the tumour. She refused to let me move back in to help her.'

She glanced at him, and her heart burner harder and fiercer. 'Her parents blamed you for that?' she whispered.

'After she died they started all sorts of dreadful rumours. My parents couldn't bear the speculation whenever they went into town—the snubs and the looks—so they moved to the coast.'

And left Luke to cope on his own! No wonder he'd buried himself out here and thrown himself into farm work.

She had to swallow down a sudden lump. 'Have you told Jason what you just told me?'

'A lot of it.'

'And is he...?' What was the word Jason used? 'Sweet about it?'

He surveyed her for a long moment. 'It really matters to you, doesn't it?'

She shrugged a bit self-consciously. 'I guess it does. Crazy, huh? I've only known you guys for all of five minutes.'

He stared out at the river, lips pursed. 'It doesn't feel crazy,' he admitted.

'Must be all those irrational conversations we've been holding in the wee small hours,' she teased.

'That must be it.'

He grinned, and Keira suddenly remembered that the sun

was shining, it was nearly Christmas, and she was having a baby. And, from the look in Luke's eyes, the future looked bright for more than just her.

'Yeah, Jason and I are good. That's thanks in large part to you.'

'I didn't really do much.'

'You opened my eyes. I will always be *grateful* for that.'

She smiled at the emphasis. His approbation felt good— better than it had any right to—but she allowed herself the luxury of basking in it anyway. Because in two days she'd be leaving this place. In the long term she suspected this man could prove a challenge to all her carefully laid plans…not to mention her peace of mind. He could lay it all to waste. She also knew that two days was not enough time to create that kind of havoc inside her.

The thought of leaving, though, darkened her day for a moment. She shrugged it off. She had a wonderful future to look forward to. That was what she had to focus on.

'Have you sorted everything out with the house?'

Another shaft of sadness pierced her. 'I've signed the last of the paperwork and found myself another estate agent. My great-aunt's house will officially go on the market next week.'

'Congratulations.'

'Thank you.' She fought to find a smile. She should be smiling! She'd done what she'd come here to do. It was just… She didn't know why, but it somehow seemed wrong to sell her great-aunt's house.

'You don't seem all that happy about it.'

She should have known he'd sense her disquiet. 'I feel a bit guilty about selling it,' she confessed. 'Like I'm returning a gift someone has given me.'

'You know…' He pursed his lips. 'Something struck me when we inspected it the other day. With just a little bit of work your aunt's house would make the perfect home business.

You could extend out the back and convert the front into that clinic of yours.'

Keira's mind instantly shot off in a million different directions. 'Are you suggesting that I move here? That I set my clinic up in Gunnedah?'

He shrugged, and sent her the kind of grin that had her pulse tripping over itself. 'Why not?'

'But…I don't know anyone here.'

'You know me and Jason. It wouldn't take you long to make friends. Country towns have a community spirit I think you'd like. Believe me, you wouldn't lack for eager babysitters.' He stretched his legs out in front of him and gestured with one arm. 'And look at all this. It's a great place to grow up.'

He loved his home. That much she could tell. When he'd outlined his plans for the farm on their drive down here she'd started to see the place through his eyes. It had given her a whole new appreciation for it. 'But to move out here…' Her heart raced.

'Medical practitioners of all kinds are in demand in rural areas like this. It's hard to lure people from the city. You wouldn't have any trouble establishing yourself.'

'I…' She tried to shake herself out from under the spell he was weaving about her.

He sent her another one of those grins. 'It's just a thought. But it's worth thinking about, isn't it?'

'I…yes.' She drew the word out slowly. 'I guess it is.'

She'd have to sit down with a pen and a pad later, and work out the pros and cons. She sucked her bottom lip into her mouth. She could always rent out her flat in the city. That would provide her with a steady source of income and—

Later, she told herself firmly. This wasn't the kind of decision she could make on the spur of the moment. It needed careful consideration.

She glanced at Luke, and warmth curled in the pit of her stomach. She did her best to banish it. This wasn't the kind of decision where she'd allow her feelings for a man to sway her—no matter how broad his shoulders or devastating his smile. This came down to a straight business decision and whether this kind of life would be better for her and her Munchkin.

Still, it would be nice to have Luke as a friend.

'If need be, would you rent your room to me for another week some time in January?' Just in case this idea warranted further investigation.

'Of course.'

Excitement billowed through her—a sense of new possibilities opening up before her. She reached for a nectarine and bit into it. Juice promptly ran down her chin. She wiped it away with a laugh. 'Stone fruit is one of my favourite things about this time of year.'

'What are the others?'

'Christmas carols.' He rolled his eyes so she added, 'Not the jingly-jangly ones—though I quite like them too. I'm talking about the slow ones. You know—"Silent Night", "The First Noel", "The Little Drummer Boy"… They're beautiful songs, and they do what all good music should do.'

'Which is?'

'They make you feel…fuller.'

He didn't roll his eyes. He didn't say anything.

Keira bit into her nectarine again, tried to catch the juice that ran down her hand. She held the fruit away from her body. 'I'm going to need a bath after I've finished this.' Even so, she couldn't remember the last time she'd enjoyed a piece of fruit so much.

She went to take another bite, but made the mistake of glancing up at Luke first. His eyes had darkened, and he stared at her mouth with such fascination it made things inside her heat up then melt down. She gulped and tried to remember the friends thing. And that this was a *rational* time of day. Dear Lord, what had they been talking about?

Um… Uh… Christmas!

'You should really do something special for Jason for Christmas, you know. All kids need Christmas—even teenagers.' Instinct told her Luke needed it too. 'There's a magic to Christmas you can't get at any other time of year.' He didn't reply, so she stared doggedly out at the water. From the corner of her eye she could discern his gaze, hot and fierce on her face. If he didn't stop that soon she'd have to dive fully clothed into the river before she burned up.

She recognised the precise moment his gaze shifted to her legs. It was as if he'd reached out and stroked her with one lean, tanned finger. A quiver ran through her. Her breathing sped up. So did his. Her nerves drew tauter, tighter, until she thought they'd catapult her into something she'd regret.

It would be something Luke would definitely regret.

'Stop looking at me like that!'

She didn't want to be anybody's regret. Especially not at this time of the year. 'Tis the season and all that. She had a lot to be grateful for: that was what she wanted to focus her energies on. Not on a pair of firm lips and a strong, square jaw, or the way tawny eyes could darken to chocolate.

Luke leapt to his feet with a cut off imprecation. 'Why don't you wash in the river? I'll go grab a towel from the car.'

He stomped up the bank in the direction of the car. Keira fled to the river. Even if men weren't off her agenda, Luke was the last man she'd ever get involved with. He didn't want any more children, for a start.

With hands that shook, she did her best to wash the sticky remains of nectarine from her fingers and face. Because she couldn't stay in the river all day, and because she wanted to project an air of nonchalance for when Luke returned, she moved back to where they'd been sitting and propped herself against a rock. She started to unroll the legs of her shorts—

And froze.

A snake stared at her from the bottom of the track that Luke had just ascended. Its black eye—unlidded—didn't reflect the light. It lifted its head, and its forked tongue tasted the air.

Oh, help!

Keira stayed frozen. She might be a city girl, but she knew a brown snake when she saw one.

Brown snakes were bad.

Adrenaline shot through her in icy waves. Could the snake sense it? *The bad brown snake.* No—*no,* some logical part of her brain tried to reason. Snakes weren't bad. They were just one of Nature's vast array of creatures.

Yeah, and the venom from the bite of a brown snake could fell a grown man in—

'Keira?'

Luke's low tones. She could sense him at the top of the track.

'Keira, look at me.'

No way was she taking her eyes off that snake. If it made so much as the smallest move towards her, she was out of here.

'Keira, I can see the snake. Please…look at me.'

Something in his voice snagged at her. Almost against her will she lifted her gaze. He was too far away for her to pinpoint the exact shade of brown of his eyes, but she couldn't mistake the intensity in his face.

'Keira, you're doing great—you really are. I need you to keep doing more of the same.'

He wanted her to stay here?

'Any sudden movements will frighten it.'

She gulped.

'I'm not going to let anything bad happen to you, okay?'

She swallowed. 'Okay,' she mouthed back, because her vocal cords refused to work. The constriction around her lungs eased a fraction.

'You're between the snake and the river. He wants to go down for a drink.'

How did he know that? Had he and the snake exchanged

pleasantries as they'd passed on the path? She couldn't help it. She slipped a hand over her abdomen.

His eyes narrowed. 'I am not going to let anything bad happen to your baby either!'

He spoke so fiercely tears stung her eyes—those darn pregnancy hormones—but she believed him. He was like some old-fashioned hero from a book or a movie. He knew how to take care of his own.

Not that she was *his*, of course.

But she did trust him—with her life. And her baby's.

'In a moment I'm going to start drumming the ground with my feet. The snake will want to avoid something that sounds as big as me, so it's going to shoot off down to the river and probably all the way across it.'

It was going to slither right by her?

'I want you to stay as still as a statue.'

She pulled in a breath. Finally she nodded. When Luke looked at her like that she had a feeling she could do just about anything. She closed her eyes. It would be easier to focus on staying still if she didn't catch sight of that snake again.

She heard Luke's thumping—she would have had to be deaf not to. She didn't hear the snake at all. She tried to empty her mind of all thought and concentrate on keeping her body as still as possible.

'Keira?'

Her name was a mere whisper on the air, and so close she had to open her eyes. Were they safe? Had the snake gone away? Had Luke been bitten?

Before she could utter a single one of her questions Luke scooped her up in his arms and strode up the bank towards the car. She couldn't help it. She started shaking as if she were cold and couldn't get warm. All that pent up adrenaline, some rational part of her reasoned.

'Did you get bitten?' she finally managed to get out from between chattering teeth

'No.'

'Me neither,' she said, which was a ridiculous thing to say, because he'd have seen it if the snake had struck her.

Luke opened the passenger door and slid onto the seat with her on his lap. She continued to shake. 'Sorry,' she mumbled, 'I can't seem to help it. What a wimp, huh?'

His arms tightened about her. 'You weren't a wimp. You were wonderfully brave.'

Keira closed her eyes and gave herself up to the comfort of being in his arms. She rested her cheek against his shoulder and drew in all the strength and reassurance she needed.

Luke's heartbeat didn't slow until Keira's shaking started to ease. He found he still couldn't loosen his arms from around her yet.

He bit back something rude and succinct. When he'd first seen that snake, and registered the fear on Keira's face, an anger so fierce and scalding had gripped him it had almost left no room for reason.

He'd remembered himself just in time.

Tell me three things you're grateful for.

Keira was alive and safe in his arms. He was grateful for that.

Snakes might be a protected species in Australia, but if it had bitten her he'd have torn it apart with his bare hands.

She adjusted herself in his arms, sat up a little. He reluctantly loosened his hold, but didn't let her go.

He'd let her go in a moment, he told himself. When he was one hundred percent sure she was okay.

Her eyes met his. 'Thank you for rescuing me.' Her hand inched across her stomach. 'For rescuing us. I didn't have a clue what to do.'

'You did great.' She had too. She'd wanted to run, he'd read that in her face, but she'd conquered her fear and followed his instructions.

Tell me three things you're grateful for.

He was grateful she hadn't been bitten.

She gestured to herself in his lap. 'What a big baby you must think me.'

He didn't think her a baby. Not at all. She was feminine and soft and, for all her slightness, curvy where it counted. Which was an unfortunate thought to have when she was in his arms like this. Very unfortunate. And bewitching.

'I think you're brave and lovely.' Perhaps he shouldn't have said that last bit.

Dammit, though, she *was* lovely!

With a smile, she reached up and brushed her lips across his cheek in the lightest of kisses. He felt its impact all the way down to the soles of his feet.

'Thank you,' she whispered.

The scent of vanilla engulfed him, and something inside him melted. He stared into her grey eyes—her beautiful grey eyes—then he leant forward and placed his lips on hers.

She didn't close her eyes. He didn't close his. He moved his lips over hers—gentle, testing, ready to draw back at the slightest hint or hesitation from her—but after a moment of stunned stillness her lips softened and shaped themselves to his.

And then her eyelids fluttered closed.

With a groan, Luke gathered her closer. She tasted so good. She tasted so…*good*!

He ran his tongue across her bottom lip. She gasped and trembled. That gasp reached right inside his chest and dragged him under. Her hand dived into the hair at his nape to pull him closer. Her lips opened under his and he lost himself in the taste, the sensation…the freedom of kissing Keira.

The taste of her, the feel of her, woke parts of him that had been dead and numb for too long. Her hand burrowed its way beneath his shirt to trace the contours of his chest. He thought his lungs might burst with need when she ran the palm of her hand back and forth across his nipple.

With one arm anchoring her to him firmly, he traced her body from hip to breast. Slowly. He cupped and teased her through the cotton of her singlet top until she writhed and arched against him.

'Oh, Luke…please,' she begged, her moans and his ragged breathing filling the interior of the car.

He knew what she meant. He'd never wanted a woman with such a savage need before.

With something midway between a groan and a growl, he swept his hand down to her hip and across her stomach to the waistband of her shorts. He wanted to touch every part of her. He wanted to kiss every inch of her. His fingers brushed across her stomach again, and something tugged at his consciousness.

Keira.

Pregnant.

Baby.

He stilled. He knew enough to know that making love would not harm her baby, but the reality brought him up short.

He met the clear grey eyes surveying him. He swallowed, then forced words out of uncooperative lips. 'I can't offer you anything more than this.' His voice came out hoarse, as if he needed a drink.

He couldn't offer this lovely woman any of the things she deserved. All he could give her was momentary pleasure…a brief affair.

He watched her consider the idea. If he were an honourable man he'd let her go, but he couldn't. God help them both if she reached up and kissed him now—gave him her tacit agreement—because he would not have the strength to hold back.

Even though she deserved so much more.

He dragged a hand down his face. When he pulled it away, he saw her answer framed in the regret that stretched through her eyes.

Be grateful for what you do have.

Grinding back a torrent of expletives, he slid her off his lap and all but fell out of the car. He closed the door before he could change his mind. He took a moment to straighten his clothes, gather himself. Gave her the time to do the same, before walking around to the driver's side and sliding in behind the steering wheel.

Be grateful for what you do have.

It didn't matter which way he looked at it—he couldn't be grateful for this. Leaving the warmth of Keira's arms was the hardest thing he'd ever had to do.

CHAPTER SEVEN

LUKE found himself whistling as he strode towards the home-stead. The light was fading from the sky and a satisfying weariness was settling over his limbs. In another hour it would be completely dark. In less than fifteen minutes he, Jason and Keira would be seated around the kitchen table, enjoying another of her superb meals.

It was her last night—on this visit at least, he knew she'd be back—and he couldn't wait to see what she served for dinner. He moved with an eager step across the veranda, pushed open the door…and immediately sensed something was wrong.

A roast chicken and vegetables squatted promisingly in the oven, but the oven itself had been turned off. A saucepan of peas and another of gravy sat on top of the stove, but the hotplates had been switched off too. The table was only half laid.

He touched a hand to the side of one of the saucepans—still warm. Keira's morning sickness must have struck again.

He headed for the bathroom.

He hesitated for only a moment before tapping on the door. 'Keira, is everything okay?'

No answer.

He tried the door. Locked. He tapped louder. 'Keira?'

From behind the door he heard a muffled movement, then the lock slid back and the door cracked open a fraction. Keira's pale, pinched face appeared, and fear clutched Luke's heart. He tried to rein in his panic, to keep his voice steady. 'Sweetheart, what's wrong?'

Her chin wobbled. She pressed her lips tight together for a moment, as if trying to get herself under control. Luke gripped the doorframe until the wood bit into his fingers.

She swallowed. 'Would you…would you be able to drive me to the hospital please?'

Her voice came out dull, weak. The sparkle had gone from her eyes.

Very gently, Luke pushed the door open. She didn't resist. He hooked an arm beneath her knees and lifted her, strode into the living room and laid her carefully on the sofa, placed cushions behind her knees to raise her legs. She didn't resist.

Jason leapt up. 'What's—?'

Luke silenced him with a look. Seizing the phone, he called for an ambulance, and then moved back to Keira's side to take her hand. It lay in his unmoving, so small and defenceless… so limp. 'They'll be here soon,' he told her.

She closed her eyes, but he'd read the expression in them.

Her fingers were so cold! He wanted to kiss them warm. A lump thickened his throat. He wrapped her hand in both his own and held on tight.

CHAPTER EIGHT

'I'M SORRY, Luke, but your friend has had a miscarriage.'

Luke stared at the doctor—a man he'd known his entire life—and tried to make sense of the words that left the older man's lips.

'I'm sorry.'

The doctor's sympathy hit him with the force of a combine harvester at full tilt. He couldn't speak for a moment. *Keira had lost her baby.*

'You're sure?'

The question didn't deserve an answer—Dr Metcalfe had been a member of the medical profession for nearly forty years—but he nodded and squeezed Luke's shoulder.

She'd lost her baby!

'I need to see her.' He'd search every room in the hospital if he had to.

'You can take her home.'

That pulled him up short. 'I...don't you have to make sure she's okay? Make her well again?' He didn't care that it was nearly Christmas and staff were on leave. This was Keira they were talking about. He would not stand for inferior medical care or—

'Luke, Keira's not sick. She doesn't have any kind of infection or disease we can treat. She's had a miscarriage. She wasn't that far along in her pregnancy, and there's very little bleeding. She might be a little tender for a few days, but there's nothing more we can do for her.'

'What caused it?' he burst out. He should have kept a closer eye on her, made her rest more.

'Sometimes it just…happens.'

Luke's shoulders slumped. Keira had lost her baby. He wanted to find her, pull her into his arms and comfort her.

He had a feeling she wouldn't let him. Or, worse still, she'd submit because she knew it was too late and it didn't matter any more. Like she had when he'd carried her from the bathroom to the sofa. She'd known then.

'Did she tell you she was undergoing IVF treatment?' He wasn't leaving until he was one hundred percent sure Dr Metcalfe had all the facts.

'Yes. I've sent a fax through to her doctor in Sydney.'

Luke closed his eyes. There was nothing…*nothing* he could do to reverse this.

The doctor led him through to the next room and pointed towards a cubicle. Luke swallowed, and then edged forward to peer around the curtain. Keira sat huddled in a chair, small and defenceless. His scowl fled. He wanted to reach out. He had to clench his hands to stop himself. This was about her and what she needed, not him.

He moved to the chair beside her. 'Keira?'

He winced at the dullness in her eyes, the grey pallor of her skin…her lack of vitality. When he reached out to touch her cheek she jerked away. Things inside him stretched tight. He wanted to howl for her. He beat the impulse down. 'Keira, I'm sorry.' He didn't add anything more. What else was there to say? Adding the other words *that you lost your baby* just seemed cruel.

And she looked exhausted.

She gave a curt nod. 'Thank you.' Perfunctory, as if he was a stranger. It stung.

'Are you ready to go home?'

'Yes, thank you.'

Luke sat by Keira's bedside all night.

She'd told him it wasn't necessary. He did it anyway. He wanted to be close by in case she needed something—a glass of water, another blanket…him. Her answer had been to pull the covers up to her neck and turn her face to the wall.

He'd switched off the lamp, but neither one of them had slept.

When the first fingers of dawn crept across the room, she slid out from beneath the covers.

Luke jerked in the chair. 'Where…?'

'Bathroom.'

He pulled in a breath. She seemed veiled behind a haze of nothingness. No colour, no bounce—nothing. And, although there was nothing wrong with her posture or with the way she walked, it seemed to him that she limped from the room—as if some essential component of her energy had been taken from her.

He dropped his head to his hands. He didn't know how to help her. And he wanted to help her. He forced himself to his feet and went to make coffee.

Keira was relieved to find Luke gone when she returned to her bedroom. She crawled back into bed, pulled the covers up to her chin. The effort of rising, of moving, had left her exhausted, and the dim grey of the dawn light filtering beneath the curtains suited her mood perfectly.

She clocked the exact moment Luke returned. He didn't say anything for a long moment. She didn't care. She welcomed the silence. Finally, 'Would you like coffee or toast?'

'No, thank you. I'll rest. Doctor's orders.' She didn't turn from staring at the wall. 'Go tend your farm, Luke. I'm not in the mood for company.'

He still hovered, but she refused to look at him. 'Promise you'll call if you need anything?'

It took a superhuman effort, but she managed to squeeze the words from between dry lips. 'I promise.' Anything to make him go away. She wouldn't need anything. She'd lost the only thing she needed. She just wanted to stare at the greyness of the wall and not move…not think…not feel.

Every movement she made only rendered her more aware of the hole that gaped through her, of the emptiness inside her. If she stayed very still, barely blinking, she might succeed in ignoring that emptiness, in preventing it from swallowing her whole.

Maybe.

Luke came back at lunchtime, but she feigned sleep and he went away again.

He came back mid-afternoon. She feigned sleep again, but this time he reached down and touched her shoulder. 'Keira?'

'Hmm?'

'You have to eat something.'

'I'm not hungry.' The thought of food made her feel sick. Not literally sick—not nausea sick—not morning sickness sick. Only yesterday—

She cut the thought dead.

To eat she'd have to move. Moving would remind her of what she'd had yesterday. And what she didn't have today. 'I'm not hungry,' she repeated.

'Keira, if you won't eat at least one piece of toast and drink a glass of orange juice I'm going to take you back to the hospital and have them readmit you.'

He kept his voice low and quiet. For that much she was grateful. She thought about the hospital—all those rattling trolleys and cheerful nurses. She forced herself into a sitting position and took the plate and glass he held out to her. She froze when he reached out a hand, as if he meant to push her hair back from her face.

He dropped it back to his side and sank into that chair again. Keira didn't look at him. She knew what she'd see in his face, and she didn't think she could bear it.

She ate the toast and drank the juice. She handed the plate and glass back to him. She didn't say thank you. She wasn't thankful. He left a bottle of water on her bedside table. She knew in his place she'd do the same. He didn't deserve her irritation, her ingratitude.

She lay back down and stared at the wall. She didn't have the energy for irritation.

When he returned later that evening, with a steaming mug of cocoa made with full-cream milk, she sat up without a word and drank it.

The food and the drink didn't make her feel better. It didn't make her feel worse either.

And at some stage during the night she even managed some sleep.

When Luke tapped on her door the next morning and entered, Keira forced herself up into a sitting position. But Luke didn't hand her a plate of toast or a glass of juice. She glanced up.

'I'm sorry, Keira, you're going to have to get up.'

He spoke briskly. It made her blink. Resentment churned through her at this invasion into her sanctuary. 'Why?'

'Because I need to clean your room.'

Her jaw dropped. 'No, you don't!'

'Yes, I do. This room gets a thorough clean once a week.' His shoulders lifted. 'As you pointed out, Candlebark has few enough attractions, but at least the cleanliness of the room is one of the things a prospective tenant can count on.'

She stared at him and tried to work out what he was talking about. She pressed her fingers to her temples. 'What day is it?'

She counted back. 'It's Sunday, isn't it? I was suppose to leave yesterday.'

She scrambled out of bed. She'd been so caught up in her own stuff she hadn't stopped to think what a burden she'd become to Luke. He didn't deserve that. He had a farm to run, a paddock to clear, wheat to harvest. While all she could do was lie in bed and make a nuisance of herself.

'I'll pack and be out of your hair in under an hour. I promise.'

Luke caught her shoulders in his hands and turned her to face him. 'No.'

'What do you mean, no?' He must be dying to see the back of her. She didn't want to notice his steady gaze or the strength of his jaw, but she couldn't help it. She envied him them both.

'What I mean is that Jason and I would like you to stay on for a bit longer…and your room needs cleaning.'

'But…why?' She couldn't think of any conceivable reason why they would want her to stay—not in her current state— unless… 'Are you feeling sorry for me?' She couldn't stand that thought. It filled her with dread. It made the darkness looming at the edge of her consciousness nudge closer.

'We are both truly sorry about your miscarriage, Keira.'

She flinched and pulled out of his grip, turned back towards the bed. No matter how much she wanted to, she couldn't crawl back beneath those covers. She pushed her shoulders back. She came from a long line of strong women. She would not be a burden to a virtual stranger.

'But that's not why we want you to stay. We've come to think of you as our friend.'

Oh! She turned.

Luke had his hands on his hips. He looked big and broad, and his size dominated the space. This might be a double-sized room, but when Luke entered it seemed to shrink.

'I know the doctor said that physically you're fine. I even

rang him this morning to make sure you'd be okay to drive home if that's what you want to do.'

He had? She tried to brace herself against the warmth threatening to steal over her at his thoughtfulness.

'He said it shouldn't be a problem. But...' Luke frowned. 'Think about it, Keira. Do you really want to return to the hustle and bustle of the city at Christmastime?'

She didn't even have to think about it. The unequivocal *no* slammed into her before Luke had finished the sentence.

'If you stay at Candlebark you can have all the peace and quiet you want.'

She had to admit it sounded tempting—a mini-haven before returning to the city and facing all her friends with her un-happy tidings. She wished now she hadn't spread the news of her pregnancy so far and wide. She bit her lip. She wasn't due back at work for another two weeks...

Luke shifted his weight to the balls of his feet, as if ready-ing himself for a fight. He'd argue with her to stay in that no nonsense way of his because he thought it was what was best for her, in the same way he'd tackled her morning sickness with his cures.

But she no longer had morning sickness.

Unbidden, a whimper left her. Luke was at her side in seconds, easing her down to sit on the edge of the bed. 'Oh, Luke. I lost my baby.'

He pressed one of her hands between both his own. 'I know, sweetheart. I'm sorry.'

'I...' She swallowed. 'I can't face going back to the city and telling all my friends yet.'

'You don't have to. Stay here.'

The pressure of his hands reassured her. She searched his face. 'That sounds...nice. I'll pay for my room of course.'

'No, you won't. Last week you stayed as my lodger. This week I'm asking you to stay as my guest.'

One glance at his face told her she wouldn't change his mind. 'Then at least let me clean the room.'

'You sure you're up to it?'

'Positive.' It might be a blessing to have something to do.

'Then you have yourself a deal.'

Luke found Jason in the barn, rubbing down Dusty, his horse. He turned the moment Luke's boots scraped against the packed dirt floor.

'How's Keira?'

Luke shrugged, not quite sure how to answer. 'Do you mind if she stays on for a few more days?'

Jason's eyes widened at the question, and it suddenly occurred to Luke that he'd spoken on Jason's behalf earlier without a second thought. In fact he'd never once bothered to ask Jason how he felt about Luke renting out their spare room. Not once.

How much else had he taken for granted?

He set his shoulders. '*Do* you mind? I mean, it's your home too.'

'It'd be sweet if she stayed a bit longer.'

Luke nodded, and collapsed onto a bale of hay. He was glad Keira had agreed to stay. It meant he could keep an eye on her, make sure she didn't neglect herself and become ill. Or, alternatively, didn't overdo things and make herself sick. He ached to do more. Her lack of colour, her lack of vibrancy, her utter lack of life, hurt him in a way he couldn't put into words. He wanted to find a way to put just a bit of that sparkle back into her eyes.

He started when Jason threw himself down on the hay bale beside him. 'You worried about her?'

'Just trying to think of something that might cheer her up.' He glanced at his son from the corner of his eye. 'Any suggestions?'

Jason scuffed the toe of one boot against the floor.

'Flowers?' In the next instant he shook his head. 'Nah, they won't help.'

They were both quiet for a while. 'That night at dinner,' Jason finally said, 'she said she liked Christmas.'

Luke lifted his head. 'She told me she loves Christmas carols.'

'Maybe we could buy of CD of carols and play it every day. And we could Christmas the house up a bit.'

Luke remembered what Keira had said to him the day of their picnic—that all kids needed Christmas, even teenagers, and that he should do something special for Jason.

'It's worth a shot, isn't it?' Jason added. 'We could try and talk her into staying for Christmas—that's only next Saturday—and we could have a nice dinner or something. I…I think she'd like that.'

Luke leapt to his feet. 'I think it's a brilliant idea.'

Jason grinned. 'Sweet.'

That grin tugged at Luke. He thought of all Keira had just lost, and how much he himself had and yet hadn't appreciated. 'You like her, don't you?'

Jason shrugged. 'She laughs a lot.'

And most of the adults in Jason's life didn't laugh—at least not much, Luke realised.

'And she likes people, and that makes it easy to like her. She doesn't brush you off because she's busy with her own stuff or anything.'

Not like him, Luke realised. He hadn't always been like that, though.

Jason moved back towards Dusty's stall. 'She's cool. She told me I should talk to you about Mum, and she was right.'

Luke blinked, but when he thought about it he realised it shouldn't have surprised him. 'She told me I should talk to you too. And she was right.'

Luke glanced down at his hands. 'Jason, your mum—she was a great mum, right?'

Jason nodded.

'She would've known what to do, known what you needed, if our positions had been reversed and she was here and I wasn't. I'm not so good at working that stuff out. I thought if I excused you from the farm chores and gave you plenty of spare time to hang out with your friends and your Gran and Grandad, and didn't remind you about your mum, that'd make things a bit easier for you. But I was wrong. I'm sorry.'

'Not sure I'm so good at it either,' Jason said, his voice gruff. 'And, yeah, Mum was a great mum, and I miss her loads and all, but I like living here better than the city.'

Luke let out a breath. 'So…we're sweet?'

'We're sweet.'

'Good.' With that, Luke started for the door.

'Dad?'

He swung back.

'Mum's not the only one who was good. You're a great dad too, you know?'

A lump formed in Luke's throat.

'And…I…uh…love you.'

Luke walked back and did something he hadn't done in a very long time. He pulled Jason into a rough hug. Jason hugged him back. Hard.

Luke did his best to swallow the lump. 'Thanks, son. I love you too.'

Keira dressed. And then she cleaned her room from top to bottom.

It didn't make her feel any worse. It didn't make her feel any better either. Eventually, though, she had to admit there was nothing left to clean in the room. If she didn't want to become a burden to Luke she had to stop hiding out in here. She glanced at her watch. It would be lunchtime soon. She could put the kettle on.

She forced unwilling legs out into the hallway and down its length to the main living area of the house. A part of her was grateful Luke wasn't in either the kitchen or the living room. The thought of making small talk had the strength draining from her arms and legs. Besides, she wanted him working those fields of his, not worrying about her.

She filled the kettle and switched it on. Drummed her fingers while she waited for it to boil and then reached for the teabags…and froze. Her mouth dried. A packet of liquorice tea sat innocuously on the counter beside all her other teas. The liquorice tea she wouldn't need again. She swung away, pulled out a chair at the kitchen table and sat.

Don't think about it!

The bright cover of a magazine drew her gaze. She reached out and tugged it towards her, desperate for the distraction. And froze again. Her pregnancy magazine! With its cover picture of a smiling baby—a chubby-cheeked baby dressed in cheerful red and…and smiling.

She slammed it face down, but that didn't help. A very pregnant woman graced the back cover, advertising a brand of stroller. Keira shoved her chair back and raced blindly into the living room, trying to block the images of that smiling baby and that pregnant woman from her mind.

She eased herself down to the sofa and closed her eyes, tried to focus on her breathing. When she opened them again they zeroed in on the tiny baby booties she'd left on the coffee table.

She couldn't move. All she could do was stare.

She'd left those booties there because she hadn't wanted to pack them away. She'd wanted to touch them, play with them…imagine the tiny feet that would wear them.

'Oh, Munchkin…'

Very slowly she reached out and gathered them in one hand. They were so very little. She lifted them and inhaled their clean woollen scent. They felt soft and warm against her face.

* * *

'Keira?'

Keira started. She didn't know how long she'd been sitting there with the booties pressed against her cheek. She pulled her hands and the booties down into her lap.

Luke moved into the room with that easy grace of his. He settled himself on the coffee table so they sat almost knee to knee. His heat and his breadth reached out to her in silent invitation. She knew all she had to do was lean across and he'd enfold her in his arms. It wouldn't make up for what had happened, for what she had lost, but she suspected it would help. She suspected that being held in his arms would make her feel safe for a bit.

But that would only be an illusion. She stiffened her spine and resisted the temptation.

'You okay?'

She didn't know if she'd ever be okay again, but she couldn't say that out loud because it would be a pathetic thing to say. Her mother would never have said it.

'I…' She pressed the booties between both hands. 'Trying to ignore what's happened isn't working.'

His eyes softened. 'Is that what you've been trying to do?'

She nodded. 'But I was just about to make a cuppa when I saw my liquorice tea sitting there, which reminded me of morning sickness and being…'

He nodded. She was grateful he didn't finish the sentence for her.

'And my pregnancy magazine was on the table, and it has the most gorgeous baby on the front cover and the most pregnantest woman on the back.' She didn't know if there was such a word, but she knew Luke would understand what she meant. 'And then when I came in here and found these…' She stopped worrying at the booties and held them up.

He dragged a hand down his face. 'I can't believe I didn't think to clear all that away.'

'It's not your fault.' He'd been too worried about whether she was eating enough, and if she was ever going to emerge from his spare bedroom or not.

She stared down at the booties and that darkness stretched through her. She curled her hand into a fist, crushing the delicate wool between her fingers. 'I'm trying to think what I could've done differently. Did I lift something too heavy? Have I been pushing myself too hard? Did I eat something I shouldn't have? Maybe that six-hour drive from Sydney—'

Luke reached out and closed his hands over hers, bringing a halt to her rush of words. 'You did everything you could to keep you and your baby healthy and safe, Keira. You didn't do anything wrong.'

'But…' That couldn't be true. If there was nothing she could do differently next time then…then there'd never *be* a next time.

'Dr Metcalfe said sometimes these things just happen for *no* conceivable reason.'

Then… She swallowed. She couldn't go through this again—not on her own. So much for priding herself on her independence!

She leapt to her feet, shoved the booties at Luke and started to pace. For as long as he sat so close the temptation to seek comfort in his arms beat at her—more proof of her weakness. 'I've let my mother and grandmother down!'

He shot to his feet. 'What on earth—?'

'They were both strong women who could do it all alone, but I'm not like that. I—'

'Garbage!'

His bluntness made her blink.

'Your mother didn't do it on her own. She might not have had your father around, but from what you've told me your grandmother was there for her every step of the way.'

Keira stared at him.

'I'm not denying that they were both strong women, but,

Keira, you're even stronger. You've shown more courage, not less. With eyes wide open you chose to have a baby without the usual support networks. That's amazing!'

But look where it had landed her!

'One day you will make a wonderful mother.'

No, she wouldn't. She didn't have what it took to travel down that path again. Not on her own.

'And it's not shameful to need other people, to rely on them. It's natural. You needed your mother and your grandmother, didn't you? People need other people—you taught me that. I need Jason. And I know I need to broaden my social network.' His lips twisted. 'I'm hoping it'll keep me more…balanced in future.'

His admission brought her up short. Had her idea of independence become skewed, affecting her judgement? Had she deliberately kept people—men—at a distance just to prove she could do it all on her own?

'Keira, you have your mother on an impossibly high pedestal.' He paused. 'Did she ever marry?'

She shook her head. 'Have you ever considered that what you took for independence was actually fear? After your father, maybe your mother was just too scared to trust a man again.'

Her voice shook. 'That's rich, coming from you.' All the same, her mind whirled.

'I'm not criticising your mother, Keira, but she was flesh and blood like the rest of us. And, like the rest of us, she must've made her fair share of mistakes.'

Her mother hadn't been perfect, of course, but…

Luke reached out and pushed a strand of hair behind her ear. 'She'd have *loved* the woman you've become, Keira. She'd have been proud of you.'

Keira's hands started to shake. And her knees. She crossed back over to the sofa and hunched up in one of its corners, arms tightly crossed to try and contain the shaking. 'I wish she were here now.'

Luke sat beside her. 'I wish she was too. I wish she could help you through this. Instead…' those firms lips of his twisted again '…you're stuck with me.'

He wanted to help her. She could see that. Somewhere in the last seven or eight days he really had come to see her as a friend.

'Is there anything I can do to make things easier?'

'Believe me, Luke, if I could think of a single thing that would make me feel better I'd…' Her voice trailed off.

His eyes narrowed. 'What?'

That gaping darkness loomed over her. She pushed it back with all her might and deliberately un-hunched her body. 'Brooding will send me mad! Is there something useful I can do? I don't know how good I'd be at digging out weeds, but I'd be willing to give it a go.'

She needed something to keep that yawning emptiness at bay. She swallowed. Deep down she knew it wasn't oblivion that lay at the heart of that darkness. It hid a swirling pit of pain and grief, and if she fell into it she didn't know how she'd ever get out again.

'I don't think that kind of physical work would be good for you at the moment,' Luke started slowly, 'but…'

She leant towards him eagerly. 'But?'

He raked a hand through his hair and grimaced. 'I'm not sure I should ask it of you.'

'Ask away,' she ordered, the swirling darkness retreating further with every passing second.

'It might seem…insensitive.'

That gave her pause, but only for a moment. 'Out with it.'

'You…um…told me that…'

His reluctance to continue started to irk her. Out of all proportion, she suspected. She gritted her teeth, clenched her hands, but the anger surging through her had become difficult to contain. 'Fine,' she snapped, shooting to her feet. 'I thought you wanted to help, but—'

'Whoa!' Luke grabbed her arm before she could flounce off. 'Christmas,' he said, before she could tug free or yell some more. 'You said I should do something for Jason for Christmas, but…what?'

The puzzle pieces fell into place. Carefully she detached her arm from his warm grip and sat again. 'I see. And you thought asking me to help might be insensitive because I might not feel much like celebrating Christmas after…after what's happened?'

He nodded.

'And I…' She moistened suddenly dry lips. 'I just went and snapped your head off.' What had got into her? 'I'm sorry.'

'Don't give it another thought. If I've asked too much, then just say.'

'No,' she said slowly, thinking of Jason and how his face had grown wistful when she'd described her Christmas plans to him. 'We don't have to go over the top, do we?'

Luke collapsed back down beside her, his shoulders slumping. 'Don't ask me. Christmas was never a big deal when I was growing up. Mum and Dad weren't really into it.'

Her heart contracted. They should have made a bigger effort for him.

'And it was Tammy who took care of all of that stuff when we were married.'

And since her death Luke and Jason hadn't had Christmas. The thought made her forget her own misery for a moment.

He frowned. 'From memory, though, it always cost a bomb.'

'It doesn't have to. A few decorations, a nice meal…a couple of small gifts.'

'Yeah? And Jason… He'd like that, you think?'

'He'll love it,' she assured him.

He stared at her for a moment. 'You really think you can bring Christmas to Candlebark?'

With her background, nothing could be easier. She nodded solemnly. 'I believe I can.'

His brow suddenly cleared. 'So you'll stay for Christmas?'

She found she could even smile. 'Yes.'

CHAPTER NINE

KEIRA glanced up from the kitchen table when Luke strode in early the following afternoon. He grabbed a bottle of water from the fridge and drank deeply. She tried not to notice the rippling muscles in his arms, or how strong and tanned he looked.

He gestured. 'You want one?' When she shook her head he closed the fridge door. 'What are you doing?'

'Deciding on the menu for our Christmas dinner.'

Interest sparked his eyes. 'Yeah?'

It almost made her smile, this latent excitement of his. She couldn't begin to thank him for the task he'd assigned her. It had helped take her mind off…other things. Whenever the darkness threatened, she threw herself into planning and list-making till it receded again. Simple.

He leant back against the kitchen cupboards. 'What have you decided—a seafood buffet?'

She shook her head. No way. Luke and Jason needed a proper traditional Christmas this year. To make up for the last three Christmases. 'We're having roast turkey with cranberry sauce, roast vegetables and Brussels sprouts.'

Luke frowned.

She bit her lip. 'You hate turkey?' They could have pork or chicken instead.

'It just sounds like a lot of hard work. I want you to be able to relax on the day too.'

'You needn't worry about that. You and Jason will be on vegetable peeling duty.' She wanted him to see how easy it all was so he could do it again next year.

'That's okay, then.'

'We've left it too late to make a Christmas pudding, so dessert will have to be either trifle or pavlova. We can vote on that at dinner tonight.'

'Sounds as if it's all coming together.'

'It is.'

'Good.' He took another long pull on his water. 'Are you busy this afternoon?'

Her ears pricked up. Did he have another task for her? Busy was good! She set her pen down. 'No.'

'Then I thought if you were interested we might go through your great-aunt's house one more time.'

Her stomach contracted.

'I wanted to show you what I meant about converting the place into that clinic of yours.'

But… Her hands snaked around her waist. That dream… it was dust now, and—

'You said you'd always planned to open your own clinic one day. There's absolutely nothing to stop you from going ahead with that plan.'

Her arms loosened. She sat back and considered his words. He was right, of course. There was nothing to prevent her from setting up her own physiotherapy practice in Gunnedah. If that was what she wanted to do.

She'd started to grow fond of the town. Whenever she popped in to do some shopping people smiled at her and made eye contact. Shop assistants and checkout operators always had time for a chat and a laugh. She pursed her lips. The relaxed pace suited her.

Plus, the countryside was pretty. That was an added attraction. Whenever she looked at that view of Luke's she had to smile, remembering the pride in his eyes and his complete incomprehension that anybody could possibly find it wanting. Frankly, she was starting to come round to his way of thinking.

And she *had* asked him to assign her a project. Turning her great-aunt's house into her dream clinic fitted the bill perfectly. After all, Christmas would only take her up till Saturday.

'Okay.' She leapt to her feet.

He planted his hands on his hips and surveyed her through narrowed eyes. 'You're sure?'

'You bet.'

Busy was good.

'This is what I was thinking…'

Keira followed Luke through the front door of her great-aunt's house and then into the large reception room on the left.

'This front room here would be your reception area.'

She turned on the spot and nodded. 'A desk there, with some filing cabinets behind.' She pointed. 'Over there would be the waiting area—a few chairs and a small coffee table for magazines.'

'It's a large room, so you'd fit all that in no problems.'

He was right.

'A bonus is this big front window overlooking the park. If for some reason mums or dads have to bring their school-age children with them, the kids could play in the park and their parents would still be able to keep an eye on them from in here.'

Keira could feel herself start to hunch at the mention of children.

'You could even put a couple of chairs on the veranda with that in mind.'

'Right.' She nodded. 'Good idea.' Her voice came out strained and high-pitched. She turned away at Luke's narrowed gaze. 'It all needs a coat of paint, of course, and new carpet.'

'Or you could rip this carpet up and polish the existing floorboards.'

She shook her head. 'Lots of patients will have mobility problems. I'd want a non-slip surface. Water spilt on a carpet will be quickly absorbed, but wet floorboards could prove problematic for someone on crutches.'

He stared at her, admiration evident in those rich brown eyes of his. 'I'd never have thought about that.'

That admiration threatened to fluster her, so she added curtly, 'It's my job to think about it. Which brings me to another issue.' She led him back outside. 'I'll need wheelchair access—a ramp.'

He strode down the front steps and surveyed the veranda, hands on hips and legs planted wide. He paced the length of the front garden, bent down a couple of times to check… something. Keira tried not to notice how utterly masculine he looked, how completely assured and confident, but it tugged at her insides, softened her lower abdomen—and what had been cold warmed and filled with anticipation.

A burst of a child's laughter killed the warmth in a nanosecond. 'Mummy! Mummy! Watch this!'

Her head snapped back. Her shoulders drew in hard.

'You could have a ramp that extended from here—' Luke gestured to the front gate '—leading straight up to the veranda, or…'

From the corner of her eye she saw him move to the right. In the park opposite a group of children played tag—their high, thin voices and laughter made her chest cramp.

'Or you could have it running parallel from here, if you wanted an easier gradient.'

In the sun, the children's hair gleamed with good health. One of them started to sing 'Jingle Bells' and the others joined in. Her heart beat in time to the pain pounding behind her eyes. Her child should have had the chance to run like that, to sing like that. She should be the one sitting on this veranda watching her child and—

'Keira?'

She started when Luke touched her shoulder. The sympathy in his eyes burned acid in her chest. She jerked away, gestured to the imaginary ramp. 'I'm guessing John will be able to give me good advice about that?'

'Yep.'

Without another word, she turned on her heel and fled back inside, the children's laughter, their vitality, mocking her with a useless series of what-could-have-beens.

She hauled in a breath. It wasn't the children's fault. And it wasn't Luke's fault. He'd been everything that was generous and kind.

It's not your fault either.

She pushed the thought away. She couldn't go there.

She crossed into the front bedroom. 'I'm guessing you thought this would be the consulting room?'

He nodded. 'Is it big enough?'

'Plenty.' She kept her eyes averted from the front window. 'Desk here.' She pursed her lips and tried to concentrate. 'Examination table here, and a couple of chairs there…' And there would still be loads of room for exercises and whatnot.

It would be the perfect set up. For a clinic. Against her will, her eyes drifted towards the window.

'If you're as good as you've been saying, Keely…'

She could have hugged him for the teasing, the lightness, and the fact that it had her swinging away from the window. Only she couldn't hug him. Ever since their kiss down at the river last week, hugging Luke had become a decidedly bad idea. The thought of their bodies pressed up close against each other—his hardness, her softness, his strength seeping into her bones, the magic touch of his hands… She shook her head. Hugging Luke was off-limits. Unless she wanted it to lead to more kissing.

Of course she didn't want that!

She glanced at him. Or did she? Heat seared her skin when he turned and met her gaze.

She dragged hers away. Stop it! Her hormones had gone haywire. It was probably to be expected given…everything. Heaviness stole over her. That darkness threatened the edges of her vision.

She shrugged off the heaviness and lifted her chin. 'Oh, I'm as good as I say, Hillier.'

'Then you'll eventually have too much work for one person. You'll need to get in another physiotherapist or two to help cover the workload. That's why this house is so perfect.'

He led her back out to the corridor and along its length. 'Bedroom two and bedroom three—' he flung their doors open as they passed '—become consulting rooms two and three.'

She bit her lip. 'Where am I going to sleep? We are talking home business, aren't we?' He didn't mean for her to rent his room for ever?

The thought unnerved her, and she shot into the second bedroom. And ground to a halt, pressing a hand to her mouth. The first time she'd seen this house she'd thought this room would make the perfect nursery. A cot sitting in the middle of the room on an oriental rug, something soft and pastel on the walls, maybe a wallpaper border of nursery rhyme characters…

That life should have been hers!

'For the moment you'd sleep in one of these two rooms, but what I was thinking is down the track you'd put an extension on the back of the house. I'll show you what I mean.' He took her hand and led her across the corridor, through the dining room and into the kitchen.

The kitchen—the hub of the house. It should ring with

laughter and chatter. The same laughter and chatter that had filled the park. She'd imagined baking choc-chip cookies in this kitchen.

'You'd extend off the back like this.' He tugged her through the back door and out to the lawn. 'There'd be a big living/family room here.'

Only she didn't have a family.

'And then a couple of bedrooms out this way.'

There should be a swing set there…and a sandpit.

'A big master bedroom here for you, and another smaller bedroom for your—'

He broke off when she flinched.

'And a spare bedroom there.' His voice sounded heavy as lead.

Perspiration broke out on her forehead, but her toes and fingers ached with cold. She couldn't help wondering if she'd gone as pale as he.

'I can't stand it,' she finally whispered. 'I know you're trying to help me see something good in the future, but…I can't stand it. Bedroom two was supposed to be a nursery.' She gestured to where she'd imagined the swing set and the sandpit. 'There were supposed to be birthday parties out here and…' Her throat closed over for a moment. 'I can't stand it, Luke.' The darkness loomed. 'I want to go back to Candlebark.'

She turned and strode around the side of the house. She couldn't bear to enter her great-aunt's home again, to walk through all its lovely rooms with all its lovely dreams.

That life should have been hers, but it had been snatched away. *Why?* That single word reverberated through her while she sat in the car and waited for Luke to lock up.

Why?

When he slid behind the driver's seat, he didn't start the car up immediately. She gripped her hands together and met his gaze.

His eyes were dark. Those grooves bit deep either side of his mouth. 'Keira, I'm sorry. I should've thought—'

'No! No, Luke—you were trying to help. I know that. You've been a good friend. I'm the one who's sorry.'

'You have nothing to be sorry for.'

Pain stretched behind her eyes. For most of the last year she'd eaten good wholesome food, taken all the vitamins her doctor had recommended, avoided caffeine and alcohol. She'd made sure that she'd exercised and that she got a little sun most days—not a lot, just a bit. She'd done all the things that would help her fall pregnant, and all the things that, once pregnant, would nourish her baby. *It wasn't fair that the miscarriage had happened to her!*

Anger ripped through her. She tried to cram it down deep inside her. Luke didn't deserve her anger. 'Please, Luke, can we just go back to the farm?'

Without another word he started the car and turned it in the direction of Candlebark. She was grateful he didn't try to make small talk on the journey home. It gave her a chance to concentrate on stifling the anger roaring through her, threatening to flare out of control and scorch all within its path.

She'd endured almost a year of IVF treatment before she'd finally fallen pregnant—endless drugs, endless procedures, nail-biting waits—all for what?

A low growl crouched in her throat. When Luke brought the ute to a halt in its usual spot by the barn, she shoved her door open and tried to leap out. But she'd forgotten to undo her seatbelt. She tugged at it furiously, that growl emerging low and guttural. Luke leaned across and released the catch.

She fell out, stumbled to her knees before lurching to her feet again. Spinning around, she slammed the car door shut and set off towards the house.

'Keira?'

She stopped to shake an unsteady forefinger at him. 'I am so angry, Luke, but *you* don't deserve to bear the brunt of it.'

She had to get out of his presence before she did something unforgivable. 'You have been lovely—utterly lovely! I'm not angry with you!'

She kicked at a tuft of grass, and then she moved up to the paling fence and slapped it—hard. Pain shot through her hand and up her arm in a satisfying wave, making it possible to ignore the ache in her chest for a tenth of a second. She clenched her hand to a fist, drew it back…

'Whoa!' Before she could punch the fence, Luke's large, warm hand closed over hers, his other arm going about her waist and lifting her bodily off the ground.

She tried to struggle free. 'Put me down, Luke. I want to smash something!'

'I know.'

'Don't try and stop me. I—'

'I'm not.'

She stopped struggling. He was taking her towards the barn. 'You're not?'

'No, but I'm not going to let you break your hand either.' His voice was grim. 'I think we've both had enough of hospitals for the moment, don't you?'

Anger hot and untempered rushed through her. 'I'll be happy if I never see another hospital as long as I live,' she bit out.

'Good.'

He didn't set her down until they were deep inside the barn. That was when she saw it, hanging from a low beam—a punching bag. She laughed, but her laugh didn't contain an ounce of mirth.

Intent, she moved towards it, but Luke grabbed her wrist and pulled her to a halt. 'Put these on first.' He handed her a set of thin leather gloves. They weren't boxing gloves, but she didn't care. She reefed them on and started towards the bag again.

A growl of rage—a sound she hadn't known she was

capable of making—emerged from her throat when Luke pulled her to another halt. 'What *now*?' she all but yelled at him.

'That bag—it's heavy. It won't move much when you punch it. That can be…unsatisfying.' He held a wooden baseball bat out to her. 'Try hitting it with this.'

She gritted her teeth and took the bat. 'Excellent.'

She moved in close to the punching bag, drew the bat back, and then let fly with all her might. It hit with a dull thud, and the force of it vibrated through her arms and into her shoulders, making the bag shudder.

That's for my stupid body, with its ovary on the blink!

She drew the bat back and took another swing. *Thud!* It set the bag swaying.

That's for making me wait almost a year before falling pregnant!

Wind up, swing…thud.

And that's for making me lose my baby!

She stared at the swaying, juddering punching bag and her legs started to tremble. The anger slid out of her and the bat slipped from her fingers. She backed up to a hay bale and sat, breathing hard.

'Did you hurt yourself?'

Luke was there, drawing off her gloves. She shook her head.

'Keira?'

'The miscarriage.' She swallowed. 'It wasn't my fault.'

'No.'

'It's…it's not fair that I lost my baby.'

'I know.'

Her face crumpled. She'd lost her baby—her beautiful baby—and all the plans she'd made for it.

She hauled in a breath and did her best to smooth out her face, to push the pain, the darkness, away. But her face refused to co-operate, and the pain beat at her, breaking over her in wave after wave, making her head bow and her shoulders shake.

The constriction around her chest tightened. She couldn't draw breath. She knew the moment she did her defences would fall. She tried to hold it, but the burning in her lungs built and stretched and scalded her until she couldn't fight it any longer.

A sob burst from her. She dropped her face to her hands, her entire body shaking. Arms went about her, holding her and rocking her. Luke. His breath warm at her temple and his arms strong, supporting her as the sobs engulfed her. Being held in his arms didn't make up for losing her baby—not one little bit—but it did help, which made her cry harder for a bit. Being here with him like this helped a lot.

When her tears had finally spent themselves she lay in his arms, tired beyond belief. 'You want to know what one of the hardest things is?' she finally whispered.

'Tell me.'

'In the eyes of the world, my baby was nothing.' She dragged in a shuddering breath, incapable of any other movement at the moment. 'I feel as bereaved as if my baby had been stillborn, and yet I can't even have a service for it. I can't honour it in that way and—'

She didn't know the words to express how bad that made her feel. When she glanced up into his eyes, though, she knew she didn't have to. He understood.

And that helped too. A little.

When they returned to the house, Luke opened the back door to discover Christmas carols belting out from the sound system in the living room.

He closed his eyes with a grimace. He knew what he and Jason had decided, and in principle he'd agreed with it. At the moment, though, it seemed the worse timing possible.

He strode through to the living room and made silent

motions, drawing his hand across his neck and shaking his head. Jason immediately leapt to his feet and all but dived across the room to hit the stop button.

'No—don't. Not on my account.'

Luke swallowed. He hadn't realised Keira had followed so close behind him. Jason hovered by the sound system and glanced from Luke to Keira, and then back at his dad. Luke didn't know what to tell him, so he simply settled for a shrug. Keira sat. Jason contented himself with turning the volume down a couple of notches, and joined Keira on the sofa.

She glanced up at Luke. 'I told you—I *like* Christmas carols.'

He found he didn't quite know what to do with his hands and his feet. That hadn't been a problem when Keira had been crying. He'd just held her, and ached right alongside her. 'I know, but I wasn't sure you'd find them appropriate today.'

'Why not? It *is* Christmas.'

He shuffled his feet, shoved his hands into his pockets. Keira and Jason looked comfortable, sitting on the sofa like that. Jason sprawled at one end in his typical lounging, slouching fashion. Keira rested her head back against the sofa's softness at the other end.

She turned to glance at Jason. 'You like Christmas carols?'

He grinned. 'Only when my mates aren't around.'

It hit Luke then that they looked like a family.

He tried to kill the thought before it could fully form. No peace—not for anyone—could be found in it.

Another thought followed swiftly on its heels—he wanted to be sitting there on the sofa with them. There was room. It was a large sofa. He forced himself towards an armchair instead. He tried to push all thoughts of warmth and softness and the scent of vanilla from his mind. What he wanted was neither here nor there. What he should be focusing on was Keira and her wellbeing.

He tried to study her as surreptitiously as he could. She was pale, and her eyes were red-rimmed, but she seemed calmer, steadier than she had been in the last three days. Letting out all that anger, followed by the crying jag—her acknowledgement of her grief—he knew was only the beginning of her grieving process. But if he and Jason could give her a nice Christmas—nothing fancy, just a bit of company and some fun—then maybe that would help her heal just a little bit more.

It was the least he could do after hauling her off to her great-aunt's house like he'd done. That had been a serious error of judgement. He'd thought it might provide her with something else to focus on—a new project. He bit back an oath when he recalled the stark whiteness of her face, the misery haunting her eyes. He should be shot for putting her through that.

His mouth dried. He should be shot because he'd pushed her so hard to set up her clinic in Gunnedah, because he wanted her to stay. It was as simple as that.

All the strength left his body, his back slumping in the armchair, his head suddenly too heavy for his neck. Keira smiled at him as if she understood exactly how he felt.

Tension shot through him. He couldn't let her misinterpret his actions. He couldn't let her rely on him for more than friendship. He'd told her it was okay to rely on other people and he'd meant it. As long as she didn't count *him* as other people.

He would let her down.

To be free to love a woman like Keira, to build a family with her—whatever shape that family took—was what he wanted more than life itself.

But he couldn't have it. A man like him couldn't be trusted with a woman's heart. Especially not a woman as loving and giving as Keira. If he ever saw the hurt and disappointment that he'd caused in Tammy spring into Keira's eyes... It would tear him to pieces inside.

She deserved better. Much better. So had Tammy. He would not risk Keira's happiness for his own selfish needs.

'So, I guess you'll be putting your great-aunt's house on the market like you always meant to?' He made his voice brusque and businesslike.

The light in her eyes faded. He told himself this was the wise thing to do, sensible—to erect a wall that would protect her from his faithless heart. 'You'll have Christmas with us at Candlebark, sell the house, and then return to the city, where Gunnedah will become a faint memory.'

She suddenly smiled, as if she'd worked out the subtext to his words. 'Are you trying to tell me that you'll miss me?'

Hell, no! Even if the answer to that question was a resounding *yes*!

'If you invite me to visit, I'll come,' she said.

'Sweet,' said Jason.

'You'll be welcome any time.' Luke made his voice deliberately neutral—polite. It made the frown spring back into her eyes.

When she left, he'd allow himself the comfort of a couple of phone calls—just to make sure she was okay—but he wouldn't invite her to visit and she wouldn't suggest it. The time between phone calls would lengthen until they eventually dwindled to nothing. He'd make sure of it. In the long run it was what would be easier for everyone.

'To be honest, Luke, I have to admit I'm not focusing on anything much beyond Christmas.'

He was pushing her again! His hands clenched. Just because he couldn't get the thought of holding her, touching her, kissing her, out of his head, it didn't mean she felt the same way.

Selfish—that was what he was, he suddenly realised. Because the boundaries were for *him*—for his benefit, his protection. He ground his teeth together. He shouldn't be concerned with anything other than providing her with whatever she needed while she remained at Candlebark. Not with what would be best and easiest for him.

In his heart he knew she'd return to the city. She knew that she didn't belong with him.

He would give her Christmas…and there was one more thing he could do for her too.

In the eyes of the world, my baby was nothing.

His jaw locked for a moment. He unlocked it to ask, 'Keira, do you have a favourite poem?'

She cocked her head to one side. 'My favourite poet is Robert Frost. *The Road Not Taken* was my mother's favourite poem. What about you?'

'Banjo Patterson's *Clancy of the Overflow.*'

She turned to Jason. 'Anything by Spike Milligan,' he said promptly.

He reeled off a nonsense verse that had sudden laughter rising through Luke. 'You used to recite that when you were five or six.'

Keira smiled. It was slow, but it had the same impact as the sun coming out from behind a bank of stormclouds. Luke couldn't look away as she recited a nonsense verse back at Jason. Then she and Jason shot nonsense verse back and forth until they both started to laugh.

Luke rested his head back and feasted his eyes on the sight. It was beyond anything to see some of her vivacity and colour returning. It eased something inside him to hear his son laughing.

'Oh, that was fun!' Keira turned back to Luke. 'But what on earth made you ask such a question?'

'Oh…uh…a poetry programme I caught on the radio,' he improvised, recalled to his original purpose. 'What's your favourite plant?'

'Let me guess—you caught a gardening programme on the radio too?'

'Every Saturday morning from eight till nine.'

'No prizes for guessing yours, I suppose?'

'Wheat,' he and Jason said in unison.

'There's lots and lots that I love. Flowers are wonderful, but scents are the best. And my favourite smelling plant is…'

She flipped out several fingers. Luke found himself leaning towards her, elbows resting on knees. 'What are you deciding between?'

'Freesias and frangipani…'

Heck, where would he get a frangipani tree out here?

'Gardenias… Oh, and roses, of course.'

'Of course,' he echoed. He could do a rosebush.

'Wattle,' she finally decided. 'Wattle is my favourite plant. It smells divine, and it looks wonderful.'

He filed that information away.

She stared at him for several moments, as if awaiting another out of the blue question. 'What? Not going to ask me my favourite song?' she teased.

He straightened. He hadn't thought of that. 'Yeah.'

But with a laugh and a shake of her head she turned to Jason. 'What's your favourite Christmas memory?'

'That's easy.'

Luke's head shot up. It was?

'The year I was seven I woke up really, really early to find Santa had left me a bike.'

The breath whooshed out of Luke as the memory swept over him. 'Man, you should've heard him. He made enough noise to wake the neighbours.'

'Dad took me down to the local park, probably so Mum could sleep in, and he taught me how to ride it. It was brilliant! I fell over a lot, but it didn't matter, 'cos the grass was soft. And Dad would always pick me up, dust me off, and away we'd go again.'

Luke remembered that morning and grinned. At seven, Jason had had boundless energy.

'And when we got home Mum was cooking blueberry pancakes, and I remember this huge glazed ham sitting on the table. One of my other presents was this compendium of board games, and I think we ate and played board games and watched Christmas stuff on the telly all day. And then on Boxing Day we got up really early and drove here. Candlebark was my favourite place in the world.' Jason paused. 'So that Christmas I got the best presents and we had the best fun...and I knew that the next day I'd be going to my favourite place.'

'That's a great memory,' Keira said.

'It was a beaut Christmas,' Luke agreed.

And it had been. But a few short years later Luke had destroyed all that. He'd made promises he couldn't keep. Tammy hadn't deserved that, and neither had Jason.

He glanced at Keira and resolution gelled in his stomach. He would do all he could to make this Christmas special for her, but he wouldn't make her any promises. He wasn't the kind of man who could be trusted to keep his word.

CHAPTER TEN

ON WEDNESDAY morning, four days after her miscarriage, Luke set a beautifully carved oak box on the table beside her cereal bowl. Keira stared at it, and wondered how long before she stopped counting off the days.

'What's this?'

She glanced up at Luke. Just for a moment he looked touchingly uncertain. She didn't know what it was about his rich brown eyes that could have her melting into a puddle in no more than the blink of an eye.

He crouched down beside her. 'Keira, I don't think your baby was nothing. Neither does Jason. What you said about not being able to have any kind of memorial service—that struck me as pretty important. If Jason and I hadn't been able to have a service for Tammy I don't know how we could've moved on.'

She abandoned her cereal to lean back and press both hands to her chest.

'Jason and I thought that if it's okay with you, if it's something you'd like to do, we could hold a service in the garden for your baby. I know it's not the same as one in a church or a cemetery, but…we'd like to honour your baby, to remember it. But only if that's okay with you.'

Her eyes filled, and hot tears spilled onto her cheeks. For a moment she couldn't say anything. Finally, she nodded. 'I'd like that very much…thank you.'

'Both of us wanted to give your baby something…a token.' He leant out to stroke the box with one tanned finger. 'This held all my boyhood treasures.' He set a carved ebony figurine of a horse beside it. 'And this was Jason's most treasured possession when he was younger.' He added a spray of rosemary to the pile without another word.

Rosemary for remembrance…

Her face crumpled. She buried her face in the hanky he handed her. When she was sure of herself again, she lifted her face, blew her nose, and stared at those simple treasures. 'That's very kind of you and Jason.'

'I figured you might like to add one or two things of your own.' He rose when she nodded. 'We'll be out in the garden when you're ready.'

Keira placed the three sets of knitted booties she'd bought from the women's auxiliary stall, a Christmas bib she hadn't been able to resist buying when she'd been waiting for the estate agent one day, and the most colourful of the pictures books, into the oak box. She added the horse and the rosemary. With a kiss, she sealed it. Then she put on her prettiest summer dress and joined Luke and Jason in the garden.

The service was simple but it poured balm on the wound stretching across her heart. Luke said a few words about how much her baby had been wanted and loved…and how much it would be missed. Then he read out a Robert Frost poem, and it was perfect. So perfect that for a moment she couldn't see because tears made the garden blur. Jason read a psalm from the bible, and then Luke pressed a button on the portable CD player he had sitting nearby and the sweet strains of 'Amazing Grace' filled the garden.

They all sang—not always in key—but Keira didn't care. A fierce love for her baby and for the two males standing either side of her filled her. When the hymn came to an end Luke gestured, and she placed the oak box with all their treasures into the fresh earth Luke and Jason had turned over. And then they covered it in and planted a wattle tree to mark the spot.

'Thank you,' she whispered, glancing up at Luke. 'You don't know how much this means to me.'

Luke's brown-eyed gaze told her he knew exactly what it meant.

They returned to the house and drank coffee, and ate a tea bun that Keira realised Luke must have bought fresh from town that morning.

'Right,' he said when they were finished, 'now we're going to make a boiled fruitcake.'

Both Keira's and Jason's jaws dropped. 'But,' she started, 'don't you have work to do?'

'Yep, I have a fruitcake to make.' When she opened her mouth he shook his head. 'There's a few chores I'll have to take care of later this afternoon, but that's hours away yet. Besides, Jason will help me with them—won't you?'

'Sure I will.'

He didn't want to leave her alone to mope herself into a depression after that memorial service, she realised. His ongoing thoughtfulness touched her more deeply than she suspected it should. She shrugged that thought off. 'But…a boiled fruitcake?'

'I know we've left it a bit late, but Christmas isn't complete without fruitcake.'

She started to laugh. 'I won't argue with that.'

'And when you were talking about Christmas memories the other day I suddenly remembered that every year I'd help my mother make a boiled fruitcake. It was always a bit of an event.'

She was glad he had at least one good Christmas memory. She watched him dig out mixing bowls from a cupboard. He handed her a sheet of paper. 'That's her recipe.' He handed Jason a measuring cup before planting himself in front of the pantry. 'You better start by reading out the list of ingredients.'

She read the items out one by one, and Luke retrieved them. Jason, reading over her shoulder, started measuring ingredients into bowls. She grabbed a wooden spoon and helped to mix. At some stage Luke put on the CD of Christmas carols and Keira lost herself in the simple pleasure of easy conversation, humming along to old favourites and making a cake.

At some point it filtered into her that she would always mourn the loss of her baby, that she would never stop missing her Munchkin and all that could have been. Motherhood might be closed to her, but it didn't mean life still couldn't be good. At least…bits of it. Like Christmas.

Luke nudged her with a friendly shoulder. 'You okay?'

'Sure.' She pasted on a smile and pushed her sombre reflections aside. To help this man and his son have their first good Christmas in three years—that would give her more satisfaction than anything else at the moment. 'I…' She gestured. 'This is fun.'

'Yeah, it is,' he said, as if it had taken him by surprise too.

That was when it hit her that she needed a Christmas miracle, because she'd gone and done the unthinkable—she'd fallen in love with Luke Hillier.

She swallowed. That was crazy nonsense! It was her haywire hormones and nothing more.

Still, it was Christmas. And if she needed a miracle Christmas was the time to ask for one.

Keira knew the exact moment Luke stopped in the living room doorway, but she didn't turn around. Her growing awareness for the man continued to disconcert her—especially as she received such conflicting signals from Luke himself.

At times he was utterly concerned and solicitous about her welfare, making sure she wanted for nothing, quietly watching to make sure she ate enough and that she didn't physically push herself too hard. It made her feel like a princess, a queen. It made her feel not alone. It made her feel...loved.

At other times, though, he was distant, gruff, almost abrupt, as if he were out of patience with her.

And then there were those times when his gaze fastened on her mouth and his eyes would darken, his hands would clench, and something inside Keira would stir to languorous life and hold its breath, waiting for him to kiss her.

He never did.

And she couldn't get the memory of their one kiss out of her mind. The feel of all that firm flesh beneath her fingertips, the rightness of his lips on hers. That kiss had transported her to a place she hadn't known existed—beyond desire to a one-on-one harmony that had made her spirit soar. Her soul hungered to experience it again.

Her lips twisted. Who was she trying to kid? She wanted to seize hold of it and never let go. Luke had experienced the desire, but that soul-to-soul togetherness hadn't reached out and stroked him with its enchanted fingertips. If it had he wouldn't be able to resist kissing her again and trying to recreate it.

So...all in all, it was just as well he didn't kiss her. And the sooner she forgot about kissing the better!

If only she could get her stupid body to believe that. And her traitor of a heart.

Maybe he's giving you time to heal after your miscarriage?

She crushed an almost hysterical desire to laugh. She was leaving for the city next week. Time was the one thing they didn't have.

She bit back a sigh and refused to turn around, even though Luke's presence beat at her and made her skin itch and prickle.

Jason, though, showed no such reticence as he brushed past

Luke to get more staples from Luke's office. 'Hey, Dad, what do you think?'

This morning she and Jason had gone shopping. They'd bought all the ingredients for Christmas dinner, and some odds and ends to make Christmas decorations. She'd wanted to prove to Luke that Christmas didn't have to cost a lot of money. So this afternoon she and Jason were making angel chains and Christmas lanterns from shiny foil paper and hanging them as they went. Their handiwork draped the mantel-piece, hung from each of the windows, and festooned the French doors that lead out to the veranda.

'It…uh…looks very festive.'

She finished cutting out her row of angels. Only then did she allow herself to turn and survey Luke's face. He stared around a bit dazed, but not in a bad way, she decided. He just needed to lighten up and let his hair down for a bit.

A ripple of mischief squirmed through her. She grabbed a wad of tack and rose, moving to where Luke slouched in the doorway. 'Here—you can help me.' She handed him one end of her angel chain and pointed to the top of the doorframe. He obediently reached up and pressed it into place, giving Keira a pleasing eyeful of broad shoulder and rippling muscle as he did so.

'My turn.' She stood on tiptoe, one hand on Luke's shoulder for balance as she reached above her head. One of Luke's hands automatically went to the small of her back to steady her, and it felt so good there she took her time fixing her foil angels into place.

'Are you almost finished?' he eventually ground out.

It made her grin. 'Not quite.'

With a flourish she pulled a spray of mistletoe from her pocket and dangled it above their heads. 'Know what this is?'

He scowled. 'Mistletoe.'

His utter lack of enthusiasm made her laugh. She tacked it

into place. When she was done, his hand immediately dropped from her waist, but she left her hand resting on his shoulder. 'Oh, no, you don't, Luke Hillier. Not so fast. You've been caught under the mistletoe.'

His jaw dropped. 'But…but that's cheating!'

'Face it, Luke.' She drew her hand down from his shoulder to his chest in a slow, lingering curve, relishing every contour and the way his muscles tightened at her touch. Beneath her palm his heart thudded, and the hot male feel of him branded itself on her skin. 'You're going to have to kiss the lodger.'

He really did need to lighten up. She shimmied in closer, lifted her face. 'C'mon, you can do it.' She sent him her cheekiest grin and pointed to her cheek. 'Right there, Hillier.'

Her grin faded, however, as Luke lifted one large hand and curved it around the back of her head, his thumb running lightly back and forth over the pulse at the side of her throat. 'You like playing with fire, Keely?'

His eyes darkened. His lips—those sure, firm lips—parted as if to allow him to draw more breath into his lungs. Oh, dear Lord! Her pulse went mad and the strength drained from her limbs. Her hand fisted into the cotton of his shirt as his mouth descended.

He pressed the lightest of kisses to the side of her neck, just below her ear, his breath teasing her overheated flesh as his mouth moved to her cheek. 'Here? Is this where you meant, Keely?'

She tried to nod, but she couldn't move. She could barely swallow as that thumb moved back and forth. Back and forth over that pulse point in a barely there skin-on-skin touch until need screamed through her. Just by the touch of his thumb!

And the warm pressure of his hand curling around her scalp.

And the dark promise in his eyes.

And those wicked lips.

'I consider myself more of a traditionalist, however.'

Those sinful lips curved upwards and her breath hitched. 'I prefer lip-on-lip contact.'

Oh, he couldn't mean—

He touched his lips to the corner of her mouth. Her knees shook. He touched his lips to the other corner, lingering until white-hot tendrils whipped through her. He drew back, gazed at her long and hard, as if he meant to savour every single moment of the lip-on-lip contact he'd promised, and it drew her as taut as a newly strung bow. With agonising slowness he eased forward again. His lips brushed hers, feather-light, magical, and then he eased back, just as her lips opened in an attempt to deepen the fleeting caress. He grinned down at her, as if he knew exactly what havoc he'd played on her senses.

'How was that, Keely? Pass muster?'

She straightened, swallowed, and unclenched her hand from the cotton of his shirt. 'You better watch yourself, Hillier.' She smoothed the cotton out. 'I'll be spending the rest of Christmas trying to catch you beneath the mistletoe.'

He threw his head back and laughed. 'I consider myself duly warned. Now, enough of this seasonal silliness.' He smiled as Jason came back in with a box of staples. 'I need the pair of you to help me unload the car.'

Keira and Jason stared at each other, and then at him.

'I...uh...' He shuffled his feet and looked deliciously out of his depth. He waved a hand at the decorations she and Jason had made. 'It appears that great minds think alike,' he muttered.

With that, he strode from the room. Keira hesitated for half a second before following him out through the back door and down the steps towards the barn, doing what she could to get her hormones back under some semblance of control. All around her the wheat waved golden in the fields. High in the sky cirrus clouds traced tracks of foam. In two days it would be Christmas...and Luke had just kissed her! She jumped up and high-fived a branch in a nearby bottlebrush tree.

Luke halted by the tray of the ute. She stopped beside him—not too close—and peered inside. 'A Christmas tree?' And by the look of its box it must have been the biggest one he could find.

Jason peered over her shoulder. 'Sweet!'

She'd wanted to buy one when she and Jason had been shopping earlier, but had been afraid of overstepping some unspoken boundary.

Luke glanced at her from beneath a lock of hair that had fallen forward onto his forehead. 'Is it…um…okay?'

'It's better than okay!' She couldn't help it. She turned and hugged him. Hard. Then she let him go, because neither she nor her body had forgotten that episode beneath the mistletoe yet. 'It's perfect!'

She stared down at the Christmas tree, and all the associated bags and boxes of tinsel and decorations. 'My favourite Christmas memory is decorating the tree with my mother every year.'

Luke planted his hands on his hips. 'Why didn't you say something sooner?'

She shrugged and risked glancing up at him. 'It didn't seem right, somehow.' But now… 'Ooh, c'mon—let's unload it.' She clapped her hands. 'Time's a-wasting.'

The genuine delight on Keira's face as they set up the Christmas tree lightened Luke's heart. A Christmas tree— such a small thing—but it gave her so much joy.

Mistletoe was an even smaller thing, he reminded himself with a wry twist of his lips, but it had nearly undone him. For a brief crazy moment her teasing had made him feel young again. He had to take serious care he didn't get stuck under that mistletoe with her again.

'Have some shortbread.' Keira held a plate out towards him, humming along to 'Deck the Halls' as it blasted out from the CD-player.

He took a break from unknotting tinsel to select a piece. He bit into the crumbly sweetness and then had to close his eyes against the vivid need that shook through him. He couldn't let all this go to his head—Keira handing out traditional Christmas treats and singing along to carols while she helped his son decorate the tree, and both of them turning to him every now and again to tell him what a stroke of genius the tree was—none of it was real.

Well, it *was* real, he amended, but it fed too closely into the fantasy. A fantasy that could never come true. This was a mirage—a temporary illusion. In a few days Keira would be gone, and she'd leave a gap in his life. He had no illusions about that. All the same, he would do nothing to stop her from leaving. He'd promote it if he had to.

If she stayed he would break her heart—just as he'd broken Tammy's. He'd make her promises he couldn't keep—just as he had with Tammy. Keira's eyes might go all soft now, when they rested on him, but if she stayed eventually they'd harden with disappointment and heartbreak. He'd put lines of care on her face.

He couldn't stand the thought of doing that. Better she left in a few days than they risk exploring the heights he instinctively knew they could scale together. Her eventual pain would not be worth it. It would be a thousand times better that he suffer the torment now than for her to suffer it later.

In the meantime, he had to work at keeping things light.

And no more kissing under the mistletoe!

'Earth to Luke?'

He crashed back to find Keira holding out a large golden star.

'You can do the honours.' And she pointed to the top of the tree.

'Me?'

'Yes, you. You were the one to surprise us so wonderfully in the first place, and…'

'And?' he asked, intrigued in spite of himself.

'And you're the only one tall enough to reach the top.'

He grinned and popped the rest of his shortbread into his mouth, wiped his fingers on his jeans and carefully took the star. He settled it into place, securing it there as gently as he could and doing his best not to dislodge any of the other decorations.

He stepped back to survey their handiwork.

'Sweet,' Jason said, moving in beside him.

'Perfect,' Keira breathed from his other side.

And just for a moment while he stared at the tree he had a glimpse of the true spirit of the season, and it eased the ache out of his chest.

'It really does feel like Christmas now,' Keira added with a satisfied sigh, and his chest expanded. His plan had worked, but it hadn't just lifted *her* spirits. It had lifted Jason's too. *Even teenagers need Christmas.* He vowed that in the future he wouldn't forget.

He stepped back before the fantasy could swallow the last shred of his sanity. 'Is there anything else we need to make Christmas perfect?' Tomorrow was Christmas Eve. That meant there was only one more shopping day left.

'I don't think so.' Keira sucked her bottom lip into her mouth before letting it go again. It glistened as bright as the tinsel and the foil angels that swayed in the breeze from the French doors. For the life of him, Luke couldn't look away. 'We've bought enough food to feed an army!'

'We're roasting a turkey and vegetables,' Jason said, practically drooling as he threw himself down on the sofa. 'Keira promised to show me how to cook it so we can make it next year.'

When Keira wouldn't be here.

Luke retreated to his armchair and pretended to admire the Christmas tree.

'And we have all the ingredients for a pavlova.'

From her tone, pavlova must be one of her all-time favourite things.

'Not to mention enough chocolate-coated sultanas, short-bread, sweets and nuts to sink a ship.'

'And fruitcake,' he added, remembering how they'd made that cake—the easy laughter and camaraderie.

'And fruitcake,' she agreed.

She settled herself in the other armchair, the one furthest from him and nearest the Christmas tree. Her hair curved around her face. He curled his hands into fists, but that didn't stop him remembering its softness. She wore the same shorts she had the day she'd paddled in the river—the day of their picnic. The day they'd—

She crossed her legs, her shorts rode up, and he forced himself to glance away.

He saw Jason surveying the tree with eyes that glowed and his heart clenched. He would never be able to thank Keira for bringing Christmas back into his son's life. He had to clear his throat before trusting himself to speak. 'Are you spending Christmas night with your grandparents?'

'Dunno.'

Something about his tone had Luke straightening. Now that he came to think about it, Jason hadn't spent any time at all with Brenda and Alf this last week. 'You want to tell me about it?'

Jason shrugged. 'We had words,' he mumbled. 'I told them they had to stop saying bad things about you in front of me—that I didn't want to hear it. I told them they were wrong about you, and that you did love Mum even if it wasn't the way they wanted you to.'

Luke stilled.

'I told them to get back to me when they'd worked out if they could do that or not.'

'Aw, hell, son, I…' He swallowed, and tried to tell Jason how much Brenda and Alf needed him, but he choked up.

Keira spoke over the top of him anyway. 'Good for you. They'll come around—you'll see.'

Did she really think so?

'Yeah, I reckon they will too.'

Luke gazed at them both in astonishment.

'Don't sweat it, Dad.'

Jason clambered to his feet, and it hit Luke just how much his son had grown up in the last couple of years. 'Do you have any idea how much you sounded like your mother just then?'

A grin spread across Jason's face. 'Yeah? Sweet! I'm going to exercise Dusty.' With that, he pushed out through the French doors, whistling.

Luke swung back to Keira. 'But Brenda and Alf...' His heart went out to them. They'd lost their only child. Their grief and anger—he understood it only too well.

'Jason has a right to ask the adults in his life to act in a reasonable manner.'

He closed his mouth. She was right.

'And maybe this is the shake-up Brenda and Alf need. They won't find any peace in the bitterness they keep perpetuating. They need to concern themselves with the living, not with the dead. It's time they started remembering all the good things about Tammy, instead of focussing on her death and the gap she's left behind.'

He couldn't help but stare at her. She brushed a strand of hair back behind her ear and shrugged, not quite meeting his eye. 'My gran told me all that when my mother died.'

His heart ached at how much she'd lost and how alone in the world she was. 'Keira, your coming to Candlebark was a stroke of good fortune for Jason and I.' He paused. 'I just wish it could've been as good and as trouble-free for you.'

She glanced away. 'My miscarriage had nothing to do with your farm, Luke, or the town of Gunnedah.'

There was something in the way she said it that suddenly

froze his blood. Something hard and unrelenting in her voice that he hadn't heard there before. He shot forward to the edge of his seat. 'When you return to the city, Keira, you will be pursuing your IVF treatment, won't you?'

She shrugged, but still didn't look at him. 'I kind of think the universe has spoken up on that subject, Luke, don't you?'

His gut clenched. So did his hands. 'You can't give up on your dream of becoming a mother!' The words burst from him.

She turned then, and met his gaze. 'It's too soon to think about it.' Her eyes were dark and shadowed. 'I don't want to talk about it, Luke. Please—it's Christmas.'

And he had promised her Christmas. He nodded, but his heart burned in protest.

She sagged. 'Thank you. Now...' She straightened again. 'What gifts have you bought for Jason?'

'I...uh...' He shifted on his chair. 'None.'

'None!' She stared at him, evidently scandalised. Then her face softened. 'Let me guess, Tammy used to take care of that side of things?'

He nodded.

She sucked her bottom lip into her mouth. 'Didn't you and your family exchange gifts when you were growing up?'

When he was very little he seemed to recall there'd been some gifts. After that... 'We had dreadful droughts out here during the eighties. There wasn't much spare cash. Everything we had went back into the farm or to the bank.'

She sucked that bottom lip into her mouth again. He wished she'd stop doing that. As if she'd heard that thought rattling around in his head, she suddenly pursed them instead, and he could have groaned out loud—that wasn't any better!

'What about now?'

Was she asking him if he had enough money to buy Jason a Christmas present?

'We're a bit cash-poor until the harvest comes in. Once it does, though…' They were on track to make a tidy profit this year. 'I can afford a gift or two, if that's what you're asking.' This should have occurred to him sooner. He scratched his head. What did one get a fourteen—nearly fifteen—year-old boy for Christmas these days? What had he wanted when he was fourteen?

Again, as if she could read his mind, she gestured towards the television unit. 'I see that Jason has one of those game consoles.' She paused and her eyes suddenly twinkled. 'Unless that's yours, of course?'

Two weeks ago he'd barely been able to crack a smile. Now she could have him grinning as easy as not.

Two weeks ago he'd have dreaded going into town. Today he hadn't given it a second thought. He'd just wanted to buy Keira and Jason a Christmas tree.

Presents, though, had completely slipped his mind.

'Well,' she started, 'I have it on very good authority that the hottest game this year has something to do with dragons… and the Gunnedah Games Shop has it in stock.'

He gazed at her in admiration. 'You're good.'

'I am.'

She said it with such deadpan seriousness he burst out laughing. 'Jason told you, huh?'

'I believe you're accusing me of cheating, Hillier. Indeed he did—but not quite in the way you think. When we walked past the Games Shop earlier today he hollered, "Sweet!" and pressed his face up against the window like a little boy.'

Her description somehow had Luke's gut tightening and melting both at the same time.

'And then there are the staple presents to fall back on, of course.'

'Staple presents?'

She nodded. 'There are the unisex chocolates and sweets. Then for men it's socks and undies. Every male should get those on Christmas and birthdays. Women are convinced that men are incapable of buying them on their own, you see.'

He knew she was teasing him. 'And what are the female equivalents?'

'Body lotions and bath bombs. Men know that women like to smell good.'

She didn't have any problem in that department—she smelt great! Still, he vowed then and there to get her some kind of body pamper-pack—vanilla-scented, of course.

The phone suddenly rang. Luke blinked. It took him a moment to realise what the sound was as it was such a rare event. And not a welcome one, he acknowledged as he hauled himself out of his chair. He'd have gladly idled away the rest of the afternoon chatting with Keira.

He ground his teeth together. All in all it was probably just as well they'd been interrupted.

'Hello?'

A cool, professional female voice asked to speak to Keira. Wordlessly, he held the phone out towards his house guest.

Keira immediately leapt to her feet, and sent him a puzzled glance before taking the receiver. 'Hello?'

Her frown cleared immediately when she realised who was on the other end, so Luke moved back to his chair and tried not to study her too closely, tried not to pay attention to her conversation.

'Oh, so soon?'

He had about as much chance of that as he did of getting the entire harvest in this afternoon. His gaze narrowed in on the way she worried at her bottom lip.

'No—no, of course not. If that's your professional opinion then I'll take your advice. You're the expert.' She swallowed. 'I'm glad there's so much interest.'

She didn't look glad.

'I just thought it would take a whole lot longer. This is... good news.'

Then why was she frowning?

'I'll pop in tomorrow. Yes—thanks, Julia.'

She replaced the receiver. She stood by the phone for a long moment, and then pasted on a smile that didn't quite reach her eyes. All his muscles tensed. 'Is everything okay?'

'That was my new estate agent. She said there's been a lot of interest in my great-aunt's house.'

Of course there had. It was a great house.

'She wants to take it to auction on the twenty-ninth of this month, while interest is running hot.'

He let out a low whistle.

'Is it okay if I stay here till then?'

'Not a problem at all. Stay until everything is settled.' He paused. 'It's moving very fast.'

She nodded.

'Are you sure you're ready for this?'

She lifted her chin. 'It's what I came here to do.'

And when it was done she would leave, and there would be no reason for her to ever return. He pressed his lips together and rose. 'I better get onto the chores.'

'Yes, of course.'

The scent of vanilla followed him all the way out to the barn.

CHAPTER ELEVEN

KEIRA woke early on Christmas morning. She tried to push her wakefulness away, and drag the mantle of sleep back over her, but as happened every Christmas morning the thrill of excitement threading through her made that impossible. As it had every Christmas morning for as long as she could remember.

Even those Christmases when she'd ached for her mother and grandmother.

Even this Christmas.

The light filtering beneath her curtains dimmed for a moment when she slid her hands over her stomach. She dragged in a breath, sat up, and threw back the covers. No moping today. Today was for Jason and Luke. She wanted them to experience just a little Christmas magic—to realise that they shouldn't shut themselves off from the joy the day had to offer.

Shouldn't shut themselves off from any of the joys the world had to offer.

She tiptoed through the house, careful not to wake anyone. She needn't have bothered. She found Luke and Jason at the kitchen table, eating fruitcake.

'Ooh, fruitcake for breakfast! Excellent idea. Merry Christmas, Luke. Merry Christmas, Jason.'

'Merry Christmas, Keira.' Luke leapt up to pour her a

coffee. He looked so fresh and bright and eager her heart expanded.

'Merry Christmas, Keira.' Jason cut her a slice of fruitcake, his grin wide and his eyes thrilling with the same excitement that rippled through her.

It took her precisely half a cup of coffee and two generous bites of fruitcake before she realised Jason and Luke had no idea how to proceed with the day. A wave of tenderness engulfed her. Across in the living room, early-morning sun poured in at the windows and the French doors, winking off tinsel and angel chains and Christmas lanterns. She nodded. 'It looks like fairyland in there.'

'I'm going to be vacuuming tinsel up for the next six months,' Luke grumbled.

But his eyes twinkled and Keira grinned at him. 'Every time you come across another piece you're going to remember what a marvellous Christmas you had,' she countered. 'C'mon.' She stood. 'I've never been able to show the least restraint on Christmas morning.'

She set a tray of mini-croissants into the oven, and then tripped into the living room. 'It has to be present-opening time!'

At different stages on the previous day, unseen by the others, each of them had tiptoed into the living room to put presents beneath the Christmas tree. It made it seem as if those presents had appeared by magic, even though she knew they hadn't. She clasped her hands beneath her chin. 'It almost looks too pretty to disturb.'

Jason groaned.

'That's what my mother would say every year,' she said with a laugh. 'And I'd always point out that she'd said *almost*... and that I harboured no such scruple.'

She settled on the carpet in front of the tree and rifled through the presents. 'Here—catch!' She tossed identical packages to Luke and Jason.

They stared at the presents in awe, and then glanced around as if figuring what they should do next. Keira shuffled along a bit, and with shrugs they settled themselves on the floor to form an arc around the Christmas tree with her.

Keira. Jason. Luke.

She tried not to notice how perfect that seemed.

A bark of laughter shot out of Luke when he tore his present open to discover the chunky three-pack of sports socks and the outrageously loud satin boxers encased within.

Jason sniggered. 'Going to model them?' Then promptly closed his mouth when he realised that his was an identical gift.

Luke leant over and placed a brightly wrapped present in front of her. She tore the package open with more speed than grace—vanilla-scented shower gel, body lotion and bath bombs! She clapped her hands and suspected her grin threatened to take over her entire face. 'You've got the hang of this, Hillier.'

'My turn!' Jason said.

His gift to her was a book of nonsense verse that made them all laugh. His gift to his father was a DVD box set of action movies, and an accompanying movie directory book.

'I've been wanting to see this movie for ages!' Luke selected one from the box and glanced at the television.

'Later,' Jason decreed, leaping up to put the Christmas CD on. When he opened his present from his father, though—the dragon game—he gazed longingly at his game console.

In unison, Keira and Luke said, 'Later!'

Keira knew Christmas wasn't about presents, but Luke and Jason hadn't had presents in three years. And to see the happiness that the presents they'd selected could bring to someone's face…and to be made to feel special by someone else's carefully selected presents…that was priceless.

As unobtrusively as she could, she retrieved the croissants and made a fresh pot of coffee, and brought the tray through to the living room. She set her other presents in front of Luke and Jason.

'Sweet!' Jason immediately immersed himself in the Manga comics she'd selected for him.

Luke's eyes darkened when he unwrapped his gift—a leather wallet with a snakeskin design. All she'd written on the tag was 'My Hero!'

When his eyes met hers she knew he remembered that day down by the river as vividly as she did. 'Merry Christmas, Luke.' Her voice came out husky, but she found she could do absolutely nothing about that.

He leant across and placed the last remaining present in her lap. 'Merry Christmas, Keira.'

She tore open the paper and laughed as she drew out a hot-pink sun hat, but nestled in its crown was a silk scarf in all the colours of the rainbow—orange bleeding into yellow and green, then violet and finally cobalt blue. 'I don't think I've ever owned anything so beautiful.'

She promptly settled the hat on her head, and wound the scarf around her throat. Jason pronounced it, 'fully sweet'.

Luke leant over to finger the delicate silk. 'It suits you.'

Her heart billowed and skipped.

They all stretched out—Jason on the floor, Luke in his armchair, her on the sofa—and munched croissants and drank coffee, becoming immersed in their books and comics. Occasionally one of them would read something out to the others.

Keira glanced surreptitiously around. This was perfect. It hit her then, with a clarity she could no longer ignore or deny—this was what she wanted. This was where she wanted to be for the rest of her life.

With one final glance at Luke, she closed her eyes and prayed again for a Christmas miracle.

* * *

Luke started when Keira leapt up with a squeak. 'It's time we got the turkey on!'

Jason scrambled to his feet. 'You said you'd show me what to do.'

'I will indeed.'

Luke pushed out of his chair more slowly, found a piece of gift paper to use as a bookmark in his movie directory book, amazed at how much he'd lost himself in the ease of the morning.

Keira and Jason's wide eyes and laughter during their exchange of gifts had told him that the whole Christmas thing was working. What he hadn't expected was that it would work its magic on him too.

Keira was right. There *was* a magic to Christmas. He moved towards the kitchen for potato-peeling duty, determined that she wouldn't be stuck with all the hard work. He couldn't remember the last time his shoulders had swung so loose and free.

'That's all there is to it?' Luke asked, stunned, when Keira set the turkey and vegetables in the oven.

She dusted off her hands. 'We put the sprouts on and make the gravy a little before we're ready to eat. And the turkey will need basting every now and again.'

'I'll do that,' Jason volunteered. 'You showed me what to do.'

She shrugged. 'So, yes, that's pretty much all there is to it.'

'I should be able to manage that on my own next year.'

At his words, he could have sworn her smile slipped, but it emerged with renewed vigour and he figured he must have imagined it. 'That's the plan.'

She wanted to set him up for all future Christmases—Christmases when she wouldn't be here. A rock lodged in his chest. Would he have the heart to celebrate Christmas next year?

He glanced at Jason and pulled his shoulders back. He'd celebrate next year if for no other reason than for his son. He would not let things slide so badly ever again. That was Keira's true gift to him.

If only he could give her something so precious.

His mind suddenly whirred and clicked. Maybe he could?

'C'mon, Jason. I'm dying to check out this game of yours.'

With a whoop, Jason shot into the living room. Keira stopped by Luke, touched his arm. 'Are you okay?'

He gestured towards Jason. 'Thank you. It's been a perfect day so far.'

'Yeah, it has.' She dimpled up at him, and all he could think about was kissing her. 'But the fun's not over yet. C'mon.'

He followed her, but kept at least three feet between them as they made their way back into the living room. It would be too dangerous to get caught under the mistletoe with her today. Christmas might contain a spark of magic, but it couldn't change the past. Nor could it change the future he'd set out before him.

Christmas dinner lived up to expectation. They all ate too much, and it all tasted so good that Luke wanted to keep eating—only he couldn't fit another morsel in.

After lunch Keira made them play charades and other party games. Luke lost every time. He'd find himself caught up in the way her hair bounced, fascinated by the mobility of her features.

He didn't enjoy himself any the less for that.

When the phone rang and no one else moved to answer it, Luke lumbered to his feet. He pressed the receiver to his ear. 'Hello?'

A tiny pause, then, 'Luke…hello.'

Brenda! Heaviness slammed into him. Guilt that he hadn't given Brenda and Alf a second thought so far today. Guilt that he was alive and healthy when Tammy was not. 'I…uh…I guess you'd like to speak to Jason. I'll get him for you.'

'Thank you. And Luke…?'

He paused in the act of gesturing to his son, and braced himself for something hard and crushing.

'Merry Christmas.'

He stared at the receiver. He couldn't have heard that correctly. He pressed it against his ear again. Swallowed. 'Merry Christmas to you and Alf too, Brenda.'

'Thank you.'

Without another word, he handed the phone to Jason. Dazed, he moved back to his chair.

Keira touched his knee. 'Is everything okay?'

'Brenda…she just wished me a merry Christmas.' He still couldn't believe he'd heard that right.

Keira's smile when it came wasn't one of those big ones that could dazzle and unbalance a man. It was both softer and deeper, and more devastating, than that. 'A Christmas miracle,' she whispered.

He didn't believe in miracles, but…

'Dad?' Luke turned to find Jason holding the phone against his chest. 'Is it okay if I spend tonight with Gran and Grandad?'

Luke nodded, and waited for Jason to call him back to the phone so Brenda could retract her merry Christmas.

Jason spoke a few more words into the phone, and then settled it back into its cradle before flopping onto the sofa. 'It's all good. They're going to collect me later this afternoon.'

'Sorted?' Keira asked.

'Sorted,' Jason said. 'Gran almost sounded like her old self again.'

Luke blinked. A Christmas miracle?

'This has been the sweetest Christmas ever.'

Luke couldn't argue with that.

Jason's grandparents collected him at four p.m. They didn't come in, but they waved from the car. Luke hugged his son, ordered him to have a good time, and waved back.

The car drove away and Luke dragged in a breath and braced his shoulders. There was only one more thing he wanted to accomplish today...

'Tired?' he asked Keira when he returned. She was curled up on the sofa, her head propped up on one hand. She'd remained inside while he said farewell to Jason. Diplomacy, he suspected. She hadn't wanted to remind Brenda and Alf of Tammy.

Not that he and Keira had that kind of relationship. He rolled his shoulders. They did have a friendship, though.

'Pleasantly so,' she said.

'Are you up to sharing a bottle of wine on the veranda? I have a bottle of Pinot Gris here that should be as smooth and mellow as anything you've ever tasted.'

'Ooh, yes, please!' She swung around to stare at him. 'That sounds *divine*.'

He grabbed the bottle and two wine glasses and led the way out to the veranda and around to the bench at the side. This spot was one of his favourite places in the world.

Keira leant against the veranda railing. 'You were right, you know, Luke. This view really is wonderful. It'd be worth quite a bit of inconvenience for the privilege of waking up to it every day.'

'So you're not sorry fate sent you here to Candlebark?'

She settled herself on the bench. The scent of vanilla rose up around him, mingling with the bouquet of the wine. She took the glass he handed her. He was careful their fingers didn't touch.

'I'm not the least sorry that I landed at Candlebark. Meeting you and Jason—that's been quite an adventure.'

'Have you had a nice day today?'

'Yes…and I didn't really expect to. I just wanted to try to make it nice for you and Jason, but…well, somehow I got swept up in it too.'

'That makes the two of us.'

He stared at her for a long moment, prayed that what he was about to do was the right thing. His gut told him it was.

She touched a hand to her face. 'What?'

He shook himself. Made himself stare out at the golden expanse of wheat. 'You've given me a lot of good advice over these last two weeks, Keira—about Jason, about myself, about Christmas. It appears you were even right about Brenda and Alf. I can't begin to thank you.'

She half-grimaced, half-grinned. 'Considering most of that advice was unsolicited, Luke, I don't think you need to thank me.'

He stared at her steadily for another long moment. 'I want to offer some unsolicited advice in return.'

Luke's eyes were gentle, and that particular shade of rich golden-brown that could make her mouth water. She swallowed. He stared at her as if he cared about her.

Of course he cares about you. As a friend.

She drew her bottom lip into her mouth. His eyes fastened on that action, darkened. Her blood quickened. Her heart skipped. Was it possible that she could get her Christmas miracle after all?

'Advice?' she whispered. She couldn't do anything about the huskiness that had invaded her voice, or the yearning that invaded her soul.

'I think you should continue to pursue your IVF treatment.'

She settled her wine glass on the floorboards at her feet, turned to stare out at all that golden wheat, rippling like a promise across the landscape, and waited for the darkness, the emptiness, to claim her.

A heavy sadness pressed against her heart, and tiredness made her want to rest her head against the wall behind, but the darkness didn't settle over her to block out the sun or the glory of the view or the presence of the man sitting next her.

She blinked and risked a deep breath. The darkness remained at bay.

And then a new thought banished her tiredness. 'It seems to matter to you.'

'Of course it matters!' He stared at her as if she'd gone mad. 'This is important.' He reached out and took her hand. 'You helped me rediscover the joys of fatherhood. And believe me, it *is* a joy. I want that for you. I want you to experience that blessing. You deserve it.'

Because he cared about her?

'You'll make a great mum, Keira.'

She left her hand in his because it felt so right. 'Luke, in the last fortnight I've learned a lot about myself. You showed me how counterproductive it's been to try and follow in my mother and grandmother's footsteps, that I've perhaps mistaken strength for necessity, and for putting a good and brave face on a less than ideal situation. I've finally acknowledged to myself something I've always been too scared to admit before.'

He leaned towards her, eyes intent.

She wanted to take his face in her hands and kiss him. She resisted the impulse. There was too much to say first. 'I don't want to be a single parent. I don't want to have to do it all on my own. If I had another miscarriage…' She shook her head. 'I don't know how I would get through that.'

He opened his mouth, but she shook her head again and held up her free hand. 'I know you're going to say my friends would help me through it, and of course they would. But it's not the same as having someone by my side who'd hoped for the baby and loved it as much as I did.'

Luke stared out at the view, but Keira wasn't sure how much of it he saw. Those grooves bit deep either side of his mouth. Grief for her and her baby? The thought made her throat thicken.

'Yes, I want a baby…babies if at all possible. But not at the expense of everything else. I have to decide if I really am prepared to do it on my own, or whether to take my chances and wait. That's not a decision I can come to in a couple of days.'

He turned and nodded.

She smiled, desperately wanting him to smile back. 'I appreciate your concern, though.'

She squeezed his hand and prayed as hard as she could for her Christmas miracle. Luke's eyes had gone gentle again, but…

But nothing. He didn't lean forward to kiss her. He didn't open his mouth to tell her he cared for her, that he wanted to keep seeing her or…anything.

A faint heart never won a fat duck.

She blinked as those words sounded through her mind. It had been one of her grandmother's favourite sayings.

It hit her then. True strength lay in going after what she wanted rather than hoping it would come to her in some magical way…waiting and hoping because she was too scared to reach out and take it for herself, too scared to open herself up and be vulnerable.

She moistened her lips and swallowed. Did she dare?

Her heart pounded so loud she could hardly believe Luke couldn't hear it. 'Luke, if I wasn't leaving next week I wouldn't mention this now, but…'

'But?'

She straightened and met his gaze head-on. 'I…Luke, I love you.'

His head snapped back. She didn't know what that meant or how to read it. She swallowed and refused to allow herself the luxury of a retreat. Her grandmother had been right. *A faint heart never won a fat duck.* 'I didn't plan on this happening—not in a million years—but I think you care about me a little... and I was wondering if perhaps we might be able to keep seeing each other and see where it might all lead to?'

Her words faltered to a halt. He'd reefed his hand from hers and she knew precisely how to read that. She gripped her hands together to stop their shaking, but there was nothing she could do to prevent her heart from shattering.

Luke jerked to his feet, banging his hip hard against the arm of the bench in his haste to move away from her and all her glorious sweetness and warmth. He set his wine glass down, wiped away the wetness that had spilled across his hand.

She was handing him everything he'd ever wanted. No—more than that. Because she was more than he could ever have imagined. But he couldn't accept it.

What he felt for Keira—it wouldn't last. He had a false heart. If he hadn't been able to give Tammy what she'd needed—the woman who'd meant most to him in the world—then he couldn't be trusted with a woman's heart at all. End of story. He would break it—break her.

His chest constricted so painfully he couldn't breathe. He couldn't do that to Keira!

As she stared at him, tears caught on the ends of her eyelashes and hung there like stars. The stars spilled from her lashes and trailed down her cheeks to the corners of her mouth. He wanted to reach out and catch them before they were gone for ever. But he could only do that if he gave her what she asked for.

Air rushed back into his lungs. He clenched his hands together to keep them at his sides. 'I'm sorry, Keira. I can't give you what you want or what you need.' No matter how much he wanted to. All he could give her was potential heartache and disappointment.

Keira dashed her tears away, folded her arms and hitched up her chin. 'Why not? I know you care about me.'

Yeah, he did. But how would she cope when he let her down the way he'd let Tammy down? He couldn't risk it.

Her chin wobbled. 'Why won't you take a risk on us?'

He didn't want to talk about this, but she'd laid her heart on the line with total honesty. If she saw him for what he really was…

Sourness filled his mouth. Her happiness mattered more than what she thought of him. 'Keira, my first marriage was hell. I didn't love Tammy.'

She didn't back away. Her eyes didn't widen in horror.

'No marriage can be happy with that knowledge pulsing in the silences.' At eighteen, he'd had a crush on Tammy. When she'd fallen pregnant he'd done the right thing and married her. But then Tammy had discovered the truth—the fickleness of his feelings. He hadn't even been able to pretend. People stayed together for their children's sakes, but he hadn't even been able to manage that much.

'Tammy knew?'

'Not at first.' He forced himself to say the words out loud. 'But when she found out it broke her heart.'

'Oh, Luke.' Her eyes turned dove-grey. 'So that's where all this guilt comes from. This is why you punish yourself.'

She knew how badly he'd failed Tammy, and yet she was still standing here. Didn't she know—?

'You told me you never cheated on Tammy, or made her feel guilty for falling pregnant, and that you weren't cruel to her.' She took a step towards him. 'You can't keep punishing yourself like this.'

He dropped back to the bench, head in his hands, and tried to beat back the darkness. She perched beside him. She didn't touch him, but the scent of vanilla drifted around him, torturing him with its sweetness.

'You don't get it. I told her I loved her. I thought I did.' If only he could relive that day, spare her. 'And we…' He lifted his head. 'I was her first and…'

'And then Jason happened?'

He nodded heavily. 'She gave up all her dreams to have him.'

'No, she didn't. You took her to the city, didn't you?'

He dragged a hand down his face. 'That didn't make up for lying to her!'

'You didn't know it was a lie at the time.'

He straightened. The pain pierced his very core. 'You didn't see her face when she demanded to know the truth—did I love her or not?' Tammy had known him so well. His hands clenched. 'It was like…the lights went out.'

Keira's eyes filled with tears. For his dead wife? 'I'm sorry,' she whispered. 'You didn't mean to hurt her.'

'Do you think that's any consolation?' The words broke from him, harsh and loud. 'I loved my home more than the woman I married. I chose *this*—' he flung an arm out '—over her. What kind of man does that make me?'

'Oh, Luke.'

No! He didn't want her sympathy. He didn't deserve it. The vision of Tammy's stricken face, her tear-swollen eyes, filled his mind. Her mute pain. Her guilt. *Her guilt!*

He gave a harsh laugh, leapt to his feet. He'd betrayed her—his best friend. He'd have laid his life down for her in an instant, but he hadn't been able to do the one thing that would have made a difference—love her the way she'd loved him.

And then she'd died and…and the despair…

And the release.

He hated himself for it.

'I don't deserve a second chance, Keira. I'm sorry, but I

can't be what you want me to be. I might love you now, but in the end I'll do to you what I did to Tammy.'

'You can't know that!'

He remained silent. There was nothing left to say.

'And the fact that I love you and that you care about me—that doesn't make any difference?'

The panic that raced across her face snagged at his heart. He couldn't let it make a difference. 'I can't be trusted.' He had to protect her.

She shot to her feet, stabbed a finger at him. 'You think you know what's best for everyone, but you're wrong!' Her finger shook. 'You'll sacrifice your happiness and mine to that belief because you're an emotional coward who doesn't have the gumption to take a risk!' She flung an arm out, swung away only to swing back again. 'How *dare* you preach to me about going after my dream of motherhood when you refuse to even dream at all?'

She dragged in a breath, and he could almost see her count to three. She took a step away from him. 'It's been a big day. I'm tired. I'm going to take a nap. There are a lot of leftovers. I propose that if we get hungry later we just make ourselves up a plate.'

With that, she turned and left. Luke realised she'd just become the lodger he'd so desperately wanted two weeks ago. And now—now all he wanted was the warm, vibrant woman that was Keira.

CHAPTER TWELVE

LUKE paced the edge of the crowd, astounded at the number of people who had shown up for the auction. Keira's estate agent had drummed up an enormous amount of interest in record time.

He wished he could feel more impressed about that.

He glanced at Keira's great-aunt's house—Keira's house—and a rock settled in his chest. She should have had the chance to live and work there, to have her baby and run her physiotherapy clinic and be surrounded by a community who would have embraced her.

His fists clenched. It should have all been hers!

It still could be.

He pushed that insidious thought away. He couldn't give her what she needed.

And he wasn't an emotional coward. He was trying to protect her!

He glanced at the house again and the rock grew. He glanced over at Keira, who was talking to the estate agent, and the rock developed jagged edges. He'd wanted to bring her to the auction today, but she'd refused to let him. She'd packed up her car, intent on returning to Sydney as soon as the auction was over. He should be out in that boundary paddock of his, demolishing weeds.

He hadn't been able to stay away.

Her red-gold hair gleamed in the sunshine. Darn it, she

wasn't wearing a hat. If she weren't careful she'd burn to a crisp.

You'll sacrifice your happiness and mine.

His happiness didn't matter, and he wasn't sacrificing hers. She'd find someone new, someone worthy of her love, and—

His thought processes stumbled to a halt. He rewound his previous thought, went back over it carefully to test its truth, its validity. Did he seriously mean that—that her happiness was more important than his?

His mouth went dry. If his happiness didn't matter... then...

His head reared back. What a blind fool he'd been! His feelings for Keira were so far beyond what he'd ever felt for any other woman as to be laughable. He'd do anything to give her what she wanted, what she needed. He'd make any sacrifice...

Including Candlebark.

He swore—low and swift—as he tried to counter the panic racing through him. Had he left it too late? Through the crowd he identified the grey hair and sloping shoulders of his bank manager. Without further ado he shouldered his way through the crowd towards him.

'I mean to bid and I mean to win,' he said without preamble. 'Will you stake me a bridging loan until I can sell Candlebark?'

The bank manager was clearly stunned. 'Are you sure?'

'Yes.'

Luke held out his hand. The other man shook it. 'Done.'

Once the bidding on Great-Aunt Ada's house had started, Keira couldn't look at the crowd. She didn't have the heart for it.

She knew Luke was in that crowd somewhere. She'd sensed

him there earlier, before the auction had started. She hadn't needed to turn around to confirm it, but she had anyway.

He'd stood tall and grim on the outskirts of the crowd, his lips tight and those grooves biting deep into the flesh on either side of his mouth. She'd swung away again, before he caught her staring.

What was he doing here?

Her lips twisted. Maybe he wanted to make sure she really did leave town, and that she no longer meant to trespass on his hospitality?

He need have no worries on that score. She'd made enough of a fool of herself over him already. She was in no hurry to repeat the performance. A girl had to have some pride. She'd be driving away from here some time in the next hour and she would *never* return.

But the thought shrivelled her heart up as hard and tight as a walnut.

Pride be damned! She'd beg him to give their love a chance if she thought it would make a difference.

Only it wouldn't.

All she could do now was studiously avert her gaze from the crowd—from Luke—and try with all her might to stop from falling apart in public. Problem was, that only left her one place to look—at Great-Aunt Ada's lovely colonial-style cottage. A reminder of the dreams that had taken seed there burned and prickled through her. As did the guilt that she was selling off part of her heritage.

She clenched her hands together and did her best to block the rapid-fire bidding from her ears. She didn't have any other options. She couldn't stay in Gunnedah. Living in the same town as the man she'd fallen in love with was not a sure-fire method of getting over him, of that she was certain. And she wasn't a masochist.

'Excellent,' Julia murmured in Keira's ear, tapping her

clipboard. 'We've reached the reserve price. Your house is now officially on the market. It will be sold today.'

Keira's eyes burned. She gripped her hands tighter.

'I don't know what's got into Luke Hillier, though,' Julia continued. 'He's bidding like a man possessed.'

The iron-bar rigidity left her body on one big out breath.

'What?' She spun around.

To discover Julia was in earnest.

Luke was bidding on her house!

What on earth…?

'Will you excuse me for a moment?'

Not waiting for Julia's reply, Keira threaded her way through the sea of bodies to where Luke stood. 'What on earth do you think you're doing?' she ground out as quietly as she could. She wanted to scream!

'Buying your house.' He spoke just as low, and then raised his hand to indicate another bid.

She grabbed it and hauled it back down. 'But… But…you can't afford it.'

'Yes, he can,' said the man standing beside Luke.

He handed her a business card. Luke's bank manager? But… Her brain wouldn't work.

One thing she did know. 'I am *not* selling my house to you,' she hissed.

'Listen here—' the bank manager pitched his voice low '—Luke's money is as good as anyone else's, missy.'

Keira gave up all pretence at discretion. 'What did you just call me? Missy? *Missy!* What kind of Neanderthal—?'

'Uh, Keira…'

Luke touched her arm. She glanced up to find everyone had turned to stare. Anger that she wanted Luke to not only keep touching her but to haul her into his arms overrode her embarrassment.

She focused on the anger, not the despair. 'Why on earth would *you* want to buy *my* house?'

She suspected she might well die a thousand deaths over making such a public display when she went back over this scene later. In fact, this was proof positive that she wasn't quite over making a fool of herself where this man was concerned after all, wasn't it?

Her chin shot up. What did it matter? She'd be leaving here in an hour, and these people would never see her again. What did it matter what they thought of her?

'How on earth can you afford it?' she demanded. 'Not by renting out that Spartan room of yours—of that I'm certain!'

He shuffled his feet and glanced around. Keira did too. The auction proceedings had ground to a categorical standstill. She gritted her teeth and reminded herself that she didn't care what these people thought of her.

Amazingly, when Luke's gaze returned to her, his lips twitched. 'I'm guessing you're not going to wait till the auction is over for an explanation?'

She shook her head. 'Not a chance.'

'I can afford to buy your house if I sell Candlebark. It's that's simple.'

She gaped at him. He couldn't sell his home. He loved it! It was a part of him. Why would he even *consider* such a thing?

He continued to survey her with that curious half-smile and her mouth went dry. 'Why would you do that?' she croaked.

'Because I was wrong.'

Her heart stuttered and threatened to take flight. She tried to rein it in. She planted her hands on her hips. 'About which bit, precisely?'

He didn't hesitate. 'The bit about not being able to give you what you needed.' His chin jutted out. He planted his feet. 'I know I've been blind...an idiot...but just give me a chance to prove myself to you, Keira, and I will.'

She had no hope of restraining the wild hope that gripped her.

'I know you dreamed of raising children here in your great-aunt's house, of establishing your physiotherapy practice and being part of a community. You deserve to have all those things, and they can still be yours. I *can* be the husband you need. I *can* be the father of your children.' He hauled in a breath. 'If that's what you still want, that is. If I haven't left it too late.'

He was prepared to sell his farm to give her what he thought she most wanted in life? Her throat grew so thick she couldn't so much as utter one word.

'What you want and what you need are more important than where I live or what kind of job I have or…or anything. I want to spend my life with you—whether that's here in your aunt's house or in the city. Keira—' he reached out and gripped her hands '—I love you.'

She couldn't help it. Her heart burst free with all its hope and joy. She threw herself at him and wound her arms around his neck. All around them cheers and applause broke out. 'You idiot,' she whispered, resting her forehead against his. 'I don't need you to sell Candlebark to prove that to me.'

'Sweetheart, after everything I've put you through I can't expect you to take me on trust.'

She drew back to gaze into his face. 'Why not?'

His eyes widened.

She threw her head back and laughed for the sheer joy of it. 'Luke, wherever you are, that's my home. All the other bits don't matter. Please don't sell Candlebark. I would love to raise our children there. My great-aunt's house will make the perfect clinic—just like we said.'

'Are you sure?' He cupped her face in his hands. 'I want you to know that I would give it up in an instant for you.'

She knew he meant it. And she knew what he was trying to tell her. She wondered if it were possible to melt from sheer happiness. 'I'm positive, Luke. Now…' She cocked what she hoped was a cheeky eyebrow, but her heart pounded in her chest so loudly everyone within a two-metre radius must hear it. 'You said something about being the husband that I needed. Was that a proposal of marriage?'

His eyes darkened. 'Yes, it was. But it was a darn clumsy one.'

He went down on one knee in front of what felt like the whole town. Heat surged into her cheeks, but whether from embarrassment or happiness she couldn't tell. 'Keira, will you do me the very great honour of making me the happiest man on the planet and becoming my wife?'

'Yes,' she said simply, pulling him back to his feet. 'Now, kiss me.'

And he did.

Then it seemed everyone was crowding around them to shake Luke's hand and to kiss her cheek and to offer congratulations.

Julia bustled up. 'Do I take it that the house is off the market?'

'Oh, yes!' Keira seized the other woman's arm. 'Julia, I'm so sorry. I've put you to an awful lot of trouble for no reason.'

'Not at all,' the agent said with a laugh, patting Keira's hand. 'I wouldn't have missed this for the world. Congratulations to both of you. I don't doubt that once word gets out our next auction will be packed to the rafters.'

'I do hope so!'

Before she could say anything more Jason came racing up, his grin wide. With a whoop, he picked Keira up and swung her around. 'That was fully sweet, Dad!' He put her down to clap his father on the shoulder.

That was when Keira saw Brenda, standing on the fringes of the crowd. She hesitated for a moment, before moving towards the older woman and taking her hand. 'That must've been terribly difficult for you to witness.'

Brenda squeezed her hand. 'It wasn't as bad as I thought it would be.'

Keira led her across the road to a park bench. 'Are you okay?'

Brenda sat. 'I think so.'

Keira sat too. She stared at the sky, at the house opposite, at the crowd. 'I don't know if this is common knowledge yet or not. I don't know how quickly news spreads in a country town…but a couple of weeks ago I had a miscarriage.' She paused. Stared at the sky again. 'I wanted that baby so much… and then I had the miscarriage…'

She let the words trail off. She knew Brenda would understand. 'But I never held my child in my arms. I never waved her off on her first day of school, waited in the emergency room while she had a broken arm set, watched her grow up and blossom into a woman with a child of her own. I can't begin to know how terrible and difficult your grief must be, Brenda.'

'And yet,' Brenda said slowly, 'we had our Tammy to love for thirty years.' She stared down at her hands. 'Jason was right. I've let my bitterness twist me. I wanted to blame someone and I fixed on poor Luke. I know what happened wasn't his fault.' She lifted her head and met Keira's gaze. 'The thing is, while I've missed Tammy more than I can say, I've missed Luke too. He and Tammy were thick as thieves when they were growing up. He spent as much time at our place as he did at his own. He was always like a son to me.'

Keira swallowed and moistened her lips. 'So…you wish him well?'

'I hope the two of you will be very happy, Keira.'

Keira's heart soared. 'And will you and Alf come to our wedding?'

'We'd be delighted to.'

'And dinner next week?'

'That would be lovely.'

Both women stood as Luke made his way across to them. Brenda reached up and kissed Luke's cheek. 'Congratulations, Luke.'

'Thank you.'

'Now I must be off, to tell Alfred the news.'

'I'll call you,' Keira said.

'You do that, dear.'

Luke's jaw dropped. Keira reached up and tapped it closed. He swung to her. 'I swear, woman, you're a witch!'

She shrugged. 'I didn't do anything.'

One corner of his mouth hooked up. 'How can you say that when you've waltzed into town and turned my life upside down?' He collapsed onto the bench and then reached out to seize her around her waist and drag her down into his lap. 'How can you say that when you've bewitched me body and soul until I can think of nothing but you?'

'Oh, Luke.' She laid her hand against his cheek. 'Are you happy? Really? Is this really what you want?'

'With my whole heart,' he vowed. 'What I feel for you, Keira, is a man's love. It's deep and true…' his eyes darkened '…and unchangeable. What I felt for Tammy was a boy's crush mixed up with friendship. It's taken me a long time to realise the difference. I couldn't stand the thought of hurting you the way I'd hurt her.'

He stared out to the front, his mouth tight for a moment. 'It wasn't until the auction was about to start that I realised I'd give up everything—including Candlebark—if only you could have what you wanted. When I realised I'd choose you over my home, my livelihood, my way of life. That's when I knew what I felt for you was something different—something I'd never experienced before. And I hoped I hadn't left it too late to tell you that.'

Keira stared at him in awe for a moment. Then she smiled.

'You didn't leave it too late, Luke. You timed it perfectly. I got my Christmas miracle after all.'

He traced her cheek with one long, tanned finger. '*You* are my Christmas miracle, Keira.'

Her heart swelled so big she could hardly breathe. 'I love you, Luke.'

'And I love you. I mean to spend a lifetime showing you just how much.'

She cocked that cheeky eyebrow again. 'You could always start right now, by kissing me.'

His grin when it came was low and sexy. 'What an excellent idea.'

THE NURSE WHO
SAVED CHRISTMAS

BY
JANICE LYNN

Janice Lynn has a Masters in Nursing from Vanderbilt University, and works as a nurse practitioner in a family practice. She lives in the southern United States with her husband, their four children, their Jack Russell—appropriately named Trouble—and a lot of unnamed dust bunnies that have moved in since she started her writing career. To find out more about Janice and her writing, visit www.janicelynn.com.

To my children, who bring Christmas alive
and are life's greatest gifts. I love you.

CHAPTER ONE

NURSE ABBY ARNOLD hid her smile behind her hand as Santa Claus grimaced at the squirming kid sitting in his lap at the children's advocacy Christmas community outreach in downtown Philadelphia.

"Smile for the picture," she said sweetly, standing a few feet from the elaborate thronelike chair and Christmas tree being used for "Pictures with Santa."

Santa Claus's deep blue eyes narrowed behind his gold-rimmed glasses, but his lips curved in a smile hopefully only she could tell was forced.

How had she talked Dr. Dirk Kelley into helping when the Santa she'd arranged for the event canceled at the last minute, leaving her desperate for a replacement? So desperate she'd asked a man she'd treated as if they were just friendly colleagues for the past two months and not more, all the while walking on eggshells at the sharp undercurrents between them.

"Ho, ho, ho, what do you want for Christmas this year, little boy?" Santa asked, sounding more like the Abominable Snowman than a jolly old man full of Christmas spirit.

Despite her awkward physical awareness of the man beneath the suit, it was all Abby could do not to snort. Did Dirk really believe that voice sounded Santa-ish? Hadn't he sat on Santa's knee as a kid? Watched Christmas television shows about jolly Saint Nick? Anything that would clue him in that Christmas was the most magical time of the year and that for these kids he was part of that magic? Something they'd always remember?

For all she knew, he hadn't.

Although they'd started out with a bang the night they'd first worked together, she really didn't know much about the handsome doctor who'd knocked her socks off from the moment she'd met him.

She knew very little about him or his past. Although, thanks to *that* morning, she spent way too much of her present thinking about him and how much she'd like to feature in his future.

The kid on Dirk's lap, around five, wiped the back of his pudgy hand across his runny nose. "An Xbox, and a cellphone, and a digital voice enhancer, and a…"

The list went on. And on. Even Abby's eyes widened at some of the items the kid listed. What had happened to a baseball glove or a bicycle?

Santa's bushy white brow rose as he regarded the kid. "Have you been that good this year?"

Another wipe of the face, then a nod. "I have. Extra-good."

"I'll see what I can do." At the mother's frantic look, Santa diplomatically added, "But Santa's on a budget. To be fair to the other good little boys and girls, I'll have to prioritize and just bring one or two of your list items."

The mother heaved a relieved sigh.

Santa set the boy off his lap but, rather than walk

away, the kid wrapped his arms around Dirk's neck and planted a noisy kiss on a high cheekbone Abby had doctored earlier with rosy rouge. "I love you, Santa."

Abby's insides melted. How sweet! This was why she'd volunteered to organize this event. Why she volunteered with so many Christmas events. To help bring holiday magic alive for others.

Only Dirk looked more like he was being cooked alive than feeling the magic.

"I...uh..." His eyes cut to her with a distressed plea for rescue. He didn't have to say anything aloud. Abby got the message loud and clear.

Not in a million years could she deny him. Not when his gaze held hers and she had a resurgence of the connection she'd instantaneously felt with him, had a resurgence of the connection they'd shared *that* morning. One so real, so tangible, she'd felt in sync with him, had comforted and been comforted.

No, she couldn't deny Dirk much of anything within her power to give. Obviously. Besides, she was good at helping others, giving to others. It's what she did. What she'd always done. What was expected of her by all who knew her, especially this time of year.

Wondering at Dirk's evident rising unease, she put her hand on the boy's back and gave him a gentle pat. "Santa loves you, too. Don't forget to keep being extra-good between now and Christmas. He'll be watching."

At the last, the kid shot a wary glance toward Santa, his face contorting in shock. "Even when I'm in the bathtub?"

"No, not then. Just when you're being good or bad." Sending an apologetic smile, the boy's mother took his hand and led him away. Several times he glanced over his shoulder, waving goodbye.

Standing to tower above her five feet, six inches, Dirk bent to whisper in her ear. "Santa needs a break. Stat."

His rush of warm breath tickling her ear filled her with Christmas magic, from her head to the tippy-tips of her toes. This so wasn't the place to be getting hot and bothered by Dirk and his overabundant male magnetism.

In a Santa costume, for goodness' sake.

How could she possibly be turned on by a man dressed in her deceased father's treasured Santa suit? Although she loved Christmas, she wasn't prone to Christmas fetishes. Then again, it wasn't the suit but the man inside it lighting up her world like the most overdecorated house in the neighborhood.

He was playing Santa as a favor to her—she had no choice but to get her feelings under control and not attack the man's lips with hers in front of all these children.

She gave a calm nod and told the waiting crowd, "Sorry, kids, but Santa needs to check in with his elves to make sure all the toys are being made just right." She smiled brilliantly at the children and their parents. "We'll be back in ten minutes."

As expected, moans and groans greeted them from the families in the long line. Despite Dirk's obvious need for a reprieve, she sensed his hesitation, liked him all the more for it. Still, he'd said he needed a break and she'd seen in his eyes that he really did.

"Come on, Santa." Smiling brightly, Abby looped her arm in a red-velvet-covered one and spoke loudly.

"Follow me, and I'll take you to where you can use your special Santa phone to call the North Pole and put in the requests for presents you've heard so far. There's only two more weeks until Christmas, so they need to get started filling the orders right away."

Gratitude shining in his eyes, Dirk nodded, pasted on a fake smile, and waved at the crowd.

"I can't believe I let you talk me into this," he mumbled under his breath while allowing her to lead him away from the masses gathered at the community center just to meet him. "This is madness. Pure commercialized madness."

She still couldn't believe he'd said yes, either. Sure, he was the one man capable of delivering her Christmas wish, but long and lean Dr. Dirk Kelley playing the role of Santa to dozens of children was another matter altogether. They'd worked together long enough for her to realize kids made him uncomfortable, that he was quiet and kept to himself. Her friend and fellow nurse Danielle called him Dr. Dreamboat. Abby called him what she most wanted for Christmas, but had never said the words out loud, not even to her tabby cat, Mistletoe.

Regardless, Dirk was doing her a huge favor and she was grateful. Smiling, she quirked a brow in his direction. "Ah, Santa, where's your Christmas spirit?"

He snorted. "I lost it somewhere between demands for a new computer and the kid who wanted a Mercedes-Benz." He shook his red and white hat and white wig topped head in dismay. "What happened to kids wanting Tinkertoys and tricycles?"

Although he pretty much echoed her earlier thoughts, Abby just shrugged. "Now, Santa, stay with the times.

It's high tech and electronics these days. You'll have to get your elves with the program."

"Apparently," he said wryly. The moment they stepped out of the main walkway of the community center and into the privacy of the employee break room where they'd left their things earlier, his broad shoulders sagged. "I'm not sure I'm going to last another hour. Christmas just isn't my thing, Abs."

"Bah, humbug, Mr. Scrooge." While trying to decide if he was serious about the Christmas comment, she gave an internal sigh at his use of his pet name for her. Did he have any idea how that sent shivers through her? That every time she heard it she was instantly taken back to being in his arms, to the first time he'd whispered the name when they'd been tangled together beneath her bedsheets? "Surely you can make it another hour." She sighed theatrically. "Guess men of endurance are a thing of the past, too."

"Don't you believe it," he warned, grinning for real for the first time in over an hour, his eyes taking on a dangerous gleam despite his costume and obvious dislike of his role. "My endurance is just fine. Better than fine."

She raked her gaze over his red fur-covered body. The padding beneath the suit didn't begin to hide the wide shoulders and abundant male charisma. Not really. Abby had caught more than one mom in line eyeing Santa as if they'd like to sit on his knee and ask for him in their Christmas stockings… If they knew Santa was none other than scrumptious Dr. Dirk Kelley, Santa would have had to beat the women off with a giant candy cane.

Besides, thanks to the particularly rough night they'd first worked together, Abby did know all about Dirk's endurance. If only she could forget what amazing stamina the man wielded at the tips of those magical fingers. What stamina the rest of him had delivered. Twice.

Dirk Kelley didn't need a sleigh and flying reindeer to take a woman to soaring heights.

Maybe somebody should thwack *her* with a giant candy cane for even letting memories of *that* morning creep into her thoughts. Hadn't they agreed they'd made a mistake? Memories like those could only cause her to want to sit on Santa's lap and tell him what she'd like to find under her tree on Christmas morning.

And that was a family.

Kids anxiously waiting to rip into brightly colored packages.

Aunts, uncles, cousins, parents and grandparents to fuss and carry on about everything from setting the table for Christmas morning breakfast to who was the most surprised by their gift.

A man to share her life with, to love her, and surprise her with something special just for her. Not necessarily something expensive, just something with meaning, something from his heart.

Like the beloved Christmas village pieces her father used to give to her mother before they'd been killed in a house fire when Abby had been seven. She wanted to experience what her parents had shared, to open a package and glance up with excitement, not at the physical gift but with the love with which it had been chosen. She wanted to see that love reflected back at her in the glow of twinkling Christmas morning lights.

But on top of all that, she wanted Dirk.

Abby sighed.

Other than her very busy volunteer schedule and long work hours, Abby led a lonely life. Oh, she had friends, lots of friends, amazing friends like Danielle, but she didn't have someone to come home to, someone to whom she was the most important person in their life, someone to love and be loved by. Only her tabby cat Mistletoe cared whether or not she came home in the mornings after working the emergency department night shift.

Oblivious to her onset of melancholy, Dirk adjusted his belly padding, scratched at his glued-on beard. "I'll never complain about a monkey suit again. After this getup, wearing a tuxedo will feel like a real treat."

Pulling herself from her unwanted self-pitying thoughts and trying not to think about how handsome Dirk would look in a tux, *out of a tux*, Abby focused on the here and now. She had a great life, a great job and great friends. She was a needed, productive member of society. At the moment she was needed to give downtown Philadelphia children a magical visit with Santa.

Abby wasn't the kind of woman to disappoint. Not when she had any say in the matter and never when it came to children and Christmas.

"Better let me adjust your beard there, Santa." She tugged on Dirk's fake white beard, soothing down the coarse lifelike hair he'd ruffled with his scratching.

Just touching him prickled her skin with goose bumps.

Glancing everywhere but at her, he fanned his face. "Man, this thing is hot."

He was what was hot. Hot as a roaring fire she'd like to warm herself next to. Oh, my! Abby turned away before she had to fan her face, too.

"You think that's why Santa's cheeks stay red?" She reached into the break room's refrigerator and pulled out a cold bottle of water.

"I thought it was from kissing all the mommies under the mistletoe," he surprised her by saying.

Abby blinked at him, at how the corners of his mouth hitched upward ever so slightly. Was he flirting with her?

Laughing a bit nervously, she handed him the water. "Well, there is that."

Twisting off the top and taking a long swig, Dirk sagged into a chair, his blue gaze lifting to hers. "Tell me I don't really have to go back out there."

"You don't have to, but you will, anyway."

He would, too. In the short time since he'd arrived in Philadelphia, just a couple of weeks prior to Halloween, Dirk had proved himself the type of man who didn't shirk a commitment. Even one he so obviously regretted having made. Why had he? Guilt at what had happened between them? At his hasty retreat into "This never should have happened" immediately afterward? She'd hid her hurt. She knew she had. And she'd told herself she should be relieved—workplace romances never seemed to end well.

"You're right." Even for a guy dressed like Santa Claus his sigh was a bit too melodramatic. "I will, but you owe me, Abs. Big-time. Any time. Any place. Any thing. You owe me. Take note."

Despite how her heart tattooed a funky beat at his

unexpected words, wondering if maybe that morning haunted him, too, Abby placed her hands on her hips. Or maybe it was because of his words she felt the need to stand her ground. "I think 'any' is a bit too general."

"Nope." He shook his Santafied head. "Any it is."

She sighed. How bad could owing him be? They'd both agreed falling into bed together had been a mistake, the result of a particularly bad night in the E.R. where three people had died due to trauma received in a multicar accident. Although they'd done everything medically possible, the internal injuries had been too extensive. An elderly man had suffered a heart attack and hit another car head-on. He'd died instantly, but a two-year-old girl and her mother had been alive, barely, when paramedics had rushed them into the emergency room. The mother had died within minutes, the child soon thereafter. Abby's heart had felt ripped out by shift change. Surprisingly, Dirk had been just as devastated. It had been the only time she'd seen his E.R. physician armor crack.

They'd ended up at her house, clinging to each other for comfort. That's all *that* morning had been. Comfort sex between two normal, healthy adults who found each other attractive.

Not that comfort sex with Dirk had been a bad thing. She supposed sex with any man of his probable experience would be fabulous. Definitely, Dirk had been fabulous. Practice made perfect, right?

Which meant there was no way his any thing, any time, any place would have anything to do with a repeat performance. He might have been well on his way to the perfect lover, but she'd been sorely lacking in practice.

As in a couple of not-so-perfect boyfriends.

So why had she asked Dirk in when he'd dropped her by her house when he'd caught her crying in the elevator and insisted on driving her home? How had him walking her to her front door ended with him carrying her to her bedroom, stripping her naked, and initiating her to the joys shared between a man and a woman that up to that point she'd only believed happened in romance novels?

"Abs?" He pulled her back to the present.

She blinked again, hoping more fervently than every kid on Christmas Eve that he couldn't read her thoughts.

He pushed the gold-rimmed glasses back against the straight slant of his nose. "Do we have a deal?"

She may as well agree. It wasn't as if Dirk would ever really need anything from her. He was gorgeous, and despite his grumblings about having to play the role of Santa, Dirk was good-hearted, an honorable man and an excellent doctor. The physical chemistry between them kept her from being a hundred percent comfortable in his presence—how could she be comfortable when she looked at him and remembered how delicious his kisses tasted, how his naked body felt gliding against hers?

Just thinking about him made her feel a little giddy. There was always a little extra bounce to her step on the nights her shift overlapped his emergency room duties.

"Fine." She met his gaze and wondered what he was up to. The man was brilliant. He was also the only Santa she had. She needed him. "For the kids. I owe you."

"Good," he said, standing. "Let's get this over with."

Dirk's smile scared her. Which felt wrong. How could a smiling Santa be intimidating? Yet, as his gloved hand clasped hers, her nervous system lit up like a twinkling Christmas tree.

CHAPTER TWO

FROM the moment his precious two-year-old daughter and his wife had been killed in a car accident on their way to an early-morning Christmas bargain sale, Dirk Kelley had hated Christmas.

He'd avoided anything to do with the holiday year after year. To the point that his family had held a well-intended but unnecessary intervention at last year's not-so-joyous festivities.

After their unwelcome confrontation, telling him he needed to deal with Sandra and Shelby's deaths, they'd continued to hound him, to try to set him up on dates, to beg him to live life. By early summer, he'd known he had to move away from Oak Park, where his family resided, before the next holiday season. Much to their disappointment, he'd accepted the job in Philadelphia, knowing he was far enough away to avoid holiday get-togethers and their piteous look, but not so far away that he couldn't make it home if there was an emergency. He loved them, just couldn't deal with the pity in their eyes, their interference in what was left of his life.

They were wrong. He hadn't needed the intervention. What he'd needed was for his wife and daughter to be alive, but that was impossible. He'd accepted that inevitability years ago, accepted that he had to move on with his life, and he had. But that didn't mean he'd ever want to be involved with another woman or would welcome the month of December and all the holiday hoopla that arrived with it.

If he could fast-forward December, he'd gladly do so. The lights, the smells, the sales, the noises, everything about the month ripped open his never-healing chest wound.

Abby's initial shocked expression must have mirrored his own when he'd agreed to be her Santa.

Mortification and panic had struggled for top seat. Yet he hadn't been able to take back his ill-fated yes. Not when the wariness she'd eyed him with since the morning after they'd met had finally disappeared, replaced with surprise and soft hazel-eyed gratitude. That look had done something to his insides. Something strange and foreign and despite knowing how difficult today was going to be, he hadn't retracted his agreement.

Not when doing so would disappoint Abby.

Thank God the deed was behind him and he could put Christmas nonsense behind him, where it belonged.

Thankfully de-Santafied, he wandered around Abby's living room. The room had been taken hostage by Christmas Past since the last time he'd been here, two months ago. He'd swear he'd stepped into a nostalgic Christmas movie scene from a couple of decades ago.

An ancient wreath hung over Abby's fireplace, a slightly thinning silver garland was draped over a doorway with faded red ribbons marking each corner. A small Christmas village complete with fake glittery snow and dozens of tiny trees and villagers was set up on a white cloth-covered table, clearly set up in a place of honor beside the tree. The nine main pieces of the village looked old, expensive.

Her live Christmas tree towered almost to the ceiling, a ceramic-faced angel's tinsel halo mere inches from it. What a crazy tradition. Trees indoors. The entire room smelt like the pine tree—like Christmas. Smells he didn't like. Smells that haunted him and took him to hellish places he didn't want to go.

There had been a Christmas tree in the waiting room of the emergency department the morning Sandra and Shelby had died. Amazing how the smell could take him back to sitting in that room, a broken man, a doctor who hadn't been able to do a damned thing to save his baby girl and her mother.

He walked over to the fireplace, eyeing the giant painted toy soldiers to each side, picking up a slightly worn wooden nutcracker. He shook his head, waiting for the nausea to hit him, waiting for the cold sweat to cover his skin, the grief to bring him to his knees.

Christmas did that to him. Sure, he'd learned to bury his pain beneath what most labeled as cynicism, but that didn't mean in private moments the past didn't sneak up to take a stab through his armor, to chip away another piece of what was left of him.

And yet, for the first time since Sandra and Shelby's deaths, he'd agreed to do something that fed into the whole commercialism of Christmas. All because pretty little nurse Abby Arnold had asked him. She'd lit up so brilliantly someone could stick a halo on her head and place her on top of a tree.

He'd definitely found a piece of heaven on earth in

her arms. Had found solace he hadn't expected in the heat of her kisses.

Solace? After the first sweep of his mouth over her lush lips, he hadn't been seeking comfort but acting on the attraction he'd instantly felt for the pretty brunette nurse. He'd been on fire. With lust. With need. With the desire to be inside her curvy body.

He hadn't been remembering or forgetting. He'd been in the moment. With Abby.

He'd wanted her the second he'd laid eyes on her, but never had he experienced such all-consuming sex as that morning. So all-consuming he'd known they couldn't repeat it. Quite easily he could see himself getting obsessed with having her body wrapped around him, getting serious when he had no intention of ever having another serious relationship. Just look at how often he thought of Abby and they'd only had the one morning where they'd made love, twice, and collapsed into exhausted sleep.

Letting out a slow, controlled breath, Dirk placed the nutcracker back on her mantel. Any time, any place, any thing. Why had he teased her into making such an outlandish promise? Better yet, why had he asked for what he had?

He turned, planning to go and find Abby, to tell her he'd changed his mind and needed to go.

A fat tabby cat in a wicker basket at the end of the sofa caught his eye. They'd been formally introduced when the cat had jumped onto the bed, waking both Dirk and Abby in the middle of the afternoon that mid-October day. The cat had been observing his perusal of the room but other than watch him with boredom the cat never moved except to close its eyes.

Realizing another smell, one that was making his stomach grumble, was taking precedence over the pine and was coming through an open doorway, he followed his nose.

When he stepped into the kitchen, he stopped still at the sight that met him, wondering if he'd had one too many kids call him Santa. Because he certainly had the feeling that he'd stepped into an old Christmas movie again.

Singing to the soft Christmas music playing on the mounted under-the-counter player, Abby had on an apron that had Mr. and Mrs. Claus kissing under a sprig of mistletoe on the front. She'd pulled her thick hair back with a red ribbon and had kicked off her shoes for a pair of worn, fuzzy Rudolph slippers.

Stirring a mixture in a glass bowl, a whimsical smile played on her lips as she swayed to the beat of "Rocking Around the Christmas Tree." She looked happy. Like she belonged in this house with its hand-me-down decorations and cozy holiday atmosphere.

Not that he found any of this cozy.

Only there was something about Abby that made him feel warmth where only coldness had resided for so long. There was also something about her that made him want to hold mistletoe over her head and kiss her.

He'd need a thatched hut with a mistletoe roof over her head to justify all the places he wanted to kiss Abby Arnold.

He wanted to do more than kiss her. Lots more. Like take some of that fudge and smear it across her…

Her gaze lifting from the glass bowl she held, she smiled, knocking the breath from his lungs with her beauty and sincerity. "I can't believe you wanted home-made fudge as your any time, any place, any thing."

Her smile said he'd pleased her with his ravings about the goodies she'd brought to the break room at the hospital and how he wanted another bite.

He wanted another bite all right.

Her dimples dug a little deeper into her lovely face. "Some men are so easy."

Smiling at him like that, she made him feel easy. Like he was cookie dough in her hands, waiting for her to mold him into whatever shape she wanted. So why was he still there? Why hadn't he told her he was leaving as he'd come in here to do?

Why was he smiling back at her? Why was he eyeing the pan of chocolate-chip cookies she'd taken out of the oven and feeling a pang of hunger in his belly? A pang that didn't begin to compare to the one below his belt caused by eyeing Abby.

"If they've tasted your homemade goodies, I understand why. Especially the peanut-butter fudge."

"Thank you." Her eyes sparkled like the silver tinsel draping her tree. "It was my mother's recipe."

"Was?"

A flicker of pain crossed her face. "She died."

"I'm sorry." He was. Death was never easy. If anyone knew that, he did. In spades. No, death wasn't easy. Not even when you were a highly trained doctor who'd been dealing with life and death on a daily basis for years.

Just look at how stupidly he'd behaved that first night he and Abby had worked together. Even now, his reaction to the motor vehicle accident victims bothered him, but he understood why, understood that when he'd been battling to save the mother and daughter, he'd been trying to save his wife, trying to save Shelby.

Only to fail.

But he'd held up fine, wearing the mask he'd perfected in those months following their deaths. Pretending he was okay when inside all he'd felt was cold.

Until he'd run into Abby.

He'd been on his way out of the hospital, had caught the elevator just as the door had started closing, and been startled to see a red-eyed Abby eyeing him in surprise.

After shift change, she'd obviously slipped into the bathroom and had a good cry, was still fighting tears. She'd looked vulnerable, needy, way too distraught to be getting behind the wheel of a car.

Way too distraught for him to let her.

He'd insisted on driving her home.

Which was all fine and dandy.

Walking her to the door, going inside, staying, was where he'd messed up.

He didn't date hospital employees, wouldn't date hospital employees.

He hadn't really dated Abby. He'd just not been able to stand the sadness in her eyes, to stand the thought of her driving upset and possibly something happening to her. They'd ended up naked, in her bed, making love until they'd both collapsed in each other's arms and slept the day away.

He shouldn't have done that.

Shouldn't have agreed to be her Santa.

Shouldn't be here now.

So why was he pulling up a chair, willingly staying somewhere Christmas tunes played, instead of beating a path to the door?

Was her imagination running wild or was Dirk looking at her like he'd rather take a bite out of her instead of the peanut-butter fudge?

Abby turned away from his intense blue eyes and took a deep breath. Needing to do something with her hands, she twisted on the faucet and filled the sink with sudsy water to wash the dishes she'd used to make the cookies and two batches of fudge—one chocolate, one peanut butter.

"This is really great."

There was no doubting the sincerity in his voice. She'd swear she heard him moan a moment ago.

Without turning toward him, Abby began stacking the dishes into the hot water to let them soak a few minutes.

"My mother had tons of great recipes, but…" But most of them had been lost in the fire. Only her mother's Christmas recipes packed away in the crates in the basement had survived. The items stored in the basement had been the only items that had survived, period. Almost every box had contained precious Christmas items. "I always bring several big platters full of goodies to the hospital every Christmas."

"Like the fudge you brought the other day?"

"That, and more." She grabbed a dish towel, turned toward him and leaned against the sink. "I like to bake.

I like how the house smells when I have cookies in the oven and candies going on the stovetop and…"

Realizing she was probably boring him, heat flushed her face. She wiped her hands more with the dish towel, wondering if the moisture was from the dishwater or from nervous clamminess. Dirk made her edgy.

"Sorry." She smiled wryly. "Christmas is my favorite holiday and I get carried away at times."

"Obviously."

Despite the amusement in his eyes, something about the way he said the word struck her as wrong. "What's that supposed to mean?"

His grin stayed in place but, still, there was something off kilter, something a bit too brittle about him. "Just that it looks like Bing Crosby should be showing up any moment to start singing about a white Christmas."

"What would be so bad about that? He was a great singer. What's wrong with you anyway? All day you've acted like you really don't like Christmas."

He shrugged. "I don't."

"Say it isn't so!" Astounded, flabbergasted, shocked, her mouth dropped open and her palm flattened against her chest, dish towel and all.

"Why?" He shrugged, looking so serious it made Abby want to loosen her apron strings. "It's the truth. I'm surprised you buy into such a commercialized holiday."

"The business world commercializes every holiday but that doesn't lessen what the day is about."

"Which is?"

"Are you kidding me?" She eyed him, wondering if he was teasing her. When he'd first told her he didn't like

Christmas, she'd thought he was just trying to get out of playing Santa. Could anyone really not like Christmas? Why wouldn't they? "Christmas is about everything good in life. It's a time when families come together and give of themselves to each other. A time when the world slows down and gives a helping hand to someone in need. It's—"

"It's a time when people run up credit-card debt they can't pay. It's a time of the highest rate of depression cases treated, the highest rate of suicide, the highest rate of—"

"How can you be such a cynic about Christmas?" Abby tossed the dish towel onto the countertop and frowned. How could someone not love Christmas? Not love the bright colors in the stores, the sounds of Christmas over the radio, the decorations along the streets? Abby even loved walking past the Salvation Army bellringers. Dropping money into their collection pails always made her feel warm and fuzzy inside.

Giving of oneself was the greatest joy of the holidays. Sure, it would be nice to have someone give to her, to share the moments with, but she'd already decided once today that she'd had enough self-pity.

"I'm not a cynic," he denied, but the more he talked, the more convinced she became that he was.

"I'm a realist," he clarified. "For most, Christmas is a major stressor with trying to come up with the perfect gift, trying to figure out how they're going to pay for that gift, and how they're going to fight the crowds to make sure they get their hands on that perfect gift."

"You're so negative," she pointed out, wondering what had given him such a slanted view of her favorite time of the year. "I see Christmas as at time when you get to search out that special gift to bring a smile to someone's face. A gift meant just for them from you that signifies who they are and how much you appreciate having them in your life."

"It's about rushing from one place to the next," he went on, as if she'd never interrupted his tirade. "Never quite satisfying family and friends with how much of your time you can allot for the festivities they planned without any consideration for your busy schedule. It's about high emotions and family bickering and—"

"Bah, humbug," she interrupted, pulling out a chair at the table and sitting down beside him, positive she was staring at a complete stranger. Who would have thought the wonderful emergency doctor was such a Scrooge? The caring man who'd been as devastated by the deaths of two patients as she had? "Say what you will, but that's not what Christmas is about. Not to me, and you should be ashamed for being so…so…Grinchy!"

He eyed her for long, silent moments, studying her as if she were an oddity. Then, as if he'd not just dissed her favorite holiday, dissed her favorite childhood memories of perfect Christmas moments, his lips curved into a crooked smile. "If it's any consolation, I really like Christmas fudge."

Taking a deep breath, relaxing the tension that had tightened her neck muscles, Abby sighed. How could she stay annoyed at him when he gave her that boyish look that made her toes curl in her shoes?

"Good thing I didn't know all this about you when I asked you to be Santa," she said, smoothing out the edge of a plain red and green table placemat. "You, Dr. Kelley, are no Santa Claus."

"You asked me to be Santa because you couldn't get anyone else to agree." Still showing wry amusement, his gaze pinned hers. "Admit it."

An unexpected giggle rose up her throat. "Okay, you're right. Everyone else I asked claimed to be busy."

"Such classic examples of Christmas goodwill and cheer."

"They were probably busy," she said defensively, although she doubted any of them could match her holiday season schedule. Every year she took on as many projects as she could fit in.

"Sure they were." He popped the last piece of his fudge into his mouth. "But if they'd known they could maneuver their way into your kitchen, you'd have had to beat Santa-wannabes away with stockings filled with coal."

"I'm guessing you'd know a lot about those stockings filled with coal." At his mock look of horror, she smiled. "You should've tried my mother's Martha Washington candy."

Memories of standing on a chair beside her mother, carefully dipping rolled candies into melted chocolate, her mother smiling down at her, praising her efforts, filled Abby's heart. How she longed for a family to spend Christmas with.

Dirk reached for a second square of fudge. His sooty ashes swept across his cheeks as he bit into it. Was it shameful she'd like to see that blissful look on his face while he tasted her lips? Yes. Yes, it was. They'd agreed anything physical between them was a mistake. She'd agreed when he'd said that.

It had been a mistake. Hadn't it? Or had agreeing with him been the mistake?

Because looking at him, being here with him, denying the way she wanted him when she wanted him so badly sure felt like the bigger mistake.

CHAPTER THREE

"If you're more into peanut butter, there's always peanut-butter balls and homemade peanut brittle," she rushed out, trying to redirect her mind away from the direction it was headed.

Eyes wide, his gaze lifted to hers. He looked like an eager little boy. *Like he'd looked that morning when he'd devoured her mouth.*

He placed his hand over his heart. "I've died and gone to heaven. You're right. I was too easy. I should have asked for peanut brittle."

She laughed out loud at his look of ecstasy.

Just as quickly her laughter faded as more memories of another time, another look of ecstasy had been on his handsome face.

When he'd been standing just inside her front door, awkwardly saying goodbye but making no move to leave. The only move he'd made had been to bend and gently kiss her lips.

Then he'd kissed her not so gently.

Oh, Lord, how he'd kissed her.

And kissed her.

No, she couldn't keep thinking of *that* morning. Not

with him here, alone, in her house, just the two of them and the bed where he'd made love to her.

No, not love. They'd just been two colleagues dealing poorly with a very stressful night in the emergency room.

Her gaze tangled with his and his good humor faded just as quickly as hers had. Was he remembering, too? Recalling that the last time he'd been in her house, he'd never seen the kitchen but had had an up-close-and-personal tour of her bedroom?

He stuck the remainder of his fudge in his mouth, stood and brushed his hands over the faded jeans he'd changed into in her guest bathroom after his shower. When he'd swallowed the mouthful, he took a step back. "I put your Santa suit on the sofa."

His words managed to pull her from memories of Dirk's last visit to further in the past. Her father's Santa suit. When Dirk had asked her about what he'd wear, she'd instantly offered her father's suit.

"Thanks for the fudge and for the loan of the suit."

"It was the least I could do as you filled in for Santa." True, but had anyone else agreed to play the role, she would have bought a cheap Santa costume from a department store. For Dirk, she'd dug out the treasured suit that had belonged to her father.

"Thanks all the same."

"If you hadn't agreed, I'd have had to play Santa." Not that her father's suit would have fit her, but she'd have made it work somehow. "I think the kids might have been scarred for life."

His gaze raked over the ample upper part of her body.

"You're probably right about that. You're no Santa." He tossed her earlier words back at her.

Abby didn't know whether to be offended or flattered. Either way, heat crept into her face.

"I'll get a dish for you to take some home." She stood so rapidly her chair almost toppled. Pulling out a Christmas patterned storage tin, she placed a generous piece of plastic wrap inside, arranged as much as would fit of the fudge and cookies, and put the lid on. "There you go."

He'd moved over next to her, standing near the cabinets. His body heat radiated toward her, luring her nearer. "I feel guilty, coercing you to make this and then taking most of it."

"You should feel guiltier if you left it here," she teased a bit nervously, playfully elbowing him, the contact shooting stars through the pit of her belly.

His gaze dropped to where she'd touched his arm then his brow rose in question of her comment.

"If you left it, I'd eat it," she clarified, not lowering her gaze despite how her blood pumped through her body at warp speed and made her feel as if she needed to call time out so she could catch her breath.

Again his eyes ran over her features, taking their time and not seeming to mind the bumps and valleys along the journey. "That would be a bad thing?"

"I'm a woman who is constantly on a diet," she admitted, sucking in her waist reflexively as his gaze traveled lower. Not that holding her belly in would do much good.

"You have no reason to be on a diet." When his eyes met hers, they were blue fire, hot, lust-filled.

A thousand carolers began to sing in her soul, louder and louder until she might explode from the sheer beauty of it, until she was sure the sound must be able to be heard in heaven itself.

"No reason at all," he repeated, his gaze burning hotter. "You're perfect just as you are."

Um, right. Perfect. If you liked a woman who was busty and hippy, with a little extra thigh thrown in on the sides. But she couldn't look away from Dirk, because he was either the most talented fibber in the world or he meant what he said. And, darn, if those carolers hadn't gone up another octave in the pit of her belly, making every individual cell vibrate in a happy dance.

"I, uh…" What could she say when he was looking at her as if a slightly fuller figure really was perfection? She shoved the fudge at him. "Thank you, but I'm glad you're taking it, all the same."

He looked as if he wanted to say more, but must have decided against doing so as he took the candy, stared at her a few moments, his gaze going from fire to almost a sad smoldering. "Bye, Abs. You working tomorrow night?"

Abs. He really shouldn't say her name like that so carelessly! Holding her breath, she nodded.

"Are you planning to go to the hospital Christmas party this weekend?" Had he winced while asking that? Or after the words had left his mouth?

"Of course," she answered slowly, watching the play of conflicting emotions dance on his face. "I'm on the hospital's Christmas committee and helped put the party together. Are you going?"

"I hadn't planned to, but…" He paused, looked as

if he needed to loosen his collar even though his black T-shirt was far from restricting at the neck.

"But?" she prompted, her eyes focusing on a bead of sweat she'd swear was forming on his brow.

He took a deep breath, as if he was about to embark on a dangerous quest he really didn't want to go on but had little choice. "If you'll go with me, I could probably tolerate it this once. When I didn't RSVP, the hospital administrator came by." Dirk sighed, looking almost as uncomfortable as he had when he'd been playing Santa. "He said it wouldn't look good for the newest member on the medical staff to not show for the hospital's biggest employee social event of the year."

Not the most enthusiastic invitation she'd ever received, but happiness spread through Abby.

Dirk had just asked her on a date to the hospital Christmas party.

Not that he really wanted to go, but he'd asked her to accompany him. On a date.

"I'd love to go to the Christmas party with you." There wasn't a man alive she'd rather attend with. Being at Dirk's side would make the party all the more special, made everything all the more special.

Would he please turn around a moment so she could happy-dance around the kitchen?

Dirk had asked her to the Christmas party! Their morning hadn't been a one-night stand after all. Er…a one-morning stand after all.

"Okay. Great." He sounded relieved at her answer.

Had he thought she'd say no or was it the Christmas party itself stressing him? Either way, Dirk had just asked her to go on a date.

Thinking this just might be the best Christmas ever, she bubbled with good cheer and found herself wanting to tease a smile out of him. "Do I need to have my father's Santa suit dry-cleaned or will you be providing your own wardrobe for the evening?"

He snorted, his mouth creeping up at the corners as she'd hoped. "You worry about what you're going to wear, Li'l Miss Christmas Spirit. I'll take care of my suit."

"So long as it's not green with pointy toes, Mr. Grinchy."

He laughed. "Deal."

They stared at each other long moments, so long Abby couldn't help but wonder what he was thinking, couldn't help but wonder what had prompted his invitation. Was it possible that she wasn't the only one with visions of more than sugar plums dancing through her dreams? Could he at this very moment want to whisk her off her feet and carry her back to her bed and have a repeat? Why bother going to the bedroom? Kitchens were always good for cooking up something hot.

He cleared his throat, coughed, shook his head a little. "See you tomorrow night at the hospital. Thanks again for the fudge."

With that, he took his goodies and left.

Abby wrapped her arms around her apron-covered waist and danced around the kitchen while singing along with one of her favorite Christmas tunes.

She was going to the hospital Christmas party with the most amazing, sexy, wonderful man she'd ever met.

God, she loved Christmastime and if she wasn't careful, she just might end up loving Dirk, too.

* * *

"Bay one has a probable UTI," Abby told Dirk when he stepped out of the exam area where he'd just been seeing a patient in. "White blood cell count is twelve thousand, with neutrophils slightly elevated. There's a trace of blood and plus four bacteria in the urine. The patient reports tenderness in the abdomen and in the mid-low back."

Dirk nodded, without glancing directly at her.

Abby sighed. He'd seemed a bit distant tonight. She'd been dreaming of dashing through the snow like lovers with him ever since he'd issued his invitation to the Christmas party. Okay, before then. Way before then. She'd been dreaming of Dirk since the morning they'd ended up in bed together. Hadn't she known not to get her hopes up after the way he'd *dashed* out of her house after they'd made love? But she just couldn't seem to help herself where Dirk was concerned.

Reminding herself that she was a registered nurse, a professional, and on the job, she followed Dirk into the bay, telling herself to keep her mind—and eyes!—off the man in front of her, even if he did look fab-u-lous in his hospital-issue scrubs.

Obviously, he didn't spend his days inside, baking. Not with the taut definition in his upper arms, the strength in his neck and shoulders, the taper of his waist, the... Abby gulped. *Focus! He is not a Christmas package waiting for you to unwrap him. He's a highly respected emergency physician.*

But she'd really like to unwrap Dirk.

Focus! Focus! Focus!

"Hello, Mrs. Youngblood," he greeted the thin lady with streaky brown-blond hair and pinched facial features. "The nurse was just telling me about your lab results. It appears you have a serious urinary-tract infection. Tell me what's been going on."

Dirk examined the patient while the lady told him of her symptoms, when they'd started and how they'd gotten much worse during the night to the point she'd decided she couldn't wait until morning to check in with her primary care provider.

"No history of kidney stones?"

Mrs. Youngblood shook her head, her expression easing very little. "My husband has them, but I never have. Are they contagious?"

"No. You can't catch kidney stones from another person." Dirk pressed on her thin abdomen, attempting to palpate organs. "Any vaginal symptoms?"

"I don't think so," she denied, her hand guarding her belly as Dirk examined her. "It just really burns when I urinate. And feels like my bladder is going to turn inside out when I go, too."

"Have the medications given since you've arrived helped?"

"Yes." Although you sure couldn't tell it by the woman's grimace. "When I first got here I was miserable. The pain hasn't completely eased, but I'm a lot better."

Dirk washed his hands then turned to his patient. "I'm going to write a prescription for some antibiotics. You'll need to follow up with your primary care provider within the next couple of days." He began writing out orders. "Do you need a note for work?"

The woman shook her head. "I work from home as a medical billing clerk."

"Great." Dirk turned to Abby, meeting her eyes for the first time since they'd entered the room, and he smiled.

A real smile that reached those gorgeous blue eyes and pierced right into her heart.

Relief flooded Abby. Did he have any idea as to the lethalness of his smile? Probably. She soaked up every drop of his potency, letting the intensity of her emotions flow through her veins.

"Mrs. Youngblood," he said, his gaze flicking back to his patient. "The nurse will get you ready for discharge. If you have any additional problems or get worse before morning, I'd suggest you return to the emergency department for a recheck."

An hour later, the emergency department was in full swing. Every bay was full. Both physicians and the nurse practitioner on duty were at full stretch.

Abby adjusted a breathing mask over an asthma patient's mouth and nose, preparing to administer a beta-agonist medication via a nebulizer to rapidly open up the restricted airways.

"You may feel a little shaky and jittery after the medication starts working," she warned her patient. "The process that causes the bronchial tubes to dilate also speeds up the heart rate. Don't let the reaction alarm you as that's a natural and expected response to the medicine."

She turned on the nebulizer and waited to make sure the patient's wheezing slowed before she stepped out of the bay to check on her next patient.

Dirk was with him—a morbidly obese man who'd woken up with a sharp tightness in his chest that took his breath. They'd started him on meds immediately on arrival, done tests, including an EKG that showed left ventricular hypertrophy and a possible blockage. They'd stabilized him while awaiting the results of his cardiac enzyme tests.

"I read your chest X-ray, Mr. Lytle. Your heart is enlarged, showing signs of your high blood pressure and congestive heart failure, but that shouldn't have caused you to wake up with chest pain. I don't see anything acute on the films, but your troponin level is slightly elevated. That's a myocardial muscle isoenzyme that elevates when the heart isn't getting enough oxygen. I'm going to admit you to the cardiac-care unit for close observation. The cardiologist on call has been notified you're here and will be by soon. He'll schedule you for a cardiac catheterization, likely for in the morning. That way, if there are any blockages, he can repair them immediately."

Abby began to prepare to have the patient transferred to the cardiac-care unit while Dirk answered the questions of the patient and his wife.

The rest of the night passed quickly. The E.R. was still bustling come shift change. An hour past time for her to have left, Abby clocked out, exhausted and feeling a little woozy.

Dirk had still been with an abdominal pain patient who'd come in minutes before shift change. Abby had offered to stay, but the day-shift nurse had taken over and had things under control.

She'd felt relieved at the reprieve, and surprised at how tired she was. The night had been busy, but no more so than dozens of others she'd worked, but she just wanted to go home, crawl into bed and pass out.

She rarely got sick, but definitely her stomach churned at the thought of breakfast. Maybe she'd just skip her usual light meal before going to bed. Hopefully, she'd feel better once she got some sleep.

She hoped she wasn't coming down with something, especially so close to Christmas.

Regardless, no way would she let a little nausea and fatigue get her down when she had a date with Dirk for the Christmas party on Saturday evening.

CHAPTER FOUR

"Don't tell me you unwrapped a Christmas present early and found Dr. Kelley inside, because if that's the case, I'm changing what I put on my wish list for this year." Medical floor nurse Danielle Booker draped her arm around Abby's shoulder on Saturday night at the hospital Christmas party being held in the ballroom of a nearby hotel.

Abby glanced away from where she watched Dirk talk with a couple of other physicians. When the conversation had turned to golf, she'd excused herself. She'd needed a few moments to breathe. Dirk had been the perfect attentive date, but the tension between them was so palpable it threatened to cut off her windpipe. Between that and his obvious discomfort at being at the party, Abby was wound tighter than a spool of ribbon.

"I'm waiting." Danielle tapped her slinky black high heels against the ballroom floor. "Were you such a good girl this year that Santa arranged for Dr. Kelley to be in your stocking?"

"Now isn't the time for details about my relationship with Dirk." Not to mention that she didn't know how to define their relationship.

"You're admitting you have a relationship with *Dirk*?"

Her friend put emphasis on the use of his given name rather than his title of Dr. Kelley.

He'd been Dirk from the moment she'd glanced into his eyes and felt as if she were drowning in a blue sea of Christmas ribbon. With all her volunteering with the community outreach program, she hadn't found the time to call her best friend and they'd been on different shifts at the hospital. She hadn't told anyone about the morning she'd spent with Dirk. Perhaps if their relationship hadn't ended almost as fast as they'd started… And if they'd ended, what was tonight about? And why did she fluctuate between giddy and the need to protect her heart?

"I'm not admitting anything. Not here." Abby's gaze shifted to him again. Just looking at him made her feel as if she was all tangled up and would never be able to free herself. "But I like him, if that's what you're asking."

"You like him? Girl, that isn't 'like' I see in your eyes," Danielle teased, her grin growing bigger in direct proportion to Abby's face growing hotter. "You are so telling me everything soon."

"Everything," Abby agreed. Which was what? Dirk hadn't called or even talked to her at the hospital other than about patients and to confirm what time to pick her up. After his Santa debut and him asking her out for tonight, she'd jumped every time her phone had rung, hoping he'd call. She'd been disappointed every time. Disappointed that he hadn't made any effort to talk to her outside the parameters of work.

Until tonight.

Tonight, he'd been a considerate date, if quiet, taking

her white faux-fur wrap and gloves to the designated coat room, ensuring she had everything she wanted to drink and eat, even making the comment that her goodies tasted better than the ones supplied by the party's caterer.

Yet that ever-present awkwardness, awareness, kept her slightly on edge, not letting her completely relax, making her stomach stay slightly knotted with tension. That's why she'd needed a breather. Being so close to Dirk, his hand occasionally resting possessively on her back, she'd been on the verge of swooning from lack of air.

On the verge of grabbing his hand and dragging him to a room and kissing him like crazy in hopes of abating whatever this burn inside her was.

Abby covered her mouth with her hand, biting back a slight smile at what Dirk would do, say, if she marched over to him and did just that. Bet that wouldn't do a thing to ease the edginess she'd sensed about him all evening. Because of her? Or the Christmas party?

Danielle eyed her a moment, taking note of exactly what Abby wasn't sure, just that her friend's smile faded. "You okay? You look flushed."

Any flush on her face was from her thoughts, not from not feeling okay. Actually, the bug that had been bothering her earlier in the week was sticking around. But, fortunately, by the time Dirk had arrived she'd been fine. When he'd looked at her as if she was more mouth-watering than any piece of peppermint candy, had told her she was beautiful, well, she'd been over the moon.

If she'd stop trying to label whatever was happening between them and could just enjoy the fact that something was happening, everything would be wonderful.

She visually sought out where he still stood with the group of golfing physicians. He wasn't saying much, just listening to the others. Dirk didn't have to say much. The man would stand out in any crowd. Not just because of his height or his good looks or even his quick intelligence. No, he'd stand out because of the confident way he held himself, the pure aura of testosterone that clung to him and demanded women take notice, even though he seemed oblivious to the fact he was gorgeous.

Abby noticed. From his thick black hair to the tailored lines of his dinner jacket and trousers to the pointed toes of his Italian shoes, she noticed. And liked. She definitely liked.

"How could I not be okay?" she practically sighed, wondering if Danielle would scoop her up if she melted into an Abby puddle. Dirk liquefied her insides. Any moment she might slosh to the floor.

"Right," Danielle replied, her gaze following Abby's. "Got to admit, that man is fine. A little quiet and brooding for my taste, but he is easy on the eye."

Very easy on the eye. She'd seen more than one envious look her way when they entered the hotel ballroom.

"Just because he doesn't like Christmas doesn't mean he's brooding," Abby defended. "Plus, he isn't quiet once you get to know him. He has a great sense of humor."

Just recalling how he'd teased her made her insides toasty warm.

"I didn't know Dr. Dreamboat doesn't like Christmas and I still think he's brooding," Danielle pointed out.

Okay, so maybe a little brooding.

"The man keeps to himself, doesn't socialize, rarely talks to anyone outside anything to do with a patient or work. That's okay, mind you. He's probably just a private person, but that's not my style. Although…" she glanced toward where Dirk stood "…in his case, I could be convinced to make an exception." Danielle gave a little shake of her head. "Seriously, he doesn't like Christmas? Talk about your opposites attracting. Does he know you're the Queen of Holiday Cheer?"

"He knows." Recalling their conversation about the holidays, Abby tried not to wince. She'd just focus on the positive. "He likes my peanut-butter fudge."

"I'll just bet he does." Danielle snickered.

Abby rolled her eyes, but couldn't keep her smile from her face. "He stepped in and played Santa the other day at the community center, too."

See, there was another positive. Dirk had been there when she'd needed him. How many people could she say that of throughout her life so far?

"You're kidding! Dr. Kelley was Santa?" Danielle's mouth dropped open. "Now I know I'm changing my Christmas wish list. You should have told me. I could have come and sat in his lap."

Um, no. If any grown-up had been going to sit in Dirk's lap, Abby had dibs.

"My Santa canceled very last minute and I couldn't find a replacement. He saved me from canceling the event. Plus, he did a good job." Abby laughed at her friend's amazed expression. "Seriously, he did."

Mostly. He hadn't seemed to enjoy himself, but he had stayed until every kid in line had gotten their time with Santa. Not every busy doctor would have given up so much of his free time.

Okay, so he professed not to like Christmas. He was here at the Christmas party. He'd played Santa. Next thing you knew she'd have him out caroling or ringing bells for charity donations. Hey, it could happen. She was here with him, wasn't she? He was taking her home, wasn't he?

As if sensing her gaze, Dirk looked up. Laser-blue fire flew from across the room, flooding her belly with the sensation of a curly Christmas ribbon having been stretched out and released.

Wow, but the man packed a wallop.

First saying something to the men he stood with, he headed toward her. Tall, handsome in his dark suit, his eyes solely trained on her, as if she were the only person in the room, the only person who mattered. His hand touched her elbow and her world shifted off its axis.

"Hi, Dr. Kelley. Great party, huh?" Danielle smiled at Dirk, taking a sip of her wine.

"I suppose." Dirk's gaze briefly touched on Danielle, but immediately returned to Abby. His eyes had the same look in them that he'd had at the "Pictures with Santa," a *rescue me, please* one. He held her gaze, his thumb stroking over her bare arm. Did he realize he was doing that? Would he please stop? The more he touched, the more she wanted him to touch. Not good. Her bosses were all here!

When she went to pull away, his hand enveloped hers, clasping her fingers in his slightly clammy ones.

Oblivious to Dirk's discomfort, Danielle sent Abby

an impressed look, smiled widely, then excused herself under the pretense of getting another glass of wine.

"I'm not going to be able to stay much longer, Abby."

She nodded as if she understood, but she wasn't exactly clear. Had he gotten a call from the hospital? Due to the party, they were operating on a skeleton staff. Both Dirk and Abby were on call, so it was a possibility. Although she couldn't imagine why that would make him nervous.

"I'm sorry."

"What are you sorry for?"

"Not wanting to stay at the party you planned."

Work hadn't called. He just didn't want to be there. Abby bit the inside of her cheek, studying him.

As his gaze skimmed over the Christmas decorations Abby had thought gave just the right touch, he winced. "If it were any other kind of party…"

Than Christmas. He didn't have to say the words.

There was something about the way his eyes darkened, the way his body tensed, that had her squeezing his hand. She didn't want to leave, but neither did she like the tortured expression in his eyes. "It's okay. We can go whenever you like. Most of the good stuff has already taken place."

"Good stuff?" He focused on her face as if using her as a focal point to stay grounded.

"When the administrators acknowledged all the hard work everyone does every day of the year, when they acknowledged what a great staff we have, and, of course, when they gave away the gifts donated by local businesses."

His expression not changing, he studied her. "Sorry you didn't win."

"That's okay." She smiled up at him, feeling petite despite her four-inch heels.

"You look like a winner." His gaze raked over her Santa Claus red dress, pausing at where the waist dipped in before flaring out just above the knees.

"Thank you." She'd seen the dress, added the white wrap and the heels that were much more daring than anything she usually wore but couldn't resist, and known she had the perfect Christmas party ensemble.

She'd even splurged on new underwear. Not the granny whites like she usually wore. No, the tiny silk and lace garments beneath her dress kept up her Christmas red theme and made her feel less like that broken-down old toy and more like the shiny new one waiting to be played with under the Christmas tree.

Just in case.

As crazy as it was, she definitely wanted to relive all the things she and Dirk had done together, all the ways he'd touched her, kissed her, loved her body. She sighed in remembrance of the ways his hands and mouth had given her pleasure. So, so much pleasure.

"What are you thinking about?"

She glanced up, curious at the slight rasp to his voice. When her gaze collided with his, heat flushed her cheeks. She might not be able to read his mind, but he'd certainly read hers. He knew.

Knew exactly what she'd been thinking. Remembering.

It turned him on. Maybe as much as she was turned on. Could that be possible? Could he really feel the same?

"Earlier, when you asked, I promised to dance before the evening ended." His gaze never shifted from hers. "With you by my side, staying doesn't feel quite so impossible. Dance with me, Abby, then we'll go."

He was really going to dance with her? She'd already resigned herself that unless she danced with someone else, she wouldn't be making her way onto the dance floor.

Smiling, she let him lead her out. He took her into his arms and they swayed to the music in gentle rhythm.

"You're a good dancer." She'd imagined he hadn't wanted to dance because perhaps he couldn't. She should have known better about that, too. Dirk Kelley was a man of many talents.

"You sound surprised." He almost smiled. "It's been a while," he admitted, endearing himself even further, "but I guess it's like riding a bicycle. One of those things you don't really forget how to do."

"Why has it been a while since you've danced?"

Instantly, his arms stiffened.

"I just don't dance any more," he finally said.

Which wasn't really much of an answer and left her with a dozen questions he obviously wouldn't answer. Resisting a sigh, Abby laid her cheek against his chest, soaking in the warmth of being in his arms.

They danced, slow and in sync, their bodies touching, brushing against each other, his body heat melting her like a marshmallow in hot chocolate. Dirk made no motion to leave when one song turned into another.

"You smell good." He nuzzled her lightly, brushing his cheek against her hair. "Like fresh berries and cinnamon."

"You smell good, too," she admitted, amazed at her vocal cords' ability to make coherent sounds when her entire insides shook like she'd been trampled by stampeding reindeer.

"Are you having a good time?"

Nodding, she laid her cheek against his shoulder. From the corner of her eye, she saw Danielle give a thumbs-up and a suggestive eyebrow waggle and shake of her hips. She also noticed several of their colleagues watching them. Some with curiosity. Some with smiles.

A low, nervous chuckle rose up her throat.

"What?" he asked in a low voice, near her ear.

"Everyone thinks we're a couple."

His feet stilled a moment, as if he'd forgotten where they were, but his hands stayed at her waist. "I don't do couples, Abby."

She raised her head, stared at him. "Okay, we're not a couple." She took a deep breath. "What are we?"

He hesitated, looking torn. "I'm not sure."

Not the answer she'd hoped to hear. Then again, what had she expected? Feed the man a little fudge and he wouldn't be able to get enough of her?

She couldn't deal with his hot-cold attitude. Not and keep her sanity intact. Her heart intact.

"Then maybe you should get sure before we go any further, Dirk." Her heart banged against her rib cage in protest of her words. She wanted to go further. Lots further. But she wasn't a fool and wouldn't pretend to be one, not even for more time with Dirk. Regardless of how she felt, she deserved better than to be at his beck and call, available for comfort sex and Christmas parties. "I like you. A lot. But I don't want to end up with a broken heart and if you're not in this with me, then…" She shrugged. "Well, whatever this is needs to end now."

He studied her, his fingers splayed against her back, stroking over the material of her dress, possessively, distractingly. "I'd never hurt you, Abby."

"Not intentionally." Why were tears pricking her eyes? Why did she feel as if he was going to tell her goodbye? Why did that hurt so much? Technically, tonight was their first date. She would not cry. "But if I'm not careful where you're concerned, I will end up hurt."

Her heart protested it was way too late to start thinking about heart protection. She was crazy about Dirk. Way too crazy to walk away unscathed. Hadn't she fought tears more than once that he'd immediately had regrets about making love to her?

"You're right." He took a deep breath and she expected him to let her go, to push her away. Instead, his hands tightened at her waist, as if he wasn't willing to let go, as if he clung to her for support. "I shouldn't have asked you here tonight."

"Why did you?"

"I didn't want to be here alone."

Had he only asked because she was convenient? Because he'd known she'd say yes? She bit the inside of her lower lip to hold it steady. He'd not made any grand promises. All he'd done was ask her to attend a Christmas party with him. She'd been the one to attach all sorts of sentimental meaning to his invitation.

Just as she'd attached all sorts of sentimental meaning to their morning together. Lord, she was a fool.

"But mostly because I can't quit thinking about you."

A soft moan escaped. That was more along the lines of what she wanted to hear. More along the lines of how she felt about him. Her breath caught, knotting in her throat.

"About making love to you." He shifted against her, holding her more closely, pressing the length of her body to his. "I want you, Abby. I haven't stopped wanting you. Seeing you tonight, like this…" his gaze moved over the curve of her neck, her upswept hair "…touching you, I can't help but want to make love to you even though I know I shouldn't and you certainly shouldn't let me. Because regardless of how much I want you, I was serious when I said I don't do relationships."

"Why not?" She swallowed the knot, wondering at the raw emotions in his eyes. Emotions she wasn't positive had only to do with her, emotions he'd rarely bared, if ever.

He shook his head. "Not everyone wants the cozy Christmas fantasy of being part of a couple, Abby. That's not what I want."

The pain in his voice overshadowed his words, words she was sure were chosen to alienate her emotionally, revealed so much more than what he said. Did he realize how much he'd just exposed to her? That he'd given her a glimpse inside him? A glimpse that undid any resolve she might have had to walk away.

"What do you want?" She held his gaze, clinging to his shoulders to remain steady on her feet as she prepared to expose her heart. "Because I'm not asking for some cozy Christmas fantasy. I just want you. So much I forget to breathe when I look at you."

He inhaled sharply, closed his eyes.

"Oh, Abs," he whispered against her forehead, sounding tortured and pleased all in the same breath. His jaw flexed. His eyes darkened then closed again. When they opened, possession shone. Possession and something so primal and needy that desire swept through Abby. His eyes asked questions much more potent than any he could speak.

She toyed with the soft hair at his nape, twirling the silky black strands around her finger, wondering if it was bad that she felt just as wrapped around his finger. "Will you take me home now, Dirk?"

He placed his thumb beneath her chin, lifted her face. "I want to leave this monstrosity more than I can say, but are you sure?"

Concern flickered that he was calling what she'd thought a lovely Christmas party a monstrosity, but hormones ruled. That possessive look had her glutes tightening.

"Yes." She was sure she wanted to give him... everything. More. Needed to give him everything and more.

What the hell was he doing? Dirk wondered for the hundredth time that week.

Little Miss Merry Christmas was getting to him. And not just a little.

He'd been right when he'd told Abby she was beautiful earlier. She was. Absolutely stunning in her party dress.

But not as stunning as she'd been in nothing at all.

Dirk had been focusing on Abby to get through the party, had hung around the golf conversation just because it had been one of the few conversations going that had had nothing to do with the holidays.

Now, if he wanted to get out of the party without embarrassing himself, he had to keep his mind off Abby, off *that particular morning*, off how he'd lost himself in her body, how he'd felt whole inside for the first time in years. Even now, with her smiling up at him, he could lose himself in everything she was and almost forget the ever-present ache inside him at this time of year.

Her big hazel eyes were striking even without make-up accentuating them. Tonight they looked huge, like luminous stars guiding him to her. Her silky brown hair had been pulled up, but rather than the tighter style she wore for work, lots of strands hung loose, curling in loose tendrils. She wore a bright red dress that demanded attention and had captivated his from the moment she'd opened her front door, smiling at him as if he really was Santa come to fulfill her heart's every desire.

And those shoes.

He didn't know how she walked in the spindly red heels, how any woman walked in heels, but he appreciated how they pumped out Abby's calves, accented the toned lines of her legs. How they made his gaze want to keep traveling up those long lines, to unveil where they met, where he wanted to be. Oh, Abby.

Since his wife's death, he hadn't been a saint. He'd tried to ease the ache inside of him, only to realize he wasn't dating material any more.

But he'd never been as attracted to anyone as he was to Abby.

He knew better than to get involved, knew there could never be a relationship between them. Not one that would go anywhere. He'd suck the goodness right out of her life, weigh her down with his heavy heart. She was right to question him. Given the chance, he would break her heart.

Yet, he'd slept with her, figuratively and literally, after the first night they'd worked together. Sure, he'd backed off after that morning, but only because of how she'd looked at him with hope of a happy-ever-after. That look had had sweat prickling his skin and his heart fluttering in a panicked rhythm. Otherwise he'd have been burning up her sheets for the past two months.

He'd gotten out of her house stat and promised himself he'd keep his distance. So why had he agreed to be her Santa? Why had he asked her to come to this party with him? Sure, the administrator had questioned why he hadn't been going, but the guy would have gotten over it if he hadn't attended.

"Dirk?" Abby prompted when he failed to respond to her gutsy invitation to take her home.

He stared down into her blue-green eyes with their golden flecks, his hands around her waist, holding her to him while Christmas music played around them.

She was sweet and wonderful and giving. The more time he spent with her, the more he craved, the more he knew he should stay away. She believed in goodness and in the magic of Christmas. She gave of herself without asking for anything in return. Hadn't he just told her he didn't do relationships? Yet here she was, willing to give what he wanted. The truth was, he didn't want to go home alone, didn't want to face the demons of being at this party, just being alive during the holiday season, dredged up from his past, not when being with Abby made him feel better, less alone. She made him forget everything but her.

Just as on the morning they'd fallen into bed together, words weren't needed.

He was going to take all she'd give, knowing he had nothing to give in return and never would.

Bah, humbug. He really was a Scrooge.

CHAPTER FIVE

STANDING on her front porch, Abby fumbled twice before inserting the key into her door lock. Her hands shook like crazy.

She was crazy.

Hadn't Dirk told her he didn't do relationships? So why had they rushed from the Christmas party like teenagers? She laughed nervously. God, she felt like a teen on her way to a heated make-out session.

"Let me," he interrupted when, although she'd gotten the key into the lock, the release hadn't caught properly.

The lock clicked and Abby pushed the door open, practically falling into her foyer and dragging Dirk with her. He pushed the door closed with a resounding snap. The sound echoed through the darkness broken only by her Christmas lights, which cast a magical aura over the foyer and living room thanks to the timers she kept them on.

"Come here," he growled, pulling her to him, taking her mouth by storm as he worked off her wrap, letting the heavy faux fur fall to the floor.

Yes, Abby thought, this was exactly how she remembered Dirk kissing her. As if she tasted sweeter than

Christmas cookies and he was eager to go on a sugar binge.

He tasted just as sweet. Sweeter. His lips were marauding her mouth, his tongue tangling with hers as his hands slid over her body, touching, caressing, *claiming*.

Abby set about staking some claims of her own. Meeting him kiss for kiss, tangle for tangle. Tactically committing the hard lines of his body to memory, committing everything about him to memory.

"I want you so much."

She'd noticed. Oh, how she'd noticed!

"I want to savor every touch, every sigh that escapes from your lips." He nibbled at her throat, at the base of her neck. Hot kisses that scorched her skin, bringing her blood to a boil.

His fingers searched out her zipper, slowly parted the back of her dress as his tongue traced over her carotid pulse, licking at the raging beat on her throat.

When his hand rested on her lower back where the zip ended, he turned his attention to the thin red straps holding up her dress.

Eyes locked with hers in the flickering colors of the Christmas lights, he looped one finger beneath the thin satin and slid the string off her shoulder, letting it dangle against her deltoid. He kissed where the strap had been. A soft, gentle, stomach-knotting kiss that shot an arrow of pleasure straight to the apex of her being. He turned to the other side and repeated the seductive gesture, his lips lingering on her bare shoulder.

"You are so beautiful, Abby. So sweet and perfect."

"I'm not perfect." Surely he knew she wasn't without

her having to tell him. Surely he was just spouting lines. Although why he would when he already had her, she couldn't fathom. And, oh, how he had her!

He trailed more kisses over her shoulders, light, reverent. "You're the closest thing this side of heaven."

Dear Saint Nicholas alive! Did he have any idea what his praise was doing? What his kisses were doing?

Apparently, because he shimmied her dress over her hips to puddle in the floor around her feet.

She stood in her foyer, dressed only in the new red underwear she'd bought to match her dress and her high heels. If not for the blaze in Dirk's eyes, she might be cold, might be embarrassed. She was neither.

His gaze burned with desire. Deep, hot desire that told her everything. More. Desire that made her warm from the inside out. Hot.

She took his hand in hers. His eyebrow rose in question when she led him into the living room, rather than toward her bedroom. But she didn't explain herself, sensing that words would ruin the magical atmosphere. Instead, she took the throw blanket off the back of her sofa and tossed it into the floor in front of her fireplace, turned the knob that lit her gas logs, and met his gaze.

Swallowing audibly, he nodded, lay down with her on the blanket, pushing her back and staring down at her in the firelight. Wordlessly, his lips brushed her temples, her cheeks, her eyes, her throat. Slowly, his mouth worked over her skin.

She shifted, grasping at the buttons of his shirt, fumbling to undo them. She ran her hands inside the parted material of his crisp white shirt, loving the feel of his smooth chest against her fingertips, loving the rapid pounding of his heart beneath her palm.

She'd done that to him, made his heart beat wildly.

Like a snowman caught in a hothouse, Abby melted.

Dirk groaned, and gave up whatever hope he had of going slowly. He'd wanted to kiss every inch of her, to take things slowly, to do things right, instead of the desperate coupling they'd had last time. *Twice.* But where Abby was concerned he obviously could only go one speed. Head-on.

He shucked out of his shirt, groaned again at the feel of her hands rubbing over skin, over his shoulders, down his back. The pleasure Abby found in his body thrilled him, had him aching for more. She craned her neck to kiss his throat, his shoulders, his chest. Frantic, quick kisses that seared his flesh.

"So beautiful," he repeated, breathing in the spicy scent of her skin.

"If anyone in this room is beautiful, it's you," she whispered, pressing a kiss to his clavicle and reaching for his belt at the same time. "Hurry, Dirk."

If he hurried, everything would be over. Fast. She was driving him crazy. Each and every cell in his body had caught fire and burned with need.

Letting her pull his belt free, Dirk slid over her, pinning her beneath him, loving how she wrapped her arms around him, clinging to him.

"Hurry," she urged. "I need you."

Dirk kissed her until he thought he might explode, until their hands locked on to each other's rather than continue the frenzied exploration of each other's bodies.

"I need you, too, Abby." More than he'd ever imagined possible. Rolling slightly to his side, he reached for his waistband, planning to strip off his pants.

That's when he heard the sound of cold reality.

His cellphone.

"Don't answer it," she moaned, taking over where he'd stopped undoing his zipper. Her fingers brushed against him, and he inhaled sharply.

He wanted to ignore the phone, but he wouldn't.

"I'm on call." How he wished he wasn't. "No one would call me this late unless there was an emergency."

Abby's face paled in the glow of the firelight. "Oh, God. I forgot."

He understood all too well. She made him forget, too.

Going into the foyer, he grabbed his jacket from the floor and removed his phone from the inside pocket. He listened to the caller for about thirty seconds then raked his fingers through his hair. "No problem. I'll be right there."

He hung up the phone and met Abby's soft, concerned gaze. She'd followed him into the foyer, stood next to him, her arms crossed protectively over her gorgeous body.

"It's okay. I understand," she said before he spoke. "My phone will likely ring at any moment."

"Probably." He went back to the living room, got his shirt, buttoned it with a lot less enthusiasm than he'd removed it, although with just as much haste. "There's been a gas leak in an apartment high-rise. One death.

Dozens suffering inhalation injuries and respiratory distress. Patients are being diverted to several hospitals."

Stooping down and providing him with a delectable view of her backside that tempted him to say to hell with everything, Abby plucked up the blanket from the floor. She wrapped it round her shoulders, as if she didn't want him to see her almost naked body now that they'd been interrupted. "I'll get changed."

He started to speak, to tell her to get some rest while she could, that perhaps they'd already called in enough nurses without her. But her phone started ringing from inside her purse.

She gave a shaky laugh. "Wonder who that is?"

While she took the call, Dirk finished dressing, got his coat. A gentleman would wait until she finished her call, but he didn't. He left.

She already knew he wasn't a gentleman. Hell, he'd slept with her the day they met and had been about to take advantage of her yet again.

Still wanted to take advantage so badly every cell in his body protested against the interruption.

She'd be wise to stay far, far away.

Perhaps that's why they'd been interrupted.

To give them both time to think about what they were doing. For Dirk to recall that Abby deserved better than what he'd give. For Abby to recall that she was young and beautiful and not bitter at the world, that she saw the goodness in life, the positive.

Things Dirk had quit doing long ago even if Abby had made him forget that for a short while.

Abby had put in eight hours of nonstop running from one patient to the next. Every bay had been full, with a rapid rate of turnover as patients were triaged into admission or treated and released.

The day shift would be arriving soon. Thank goodness. Her lower back ached and she felt more tired than she recalled feeling in a long, long time.

Surprised to find there wasn't another patient waiting, she took advantage of the unexpected reprieve. Just a couple of minutes to disappear into the break room, lean against the wall and close her eyes, then she'd recheck the pneumonia patient in bay five.

"Things are starting to slow down. You should go home and get some rest. You look tired."

"Dirk." Abby's eyes shot open, surprised to see that he'd followed her. Not that she'd really expected otherwise, but he'd been the consummate professional all night. Not once had he let on that there was anything between them other than a doctor-nurse relationship, not once had he let on that had they not been interrupted they'd have made love most of the night.

Not once had he mentioned that when she'd come out of her bedroom, he'd left, breaking her heart into a thousand tiny shards that he'd left her without so much as a word.

"The others can handle the remainder of the shift." His tone was brusque, paternalistic. "Go home and get some rest, Abby. You look tired."

"I am tired, but I'll be fine until the end of shift." She would. Already, just looking at him, she could feel her energy level rising. Or maybe that was her hurt and anger coming to a head. "Are you coming back to my place?"

He sighed, raked his fingers through his dark hair,

and glanced around the otherwise empty break room. "We need to talk."

Trying to read his expression, Abby searched his face. "I understand if you're too tired. It's just, well, I wanted you to know that if you want to come back, that's good by me. I could cook us something."

At least, she could cook him something. The thought of food made her stomach recoil. Or maybe it was the thought that he'd left her and she knew she wasn't going to like what he had to say.

His jaw worked back and forth. "I've been thinking about last night."

"Me, too," she admitted unsteadily. She couldn't quit thinking about last night, how they'd touched.

He grimaced. "Not like that, Abby. I've been thinking about what you said at the party about me needing to be sure before we went any further."

A feeling of impending doom crawled up her spine. Doom that made her stomach pitch so high it could have capsized a tanker.

"And?" she asked, not really wanting to hear his answer. Why was he backpedaling? She'd thought they'd come so far last night. Had everything only been physical? Was she really so naive as to have misread his looks, his touches so drastically?

"You were right to say that." He didn't meet her eyes, stared somewhere to her right at the wall. "If we continue on that path, I will hurt you and that's not what I want. I think we should just be friends."

"You're kidding, right?" She could tell by the look on his taut face that he wasn't. *Friends?* "If your phone hadn't rung, what we'd have been doing was a lot more than what just friends do," she pointed out, not willing to let him backtrack so easily.

"Which means we shouldn't have been doing what we were about to do. Fate stepped in."

Chin lifting, Abby's hands went to her hips. How could he be so dense? "Fate had nothing to do with that gas leak."

"But fate did rescue you from making a mistake, Abby. I have nothing to offer you beyond friendship. Nothing."

Did he really believe that? Looking at him, she realized he did, but not because he didn't want to offer her more, just that he didn't believe himself capable. What had happened to make him so cynical? To make him see the glass as half-empty? How could she look at him and see so plainly that he had so much more to give? So much more life in him than he saw in himself?

Why was it that when she looked at him she saw a world full of good and amazing things? A world full of Christmas every single day just because he was a part of her life?

She closed her eyes and counted to ten. "Okay, if you want to just be friends, we'll just be friends."

She couldn't make him love her. Couldn't make him want to take a chance on loving her. She'd spent years living with her great-aunt, doing everything she could to earn the woman's love. In the end, she'd realized you can't make someone love you. Either they did or they didn't.

"I'm glad you understand." He let out a slow breath, looked relieved that she wasn't going to make a scene.

Had he expected her to stomp her feet and throw a

fit? Wrong. But neither would she pretend everything was fine, when it wasn't.

"No." She shook her head. "I can't say that I understand, because I don't. Obviously I misread your feelings for me."

"Abs—"

"Don't," she interrupted, holding up her hand. "Don't say things you don't mean in the hope of making this easier. I like you, a lot. You obviously don't feel the same so, fine, end of story. We'll be friends."

So why didn't she believe he didn't feel the same? Why did she believe that something else had prompted him to back away? Something that ran so deeply through him he believed he had nothing to offer her but heartache? Something that had to do with his dislike of the holidays?

"You deserve better."

She nodded. "You're right. I do."

This time she was the one who left.

By the time she got home, she was throwing up. No doubt from the stress of the night and the sickening feeling that had crept in during their conversation.

Friends. He wanted to be friends. *Liar.* Who did he think he was kidding? He didn't look at her the way her *friends* looked at her.

Neither did she have sex with *friends.*

Or even almost have sex with her friends.

Really, she'd just like to know how it was possible for a man to look at her with fire in his eyes and ice on his tongue? Because his words had bit into her bitterly coldly. Frigidly. *Friends.*

Fine, if that's what he wanted, she'd be his friend.

She told herself all these things and more right up until that night, when she was scheduled to work with him.

Then she admitted the truth.

She couldn't be Dirk's friend. Not when she felt the way she did about him. If she didn't protect her heart, she'd end up wearing battle scars from their *friendship*. Scars that ran so deep she wouldn't ever recover.

No, she couldn't be his friend, but somehow she had to be his colleague, his nurse. She had to work with him and be the professional she was. Somehow.

Almost, she called in sick, but her illness had passed, had just been from a morning spent longing for what might have been. So she'd go to work and come face-to-face with a man who seemed determined to be *friendly*.

Seriously, it was enough to send her stomach into Churnville all over again.

CHAPTER SIX

DIRK hadn't slept much between ending his emergency call the morning following the Christmas party and reporting back in for a half-shift that evening. How could he when he couldn't stop thinking about Abby?

She'd agreed to his friend proposal, but he'd seen the hurt in her eyes. The confusion. She didn't understand.

Why had he let things get so out of control the evening before? Not that Abby had given him much choice. He'd looked into her eyes, heard the truth in her voice when she'd told him she wanted to make love, and he'd ignored all the reasons why they shouldn't.

Just as he'd ignored the reasons why he shouldn't have asked her to the Christmas party to begin with. Not that he'd meant to. The invitation had just slipped out of his mouth and she'd looked so happy when she'd said yes, he hadn't taken the words back.

Just as he hadn't taken them back when he'd agreed to be her Santa.

Seeing Abby happy did something to him, made him do things he ordinarily wouldn't do. Made him want things he shouldn't want.

When he had slept, he'd been haunted by treacherous

nightmares. Had they been triggered by attending the Christmas party? Or just by the season he could never escape? Or from walking away from Abby when she was the best thing to enter his life in years?

Regardless, he'd welcomed the evening and the start of his abbreviated—due to the holiday party—shift. Right or wrong, he'd also welcomed seeing Abby again, welcomed everything about her, including the tray of goodies she'd left on the break-room table.

Mostly he just wanted to make sure she was okay. During the night, as they'd worked on patients, he'd felt her gaze on him, felt her studying him, trying to see beneath his surface. If she only knew what darkness lay beneath, in the depths of his soul, she'd have turned away, never wanting to look again.

If he wasn't careful, he was going to hurt Abby.

That and that alone should accomplish what he hadn't previously had the willpower to do.

He would ignore the attraction between them before he hurt her. Otherwise he'd end up taking every drop of sweetness from her and leaving her with nothing more than a barren tree with a few empty hangers where shiny ornaments had once glistened.

Abby deserved fullness of life, color and brightness, glittery packages, and tinsel, and twinkling lights. All the things he wasn't.

Having finished with the patient he had been tending, he stepped into the next bay, pausing in mid-step. Abby was cleaning the room, preparing for the next patient. She had to know he stood there, but she didn't look up to acknowledge him.

He turned to go, but the fact she ignored him irked.

She'd been polite all evening, courteous when discussing a patient. But other than regarding a patient, she hadn't spoken a word to him.

He didn't like it. They were friends, right?

"I saw you'd brought more goodies." He'd snagged a couple from the rapidly disappearing tray. "Those haystack things were great."

She nodded, not looking up from where she spread out a clean sheet. "I always bring lots of goodies this time of year. It's tradition."

She kept her tone even, but she was upset. She'd invited him to stay the day with her and he'd left her high and dry, told her he just wanted to be friends.

Idiot.

Dirk grabbed the corner of the sheet closest to where he stood and spread the material out, eliciting a surprised look from her. "You have a lot of Christmas traditions, don't you, Abby?"

"Yes." Taking a deep breath, she tucked the clean sheet in around the hospital bed. "Christmas traditions are important to me." She straightened, held his gaze then sighed. "Before you give me a lecture on all the woes of the holidays, let me just warn you that I'm a little cranky so you might not want to do that. Not tonight."

Dirk took a step back. Abby was cranky? Because of him. Because he'd refused to go with her. Because he'd said he just wanted to be friends.

"I'm sorry, Abby."

She snorted, rolling her eyes. "It's not that."

"Then what? Is Macy's all sold out of that gift you just have to buy still?" He tried to keep his tone light, to make a joke in the hope some of the usual sparkle would return to her eyes, but when he spoke of anything to do with Christmas a brittle edge always seemed to be present.

"Ha-ha. Too funny." Rather than sparkle, she rolled her eyes again. "For the record, I finished my shopping weeks ago."

She was probably one of those women who started next year's shopping the day after Christmas. That seemed like the kind of thing Abby would do.

"If you must know," she continued, smoothing out an imaginary wrinkle on the expertly made bed, "I haven't felt well."

Her hand popped over her mouth as if she hadn't meant to say that out loud, as if she regretted that she had.

"What's wrong?" All desire to keep the conversation light vanishing, Dirk studied her. She didn't look ill. She looked…beautiful, almost ethereal, like the delicate angel on top of a Christmas tree.

"Don't look at me like that. I shouldn't have said anything," she huffed, but when he only stared, waiting for her to elaborate, she continued. "I'm fine. Really. Just a virus."

But she didn't meet his eyes and he placed his hand on her forehead.

"I don't have a temperature." She gave an exasperated sigh.

"Tell me what's going on. I'm a doctor, remember?" Again, he strove to keep his tone light, but her evasiveness worried him. The thought of her being sick worried him. "Maybe I can help."

He wanted to help. As a doctor to a patient, he told

himself, even as he acknowledged his concern went beyond that of doctor-patient. As a friend to another friend, he corrected, but even that didn't cover the protective feelings the idea of Abby being ill spurred within him.

"Fine. I'll tell you, but just remember you asked for this." She picked at the pristine bedding, rubbing her fingernail over the white material. "I've been feeling tired. A little nauseated at times to where my appetite just isn't what it should be. I threw up this morning, but that's because I crie—" She paused again, flushing.

She must have spent as restless a day in bed as he had. Guilt hit him. He didn't want Abby to suffer because of him. He'd wanted to keep from hurting her, but he'd waited too late.

"You should have taken sick leave tonight."

"Why? Nursing staff are almost always shorthanded as is." She frowned. "Besides, it's nothing much, really. I don't feel myself, but that's my own fault, isn't it?" Glancing up at him, her weak smile almost knocked him to his knees. "I do realize that I shouldn't have read so much into you asking me to the Christmas party, Dirk."

"I'm sorry I gave you the impression we could be more than friends." He wanted more than friendship. He wanted to be her lover. Without strings. Without having to worry about hurting her.

She lifted a shoulder in a mock shrug. "I should have known better."

"Why should you have known better, Abby? I was sending mixed signals." Saying one thing, wanting another. Why was he admitting this to her? Wasn't he only sending more mixed signals by doing so?

"Were you?" Her brow lifted. "I hadn't noticed."

The way she said it, so sarcastic, bugged Dirk. Abby was happy, bubbly even. Not today. Nothing about this conversation felt right. Sure, he'd expected tonight to be awkward, but they'd done awkward before. Had done awkward for two months with only a break when he'd agreed to be Santa. This went beyond that.

Something was wrong with Abby.

He thought of the long hours she worked, of all the volunteer work he knew she did. No doubt she was spending the time she should be sleeping baking Christmas candies.

"You're not getting enough rest."

She pushed an empty IV stand against the wall, out of the way. "I slept eight hours each of the past couple of days. I'm getting plenty of rest, Dr. Kelley."

His name came out with emphasis, coated with annoyance.

He followed her around the room. "Obviously your body needs more rest."

"Obviously," she agreed wryly, picking up a stray alcohol pad package from the counter. "But it's choosing the wrong time of year to tucker out on me. I've got too much to do to get sick right now."

"Like what? More spreading Christmas cheer stuff?"

Her eyes narrowed into an outright glare. "I like spreading Christmas cheer. If anything, volunteering makes me feel better about life. Not worse. Maybe you should try it sometime instead of all that bah-humbug stuff."

"Maybe when you're healthy, but at end of shift, you need to go home and get some sleep. Doctor's orders."

"This morning, after my shift ends, I'm picking up boxes of food to deliver to the poor." Her expression dared him to say anything. "After I finish that, I'm delivering fruit baskets to a nearby nursing home."

Boxes of food. Fruit baskets. Hadn't she mentioned something earlier in the week about volunteering in a soup kitchen, too? Plus, she'd been doing all this baking.

"Aren't you on schedule to work again tonight?" He knew she was. He knew each and every night they'd be working together. And the ones they wouldn't.

"I'm due here at seven. For the record, you're not my doctor and I didn't ask for your advice, neither do I want it."

He crossed his arms, pinning her beneath his gaze. "So when are you planning to sleep?"

"After I get the fruit baskets delivered." She winced, confirming what he already suspected. She hadn't left much time for sleep. "Normally, I can do this and more without so much as blinking my eyes. Getting called in to work on the night of the Christmas party threw off my rhythm a little, that's all."

She didn't comment that he'd played a role in her rhythm being thrown off. She didn't have to. She had to be on the verge of exhaustion and whether she wanted his advice or not, she was going to get it.

"No wonder you're coming down with something," he scolded. "Didn't they teach you anything about taking care of yourself while you were in nursing school? Sleep is important."

Said he who had slept very little over the past few weeks. How could he when every time he closed his eyes his dreams took him back to the morning he'd made love to Abby? A morning where he'd felt guilty for taking advantage of her goodness. After that, he'd done all he could to avoid her, to keep things completely professional between them. Abby hadn't pushed, hadn't asked anything of him. Not until she'd asked him to play Santa.

He should have said no.

None of this would be happening if he'd just said no.

"I do this every year," she insisted, sounding more and more annoyed. "I just have a light virus or something. It's no big deal and really none of your business."

Dirk gritted his teeth, took a steadying breath, and managed to keep from pulling her into his arms to shake some sense into her.

"Yeah, well, you might try to kill yourself every year, but I've never been here to watch you run yourself ragged in the past," he reminded her, moving in front of her, placing his fingers on her chin and lifting her face so she had to look at him. "I'm going with you."

Her forehead wrinkled as her brows lifted high on her heart-shaped face. "Do what?" she scoffed, her hands going to her hips.

Yeah, that's pretty much what Dirk was wondering, too. *Do what?* But the thought of her pushing herself all day after working such long shifts back to back bothered him. Especially knowing she planned to come in and work another long shift despite the fact that she wouldn't be able to squeeze in more than a few hours' sleep at most.

None of his business? That bothered him, too. Right or wrong, he cared about Abby, didn't want her pushing herself so much. Friends could care about friends, could want to help each other.

"I'm going with you," he repeated, his tone brooking no argument. "You'll finish quicker and be able to get some of the rest you obviously need."

She regarded him a long moment, then her lips twisted into a rather sinister smile. "You're welcome to go with me, Dirk. Not because of me, but because you need a lesson in what Christmas is really about. Helping the needy is a great way to learn that lesson."

He didn't need to learn any such lesson.

"That's not why I'm going." He was going because she needed him, whether she was too stubborn to admit it or not. If easing Abby's self-imposed load counted as helping the needy, so be it.

"No, but it's definitely what you're going to learn. Come on, Scrooge. Let's finish our shifts so we can go make a difference in the world."

Abby snuck a glance at where Dirk helped pack more canned food and basic household supplies into a box that would later be given to a needy person.

She hadn't wanted him to come with her, didn't want him being nice to her, didn't want to be near him, period. How was she supposed to protect her heart when he insisted on helping her?

As much as she hated to admit it, he was right. She

had overstretched herself, and appreciated his help so that she'd finish earlier. But there was so much to be done at this time of year. So much important work. Besides, sitting at home gave her too much time to contemplate that when she went home only Mistletoe cared. That she had no family to come home to, no family to share Christmas dinners, no family to sit around the tree with and open packages.

No one.

Her gaze lifted from the box she was packing, landing on the man across the table.

Why did looking at him bring how alone she was into focus so clearly? Why did looking at him make her see what she'd been able to hide from herself in the past? That, although she loved volunteering, she didn't do so selflessly. No, she also volunteered because doing so prevented her from thinking about how she'd spend another Christmas alone.

"You okay?"

Abby blinked at Dirk. Although he'd been terse when they'd first arrived, he had quickly impressed the other volunteers.

Volunteers who kept sending Abby sneaky smiles and suggestive eyebrow wiggles. After her first few attempts at convincing her longtime friends that she and Dirk were only coworkers, friends, she'd given up. After all, she didn't buy the friends bit any more than they did. Besides, the more she'd protested, the bigger their smiles had grown.

"Abs? You okay?" he repeated.

She glanced at where Dirk had finished with his box and had lifted another to fill. A wave of dizziness hit her and she grasped hold of the table. What was wrong with her? To get sick right now would be so unfair.

"I'm fine," she lied, hoping she was imagining the sweat beads popping out on her forehead.

Maybe she should have said no for once, asked the ladies to get someone else. Anything so she didn't get ill in front of Dirk.

What was she thinking? Of course she couldn't have done that. Not when it would mean that someone's Christmas wouldn't be as special, as magical.

When it would mean going home and being alone.

She was fine. Or would be if Dirk would get back to packing and quit staring at her. It wasn't as if he knew she was struggling to keep up. She would not let him know just how much effort she was putting into this.

"Maybe you should rest for a few minutes," he suggested, boxing up more canned goods. "I'll finish this."

Or maybe she didn't have to tell him how much effort she was putting in. Maybe he already knew. Somehow. Probably that crazy connection they shared. The one he insisted on calling friendship.

She sighed.

"Or better yet…" He stopped what he was doing to pin her beneath his azure gaze. "Let me take you home where you can get proper sleep before you drop."

The two volunteers elbowed each other. Abby bit back another sigh, this one from fatigue, and straightened her shoulders. "There's no reason I can't finish, Dirk."

How dared he tell her what to do? Try to tell her what she needed? The only reason she'd agreed to let him come with her was because he needed a lesson in helping others, on what Christmas really meant. She should have said no. Him being here obviously stressed her.

"No reason except you need to rest."

She ignored his comment. Drawing on all her inner strength to hide just how woozy she felt, she smiled at the ladies watching them curiously. "Once we get these packed, we'll divvy them up and take the ones on my list to deliver. Dr. Kelley can go home and rest."

Eyeing her like a kid studied a sole, tiny package labeled for him under the Christmas tree, Dirk frowned. A tightly controlled muscle jumped at the corner of his mouth. "This is too much after working all night. Call and cancel the fruit basket delivery."

Tempting, but then who would deliver the baskets? Besides, she was pretty sure it was the stress of being near him making her feel so bad. That and the virus. If he'd just quit looking at her...

"No." She couldn't cancel her activities. Sure, she'd been a little out of sorts. That wasn't any reason to let down those depending on her. They needed her help to make their Christmas all it should be, all hers wouldn't be.

"Abby, if you're not feeling well, Joyce and I can finish this up," Judy, the lady in charge, offered, placing her hand on Abby's shoulder.

Dirk smiled smugly, obviously viewing the woman's offer as reinforcement that he was right, that she should do as he wanted. Enough was enough.

"Seriously." She made eye contact with the elderly lady she'd bonded with while still in nursing school on her first volunteer project. "I'm fine. I just made the mistake of mentioning to Dr. Overprotective—" she flicked her thumb toward Dirk, hoping how much he meant to her didn't show "—that I'd been feeling under the weather."

"Nothing serious, I hope," Judy said sympathetically, completely ignoring that Abby had said she was fine.

"Of course not. I've just had a little nausea and fatigue for a few days. No big deal." At the woman's look of concern, Abby added, "Nothing contagious."

At least, she didn't think so. If so, surely some of her coworkers would be having symptoms by now since she'd been fighting this for more than a week. For that matter, Dirk would be having symptoms. He'd definitely had up-close exposure the night of the Christmas party.

"I'm definitely not contagious," she repeated, hoping to reassure her friends.

Her face brightening, Joyce clapped her hands together gleefully. "Ooh, when you walked in today, I just knew there was something different about you. Beside the fact you brought this gorgeous man with you." The older woman sent a knowing smile Dirk's way then returned her attention to Abby. "Just look at how you're glowing."

"Glowing?" Abby's mouth dropped just as Dirk's can crashed to the concrete floor as the woman's meaning sank in. The sharp intake of his breath almost drowned out the loud clang. Abby was surprised the thunderous beat of her heart didn't deafen them all. "If you're implying... I think you're making a wrong assumption."

The two smiling volunteers looked at each other, then

back at Abby and Dirk, their smiles fading as realization dawned. "You're not pregnant?"

"Uh, no." Abby coughed into her hand, trying to make sure she worded this correctly so she didn't end up as before, protesting to the point that she was only convincing her friends of the opposite. "Of course I'm not pregnant. I can't be."

Dirk had used a condom. Although she'd been wrapped up in what they'd been doing, she was sure he had used protection. She'd found two opened foil pouches.

She faked another cough, whether to show her symptoms were from something else entirely or just to buy a few more seconds to think of what to say she wasn't sure.

"You ladies are as bad as Dirk about overreacting." She laughed as if their suggestion was preposterous. It was preposterous. Pregnant. Her. No way. "I've just been pushing myself a little too hard with the holidays and have picked up a minor bug of some sort at work. You know how I'm exposed to everything in the emergency room. It's a wonder Dirk isn't sick, too."

But even as she gave the excuse she counted back the days since her last menstrual period and came up with a too-high number. Way too high a number. Oh. My.

This time she inhaled sharply, would have dropped a can if she'd been holding one. Her fingers curled into her palms, her nails digging painfully into the soft flesh.

Could she be? Was it possible? She'd never considered the possibility, hadn't dared to consider her lovemaking with Dirk might leave her pregnant. They were consenting adults who'd used a condom. Not overzealous teenagers who'd had unprepared-for sex.

She wasn't pregnant. Or was she?

She wanted kids. Someday, she wanted kids a lot. But not while unmarried and by a man who said he wanted to just be her friend. She wanted the dream. Snuggling in front of the fireplace together, sipping hot cocoa, enjoying each other's company. She'd take his hand and place it over her much, much thinner belly from where she'd finally stuck to that exercise routine and, with hope in his eyes, he'd ask if she was. She'd nod. They'd fall into each other's arms and be so happy together. A family. No more lonely Christmases. No more lonely ever.

But never had she imagined being pregnant, unwed and finding out while volunteering at a food bank with the prospective father having told her just the day before that they were only friends. By the look on Dirk's face, this obviously wasn't how he'd envisioned the moment, either.

Powerless to stop her hand, her palm settled over her abdomen. Was Dirk's baby growing inside her? Would she give birth to a little boy or girl with eyes so blue they left the sky envious? With hair so inky black the night paled in comparison?

If so, what in the world would she do about an unplanned pregnancy by a man who she technically barely knew, but felt as if she knew better than anyone she'd ever met? A man who said he only wanted to be friends and professed not to even like Christmas?

CHAPTER SEVEN

DIRK's ears roared with the intensity of a jet taking off inside his head. Any moment he expected the backdraft to knock him off his feet and send him crashing against the wall.

Mentally, he was already thrashing about the room. Emotionally, he'd already crashed and gone up in flames.

Abby's big hazel eyes had widened with shock, had darkened with unwanted possibilities, with fear, then softened as her hand pressed her lower abdomen.

Hell, no. She couldn't be. He'd used a condom both times they'd made love. He always used a condom. Always.

But, hell, how old had the condoms in his wallet been? Although he hadn't lived the life of a monk over the past four years, he hadn't exactly had a high prophylactic turnover rate, either. He'd never considered checking the condoms' expiration date. They'd been, what? About a year old, maybe? God, it was possible they'd expired.

He should have checked. He should have known better. He was a doctor, trained not to make the mistakes a seventeen-year-old boy would make.

Abby might be pregnant, and it was his fault.

He didn't want her to be pregnant.

The two women who'd hovered over them both like mother hens were obviously drawing the same conclusions.

Despite her protest, Abby might be having a baby. His baby. The slightly stunned expression on her pretty little face said so.

Another woman, another pregnancy, swept through his memories. Sandra excitedly telling her news. Lord, he'd been scared. After all, he'd still had a few years of residency left. But he'd looked into her eyes and he'd hidden his fear, had swept her into his arms and spun her around. A baby. Shelby. And now, would there be another baby?

Sharp pain zigzagged across his chest at the thought.

Both volunteers turned to him, expectation and protectiveness of Abby in their eyes. He couldn't blame them. He felt like beating the crap out of him, too, for doing this. He deserved worse if he'd made her pregnant.

Judy crossed her arms over her chest, her head bent slightly to one side, as if to say, *Well?*

Uh-huh. He wasn't going to have that conversation with two strangers watching, listening to every word.

Abby wasn't pregnant. And if she was… Hell, he didn't know what they'd do if she was.

Regardless, that was a private conversation. Not one for women he'd just met, even if they were longtime friends of Abby's and treated her like a favorite niece.

Following Abby's lead, Dirk drew on acting skills he'd honed in the days following Sandra and Shelby's deaths, days in which he'd been dead inside but had had to go on, puting on a front for the world. Had put on a show for his friends and family who'd not been able to look at him without pity in their eyes. Pity he'd tired of and left behind. In late spring he'd started searching for another position, knowing he couldn't face another holiday season under their watchful gazes. In June he'd accepted the position in Philadelphia, finished up his Oak Park contract, and had started in the emergency room in October.

And met Abby. Possibly impregnated her.

"This is the last of the boxes, Abby. You ready to pack them into my truck so we can go?" God, he hoped so, because he wanted away from the prying eyes. "We've still got to go pick up those fruit baskets and get them delivered. Unless I can convince you to cancel out so you can rest and properly get over this *virus*."

Did his voice sound normal? Or could everyone in the room hear his panic? See how his insides quavered at the thought he might have made Abby pregnant?

"I, uh…" Her hand fell away from her belly. She turned to him, her expression so tentative and vulnerable that something fragile deep in his chest cracked open and bled freely, gushing, leaving him weak. "Yes, I'm ready. Let's get these loaded."

Stunned by the rush of emotions, Dirk just stood, unable to move, unable to put on a show, only able to watch Abby smile briefly at the other volunteers and walk over to a far corner of the room. She had a dolly in her competent little hands within minutes.

"It's not much," she said, rolling the dolly toward him. "But it will do at a pinch."

He would have welcomed any excuse to get away from the mother hens' knowing looks. He hightailed it, boxes in tow, moving at record speed, leaving the three women alone.

Even before he'd made it out the door Judy's excited squeal echoed throughout the building, across the city, across his stampeding heart.

"Tell me the truth. You're pregnant, aren't you?"

He turned, waiting at the doorway to hear Abby's answer. The two women had practically pounced on her, were holding her hands and excitedly asking her questions.

As if sensing he still stood there, she glanced toward the doorway, met his gaze. Deep emotions shot across the room, deep pleas. Pleas for exactly what Dirk wasn't sure, neither was he sure he wanted to know.

Abby needed him. How could he be there for her when there wasn't anything left of him to give?

"Tell us." Judy wrapped her arm around Abby's shoulder in a motherly hug. "Are you pregnant or not?"

"Regardless, we love you and are here for you," Joyce added. "You know that."

Did they even know he still stood here? He held his breath, waiting, wondering, knowing it was impossible, knowing it was damned well possible. He'd made love to Abby quite vigorously. Twice.

"Don't be silly and start rumors," she said with a falsely bright voice, looking from one of the ladies to the other, then at him. Their gazes met, clung to each other.

Don't say it, Abby. Don't say that there is any possibility you might be pregnant.

"Of course I'm not pregnant."

Which should have relieved him, but her eyes told a different story.

All eight of Santa's reindeer drop-kicked Dirk in the gut at once, knocking his breath out of him and stomping him to smithereens while he was down.

Abby might be pregnant with his baby.

What had he done?

"This is crazy," Abby protested when Dirk pulled his truck into a parking space at the pharmacy.

After his terse "We'll talk when we've finished delivering" they'd continued in virtual silence. They'd delivered to the public housing residents on her list. They'd smiled and said all the appropriate things to the grateful recipients, but there had definitely been underlying tension.

Abby didn't feel tense. Not really.

She felt numb. Perhaps in denial. Yes, she'd missed her period. Two of them. But she'd been irregular on occasion in the past, so that was the likely explanation. Certainly, she hadn't thought anything of her missed periods. They'd always come and gone as they pleased.

Plus, there were the increased demands on her time with her Christmas volunteering. Although she loved what she did, believed one hundred percent in making the holidays brighter for others, the workload was stressful.

Stress. Stress did a lot of things to the body and could be the reason for the missed periods. She hoped it was. Really hoped it was.

Which was why she didn't want to walk into the drugstore and buy the item she knew he'd come for, although, from the moment he'd turned off the ignition, they'd just sat in silence.

What if she was pregnant? What if the test came back positive? Then what? Hadn't he already told her he didn't do relationships? Yet he'd gone with her today. God, the man confused her. She really couldn't be pregnant.

"I'm probably not." She battled the tightening of her throat that she might be. "You used condoms."

She was twenty-five years old. Why was her face on fire at saying the word "condom" out loud? Here they were discussing the possibility of having a baby and she was blushing over contraceptives?

Gripping the steering wheel, he stared out the windshield at some unknown object. "Women get pregnant all the time despite having used a condom."

God, he sounded so terse, so like he hoped she wasn't pregnant. Despite understanding and feeling exactly the same way, his reaction stung. No doubt having her pregnant with his child would be a nightmare to Dirk. After all, he'd only slept with her because they'd been grieving. Although, admittedly, the intensity of his grief had caught her off guard. But there had been sexual attraction between them, too. Lots of sexual attraction. She hadn't imagined the sparks, the way his gaze had lingered when they'd first made eye contact, the way he'd seemed shocked by the physical awareness zipping back and forth. But women used for sex weren't supposed to end up pregnant.

Oh, God. Dirk had used her. Two months had passed before he'd asked her out again. That had only been after she'd initiated contact outside work, after getting him to be Santa. The physical attraction was there, but obviously Dirk wasn't interested in a relationship.

The morning they'd made love, they'd shared a physical attraction, an emotionally wrenching work experience, sex, a budding *friendship*, and, possibly, made a baby.

Just the thought had her hand going back over her belly. Was Dirk's baby nestled inside her, growing and wanting to be loved? If she was pregnant, and, God, she hoped she wasn't, but if she was, she would love this baby. A baby she and Dirk had made.

Maybe made.

"Don't do that," he snapped.

"What?" Startled by his outburst, she jerked around in the passenger seat to look at him.

His blanched white fingers clenched the steering wheel. His face looked just as pale. "Cover your abdomen as if…as if you are."

Was the idea that repugnant to him? Of course it was. She was the one longing for a family, longing for someone to love, and the idea of an unplanned pregnancy left her in a cold sweat. No wonder Dirk was pale. Such a gorgeous man probably had loads of people to love, loads of people who loved him. A baby with a woman he'd used was the last thing he'd want or need.

Then another thought hit her. Was there someone already in his life?

Oh, God. Was that why he was so upset? Although she'd never heard of anyone special in his life, she wasn't privy to the intimate details of his life. Actually, his private life was just that. Private. She'd never heard anyone

speak of outside work activities involving the man gripping the steering wheel so tightly there was likely to be
finger impressions when he let go.

"Is there someone in your life, Dirk? Someone who
will be upset if I'm pregnant?"

He didn't answer her, just gripped the steering-wheel
all the tighter, his fingers digging into the dark leather.
"*If* you're pregnant. We need to know what we're dealing
with."

A baby. That's what they were dealing with. She
wanted to scream at him. But she bit her tongue, reined
in her anger. She couldn't lash out. Not when deep down
she didn't want a pregnancy any more than he did. It
was just…just what? She wanted him to be happy he'd
made her pregnant when she wasn't happy about the
idea herself?

Wasn't that irrational? Could she blame it on hormones? She winced. She could, but she wouldn't believe
it. But if she wasn't pregnant, this was all immaterial,
all stress and angst for nothing.

She sighed. As much as she didn't want to walk into
the store and purchase a pregnancy test, he was right.
They had to know. Had to figure out what they were
going to do if she had gotten pregnant *that* morning.

There went the rest of her life, all riding on the results
of a plastic stick.

She reached for the door handle, but Dirk's hand shot
out, stopping her.

"No, that's not fair to you. I'll go and buy the test."
He squeezed her hand, held on another few seconds, as
if for his own reassurance. "I'm sorry I snapped at you,
Abby. This isn't easy. Just…just wait here."

With that, he leapt out of the truck and flew into the store as if he'd been snacking on Santa's reindeers' magic corn.

Dirk supposed it was only appropriate that he be surrounded by Christmas hell while he waited on Abby's sofa to find out if he'd made her pregnant.

That he should be reminded of how he'd taken off her red dress, lain on the floor in front of her fireplace the last time he'd been in her house.

Had that really only been two nights ago?

Everything had seemed so right. But it hadn't been. Later, when not driven by surging testosterone, he'd been glad his phone had interrupted them. Too bad his phone hadn't rung the morning they'd had sex.

Abby might be pregnant.

His brain kept telling him the test would be negative. But his heart, his heart had seen the very realistic possibility on her face.

He suspected Abby didn't need the test to know the results, whether she'd admit as much to herself or not.

Hearing the bathroom door, he glanced up, waiting for her to reappear, to tell him the bad news.

Carrying the slender plastic test, she sat on the sofa beside him and placed the test on the coffee table.

"Well?" he asked, unable to wait another minute without knowing and unable to decipher her expression.

Her cheeks pink, she shrugged. "It's not been long enough. I came straight out here after doing the test. The instructions said to wait three minutes."

Three minutes. A hundred and eighty seconds. The

difference between knowing and not knowing what the rest of his life entailed.

Knowing he was being a selfish bastard, he took a deep breath and clasped her hand. "Abs, I want you to know that regardless of what this test shows, I'll be here for you."

He didn't know how or what exactly he meant by his comment, but if he'd made her pregnant, he wouldn't abandon Abby. He might be a heartless bastard, but he'd do the right thing. Whatever the right thing was.

"I know you will." She sounded on the verge of tears. Her hand trembled and he clasped her fingers more tightly.

"If it's positive, I'll do whatever you want." What would she want? Marriage? An abortion? Child support? To castrate him for being so stupid as to get her pregnant?

"Okay, Dirk. That's fine."

Her voice was so flat his gaze lifted to hers. Unshed tears shone there and her lower lip quivered. Her fingers shook. Her whole body shook. He squeezed her hand, hoping to offer reassurance and wishing like hell someone would reassure him.

"Aw, honey, don't cry." He'd done this to her. It was his fault they were sitting here, wondering if they'd created a life. If only he'd not instantly been attracted to Abby. If only he'd not let the death of that little girl and her mother get to him. If only he hadn't found such comfort in Abby's arms. Sweet solace like none he'd known since Sandra and Shelby's deaths.

He could "if only" all day to no avail. If onlys wouldn't help them. Not at this point.

He wiped his finger along Abby's cheek, catching a runaway teardrop. "It'll be okay. One way or the other, it will be all right," he promised, although he wasn't sure he believed his words.

If Abby was pregnant, nothing would be all right.

She stared at him, opened her mouth, but no words left her tremulous lips.

"I'm sorry, Abs. So sorry." He leaned over and kissed her, gently, hoping to make the trembling stop, reminding himself that this was what had caused what they currently faced. Still, he wasn't able to stop.

Her mouth was warm and pliant, accepting his kiss, accepting him despite the fact he didn't deserve her.

"Oh, Abs, what have I done to you?" he whispered against her lips, threading his fingers into the soft waves of her hair.

"You didn't do anything to me, Dirk," she assured him, her voice catching slightly. "Nothing I didn't want."

"You didn't want this," he scoffed, gesturing toward the pregnancy kit.

"No, I didn't." She pulled back from him. Her eyes glistened with tears, but he'd never seen her look more sure of herself. "Not like this. Never like this. But if that test is positive, I will be okay."

"You'll keep the baby?"

She nodded.

"I'm sorry."

She stared him in the eyes, overflowing tears silently streaming down her cheeks. "For?"

"This. Taking advantage of you that morning."

"You didn't take advantage of me any more than I took advantage of you. We needed each other."

"What we did shouldn't have happened," he reminded her, so why was he holding her, leaning in to press another kiss to a teardrop on her cheek?

"No," she agreed, "but it did happen and we can't change the past."

"Or the consequences of that past." If only he could. Damn, there he went with another if only.

"True." She sighed, closing her eyes, opening them with strong resolve replacing her tears. "A baby wouldn't be the end of the world. Regardless of what the test shows, I will make the best of what life gives me."

She would, too. Dirk could see the determination and willpower reflected in her eyes. Knew enough about her to know Abby always made the best of any situation life presented. She was a glass half-full kind of woman.

Dirk had moved beyond glass half-empty years ago. His glass had been drained dry the moment his wife and daughter had taken their last breaths. After that, he'd tossed the cup against the wall, shattering the remains to bits.

"That's big of you, considering you're talking about the rest of your life." He couldn't keep the pain out of his voice. "A child is a big responsibility."

An odd expression on her face, Abby searched his eyes. "The biggest, really." She gripped his hand tightly in hers, a glimmer of uncertainty surfacing. "Promise me you'll try to be happy, too. Maybe it's crazy, but I need to hear you say that before we know, Dirk. Please."

Happy? She had no idea what she was asking of him. How could he be happy if he'd made her pregnant? He'd given all his love to his wife and a beautiful little girl with straw-colored hair and big blue eyes, and that love had been ripped from his soul. He couldn't do that again.

When he didn't answer, Abby sighed, dropped her forehead against his. "Maybe it'll be negative and all of this will have been for nothing. It's probably been three minutes."

Dirk was sure it had, but he didn't move away from where he stared into Abby's eyes. He wasn't a fool. He could see that she did need to hear him say he'd try to be happy. He didn't understand why, couldn't begin to fathom why, but in her eyes he saw beyond the happy front she put on to the world and saw real need. Need unlike any he'd ever experienced. Need that made him feel emotionally impotent and protective at the same time. Abby's need gutted him.

The thought of disappointing her filled him with mixed emotions. She was the kind of woman a man felt inclined to protect, a sweet, wonderful, generous woman who gave a hundred and ten percent of herself to those in her life.

She'd welcomed him into her bed when he'd needed her.

Sex with her had been phenomenal and had provided his first moments of peace in years. Yet he'd known Abby didn't give her body lightly, that if they continued, she might fall for him and want things he didn't.

But whether or not he wanted those things, if Abby was pregnant, he'd be forced to accept what fate dealt him.

She wanted him to say he'd try to be happy if the test was positive, if she was pregnant with his baby.

He couldn't do it.

"You read the test," she urged, her eyes searching his.

Without a word, he picked up the test, registered the unmistakable plus sign and felt his stomach drop down the chimney lickety-split. "You're pregnant."

"I am?" Abby grabbed the test from his hand, studied the results. "I'm pregnant."

He'd said that.

"I'm pregnant, Dirk." Dropping the test back onto the coffee table as if the plastic had scalded her hand, she turned to him, wide-eyed and stunned, grabbed his hands and squeezed. "We're going to have a baby."

A baby. What could he say? He couldn't hurt Abby, couldn't suggest they consider their options, because even if he could ask, she wouldn't do that. He didn't have to hear the words to know that.

"Oh, God, I'm going to have a baby." Her chest rose and fell rapidly. Her eyes grew bigger and bigger. Her face grew paler and paler, as if she was on the verge of a panic attack. "What am I going to do with a baby?"

"You'll be fine." Had that really been his voice? Had he really sounded normal? He didn't feel normal. He felt as if he'd been dipped in ice water and stuck to the North Pole.

"Other than from nursing school, I don't know anything about babies. Nothing." Was she even talking to him? Or just thinking out loud? Talking to herself?

She grabbed his arm, shook it as if to get his attention. "What if I don't know how to take care of him or her? Then what?"

"You'll be fine," he repeated, unable to think of

anything better. Unable to think, period. Abby was pregnant. With his baby. He was going to be a father again. He didn't want another baby.

Yet he couldn't look away from Abby's pleading eyes, couldn't shut out the need he saw there.

But he wanted to. He wanted to run from her Christmas-filled house and never look back. Never have to face the fact that he'd fathered another child when he didn't have a heart to love him or her with.

Leaving Oak Park to escape his family and friends this holiday season had backfired. He'd jumped out of the frying pan and into the fire.

He pulled his hands free, turned from her to stare at her Christmas tree. God, he hated Christmas. Hated having to dredge up the past, but since she was having his baby, there were things Abby needed to know. Things she wouldn't like. By the time he was finished, she wouldn't like him. Which was fine. He hadn't liked himself in a long, long time either.

"I was married."

CHAPTER EIGHT

"Married?" Jack Frost zapped a frigid coating of ice over Abby's spine. Surely she'd heard Dirk wrong. Hadn't she been thinking earlier about how little she really knew about him? For all she knew, he could still have a wife and family back in Oak Park where he'd come from.

How could she be pregnant by a virtual stranger?

Only when he'd kissed her, made love to her, he hadn't been a stranger. Far, far from it. He'd known her better than anyone, had touched her soul right along with her body. She'd looked at him and felt she'd known the essence of who he was, all she'd needed to know.

But she hadn't. She hadn't known he'd been married.

She was pregnant. Dirk had been married. Why wasn't he saying more? Why was he sitting there with his hands tightly fisted in his lap, with his jaw clenched and his eyes glazed over as if he were fighting demons? Had his marriage been that bad?

Was. That meant he wasn't still married, right? Why wasn't he explaining his bombshell statement?

"You were married?" she prompted.

He took a deep breath, raked his fingers through his hair. "Sandra and I married too young. I was still in medical school, gone most of the time, didn't have two nickels to rub together, but we loved each other. Then Shelby came into the picture."

Another layer of ice settled over Abby's nerves.

"Shelby?" Was she a girlfriend? A mistress? A brief fling he'd had on the side? A—?

"My daughter."

His daughter? Abby blinked, sure she'd heard wrong. He had a daughter? Why hadn't he mentioned a daughter? How could she have not known such pertinent details?

Then again, why would she have known? She wasn't important to Dirk. Why would he have told her? Disgust filled her. How could she have been so foolish?

Outside work she'd spent a total of four—*four!*—days with him. The day she'd gotten pregnant, his Santa stint, the Christmas party, and today, the day they'd found out she was pregnant.

God, what must he think of her?

Then again, she hadn't been alone in that bed. She refused to abide by some double standard that said it was okay for him to sleep with a woman he barely knew, but that for her to do the same made her less of a woman.

He had a daughter. A wife, hopefully former wife, but the fact he'd not clarified that point worried her. He had a whole other life she knew nothing about. A whole other life he hadn't shared with her. Would he ever have if she hadn't gotten pregnant?

God, she was going to throw up.

"Do your wife and Shelby live in Oak Park?" She asked each word slowly, controlling each breath to keep from gasping air into her aching chest.

Was that why she occasionally saw the look of pain in his eyes when he treated a child? Was that why he never seemed completely comfortable in a child's presence? Because seeing children made him miss his daughter? Had he and his wife had problems? She should have suspected something the moment he admitted to not liking Christmas!

"No, Sandra and Shelby don't live in Oak Park. They don't live anywhere." His voice caught, his jaw flexed, he swallowed. "They died in a car accident four years ago. Shelby was only two years old."

"Oh, God." Which explained why he'd reacted so emotionally on the day they'd made love. The mother and daughter dying in the car accident must have stirred up memories of his own losses. Dirk had had a daughter who'd died. A wife who'd died. Abby's heart twisted inside out at the thought of how much that must hurt, at what he'd been through. "I'm so sorry, Dirk."

She placed her hand over his, hoping he sensed how she wanted to comfort him.

"It's not your fault." He pulled his hand free, raked his fingers through his hair, looked tormented, as if he was erecting every defensive wall around himself. "Just as this pregnancy isn't your fault. I'm the one who's sorry."

She had a thousand questions, things she wanted to know, to understand him better, really know this man whose baby grew inside her. But he'd closed his eyes and, she suspected, the subject of his past as well.

Still, she ached for him and, as awkward as she felt doing so given their current predicament, she wrapped her arms around him and gave him a hug. A big hug. She held on to him, hoping he knew how much she wanted to ease his burden. He sat stock still, never moving, never budging, never talking. Just sat.

"I don't blame you for my pregnancy," she assured him, "if that's what you're wondering. We're both consenting adults. We used protection. Neither of us could have known this would happen."

She traced her finger over his, laced their hands. Although she wasn't sure he welcomed her hold, she squeezed. "We'll figure this out, Dirk. Somehow, all this will work out okay."

But even as she said the words, Abby wondered if they were true. Wondered why she was having to play the role of the strong one when really she just wanted to curl up against him and cry. She wanted his arms to be wrapped around her, to have him holding her, giving comfort. She wanted to be the one taken care of, the one who got to let her emotions loose, and be comforted.

Instead, she'd be raising a baby, possibly by herself, and would never have the dreams she'd clung to since childhood.

Dreams of magical Christmases with a man who loved her and their happy family. Dreams of someday sharing the magical news of a pregnancy with a life partner who would rejoice with her at the news. Dreams of a happily ever after written just for her and her special Prince Charming.

From the first, she'd hoped Dirk would be that man, but not under these circumstances. Unable to hold back the erupting emotional volcano, Abby burst into tears.

And although Dirk wrapped his arms loosely around her, she found no solace in his embrace.

How could she when he was only holding her because he was trying to do the right thing and not because he loved her or wanted her pregnant with his child?

Did Dirk really think no one was going to suspect something was up when he kept babying her? *Argh.* Abby was going to strangle him if didn't quit treating her so differently. Their coworkers weren't stupid.

And neither was she. After the halfhearted way he'd held her while she'd cried, she'd known she had to protect herself. After he'd left, she'd cried more, this time for the great grief rocking her insides, grief that she'd entangled her emotions so irreversibly with a man incapable of returning her sentiments. Even if he wanted to, he'd locked his heart away years ago and thrown away the key.

Dirk was a good man, but one without a heart to give, which meant she needed to guard hers with all her being.

"Here, let me do that." He stepped into her personal space, taking over where she was helping to transfer a patient from a gurney onto an exam table.

Biting her tongue because she didn't want to draw more attention to what he was doing, she shot him a back-off look and tried to continue with her job, to no avail since he didn't step away as they vied for a hold on the patient.

As their coworkers were looking back and forth between them, and even the patient had a curious look on her face, Abby held up her hands.

"Fine, Dr. Kelley. I'll go check on bay three's X-ray

report." At least she sounded professional, even if he was making her look like an invalid.

What was wrong with him anyway? Why was he acting like she couldn't do a thing for herself without his help? She was pregnant, not disabled.

"He's quite taken with you, isn't he?"

Abby spun to look at the medical assistant who'd only been working at the hospital for a few weeks. "Who?"

The girl, who couldn't be much older than high-school age, smiled. "Dr. Kelley, of course. I saw you together at the Christmas party. You make a lovely couple."

Abby swallowed the lump in her throat. She'd thought they made a lovely couple, too. Now, she knew they'd never be a couple. Perhaps if they'd had more time prior to her pregnancy, perhaps if they'd met years ago, before Dirk's marriage. Now it was too late.

"We're not a couple."

Dirk didn't do couples. Just because she was pregnant it did not mean she expected that to change. Neither did she want it to change because of her pregnancy.

She wanted Dirk to care enough for her to want to be a couple with her. Because of her. Because of his feelings for her.

She wanted him to love her.

The young girl frowned. "Really? I'm surprised. You looked like you were having a good time together."

That had been before they'd been interrupted and he'd said he wanted to just be friends. Before they'd known they were going to be parents. Before she'd realized Dirk was incapable of giving his heart to her.

"We were having a good time. As friends."

"Oh." The assistant didn't look as if she knew what else to say.

"No problem," she assured the girl, keeping an "it's no big deal" smile on her face in the hope of waylaying more curiosity. Particularly in light of Dirk's odd behavior since she'd clocked in. "Do you know if the X-ray reports are back on the fall patient in the next bay?"

Looking chastised, although Abby hadn't meant her to, the girl nodded. "They are."

No wonder the girl had thought they were a couple as they'd left in such a heated rush from the Christmas party and with the way Dirk had acted tonight.

She really was going to have it out with him the first private moment they got. Although they'd have to establish some type of relationship for the future, his overbearing, almost paternalistic attitude had to go. Besides, for now, Abby wanted a break from him. Later, after the holidays had passed, she'd figure out how she and Dirk could coexist in the world of parenthood.

"Hello, Mrs. Clifton," she greeted her patient, a friendly smile pasted on her face in the hope of reassuring the woman. "Dr. Kelley will be by in a few minutes to give your X-ray results." She pulled up the tests and flagged them for his attention. "How are you feeling?"

"Foolish." The woman in her early sixties gestured to the arm she held very still. "I still can't believe I slipped and did this."

"Unfortunately, falls happen." Abby lightly pinched each of the woman's fingertips, observing how quickly the blanched skin returned to its natural pink color. Almost immediately. Excellent.

"I guess this will teach me to be more careful of ice." The woman shifted, trying to get comfortable.

"Who knows, this might save you a much worse accident later down the line." Abby checked the automatic blood-pressure cuff that was wrapped around the woman's uninjured arm. One twenty-six over seventy-eight. Great. A normal reading.

The woman laughed lightly. "You're one of those positive people who always sees the best in everything, aren't you?"

"Usually." Only she hadn't been seeing the positive in her pregnancy. Only the negative. Only that her dreams for her future were undergoing a drastic transformation.

She was going to have a baby. A beautiful, precious baby that she and Dirk had made together. A baby to share her life with. To be a family with. To share Christmas with. Abby had never met anyone other than Dirk who she'd want to have a baby with. No one she'd want to share the rest of her Christmases with. Just Dirk.

If they weren't meant to be more than friends, then she'd deal with that, would love and cherish their baby without letting Dirk break her heart. Somehow.

"Nurse?" Mrs. Clifton eyed her curiously.

Pulling her thoughts together, Abby smiled at the elderly lady. "Thank you."

The woman's forehead creased. "What for?"

"For reminding me that it's much too wonderful a season to be down."

Especially over something that so many women would consider a blessing. She'd been given a gift, an unexpected, unplanned-for gift, but a gift all the same.

Just because that gift hadn't come at the time in her life she'd planned or in the way she'd hoped for didn't make a baby any less of a blessing.

Yes, there was still that part of her that didn't want this, wanted her and Dirk to have the opportunity to get to know each other without a pregnancy shadowing their every thought and word. She didn't have that luxury.

She was going to be mother to Dirk's child.

"Were you down?"

Abby considered the question. "Not really. I just wasn't seeing the miracles of Christmas clearly."

"Christmas is the best time of year, isn't it?" Her patient's gaze fell on her immobilized arm. "Only this year someone else will have to do the cooking because I suspect I'm not going to be doing much of anything."

Helping reposition her pillow, Abby nodded her agreement. "I suspect you're right. I hope you have your shopping finished."

"Mercifully, yes. I'm one of those crazy women who gets up before dawn and does all my shopping on the day after Thanksgiving." The woman chuckled self-derisively. "Fighting the crowds is a bit rough at times, but the bargain buys are worth the effort."

"Aren't they just the best? I do the same thing."

Dirk stepped into the area, his face going pale.

Abby bit back a sigh. Did he really dislike Christmas so much that just hearing a discussion about shopping bothered him? How would she explain to her child that his or her father didn't like Christmas?

Avoiding looking at him, Abby entered her nurse's notes while Dirk went over the X-ray results with Mrs. Clifton, explaining that she needed to schedule an appointment with her primary care provider in addition to seeing the orthopedic surgeon the following day.

He left the room long enough to grab some patient education materials, flipped the pamphlet open to a page with a photo of magnified images of a normal bone and an osteoporotic one.

"Your arm broke more easily than it should have because your bones are thinning due to a condition called osteoporosis," Dirk explained, pointing out the difference in the bones in the pictures. "This happens when the bones lose mass, weakening, leaving them in a state where it takes much less force to cause a fracture. Sometimes even something as simple as taking a step can cause the bones to crush in on themselves when the bones have weakened."

"Crush in on themselves? The bones can break without me even falling?"

"Yes, it's possible in osteoporosis, but falling or taking a hit is much more likely to be the culprit of a break."

"I have this?"

"You do." He nodded. "Have you ever been told you have osteoporosis?"

"At my last physical, my nurse practitioner mentioned that I should be taking calcium." The woman gave a guilty shrug. "She tried to get me to go onto a medication to make my bones stronger."

Dirk's brow lifted. "Tried?"

The woman sighed, shrugged her good shoulder. "The medicine gave me bad indigestion so I only took a couple of doses."

Dirk frowned. "Did you let her know you'd stopped taking the medication?"

She shook her head, careful not to disturb her arm. "No, I figured I'd discuss it with her at my next visit." She gave him a thoughtful look. "If I'd been taking the medicine, would my bone have broken from falling tonight?"

"It's impossible to know for sure," Dirk replied. "Medications can add around ten percent back to the bone strength, which is a significant amount and can mean the difference between a break and no break." He pointed to the X-rays again. "The medicine rebuilds those tiny connections, adding strength. With bones as thin as yours are, you do need to be on some type of bisphosphonate."

"Putting up with a little heartburn would have been better than this." She gestured to her immobilized arm.

"You should discuss your options with your nurse practitioner. There are a wide range of treatments for osteoporosis, including a once-a-year intravenous infusion of medication. With the IV method, you wouldn't have to worry about taking a pill or having indigestion as that alternative would bypass that system and the side effects of pills."

The woman asked a few more questions which Dirk patiently answered. Watching him, watching his seemingly infinite patience when the woman became repetitious in her efforts to understand, gave Abby insight to Dirk. She'd witnessed his patience, his kindness, his caring time and again in the emergency room while he dealt with patients from all walks of life. Not once had he lost his temper or behaved unprofessionally.

She didn't have to wonder if he'd been a good father. He had. Although, no doubt, with completing his residency, he'd probably been so busy that he'd missed out on more of his daughter's short life than he'd have liked. Sandra Kelley had been a lucky woman to have Dirk's love, to have had his baby, and experience the joys of pregnancy and motherhood with Dirk by her side, loving her.

Despite his aversion to Christmas, Dirk was a good man. The best Abby had ever met, really.

Honest, honorable, giving, strong in character.

Why didn't he like Christmas? Did the holidays remind him of all he'd lost? Of Christmases he'd shared with his wife and young daughter?

Would she and their child forever live in the shadow of his former life? God, she prayed not, but deep down she wondered if that wouldn't be the case.

If that happened, how would she prevent that overshadowing their child's well-being? Just the thought of their child being made to feel inferior made her neck muscles ache and her stomach clench.

She finished her notes, left the bay and entered the next, determined to stay on task. A patient she'd triaged had discovered a large amount of blood in their urine and had been having tremendous back pain. She'd put him into the bay, and initiated protocol hematuria labs.

When Dirk stepped out of the fractured arm patient's bay, Abby caught him and without meeting his eyes gave him the stats on the patient. "Do you want to get a renal protocol CT scan?"

"Yes. Thanks." When she started to walk away, he grabbed her wrist, causing her to turn to look at him. "You holding up okay? You're not overdoing it, are you?"

That did it. She'd had enough of him interfering with her work.

"No." She pulled her arm free, hoping no one noticed. "My back hurts. My feet hurt. I'm tired. My stomach hasn't felt right in days. But the main reason I'm not holding up is *you*."

His forehead wrinkled. "Me?"

"You're driving me crazy. You've got to stop treating me differently than you were before, well, you know."

His jaw worked back and forth slowly, as if he was trying to categorize her words and having difficulty knowing where to stick them. "I'm concerned."

"I appreciate your concern, but work isn't the place. I've got a job to do and if you keep making a difference, people are going to complain."

"People?"

"Our coworkers."

"I don't care what anyone thinks, except you, Abby."

He was saying all the right things, but Abby didn't want to hear them, could only hear his "let's just be friends" speech echoing through her head. She didn't want or need his overbearing behavior.

In his "concern," he was exposing her to her colleagues' curiosity. Her volunteer friends suspecting she was pregnant was one thing. Her coworkers another matter entirely. Not that they wouldn't know soon enough.

Everyone would know soon enough.

But she wanted a few weeks of having the knowledge to herself, to completely come to terms with her future plans prior to having to answer other people's questions.

"Well, I do care." It wasn't asking too much for him to give her time to work through this in privacy. "A lot of my closest friends work here. I won't have you undermining me."

His gaze narrowed. "No one would say anything if you needed an extra break."

Abby's jaw dropped. "Why wouldn't they?"

He looked away, guiltily, not answering her.

"Dirk?"

When his eyes met hers, a bit of arrogance she hadn't previously witnessed shone there. "I'm a doctor, Abby. If I give a nurse permission to take an extra break because I think she needs one, no one is going to deny that right."

Oh, no. That so wasn't going to happen. He'd do irreparable damage to her working environment. With a baby on the way, she needed her job.

"I can't take extra breaks just because you think I should." She paused, acutely aware they stood in the busy emergency room. No one was near them, but when Abby glanced around, the medical assistant was watching them curiously, a "yeah right, just friends" expression on her young face. "We can't discuss this here. Just let me do my job, okay? That's all I ask."

"Abby—"

"Dr. Kelley," an assistant interrupted, looking back and forth between them. "There's a myocardial infarction patient on his way in. The ambulance is en route and should arrive in two minutes."

Grateful for the interruption, Abby jumped into action. "I'll get the renal protocol CT scan entered into the computer and have everything ready for the MI arrival."

"Abby—"

"Take care of your patients, Dr. Kelley, and leave me alone. I can take care of myself and don't need or want your *friendship* after all." With that she spun on her heel and walked away from a man capable of breaking her heart.

When the paramedics rushed the man in, a team was ready in the emergency room to take over trying to save the man's life.

Abby stayed busy for the rest of her shift, working straight through her break, grateful for the mental reprieve from her personal life due to the intensity of their patients' needs.

Definitely meeting Danielle's definition of brooding, Dirk never said another word outside anything to do with their patients. However, when he realized she'd not taken a break, not eaten, he'd disappeared and come back with a cup of yogurt, bottled water and an apple, thrust them toward her and walked away without uttering a single word.

His expression hadn't been a pleased one. Actually, he'd looked irritated.

Part of her had wanted to toss the items at the back of his retreating, arrogant head. He deserved a good wake-up thwack. How dared he be so high-handed? Just because she was pregnant it did not give him the right to dictate what she should and shouldn't do. He'd said he just wanted to be friends, giving up any potential right to have a say in her life.

She was her own woman, could do this on her own, would forge a good life for her and her baby.

Abby desperately clung to that thought as a shield against the hurt Dirk's rejection had caused.

Clung to her mounting anger at his hot-cold attitude to prevent more pain from seeping through and jabbing at her vulnerable heart.

CHAPTER NINE

IF ABBY didn't open her door soon, Dirk was going to jemmy the lock. Or break down the door.

Was this his fourth round of knocks or his fifth?

Where was she?

Finally, he heard a scratching at the other side of the door. At least Mistletoe was up and about. Abby should be, too. If she'd gone home and gone to bed, she'd have had a good eight hours.

Was she okay? She'd looked so tired and pale when she'd left the hospital and hadn't acted like her normal self. He'd been tied up with a patient when she'd clocked out, hadn't been able to believe she'd left without telling him she was going.

As if she was truly angry with him. He'd have understood anger on the day they'd found out she was pregnant, would have understood if she'd beat his chest with her fists, but last night? Hell, he'd made a conscious effort to take care of her, to let her know he planned to be there for her and their baby even if the mere thought gave him hives. Didn't she understand how difficult this was for him? How hard he was trying?

The lock clicked, and the door swung open. Abby squinted, putting her hand up to block the fading sunlight filtering onto the porch. "Dirk? What are you doing here?"

"You look awful."

Standing in her doorway wearing baggy sweats, her hair wild, dark shadows bruising her eyes, Abby did look awful. Like she hadn't gone to bed after leaving work.

"Nice to see you, too," she mumbled. Her cat rubbing against her leg, meowing, she moved aside for Dirk to enter.

Carrying a bag of groceries he'd brought because he seriously doubted she was taking care of herself, he stepped into her foyer. He eyed her more closely, taking in the pallor of her skin, the redness in her eyes. "Did you volunteer somewhere after work this morning?"

She shut her front door, turned to face him. "You're not my boss. Not outside the emergency room. If I want to volunteer somewhere, I can."

"Which means you did." He let out an exasperated sigh, assessing her like a bug under a magnifying glass. "Why didn't you tell me? I would have gone with you."

"Have you considered that maybe I didn't tell you because I didn't want you to go?" She yawned, stretched her arms over her head, raising the shapeless sweat shirt up to expose a tiny sliver of ivory skin.

"No, I haven't considered that. Why wouldn't you want my help?" Forcing his gaze away from that glimpse of flesh, Dirk swallowed, shifted the groceries in his arms. How could he be looking at her one minute, thinking how tired she looked and wanting to throttle her for not taking better care of herself and the next be fighting the desire to pull that sweatshirt over her head to expose a whole lot more of her delectable body?

"Go away, Dirk," she continued, gratefully oblivious to the effect her stretch had had on his body and mind.

"No." After a few minutes of lying in his bed, thinking about Abby and her uncharacteristic snippiness, he had crashed into a dreamless sleep and awakened with only one thought. Seeing Abby, making sure she was okay. "You need someone to look after you."

"I can look after myself just fine." Her lower lip puckered in an almost pout.

His gaze zeroed in on that full bottom lip. He wanted to kiss her. To take her in his arms and kiss her until she sighed in contentment.

"Since when?" Dirk fought wincing at how brusque his tone was. Just because he was fighting sexual awareness he shouldn't be feeling when she looked exhausted, it didn't mean she'd understand that's what was causing his irritation. What was it about the woman that drove him so physically crazy? Taking a deep breath, he tried again in a calmer tone. "You pulled an exhausting twelve-hour shift, Abby. What was so important that you couldn't have rested first? Something to do with Christmas again?"

Mixed emotions flashed across her face, mostly irritation. "Just because you don't understand my love of Christmas, it doesn't mean you get to prioritize my activities. Volunteering is important to me."

Shifting the grocery bag, he gave her an exasperated look. "What about our baby's well-being? Doesn't that count for something?"

"I'm not going to dignify that with an answer." Turning away, she walked over to the sofa, sat and wrapped a blanket around herself. The same blanket she'd wrapped around her almost naked body just a few nights ago.

Dirk swallowed. Hard.

"Christmas makes me happy." She looked like a vulnerable child, one he wanted to take into his arms and hold. But she wasn't a child. And if she were in his arms, he'd want much more than to hold her. She was a grown woman, a woman who he'd thought about almost non-stop since the night they'd met, a woman he desperately wanted. Why did he get the feeling Christmas meant more to Abby than the obvious?

"Look, you don't have to check on me just because I'm pregnant." She pulled the blanket more tightly around herself, causing the cat, which had jumped up next to her, to look annoyed. She picked up the fat cat, placing the animal in her lap and stroking her fingers over his fur. "Actually, I'd prefer it if you didn't."

"Why not?" He moved into her line of sight, but didn't sit down, just stood, watching her, wondering why she was shutting him out. His reaction on the day they'd found out she was pregnant hadn't been the greatest, but the news had caught him off guard. Way off guard. He'd have sworn she understood, that she didn't want a baby any more than he did. Finding out she was having a baby, that the rest of her life was going to be vastly different than she'd thought couldn't have been any easier for her than it had been for him. Probably, the news had been more stressful to her. But he was trying. He was concerned, wanted what was best for her and their baby. Why was she being so difficult?

"We're not a couple, Dirk. We weren't before this and we aren't now," she pointed out, scratching behind her cat's ears. "People are getting the wrong idea."

"What?" Was she serious? "How could they get the wrong idea? You're pregnant with my baby."

"Neither of us wanted this baby."

He winced. What she said was true, and yet to hear the words come out of her sweet lips so bluntly felt wrong. He'd never considered having more children, never considered starting over. He didn't want to start over, but neither did he want to father an unwanted child.

"Whether or not we want to be parents, Abby, we're going to be. We have to do what's best for the baby." God, he sounded so logical, so clinical. Did she have any idea how awkward this was for him? Standing above her, holding the groceries he'd brought to make her something to eat, her refusing to even look at him.

Her gaze remained fixed on where she petted her purring cat, her long fingers stroking back and forth. Lucky cat.

"I'm not stupid, Dirk. I will do what's best for the baby. But for now I want time."

"We don't have to tell anyone for a while, but you won't be able to hide your pregnancy for long, Abby. Decisions will have to be made. Soon."

Looking unsure for the first time since he'd arrived, she pulled her knees up, dropped her head onto them, burying her face in the folds of the blanket. "I hate this."

Helplessness washed over him. She looked so alone, so stressed. He wanted to take her into his arms, to hold her and never let go. But he just stood there. Taking her into his arms would accomplish what? Other than send his libido through the roof? Besides, he wasn't so sure she'd welcome his embrace.

As if sensing his thoughts, sensing his need for her to look at him, she glanced up with red-rimmed, watery eyes. "You seem to be handling this fairly well this morning."

Dirk felt as if a string of Christmas lights had been twisted around his throat and cut off his air supply.

Looks could be deceiving. He wasn't handling anything. But not wanting to deal with something didn't mean one could just ignore life's realities. He'd learned that lesson well.

"There's really no choice. Which means we have to make plans."

She inhaled deeply and let her breath out slowly. "Plans?"

"To protect you and the baby."

"No." Her jaw dropped and she shook her head in short little jerks. "I'm not going to marry you, Dirk. Don't even ask. That would just be compounding our mistakes and, honestly, if you did I think…well, just don't."

Ouch. She had a way of striking beneath his armor. "I didn't plan to ask you to marry me, Abby. Although if that's what you wanted, I wouldn't deny your request under the circumstances."

"My request? Under the circumstances?" She snorted. "I'm pregnant, Dirk. Not dying. I'm a big girl. I can take care of myself and this baby, too. I don't need you."

Did she think he'd just walk away and forget she was

having his baby? Then the truth hit him. For all her bravado, Abby was scared. She did want his concern, but didn't know the first thing about accepting that concern. He'd gotten the impression her family had been close before her parents' deaths. What had happened to her after that? Had she been taken care of? Loved?

"Yes," he said softly, "you do."

She glanced up again. Surprise flickered in her eyes. "How dare you presume you know what I need? You know nothing about me."

He knew she was a prickly little thing when she was on the defensive. But why was she on the defensive with him? It just didn't feel right. Didn't she know she could trust him? That he'd never hurt her?

What was that she'd said at the Christmas party?

Maybe not intentionally.

She'd been right. He had hurt her. They just hadn't known it at the time. But he refused to accept her assessment that he knew nothing about her.

"I know more than you think. You're a great nurse. A caring woman. A fantastic lover." Her lower lip disappeared into her mouth, vulnerability shining so brightly in her eyes it almost blinded him. "And I believe you're going to be a great mother to our baby."

The tears Abby had been fighting pricked her eyes. How dared he come into her house and spout off sweet words like that after the awful morning she'd spent tossing and turning on the sofa? The sofa because she hadn't been able to get comfortable in her bed, had given up and curled up in the living room, staring at her mother's

Christmas village pieces, wishing she could lose herself in that happy little world. Finally, she'd dozed a little.

She loved nursing and liked to believe he was right, that she was a great nurse. She could also go with the caring woman. She did care about others. But a fantastic lover? What a joke.

"We both know I wasn't a fantastic lover." She snorted softly at the mere idea of him thinking her fantastic. Not that he'd complained but, still, she doubted she'd been fantastic or anywhere close.

"Yes, you were, Abby." He set the bag on her coffee table, squatted next to her and reached for her hand.

"So fantastic you couldn't run away fast enough." She stuck her hands under the blanket, anywhere to keep him from touching her. She couldn't think when he did that. Not that she was thinking clearly anyway. Not after discovering she was going to be a mother, not sleeping much, and crying a whole lot.

He touched her anyway, running his fingers along the side of her face, into the edges of her wild-about-her-head hair. "So fantastic just remembering takes my breath away."

Why did she want to lean against him? To toss the blanket away and fall into his arms and cry until there were no more tears left?

"Why are you here, Dirk?" she asked, wishing he'd go, would leave her to what so far had been a less than stellar day. "Just go home."

"Can't do," he said, shaking the burgeoning plastic bag he'd put on the coffee table. "I brought you breakfast. Or lunch." He glanced at his wristwatch. "Or dinner. Whatever you want to call it. Regardless, I'm going to make you a healthy meal."

Just the thought of breakfast made her stomach heave. She grimaced. "Food is the last thing I want right now."

"You have to eat."

She rolled her eyes. "What would be the point?"

He stared at her for long moments and when she met his gaze, his were so intent she couldn't look away even though she desperately wanted to.

"Abby, you've got to stop arguing with me."

She bit the inside of her lip. "Who's arguing?"

Stroking his fingers along the side of her face, he sighed. "This is certainly a side of you I've never seen."

She was sure it was a side he wished he still hadn't seen. Unbrushed hair, makeup-less face, nauseated-all-morning pallor. She wouldn't win any beauty prizes on her best days. Today she might send small children running for the hills.

"No one invited you here or is making you stay," she reminded him, chin lifting.

But rather than take offense at her unusual surliness, he just smiled, as if he knew some secret she didn't.

"Go take a shower. You'll feel better." Another of those dazzling smiles that it really wasn't fair for him to be flashing when she felt so… What was it she felt? Hadn't she decided the other night at the hospital that their baby was a gift? One that she'd treasure? But right now Dirk's smile, his gorgeous face and body, just annoyed her. How dared he look so wonderful when she felt so awful?

"I'll slice fresh fruit and cook breakfast." He leaned forward, dropped a kiss at her temple, lingered a brief moment.

Oh, my. If she didn't know better she'd swear he was breathing in her scent.

"How do you like your eggs, Abby?" Oh, he'd definitely nuzzled her just then, his hot breath caressing her cheek, burning her all the way down to her toes.

"Have you not heard a word I've said? I don't want breakfast. I don't want a shower." Well, a long shower would be nice and the hot water might ease her achy body. "I just want to be left alone."

He cupped her face, holding her gaze to his. "No."

Abby gawked, not believing his high-handedness. "No?"

"I'm not leaving, Abby." This time his lips brushed her face, trailing light kisses on her cheek. "Not when you're like this."

Shivering from his touch, she took a deep breath. "Like what? I'm fine."

He didn't laugh, but he could have. She was so far from fine that no one would have thought less of him if he'd had a good chuckle at her comment. She felt on the verge of screaming, crying, laughing hysterically, throwing herself into his arms and begging him to love her, an entire plethora of heightened emotions all surging at once through her hormonal system.

"It's going to be okay, Abby." He brushed her hair away from her face, stared into her eyes and warmed a place deep inside her that she hadn't realized had chilled the moment he'd said she was pregnant. "I'm as scared as you are about this, but somehow this is all going to be okay. We'll make it okay. Together."

When his lips covered hers, she let herself believe him. Let herself give in to the temptation of his touch, the warmth of his caresses, the power of the emotions between them.

She couldn't exactly recall how Mistletoe ended up in the floor and Dirk stretched out above her, his weight pressing her into the sofa, his mouth drawing out her every breath. She clung to him, loving the weight of him covering her, loving his strength, the need in his kisses, his touches.

Rather than the frantic way they'd made love on that morning, or even their desperation the night of the Christmas party, their touches were slower, more drawn out, more *everything*.

Her brain screamed in protest, reminding her she was supposed to be protecting her heart against him, not kissing him, not helping as he pulled her sweatshirt over her head, revealing her naked breasts to his eager inspection. His eager kisses.

"I want you, Abby," he breathed from between her breasts. "Let me love you."

Despite knowing she should stop him, should not expose her all too vulnerable heart, she couldn't deny Dirk, not when his hot mouth felt so good on her body, not when she suspected he already owned her heart. All of her heart.

She wanted his love. More than she'd ever dreamed of wanting anything in her whole life, she wanted this man. All of him. His mind, his body, his heart. Yes, she definitely wanted Dirk's heart.

She tugged his T-shirt free, helped pull the material over his head, bit back a groan at the beauty of his naked torso. He removed his jeans, her sweats, and was inside her in what seemed a single breath. No condom. What would be the point? Body to body. Soul to soul.

"Abby," he breathed against her mouth, staring into her eyes, moving inside her. "I'm not going to last long. Not like this. I—I need you so much. So much."

Clasping her hands with his, he drove deeper, so deep Abby lost where she ended and he began, gave herself over to the emotions flooding through her body, her heart.

Not her heart, Dirk's.

If she'd had any doubts before, she no longer did. Her heart, all of her, belonged to him, completely and irrevocably.

She wrapped her legs around him, drawing him deeper, deeper still. "I need you, too."

Saying the words out loud somehow made them more real, somehow made her feel more vulnerable. But looking into his eyes, seeing matching need, real need, she could only expose herself further.

I love you.

She wasn't sure if she said the words out loud or just in her heart. Regardless, she felt them with all her soul, with everything she was.

She loved Dirk.

Much later, Abby didn't eat any of the turkey bacon Dirk fried, but she did have a healthy portion of the freshly sliced cantaloupe, scrambled eggs and buttered toast. And didn't dry heave once.

Amazing what good sex did for a body. Not good sex. *Great* sex.

No, not sex. No way could what they'd just shared be called mere sex. No, what they'd just done transcended everything.

"Apparently—" she smiled, feeling a little shy "—I like your cooking better than my own."

"Impossible." His grin was contagious, complete. Real. "I've had your fudge, Abby. You're a whiz in the kitchen."

"Thanks." She watched him feed Mistletoe the left-over bacon. The cat purred against his leg, brushing against him time and again. Mistletoe wasn't the only one wanting to rub against Dirk. "My cat will forever be begging for more."

Just like she worried she'd be begging for more of the attention he'd shown her this morning. Wow.

Lord help her! She loved him.

The man had cooked her breakfast, made wonderful love to her until they'd both cried out. Afterwards, he'd held her. Held her tightly to him, stroking his fingers across her belly. She'd wished she'd known what he'd been thinking, wished she'd known if his caress had been incidental or if he'd purposely touched her where their baby grew.

She stood, intending to help clear away the dishes, but Dirk motioned for her to sit.

"I'm pregnant, Dirk, not disabled. You cooked. I clean."

"No." He shook his head, pointing at her chair. "My treat."

Okay, part of her thrilled at the idea that he was

pampering her. Had she ever been pampered in her life? She didn't think so. Not since her mom and dad had died.

"I can wash dirty dishes," she assured him, not wanting the way he'd treated her at work to extend into her home. She wasn't an invalid. "Besides, you really didn't make that much of a mess. It won't take but a jiffy to clean."

"Probably not, but today is my treat. Take a load off, Abby."

She stood next to her chair, eyeing him, yet again wishing she could read his thoughts. "Why?"

"What do you mean, why? Can't I do something nice for you without you questioning my motives?"

She bit into her lower lip. "Is it because you feel guilty?"

"I am guilty, but that's not why I'm here."

His blue eyes looked so sincere. "Then why?"

He leaned back in his chair, looked perplexed, then shrugged. "I want to spend time with you."

"Because I'm pregnant?"

He studied her a moment. "I've wanted to be with you from the moment we met, Abby. That's how you ended up pregnant."

"I'm pregnant because we had a horrible night in the E.R." She didn't remind him of the similarities to his own tragic losses. She understood why he hadn't wanted to be alone, forgave him for using her, found herself wanting to comfort him even more now that she understood why he'd been so deeply affected. But that wasn't what earlier had been about, was it?

"I've had horrible nights in the E.R. before and never slept with my nurse."

Why did that admission make her feel better, lighter, less used?

"If the attraction hadn't been so strong between us, no tragedy would have brought us together like that." His confident tone left no room for doubt. "I made love to you because I wanted to make love to you. Just as I wanted to make love to you today. When I look at you, I can't think about much of anything except having you."

Had he really just admitted that he wanted her? She'd thought so, but then the whole pregnancy issue had clouded her thinking yesterday and this morning. But he had wanted her. He'd said made love, not have comfort sex or one-night-stand sex or guilt sex.

"And now?" she asked, grabbing at the rope he was throwing her, hoping it was long enough to save her, hoping she wasn't grasping at straws. "Months went by with you barely acknowledging I existed outside work."

"I want you, if that's what you're asking. I never stopped wanting you. After what we just shared, surely you don't doubt that." His eyes caressed her face. "You're beautiful, Abby."

"You told me I looked awful," she reminded him.

"That was pre-shower." His tone was teasing, but his eyes remained dark, stormy. "You're always beautiful, Abby. You must know that."

"Thank you," she said. How could she not believe him when his gaze echoed his words? Dirk really did find her beautiful. He really did want her and really had made love to her.

Christmas miracles never ceased.

"But we can't repeat what just happened. Not when we're just friends."

She stood corrected.

Apparently, Christmas miracles did cease.

CHAPTER TEN

HAVING made it clear that he planned to lighten her load whether Abby wanted him to or not, Dirk went with her to her volunteer stints, becoming more and more involved in her day-to-day life, more and more involved in her Christmas charity events.

Although he didn't pretend the Christmas aspect didn't bother him, he no longer winced when she told him what they'd be doing for the day.

As she'd just done.

He'd come over, insisted upon bringing bagels, cream cheese and fresh fruit. They'd eaten and addressed Christmas cards to be distributed to nursing-home residents. When they'd finished, running his finger over the steepled church to her mother's Christmas village, Abby's favorite piece, he'd asked what was next.

"It's called Toys for Toddlers. Various businesses have set up stations for people to donate toys to be given as Christmas gifts to needy children. Our job is to go by the various drop-off points and pick up the toys. We'll deliver them to the headquarters and volunteers will wrap them at a later time, probably tomorrow."

His face remained impassive as he picked up a village figure of a couple holding hands on a park bench. "When and how do the toys actually get to the kids?"

Purposely trying to look impish, Abby smiled. "Santa delivers them, of course."

His gaze narrowed suspiciously and she'd swear he'd have tugged on his collar if he had one. She bit back laughter, enjoying teasing him, enjoying this budding aspect to their relationship.

"Santa?"

Watching as he carefully replaced the figure where she'd had it, she gave in. "No worries." She placed her hand on his arm, loved the sinewy strength there, but wondered at herself for touching him when she usually so carefully avoided doing so. "You're safe. I'm not in charge of Santa."

At least he was safe from playing Santa. Safe from her was another matter altogether. The contact of their skin touching was frying her brain cells, making her want to push him down on the sofa and leap into his lap for a little Santa role playing. She had all kinds of things on her wish list—naughty and nice.

She wanted him to kiss her, believed he wanted to kiss her, too. As frustrating as she found his insistence that they were just friends, she believed he had his reasons. But if he didn't work through them soon, she was going to make herself a mistletoe halo and wear it at all times.

"That's good to know." He sighed with real relief.

She observed him closely, noted that his shoulders had relaxed with her answer. "I was teasing. Maybe I shouldn't have, but I couldn't resist. Was being my Santa really that bad?"

He closed his eyes and took a deep breath. When he spoke, his voice was low. "Anything to do with Christmas is that bad."

His words startled like gunshots fired through a silent night. The true depth of his dislike of the holidays struck her with guilt that she'd teased him. Yes, she'd heard him say he didn't like Christmas, had seen his discomfort, but she hadn't truly appreciated how deep his dislike ran, hadn't fully appreciated that he repeatedly set that dislike aside to help her with holiday projects.

"Why?" Why didn't he like Christmas? Why was he willing to set aside that dislike for her? Even before they'd known she was pregnant, he'd played Santa. Because she'd asked him to. He'd also volunteered to help her at the food bank. Because he'd thought she was ill and needed his help.

Looking at him, his handsome face clouded, his eyes full of pain as he stared at the ceramic village, she wavered between reminding herself to protect her heart and risking his rejection by wrapping her arms around him. But she only held on to his arm.

"I don't like Christmas."

If she understood, maybe she could understand him, could understand why he insisted on calling them friends. Out of misplaced honor to his deceased wife and daughter?

"Tell me why you don't like Christmas. Please." She squeezed where she held his arm. "I want to understand you and can't fathom why anyone wouldn't love the holidays."

Silence. More silence.

With his free hand, he raked his fingers through his

dark hair. His jaw rotated, then clenched. "Sandra and Shelby died on their way to a Christmas sale."

"Oh, God, no," she gasped. She'd known they'd died in a car crash, had known he professed to dislike the holidays. Why hadn't she put two and two together and come up with the right answer about why he didn't like Christmas?

"It was early morning, before dawn," he continued, staring straight ahead, but she suspected he saw nothing, that he was locked away in a different time. A time where he had endured a horrible tragedy. Had hurt in ways Abby couldn't fix with a little Christmas magic.

Her heart bled for him, at the pain still so evident on his face, at the hollowness in his eyes.

"I'd pulled an all-nighter at the hospital, was still there and didn't know she was going to the sale. When they wheeled her in, I couldn't believe it was her, couldn't fathom why she'd be out that early."

"Oh, Dirk." She wasn't sure he heard her. He didn't appear to even be in the same room with her, his mind was so far removed from the present.

"She'd dragged Shelby out at that godforsaken hour so she could go and buy my Christmas gift." Anger cracked his voice. Deep, hoarse anger that chilled Abby to the core.

She clasped his hand, squeezed. "I'm so sorry, Dirk."

"Yeah, me, too." He looked toward her, met her gaze, and possibly saw her, although she still wasn't sure he wasn't too far lost in the past. "I'd rather have had my wife and daughter than anything any store sold."

"I know you would." Beyond caring about protecting

her heart, she moved to where she could wrap her arms around him, hold him close. "Of course, you would."

He remained stiff in her embrace, not relaxing, not making any move to take her into his arms or acknowledge that she held him.

"There was a Christmas tree in the emergency department's office where they put me after…Christmas music played." His face twisted. "I felt as if Christmas mocked me. The best part of my life was being ripped away when the world was celebrating peace, love and happiness. It didn't seem right."

"What happened was an accident. A tragic accident." She reached up, brushed her fingers over his face, smoothing the tension lines at his temples. "But Sandra and Shelby wouldn't have wanted you to be unhappy, to lose the spirit of Christmas, the spirit of life."

He blinked. "You don't know that."

"Your wife was on her way to purchase a gift for you. Not because of whatever that gift was, but because she wanted to buy you something special. That doesn't sound like a woman who would want her husband to be lonely and miserable at the holidays."

But it wasn't just at the holidays, she realized. Dirk had closed off his heart. Permanently.

"As if my family would let me be lonely at the holidays," he snorted.

He'd never mentioned a family. Only Sandra and Shelby. "Your family?"

Why had Dirk mentioned his family? Just because his mother had called repeatedly over the past week wanting to know if he was coming home for Christmas, attempting to change his mind when he repeatedly said no.

Apparently, she'd also put his brother and sister on the task as well, as both had been using various technologies to insist he come home so the family could all be together for the holidays.

As if he'd want to set himself up for another miserable confrontation. As if he'd want to give them the opportunity to force him down memory lane with photos and movies like they had the year before until he'd had enough and walked out.

A Christmas intervention. Who ever heard of anything so foolish? Anything so humiliating and embarrassing? Anything so hurtful? He'd been emotionally ambushed and, no matter how well intentioned, they'd ripped away what little balm he'd coated his raw heart with.

They just didn't understand the ache inside him.

No one did.

How could they when they still lived inside their safe little world? Sure, they'd mourned Sandra and Shelby, but they'd moved on, forgotten. Only his mother seemed to have some understanding. She put up Christmas ornaments in honor of Shelby. A baby's first Christmas ornament that had his precious little girl's photo inside.

As much as he wanted his mother to keep Shelby's memory alive, being surrounded by family only brought home just how much he'd once had. How much he'd lost.

Why had he brought up this subject? He didn't talk about Sandra and Shelby. Neither did he discuss why he didn't like Christmas. Not with anyone. Ever.

He'd never told anyone the details of his wife and daughter's deaths. His family knew, of course. Sandra's sister had shared that they'd planned to meet early at the department store. So early another car had crashed into her head-on when the driver had fallen asleep behind the wheel. A driver who'd also been on her way to an early-morning Christmas sale. All for a few sale-priced items that the recipient hadn't needed to begin with.

If Christmas never came again, Dirk wouldn't care, would be glad to not have to face all the reminders, would be glad not to have his family put so much pressure on him to "live life." What did they think he was doing?

"Dirk?" Abby touched his face, pulling him to the present. Her palm was warm against his face. "Do you have a large family?"

Closing his eyes, trying to focus on the present, he sighed. "Huge."

When he opened his eyes, Abby's had widened with delight. "Really?"

His stomach ached. "Unfortunately, yes."

She blinked, clearly confused. "Unfortunately?"

"Obviously you've never had a big family."

Looking a little sad, she shook her head. "No, my parents were both only children of older parents. I sort of remember my grandmother, but she died when I was five and the others had passed before her. When my parents died, I went to live with my great-aunt. She died while I was in college. I always wanted a big family."

Dirk studied her, a woman who had no family, had lost a great deal, and thought of what a bright light she was to those who knew her. "How is it you remain so positive when you've had so much loss in your life?"

"Everyone faces loss, although certainly there are

varying degrees. Attitude is a choice and I choose to be happy."

"Even though you're pregnant with my baby?" He hadn't meant his question to sound so negative. Neither had he meant to hold his breath while he waited for her answer.

A smile softened her expression. "This baby is a blessing. I might not have thought so when I first found out, but that was foolishness. Our baby is a miraculous gift. All babies are."

He let out the breath, relaxing a bit that their baby would be loved, that Abby would be able to wrap this baby in her goodness, that she'd make up for the hole where his heart used to be. "You're the gift, Abby."

Clasping his hand, she lifted it to her lips, pressed a soft kiss to his fingers. "I'm thankful for you, too."

Her eyes glittered with compassion, which usually sent him running for the hills, but there was more in Abby's gaze. So much more.

In her eyes he saw hope. Hope that he could be what she needed. Hope that was a waste of her goodness since her hope centered around him.

Dirk's apartment stood out in stark contrast to Abby's house. No brightly lit Christmas tree. No wrapped packages. No Christmas spice candles. No garland or bows. Nothing.

For that matter, his apartment was stark when not considering the Christmas season. The bare necessities interlaced with a few high-tech niceties. Nothing warm and inviting.

A sofa. A fully loaded entertainment center worthy

of hosting all sporting events. A square coffee table with a few sporting and medicine magazines tossed onto it. The area of the room meant to hold a dining table held a weight bench and an elliptical stair machine instead. Two stools sat in front of the bar that divided the kitchen from the open floor plan. The kitchen looked just as barren as the rest of the apartment. As if he barely lived here.

He'd been here, what? Two? Three months? Not a real long time, but enough that a home should begin to reflect its owner. Perhaps this bare one did.

Glancing toward her, Dirk paused, obviously reading her expression. "It's a place to live, Abby."

She nodded, aching more for him than she had since the morning he'd told her about his wife and daughter's deaths. Emotionally, she'd continued to waver back and forth between her growing feelings for Dirk and the pending sense that she needed to ship her heart to the North Pole in the hope of keeping it out of Dirk's clutches.

"It's a nice building."

He threw his head back in laughter. "Which is your way of telling me my apartment is sadly lacking."

Glancing around the sparse rooms again, she shrugged. "Well, at least I know what to get you for Christmas."

Christmas was Tuesday, just a few short days away, and she'd not bought him anything, hadn't known what to get him. She'd figured she'd make him a tin full of peanut-butter goodies, but she wanted to give him something more.

His laughter faded. "I don't want you to get me anything, Abby."

"I know." She bit her lip. She hadn't meant to say that, hadn't meant to mention Christmas at all.

They'd just stopped by his apartment so he could grab a shower and clean clothes, then he'd promised to take her out for dinner. When she wasn't nauseated, she was starved. Today had been one of those days where she couldn't get enough to eat.

"I mean it, Abby. No presents." Of course, Dirk would say he didn't want anything. She understood that, planned to get him something anyway. After seeing his apartment for the first time today, she had a much better idea of things he could use.

"But—"

"No buts. I'm serious. Do not get me a present. I don't celebrate Christmas."

She didn't say anything. How could she? Dirk was the most important person in her life. She couldn't not get him a present.

He eyed her as if waiting for her to argue. When she didn't, he gestured toward the entertainment center. "Make yourself at home. Watch whatever you like. There's drinks in the refrigerator. I'll only be a few minutes."

Abby nodded, but rather than sit on the oversized leather sofa she wandered around the barren room. No pictures hung on the wall. No little knickknacks sat on the coffee table. Anyone could have lived here. But Dirk did.

Her heart ached for him all over again. He really had cut himself off from the world after his wife and daughter had died. If not for work, she wondered if he'd have any contact with others. Until her.

She'd definitely pushed him outside his comfort zone with her Santa requests and numerous volunteer stints.

Now they were going to be parents, which definitely pushed his limits. Dirk needed her. Needed this baby. Maybe he didn't realize just how much but, looking around this apartment, Abby did realize.

A loud ring sounded throughout the room. Abby jumped, looked around and spotted Dirk's house phone.

Should she answer? Probably not.

But as the shrill ringing sounded time and again, she decided whoever was calling must really need to talk to him, could possibly even be the hospital as he wouldn't have heard his cell while in the shower.

"Hello?" she said, hoping she was doing the right thing by answering, but knowing at the moment she was the one outside her comfort zone.

Silence.

"Hello?" she repeated, guilt slamming her as surely as if she'd peeked inside a Christmas package. She should have just let the phone ring.

"I was trying to get in touch with Dirk Kelley," a female voice said, sounding a little uncertain.

Whoever the caller was, she hadn't said Dr. Kelley. She'd said Dirk. Abby's guilt over answering the phone skyrocketed. As did her curiosity and some other green monster taking hold in her chest.

"Um, this is Dirk's number. He's not available at the moment. Could I take a message?"

A woman was calling Dirk. Who was she? Why was she calling? What right did Abby have to answer his phone, to take a message?

Every right, her heart shouted. She was pregnant with his baby, had spent the past several days in his company, working, volunteering, getting to know him, and he her.

Silence, then, "Who is this?"

Just exactly what Abby wanted to know, in reverse. But she bit her tongue. Dirk had had another life in Oak Park. Although they'd talked a lot over the past several days, he'd shared very little of that life with her. Had there been someone special? Someone he'd left behind?

The hurt she'd felt when she'd discovered he'd been married, had had a child, and she hadn't known came back. Why had Dirk revealed so little of his past?

"Abby. I, uh, work with Dr Kelley." Why had she called him Dr. Kelley? "We're friends." Why had she added that last? What she really wanted was to insist on knowing who the caller was and why she was calling Dirk.

"Oh," the woman said, slowly, as if digesting Abby's answer. "That's nice. Where is my son that he can't answer his cell or his home phone?"

Her son? This was Dirk's mother!

"Uh," Abby hedged, her face flaming. "He's in the shower."

"Really? Or is he just trying to avoid me insisting on him coming home for Christmas?"

"Dirk's not planning to come home for Christmas?" Abby couldn't fathom having a family and not wanting to spend the holidays with them. Was he not going home because of her pregnancy? Or because of the past?

"He's volunteered to work on the holidays, hasn't he?"

"He's working on Christmas Eve," she admitted. They both were. "He gets off at seven on Christmas morning."

"I'd hoped…" His mother sighed. "No matter what I'd hoped. I'm going to have to face facts. If he refuses to come home, we'll just have to bring Christmas to him. Tell me, Abby, just what's your relationship with my son and how good are you at planning surprises?"

CHAPTER ELEVEN

ON SATURDAY, December twenty-second, Abby watched Dirk spoon a helping of green beans onto a cheap paper plate held by a rough-looking, unshaven, dirty man wearing multiple layers and carrying a toboggan.

Was he the last person to be served lunch?

They'd fed over two hundred today. Too many people with no homes, no food, no family, no Christmas.

She glanced around the dining area of the shelter. Smiling faces. Lots of smiling faces. And chatter. Being warm and having food in their bellies seemed to have turned up the noise level. Along with gift packages that included several basic amenities, baths were being offered. Several had taken the shelter up on that offer, but most had declined.

"This was a good work."

Surprised at Dirk's comment, she turned to him. "Yes. All the charities I volunteer with are good works."

He met her gaze. "You're a good person, Abby."

Slightly uncomfortable at the intensity in his eyes, she shrugged. "I'm no different than anyone else."

The corner of his mouth hitched up in wry amusement. "You're the most giving woman I've ever met."

Ignoring the depth of his look because she quite

simply wasn't sure how to take it, she winked playfully. "Thank you. I try."

"Why is that?"

"Why is what?" She wiped the metallic serving area with a washcloth, more to busy her hands than because of any spilt food.

"Why do you do so much for others?"

Feeling her face go warm, she shrugged. "My parents worked for Second Harvest. Both of them. It's how they met. After they died, a lot of people did a lot of things to help me. I want to do my part to give back."

"And?"

And she didn't want to dig any deeper than that. Didn't want to look beyond the obvious reasons for volunteering. "And so I have."

"Why so focused on Christmas?"

She took in his confused expression. "My fondest memories of my parents all revolve around the holidays."

He nodded as if he understood, but she doubted he did. After all, he still had a family who loved him, a family who craved to spend time with him and celebrate special occasions. A family he held at arm's length despite their continued efforts to be close to him.

"The Santa suit you wore was my father's." She wiggled her fingers inside their plastic serving gloves.

"You mentioned that the day you loaned it to me."

"He played Santa every year for various charity groups." How she cherished memories of seeing her father dressed up, of him scooping her into his arms and telling her he was off to be Santa's helper. Once upon a time she'd believed he really was Santa and just couldn't tell her. The times she and her mother had gone with him had been magical. He'd always made her feel special, loved.

"Good for him," the man who'd also played Santa for her said a bit wryly.

Abby just smiled, continuing her blast from the past. "Every Christmas Eve my father would put the suit on and put out my presents. He didn't know I knew, but the last two years, I snuck up and watched."

"You snuck up?" That brought a smile to Dirk's face. "Okay, so you've not always been on the nice list."

"Of course I have always been on the nice list. No way would I ever be on Santa's naughty list." She gave him an innocent look. "When my father had finished putting out my presents, my mom would offer him the cookies we'd made. My last Christmas with them, he pulled her into his lap on the sofa instead. They laughed and giggled and…kissed."

"So you literally saw your mommy kissing Santa?"

She laughed. "Yes, I literally did. I thought it wonderful how much they loved each other, how much fun they had with Christmas. All I ever wanted was to grow up and be like them."

He didn't say anything for a few moments. "Yet you chose nursing instead of going to work in philanthropy?"

Abby stared at him, amazed at how much he saw. She had always planned to go into philanthropy. "My aunt was a nurse. She convinced me I needed career skills to see me through life. I wasn't sure at first, but once I started school, I loved nursing."

"And the philanthropy?"

"I love that, too. Nursing is philanthropic work in many ways. It makes me feel better inside."

"Because you feel closer to your parents when you're helping others?"

Abby wondered how he'd seen what she'd rarely acknowledged herself, that volunteering made her feel less alone. Particularly at the holidays, when she'd otherwise be trapped inside her house with nothing to distract her from the loneliness of having no family.

"Yes," she admitted, "I guess it does make me feel as if I still have a connection to them."

"That's why the mad rush at Christmas? Because you want to feel closer to your parents?"

"I, well, I don't know. Possibly." She bit the inside of her lower lip, not wanting to admit the depth of her reasons. "They were wonderful parents. I missed them so much after they were gone."

"How did they die?"

"A house fire. Electrical wiring gone bad, according to the fire report. I was at a schoolfriend's house for the night. Everything was destroyed except a few storage bins in the basement." She gave him a blurry-eyed smile. "Those bins had Christmas decorations in them."

His expression softened. "The decorations you have up in your house?"

She nodded, surprised that he'd made the connection, then mentally scolded herself. Of course Dirk would make the connection. The man was brilliant.

"I've added a few pieces over the years, especially to the Christmas village as it's my favorite, and I've had to repair things, but, yes, my decorations are mostly all items that were part of my childhood. The only tangible parts left, actually."

Which explained a lot about Abby's love of Christmas. Dirk sighed, glanced up to see a latecomer standing in the food line, and forced a smile at the unkempt man.

"Green beans?" he asked the man, who was of indeterminate age. Could have been in his forties, could have been in his seventies. A lot of the homeless were like that. They lived such a rough life with exposure to the elements aging them more rapidly and were so rumpled that it was impossible to estimate an accurate age.

The man nodded, extending his plate. Dirk scooped a big spoonful onto the plate, which was already burgeoning with food.

"Roll?" Abby held one out with her tongs.

Again, the man flashed a toothless grin. "Thanks, pretty girl."

Abby blushed. "You're welcome."

"He's right, you know," Dirk commented when the man walked over to a vacant seat at a half-occupied table. "You are a pretty girl."

"Thanks." But rather than smile at him, as he'd expected, she averted her gaze, wiping at the counter again as if she wasn't quite sure how to take his compliment.

He understood. He didn't know quite how to take his compliment either. Wasn't he the one insisting that they were just friends? Yet he fought the desire to take her into his arms constantly.

She was right to be wary. He didn't want to hurt her, battled with the need to put distance between them.

But she was pregnant with his baby and he couldn't turn his back on her. Wouldn't even if he could.

Soon decisions would have to be made. Decisions Dirk wasn't sure he was ready to make, but he had little choice given the circumstances.

Abby had cooked most of the previous day while Dirk had been at work at the hospital. She'd only had to do last-minute items that simply couldn't be done ahead of time for dinner to taste right.

He should be arriving any moment. Would he be upset with her? He had no idea what she had planned, just that he was coming over for dinner.

Nervously, she swept her gaze around her living room. The tree blinked in multicolored magic. Her village houses glowed invitingly, making Abby imagine strolling along between them, hand in hand with Dirk as they peeped into shop windows and snuggled together to stay warm.

Despite being on edge, she smiled at the memories attached to each one of the special pieces to her mother's Christmas village. She ran her hands over the church's steeple. The first piece her father had given to her mother because it had reminded him of the small church where they'd married.

Mistletoe was in his basket next to her lit fire. Candles burned on the mantel and coffee table, blending with the pine of her tree to add a spicy Christmas scent to the room. Dinner and company waited in the kitchen.

God, she hoped everything went as planned, that his mother hadn't been wrong. But deep in her heart Abby wondered if she'd made a mistake in going along with this Christmas surprise. What if Dirk was upset? What if he thought she'd overstepped her boundaries?

Which was the crux of the matter. What were the boundaries of their relationship? He kept insisting they were just friends, yet he looked at her with desire in his eyes, looked at her with possessiveness in his eyes. She was pregnant with his child, crazily in love with him, and wanted to share her life, their baby's life, with him. But the him she saw, not the broken man he saw reflected in his mirror. She deserved better than walking on emotional eggshells for the rest of their lives.

On cue, the doorbell rang, causing Mistletoe's eyes to open. He yawned, but didn't budge from his basket.

"Nothing fazes you, does it, big guy?" she said to the lazy cat as she walked into the foyer. Pasting a nervous smile on her face, she opened the front door.

A freshly shaven and showered Dirk stood there, looking more handsome than she'd ever seen. Perhaps because he was smiling and running his gaze up and down her.

He held up a bottle. "I'd have brought wine but I figured apple cider was more appropriate considering."

"Um, apple cider is fine." Casting a wary glance over her shoulder toward the kitchen, she motioned him inside, closing the door behind him to block out the cold air rushing in. It hadn't started snowing yet but the weather forecast predicted there was a good chance of it.

Abby took the bottle. "I'll just put this in the kitchen while you remove your coat."

Slipping his coat off, he glanced around the room.

"Wow, you've really gone to a lot of trouble for just the two of us."

"About that…" She waited until his eyes connected with hers, trepidation bubbling in her belly.

Only his gaze shot past her to where he could see into the small dining area, could see the table set with eight place settings. His smile faded. "It's not going to be just the two of us? Did you invite some of your friends from the hospital?"

She shook her head. "No, I have a Christmas surprise for you."

Furrows dug into his forehead. "You know how I feel about Christmas."

"I do know." *Please don't let him be upset that she'd gone along with his mother's suggestion. Please.*

"Okay." He exhaled slowly, moving close to her, close enough to touch. "I'm trying to deal with your Christmas excitement, but no more surprises."

Cupping his handsome face, she stared into his eyes, knowing she loved him, knowing she wanted him for ever, to spend all her Christmases with him and their child, and any future children that might come along. "Dirk, I—"

"Dirk! You're here!"

His expression instantly transformed to terseness, instantly tightened with cold accusation before turning toward the woman who'd entered the room.

What the—? Dirk rotated his jaw, counted to ten, inhaled and exhaled, anything to try to keep his mounting anger under control.

"Hello, Mother." He'd never mentioned Abby to his

family, so his mother couldn't have been the one to make contact. But how? Surely Abby wouldn't have gone behind his back? This would explain why his mother's calls had eased.

Clearly having no clue as to the enormity of what she'd done, Abby's fingers clasped his arm. "Dirk?"

Seeing the stricken look in her eyes, he fought the need to reassure her. How could he reassure her when panic gripped his throat, cutting off his airways?

"I'm surprised to see you here, Mother."

She walked to him, turned her cheek up to him. Automatically, he bent to kiss her in spite of his displeasure at her invading his holidays. God, he wasn't up for Christmas Intervention II.

"I can see why you like Philadelphia so much." His mother beamed in Abby's direction. "Your Abby is quite lovely."

"She's not my Abby." But she was quite pale, looking back and forth between them, clearly trying to size up the dynamics taking place. How could she have done this?

"Are the rest of the crew here?" But he could hear that they were. Over the sounds of the Christmas music playing, he could hear his nephews chatting back and forth, hear his sister shushing them.

"Holidays are meant to be shared with your family. We wanted to spend ours with you, Dirk, because we love you."

He raked his fingers through his hair. "So you invited yourself to Abby's?"

"No," his mother laughed, wrapping her arms around him to give him a hug. "I mentioned how much we wanted to see you over the holidays, that we planned to surprise you with a visit, and asked your lovely Abby to help. She invited us here. Such a good girl, Dirk. I like her."

Dirk struggled to process his mother's words. "When did you talk to Abby?"

His mother gave him one last squeeze, starting to look a little nervous herself. "We've talked several times over the past week. She's absolutely lovely, son."

"Yes, you've mentioned that a time or two," he bit out tersely. God, what were they up to? If they brought out video tapes and photo albums again, he was out of there.

"I'll, uh, I'll go check on dinner." Abby gave him one last look, her lower lip trembled, then she disappeared into the kitchen, the low rumble of his brother's voice greeting her.

Abby had had no right to invite his family, to plan a Christmas dinner with them behind his back. Just what had his family told her? That he was a broken man? Pathetic and weak at the loss of his wife and child? That he might as well have died in that car wreck, too?

He should have. Sandra and Shelby should have lived. He should have been the one taken that morning.

"Dirk." His mother gave him a look that would have stopped him in his tracks during his younger years. "When I spoke with Abby, I'd hoped Philadelphia had been good for you, had removed the blinkers you've worn for the last four years. It's time you dealt with this."

Something inside Dirk snapped.

"Have you ever considered that I have dealt with this,

only not to everyone else's satisfaction? Guess what, Mother, I'm the one who has to wake up every single day knowing that I will never look into my wife's eyes again, that I will never feel Shelby's fingers wrapped around mine again. You should respect that I've dealt with this and let me be."

"If you'd dealt with this, we wouldn't be having this conversation, would we? Because you would have come home for Christmas."

"What? And be put through the hell of last year? I don't think so."

"We hired a top psychiatrist, Dirk. We followed her recommendations to the letter—"

"A psychiatrist?" Oh, God, that was rich. "I'm not crazy."

"No one thinks you are."

He paced across the room, spun to meet her gaze. "I was ambushed last Christmas."

She took a deep breath and didn't back down. "You were surrounded by people who love you and want what's best for you. People who want you to enjoy life again."

"What was best for me is lying in a cemetery in Oak Park." Dirk couldn't stop the words from streaming out of his mouth. Couldn't stop the feelings of hurt and betrayal streaming through him. "Something you conveniently forgot when you planned last year's fiasco. Tell me, what Christmas torture do you have in store for me tonight? Pictures? Home movies? Personal recollections of my wife and daughter? Because if that's the case, you should leave now, and take the rest of the family with you."

A loud gasp caused both Dirk and his mother to spin

toward the kitchen door. Abby held on to the door frame as if she might slide to the floor if she didn't.

Sharp pain zig-zagged across her face.

Hell. He raked his fingers through his hair. What was wrong with him? He'd never verbally attacked his mother before. Not even last year during the worst of the intervention, right before he'd walked out on them. No, he'd just calmly gotten up, informed them that they were mistaken about him and that he was leaving. And he'd left.

His mother recovered before he did, pasting a weak smile to her face as she regarded Abby. "I'm sorry, dear. It's rude of us to come into your house and squabble over family disagreements."

Family disagreements? Dirk wanted to laugh. Was that what they were calling invading his life?

"I came to tell you dinner was finished if you're ready to eat." Disillusionment shone on her face and when their eyes met, she quickly averted her gaze from his.

"Dinner would be lovely." His mother took him by the elbow, gave him a look meant to put him in his place. "Everything smells wonderful. Right, son?"

Dirk gritted his teeth, seeing right through his mother's ploy. She wanted to pretend everything was okay for Abby's sake. If they'd cared about him, or Abby, they'd have stayed in Oak Park, wouldn't have come to stir up the past.

"Right," he finally agreed, knowing this was going to be a long, long night.

Abby's face hurt from keeping her fake smile in place, just as she'd kept her smile in place all evening.

"It was so lovely to meet you, dear." Dirk's mother leaned forward, engulfing Abby in a giant bear hug. One so real and heartfelt Abby wanted to cry. "At least we know Dirk has someone to look out for him here in Philly."

Right. But during the terse evening Abby had realized she didn't want to look out for Dirk. Not under the current circumstances.

Having watched him with his family had only made obvious what she'd admitted to herself weeks ago but had shoved aside, hoping that Dirk could love her. He couldn't. He had closed off his heart to the world.

If he wasn't willing to let his own mother in, how was Abby supposed to believe he'd ever let her?

Which was the crux of the matter. After tonight, she didn't believe.

Dirk had stolen her belief in happily-ever-after, her belief in Christmas miracles. Her belief, period.

In place of the hope-filled woman she'd once been was a disillusioned woman but one determined to be strong woman who'd do what was best for her child.

"Dinner was lovely," said the next woman in line to head out the front door. A tall, dark-haired woman with eyes identical to Dirk's. His sister, Jolene. She held a well-bundled toddler in her arms. A toddler who shared the Kelley eyes. Would Abby's own baby have a similar blue gaze? Would she forever be haunted by the man she'd loved but who hadn't been able to love her in return?

"Thanks so much for inviting us." The woman leaned over and kissed Abby's cheek. "I hope to see you again soon. Maybe Dirk will bring you to Oak Park."

Abby felt tears pop into her eyes. What kind of man could have a family like this and shut them out?

Oh, he'd lightened up a bit as the evening had progressed, but he'd been out-and-out rude when he'd first arrived. So much so that Abby had planted the fake smile on her face and tried to make his family feel welcome despite his cold regard. Even now, as his mother pulled him into her arms, he wore a slight grimace, stood stiffly rather than embracing her in return.

Abby wanted to hit him. He had this beautiful family, her baby's family, and he ignored them, held them at arm's length.

No doubt after his wife and daughter's deaths things had been rough, but shouldn't he have leaned on his family, not shut them out?

His brother shook his hand, pulled him into a half-embrace. "Good to see you, man. If you can swing it, we'd love to have you at Christmas."

Dirk didn't comment. By his brother's sigh, Abby figured John knew Dirk had no intention of showing up in Oak Park on Christmas Day.

"He'll probably sleep most of the day. After all, he'll have just pulled twenty-four hours in the emergency room." Why was she defending him? This was his family. Not hers. She shouldn't be the one working so hard to make things go smoothly. "Driving long distances after working such a long shift really wouldn't be wise."

"You're right, of course." His mother's chest rose and fell beneath her heavy coat. "At least he won't be spending Christmas alone." She sent Abby a warm smile. "It really was lovely to meet you. Come on, children. Let's get this show on the road so Abby can prop her feet up. She looks tired."

Something in the way Dirk's mother said the words made Abby meet the woman's gaze, made her look away because she was sure the woman could see into her soul and see all her secrets.

Besides, she *was* tired. After pulling a twelve-hour shift at the hospital, coming home and grabbing only a few hours' sleep then finishing dinner, she was tuckered out.

It took Dirk's family another five minutes to completely get out the door, between more goodbyes, hugs, kisses to the cheeks, and kids dashing back in for a cookie for the road.

When the door closed, Abby sagged and didn't bother to try to hide her fatigue from Dirk. As his family had exited, she'd sensed his mounting tension, had seen the building fire in his eyes, had known they'd argue and was ready to get it over with.

"How could you treat your family that way, Dirk? They love you, drove all that way to spend the evening with you, and you lashed out at them every chance you got." Her heart had ached for the whole lot of them. Even Dirk. Because in his grief he'd lost much more than his wife and daughter. He'd lost everything that mattered and had no one to blame but himself.

"They had no right to show up here. How could you have invited them without discussing it with me first?"

"This is my house. I can invite whomever I want," she reminded him, chin lifting a notch. "Besides, your mother wanted to surprise you. I thought you'd be happy to see your family over the holidays."

"Well, I wasn't. You want to know why? Because I'm not you. I'm not little Miss Christmas Spirit, spreading good tidings to the whole world. I'm a man who lost his wife and daughter and the world, including his family who should understand, expects him to go on and forget."

"You weren't the only one who lost someone they loved when Shelby and Sandra died. Your family loved them, too."

"You have no idea what you're talking about," he scoffed.

"Whose fault is that, Dirk? I'm pregnant with your baby and yet you'd never introduced me to your family. Even tonight, you acted as if I was no one special."

"How did you want me to act? You went behind my back."

"It was supposed to be a pleasant surprise! Something to give you good memories to replace the ones you refuse to let go of."

"You'd have me forget my wife and daughter?" His eyes blazed, the veins on his neck bulged, his breath hissed.

Needing to put distance between them, Abby turned away, walked over to her Christmas village table, hoping to find comfort in the heirlooms she loved.

"Answer me." Dirk followed her, gripped her arm, turned her toward his angry face. "Is that what this was about? Making me forget Sandra and Shelby for your own purposes? Being pregnant doesn't give you the right to go behind my back, Abby."

"My only purpose was to give you a special Christmas

memory, which you ruined for everyone by closing yourself off to any possibility of having a good time."

"I have all the special Christmas memories I need."

"Well, good for you, Dirk," she bit out, tired, frustrated, hurt, angry at him for his callous attitude. "Maybe you should stop to think about everyone else who might still want new special Christmas memories instead of being such a selfish jerk!"

She jerked back, freeing herself from his grasp and losing her balance. She stumbled, reached out to steady herself. And failed.

CHAPTER TWELVE

IN HORRID slow motion Dirk watched disaster unfold, unable to stop what had been set into play, only able to do damage control by reacting quickly.

Reaching out to keep from falling back, Abby had grabbed hold of the table her village sat on. Only she didn't catch the table. She caught the steeple of the church and kept going, the church traveling with her, knocking pieces of the village left and right.

"No," she cried as she kept going back, too off balance to do a thing to stop the pending catastrophe as the table tipped. "My mother's village!"

But rather than saving her houses, Dirk caught hold of her, righting her while the table and its contents crashed to the floor.

The sound of glass crashing into glass sent her cat tearing from the room with a screech.

"Are you okay?" he asked, visually checking her, grateful not to see any blood as she could easily have cut herself on the broken pieces.

"My mother's village!" She pulled free of him and dropped to her knees, picking up the pieces.

"Those are just things. Are you okay? The baby?"

When he'd watched her falling back, his anger had

dissipated into fear. Fear that she might be hurt, that she might lose the baby.

Abby ignored his questions about her well-being and righted the table. She picked up the church first, noted the missing steeple, the chip at the base. She dug her fingernail into the chipped area and took a deep breath, then continued to pick up piece after piece.

Dirk knew that she connected the decorations with her family, with the connection the three of them had once shared.

He bent to help her, picking up the pieces of the train set and placing them back on the righted table, carefully reconnecting the track, the train engine and cars. Two of the houses were intact, so was the schoolhouse. The carousel had a tiny chip at the base. All the other village houses had larger breaks.

Dirk took her hands into his. "Sit down, Abby. This is only upsetting you. I'll do the rest, save what can be salvaged."

"No. I think you've already done enough, don't you?" Her chin lifted. Her eyes blazed, blazed so intently that Dirk winced. He'd never seen that anguish, that pain, that accusation in Abby's eyes before.

"I didn't do this, Abby." But he hadn't been innocent. He'd been so wrapped up in his own emotions over his family's "surprise" that he hadn't considered Abby's emotions, hadn't acknowledged that she'd been trying to do something good by having his family there. Instead, he'd attacked the moment they'd walked out the door.

"No, I did this," she admitted, glaring at him. "I ruined my mother's Christmas village."

A coldness had crept into Abby's voice. A coldness he'd never heard from her. A coldness that held finality.

Her fingers clasped tightly the church steeple she held. She looked ready to snap into as many pieces as the village collection had.

She looked like she wanted to snap him into a zillion pieces and toss him out with the trash.

Abby didn't say anything more. She couldn't. Her throat had swollen shut with emotion. Her voice gone. Perhaps for ever.

She stared at the church's steeple in her shaking hands. Her entire insides shook. Her mother's Christmas village. Broken.

How could she have been so stupid as to fall into the table? How could she have been so stupid as to fall in love with a man who could never love her back?

"Abby?"

She sucked in a breath, knowing she couldn't just keep sitting here, staring at the shattered remains of the only tangible things she had of happier times, of her childhood.

The damage was done. There was no undoing it. She'd make do with the best she could, to repair the pieces she could repair. Try not to wonder if fate wasn't trying to tell her something.

That she might dream of the wonderful Christmas village scenario with Dirk, but all she was going to get was shattered dreams, and the sooner she accepted that, the less she'd have her hopes crushed.

"These are just things. You still have your memories of the Christmases with your parents. That's what's important."

Hearing Dirk say that made something snap inside Abby. Something that perhaps had been on edge from the moment she'd found out she was pregnant. From the moment she'd realized she'd never have her happily-ever-after dream. Never have magical Christmases of her own. Never have what her parents had had. Tonight, watching him with his family, had shattered all hope.

"How dare you call my mother's Christmas village 'things'?" she accused. "You, the man who could care less about his family."

"I care about my family."

She rolled her eyes at him. "You have an odd way of showing it."

"You don't understand my relationship with my family."

"Your family doesn't understand your relationship with them. Nor do they like it. God, you are so lucky to have a family to love you, but you know what? You don't deserve them, Dirk."

His jaw worked as he regarded her. "My relationship with my family is none of your business."

Unable to sit still another moment, she stood, glared down at him. "You're right. It's not. I'm just pregnant you're your child. A fact you haven't bothered to share with your family."

He stood, did some glaring of his own. "I thought you didn't want anyone to know."

"Great excuse, but we're not talking about anyone. We're talking about your family. Our baby's family." She'd never wanted to shake another human being before, but at that moment she wanted to shake Dirk. To jar some sense into him. "Are you embarrassed by me? Or were you not planning on telling them about me ever?"

Oh, God. Was that what the problem had been tonight? Dirk hadn't wanted his family to know about her? Hadn't wanted them to know he'd knocked up some naive nurse who'd fallen in love with him at first sight? Oh, God. She had fallen in love at first sight. Just as her parents had. Only Dirk hadn't fallen in love with her. He didn't even want his family to know she existed, had been a jerk because she'd invited them for Christmas dinner.

"It's not like that." He looked as if he'd like to wrap his fingers around her and do some shaking of his own.

"They don't understand how I feel. No one does."

Which said it all. Said exactly where she fit into the grand scheme of things. She'd given and given to him. Of her time and her heart. And although Dirk had given of his time, had helped her at her volunteer stints, he hadn't given her of his heart. Not once.

"Maybe it's because you keep your heart locked up inside and won't let anyone close, including your family."

"You don't know what you're talking about."

Abby just stared at him.

His look of annoyance grew. "You have no idea how much trouble you've caused me by inviting them here."

Trouble as in they'd be asking about her?

"Well, I'm sorry to inconvenience you."

His jaw clenched, and he exhaled slowly. "Quit misreading everything I say."

"Or maybe, for the first time, I'm reading everything the right way," she said, knowing in her heart that it was true. She'd believed in Dirk's inner goodness. Had even believed that he'd come around regarding Christmas.

She really had been naive.

If not for her pregnancy, Dirk wouldn't be there. It was only his sense of responsibility that kept him coming round. Which wasn't nearly enough to base a future on.

Not nearly enough for her heart.

Abby longed to sob at her loss, but she wouldn't cry in front of him, wouldn't let him see how much she hurt. Instead, she turned her back toward him and went to the sofa and collapsed onto the plush upholstery.

"Leave, Dirk. I don't want you here." She hadn't known she was going to say the words, but once they left her lips she knew they were right, the only words she could say. Just like the Christmas village, her dreams, any hope of a future between them was shattered.

Silent, he walked over and sat down on the opposite end of the sofa. "You don't want me to go."

She gawked at his audacity. "Actually, I do. I saw a side of you tonight I never want to see again. You have no idea how lucky you are to have those people. They love you and want to be a part of your life."

"They are a part of my life."

"On the periphery perhaps."

"I've already told you, I talk to them routinely."

"About what? The weather? Sports? What is it you

talk to them about? Because I got the impression they didn't know quite what to say to you tonight."

"There were no conversational lulls."

"No, there weren't, but no thanks to you."

"I warned you that I wasn't big on company."

"Family is not the same thing as company. Family is everything." But not to Dirk. He'd lost the only family that mattered to him, couldn't see what was within his reach. And Abby had had enough. More than enough. She leapt from her sofa, flung open her front door. "Get out of my house, Dirk."

"Abby—"

"Leave!" she shouted. "And don't ever bother me again."

Without another word, he gave her one last angry look, then left.

Abby started a hep lock while Dirk shined a light into their patient's eyes.

Since he'd left her house the night before, she'd been fighting melancholy. She'd hoped he'd say he wanted to change, that he wouldn't leave, that he planned to spend Christmas Day with her. Every day with her for the rest of his life. But she'd known better.

With as much time as they'd spent together over the last week, she'd thought she wouldn't be alone this Christmas, had believed deep in her heart that she'd spend the day with Dirk. How could she have been so foolish as to get her hopes up? Her hopes had been higher than the North Pole.

What would Dirk do today? Sleep? Flip through television channels? Pretend it was no different from any other day of the year? He wouldn't be driving to his mother's for Christmas, wouldn't be embracing the wonderful family she envied. More the pity for him.

But that wasn't her problem. Not any more. She'd meant what she'd told him. She didn't want him in her life. Not when he refused to acknowledge that what they'd shared had been more than friendship. Not when he refused to open his heart to love again. To open his heart to his family.

Which was why she'd ignored his phone calls today. Why she'd ignored his attempts to talk to her tonight. What was left to be said between them?

She loved Christmas.

He hated Christmas.

She loved family.

He'd shut his out.

Could they be any further apart? She didn't think so.

"How did you fall?" Dirk asked the patient, pulling Abby back to the present. She bit the inside of her lip. She had to stay focused just a little while longer. Her shift was almost at an end. She could do this. Would do this. Then she'd talk to the nurse supervisor about having her schedule changed, changed to dates when she wouldn't have to work with Dirk.

"My wife was complaining about the angle of the star on top of the Christmas tree. I climbed a stepladder, and it tipped."

Dirk's lips compressed into a tight line. Clearly, he blamed Christmas for the man's tragedy. Was it easier for him to blame the holidays than to accept that accidents happened? He'd sure been quick enough to point out that accidents occurred when it had been her village pieces involved.

Village pieces that she'd painstakingly spent the day trying to glue back together.

"Do you recall how you landed? What you hit? How your weight was distributed?"

"It happened kind of fast, Doc." The man scratched his head with the hand Abby didn't have stabilized. "I know I hit my head." The pump knot on his forehead attested to that. "And my right ribs are sore."

"This happened about eight last night?"

The man nodded.

"What made you decide to come to the hospital this morning?"

"I woke up and couldn't breathe. I think that's what woke me."

"Are you still short of breath?"

The man nodded. "Not as badly as at the house. My wife says I had a panic attack."

"Your oxygen saturation is ninety-two percent. That's not too bad," Dirk explained. "But it's not as high as it should be in an otherwise healthy person either. I'm going to order a few tests just to check you out and make sure you haven't fractured any ribs or worse."

"Worse?"

"Fall injuries can result in serious damage to a person's body."

The man nodded. "Tell me something I don't know."

As always, Dirk responded to his patient, making Abby wonder how he could smile so sincerely at a virtual stranger and not his own kin. "Maybe you should stay off ladders for a while, too. Ask someone to help you with anything that requires climbing."

"Tell that to my wife. She has no patience and had to have that star straightened before the kids and grandkids show up in the morning for Christmas celebrations."

Finishing what she was doing, Abby excused herself and disappeared out of the bay.

The moment she finished giving report, she rushed away, determined to somehow find joy in the most magical day of the year.

Her favorite day of the year.

His least favorite day of the year.

A day she'd spend alone yet again.

Christmas Eve shouldn't be a busy night in the emergency room, but this one was. Midnight had come and gone, so technically Christmas morning had arrived.

The only thing Dirk liked about Christmas was it meant the end was near. The end of the season, the decorations, the smells, the aggravation and harassment from family.

Yes, the signal that the end of the season was near was the best part of Christmas Day.

Or it had been.

Now he wasn't so sure. Somehow he'd tangled thoughts of Abby up with Christmas and the thought of the end put his insides in a viselike grip.

The end of Christmas. The end of his relationship with Abby. No, he wouldn't accept that. Not under the circumstances.

God, his family would be ecstatic when they found out she was pregnant. How many times had they attempted to set him up with someone when he'd lived in Oak Park? How many times had they told him to find someone new and start over? How many times had they called to say how much they'd liked Abby, what a great cook she was, what a warm house she'd had, what a generous person she'd seemed? And he'd let them, because Abby's accusations had kept playing over and over in his head.

None of his family had understood that he hadn't wanted a new start, that he'd wanted his old life, a life that had been snatched away.

A life that had ended on the day his wife and daughter had died. Dirk had buried himself right along with them.

He hadn't been happy in years. Hadn't even really wanted to be. He'd preferred to wallow in his grief.

Until Abby.

In moving away, he had started over.

Quite frankly, that had scared the hell out of him. Had put him on the defensive. Had caused mixed emotions to surge. Emotions that made him want to cling to Abby and the hope she gave him. Emotions that made him want to pack up his bags and get out of Dodge. Emotions that had made him hold her at arm's length, just as she'd nailed him for doing to his family.

But he and Abby had a baby on the way.

A baby.

A precious new life that he and Abby had made.

When she'd fallen into her Christmas village table, he'd only been able to think of her safety, their baby's safety. Maybe he could have righted the table had he gone for it instead, but all he'd been concerned about had been keeping Abby from falling to the floor.

Because he wanted to keep her safe. Wanted to keep their baby safe.

He'd left when she'd asked him to, seeing she had been too upset to have the talk they needed to have, sensing that the emotions of both of them had been running too high. He'd been fine on his drive home. Fine when he'd walked through the front door. But when he'd crawled into his bed, alone, he'd done what he hadn't done in years. Not since right after Sandra and Shelby's accident. He'd been fairly positive there were no tears left inside him. The night the woman and her daughter died in the E.R. had been his first clue he might be wrong. He'd felt a crack in the protective wall that guarded his heart. Making love with Abby had sent a whole lot of bricks tumbling to the ground. Bricks he'd needed to keep himself safe.

But with Abby, she came first. Her and their baby. In that, she'd bulldozed right through the barriers around his heart, leaving him vulnerable.

Leaving him exposed to her warmth. Exposed to needing her. He'd been fighting to keep from making love to her every second they were together but as much as he'd enjoyed the passion they'd shared, he hadn't enjoyed how much he'd needed her, how connected he'd felt to her, how much he'd hurt if something happened to Abby.

She'd been right about him. He had kept his family at a distance. Had kept them at arm's length. How could he not? He'd always been the strong one in the family, but after Sandra and Shelby's deaths, he hadn't been strong.

He'd hated them seeing him that way.

Hated anyone seeing him that way.

So he'd shut them out.

No wonder they'd held an intervention.

He'd needed one. And more.

He'd needed Abby, so much so that he'd tried to hold her at arm's length, too, for fear of loving again, of possibly losing that love again.

Need had won out. Need and so much more.

He loved Abby. And wanted to risk holding her and the baby they'd made close to his heart.

But judging by the way she hadn't returned his calls, had all but ignored him since her arrival at shift change, he might have realized too late.

God, he couldn't lose Abby. In her, he'd found his salvation. Had found himself again.

If he'd lost her, he had no one to blame except himself. But he refused to accept that she wouldn't forgive his ignorance.

It was Christmas. A day of miracles. A day meant to be with the ones you loved. Somehow, he'd show Abby he could be the man she and their child needed.

A man who could be whole and start living again.

A man he desperately wanted to be.

Abby's man.

If he had to go to drastic measures to make that happen, then so be it.

CHAPTER THIRTEEN

IF EVER Abby would forgive him, this had to be the way. Hell, he hoped he wasn't wrong. Otherwise he was going to look like the biggest idiot who'd ever walked the face of the earth.

Which didn't bother him near as much as the thought of not winning Abby's forgiveness, of winning her love and trust.

It had taken him several hours to make arrangements for what he wanted to do.

But, finally, here he stood. Most likely she'd already gone to bed, would sleep for several hours.

Maybe it was wrong of him, but Dirk helped himself to the hide-a-key she'd told him where to find on the day he'd knocked and knocked without her answering.

Her house was quiet. Just as he'd expected it to be.

Not even Mistletoe was anywhere to be seen.

Quietly, closing the front door behind him, Dirk set into play what he hoped would show Abby everything in his heart.

"Meow."

Abby groaned, rubbed her face at where a paw

swatted at her. "Go back to sleep, Mistletoe. Didn't you get the memo? I'm going to sleep through Christmas this year."

"Meow." Another swat at her face.

Abby rolled onto her side, pulled her pillow over her head, hoping to gain a few more minutes of sleep before having to get up and face the reality of another Christmas spent alone.

That's when she heard another noise.

What was that? Music? Singing?

She stretched, pushing the pillow away from her head and straining to hear.

Definitely Christmas music.

Coming from somewhere in her house.

She had not left music on.

She knew she hadn't.

Someone was in her house.

Panic squeezed at her throat. Then, climbing out of her bed, she laughed at herself. What? A burglar had broken in and put on Christmas music? Right.

She must still be asleep, be dreaming.

Either that or Dirk had used the hide-a-key and if that was the case, she knew she was dreaming.

Dirk wouldn't be playing Christmas music.

But apparently someone would. Maybe Danielle had taken pity on her and come over to surprise her.

Tiptoeing down the hallway, Abby rubbed her eyes, certain she wasn't seeing clearly. Mixed emotions hit her at the sight of the man arranging Christmas packages under her tree.

The man she'd told to get out and not to come back.

How dared he come into her house and, well, whatever it was he was doing?

"I should have you arrested for breaking and entering."

At the sound of Abby's voice, Dirk turned from where he worked. Hell, he hadn't finished with what he'd wanted to do.

Still, he'd made great headway.

"Ho. Ho. Ho." Yes, he sounded stupid even to himself, but he had a lot riding on this. He'd seen the look in Abby's eyes, had seen that she'd given up on him. It was going to take a desperate act to win her back. This stunt was about as desperate as desperate got. He wished he'd been able to finish. "You're not supposed to be out of bed yet."

Her glare didn't let up. "You need to leave."

He'd meant to change into her father's Santa suit, had meant to give her the kind of Christmas Day she longed for, one like her parents had shared. "I will, but let me finish what I came to do first."

She crossed her arms over her flannel-pajama-covered chest. She glanced around the room, took in the presents he'd arranged, the Santa suit he had draped across the back of the sofa.

"What are you doing?"

"Delivering presents." Lots and lots of presents. Packages of various shapes and sizes were brightly wrapped and overflowing beneath the tree. It had cost him a small fortune to hire the personal shoppers to find stores open on Christmas morning, but if you were willing to spend enough, a person could do most anything.

Even do major Christmas shopping on the great day itself.

"Why would you do that? You don't even like Christmas." She stood in the doorway, staring at him as if she really had caught Dr. Seuss's Grinch stealing her Christmas rather than him in jeans and a T-shirt and a bundle of good intentions.

Obviously, he'd become overzealous when he'd turned on the Christmas tunes, thinking she was tired enough that the low music wouldn't disturb her and she'd sleep a few more hours. He'd just have to go forward as things were and pray for the best, pray for Abby to love him.

"Women aren't the only ones allowed to change their minds. Apparently I just needed to be reminded of the real meaning of the holiday."

"Oh, you needed that all right," she scoffed, eyeing him suspiciously. "So you've supposedly changed your mind about Christmas? Why?"

"You."

"Me?" This time she laughed with a great deal of irony. "I changed your mind about Christmas?"

"You changed my mind about everything, Abby. About life. My life. And the life I want with you."

This had to work. If Christmas magic didn't open Abby's eyes to the man he wanted to be for her, nothing would.

Abby crossed the room, stood next to him, but didn't sit, just stared at him with her forehead creased. "What about Sandra? Shelby? You still love them."

"You'd have me not love them?"

"No," she began hesitantly.

"I realize that part of my life is in the past, Abby.

I've accepted that. I'm ready to move on to the future. With you."

She glanced away, closed her eyes. "That's too bad, Dirk, because I don't trust you with my future."

He winced, but wasn't ready to admit defeat. Not when he was battling for the most important part of his life.

"Someone once told me that Christmas Day was the most magical day of the year. A day when miracles can happen." He prayed some of that Christmas magic would shine on him, would help Abby to see how much he loved her. "Trust me, Abby. I won't let you down. Never again."

She didn't say anything for a few moments then met his gaze warily. "How can I believe you? How can I know this isn't some ploy out of a sense of responsibility because I'm pregnant?"

Dirk's ribs squeezed his lungs. He'd hoped she'd say that she did trust him with her heart. That she wanted him and wanted to be a family with him and their baby.

Instead she looked at him with distrust shining in her hazel eyes. God, he'd been such a fool. How many times had Abby opened up her heart to him and he'd pushed her away out of fear? Fear of feeling again. Fear of loving and losing that love. Fear of feeling because with feeling came the risk of pain.

But there came a point when a man had to overcome his fears, had to risk that pain, had to risk rejection, because the alternative wasn't acceptable. Regardless of the risk of pain, not telling Abby the truth wasn't acceptable.

He took her hand in his. "You've had me from the moment we met, Abby. I tried fighting it, but I think I fell for you in the E.R. that first night. I know I wanted you in that instance. And every instance since."

Her gaze lowered to their interlocked hands, then lifted back to his. "Why are you saying these things? Why now?"

"Because I can't bear the thought that I might have lost you. Tell me you'll give me a chance to prove to you that I can be the man of your dreams."

A tear trickling down her cheek, she closed her eyes. "I didn't really wake up, did I? I'm still asleep and am dreaming."

Dirk lifted her hand to his lips, pressed a kiss to her fingertips. "Then don't wake up quite yet, because this dream is far from over. You have a lot of presents to open."

As if hearing Dirk say he wanted to be the man of her dreams wasn't enough to convince Abby that she was dreaming, the number of packages under her tree clinched the deal.

Never in her life had she had so many presents.

But why was he doing this?

Sitting on the floor, she picked up a box, shook it prior to carefully unwrapping it to reveal a beautiful aqua-colored baby blanket.

He'd bought a gift for their baby. For her. God, could he be serious about wanting to share a future?

Running her fingers over the soft, fuzzy material, she lifted her gaze to his. "This is beautiful."

He reached for the next present and handed it to her.

They repeated the process until she was surrounded with baby items. Some pink. Some blue. Some a mixture of pastels.

"You've been busy," she mused, biting into her lower lip, trying to decipher the meaning behind his gifts.

"I had help, but don't hold that against me." He gave a crooked grin. "Even Santa utilizes elves."

"Ah," she said, not quite believing he'd gone to so much trouble to bring her Christmas alive, to give her a magical day despite the fact they'd argued the last time they'd really talked, that she'd told him to leave. "Thank you, Dirk. I love everything."

She did. Not only because these were the first baby items for their child but because they'd come from Dirk. But what did all this mean? Why was he here? Giving her presents?

"Do you, Abby?"

She lifted her gaze to his in question.

"Love everything, that is?"

Abby's breath caught at the intensity in his blue eyes. At the vulnerability she saw shining there.

No protective walls. No barriers. No hanging on to the past. Just a man asking if she loved him.

A man who she loved with all her heart, but…

Glancing away when she didn't immediately answer, Dirk scratched his chin. "Um…" His voice broke slightly. "Better let me check my bag. Seems like there might be another present for you."

Abby wanted to stop him, to explain her pause, to ease what had put that break in his voice, but the moment had passed and she wondered if some of those fallen walls had been re-erected.

"You shouldn't have."

"Might not want to shake this one," he warned, causing Abby's curiosity to grow as she took the package.

She unwrapped the present, lifted her gaze to his, and caught her breath at what she saw reflected in his eyes.

He hadn't re-erected any walls, had left his heart bare for her to see, for her to take if she wanted.

She swallowed, glancing back down at the gift in her hands. "I can't believe you had someone find this for me."

"Actually, I had this one in my truck on Saturday night," he explained. "I'd meant to give it to you after our quiet dinner."

"Only we didn't have a quiet dinner." She pulled the piece from the box, carefully removed the protective wrapping, stared in amazement at the antique village piece. A piece that matched her mother's pieces. How had he known? And that he'd bought it before the crash made it all the more special. He wasn't trying to replace something he felt responsible for breaking. He was giving her something from the heart, giving her something because he'd known it would mean something to her, would make her happy.

"I love it," she whispered, leaning forward to kiss his cheek and hoping he couldn't tell she was choking back tears.

"And I love you, Abby."

She almost dropped the house. "Dirk?"

"I love you, Abby," He repeated words sweeter than any melody. "With all my heart. I didn't think I'd ever love again, that I could ever love. But I do. I love you.

And our baby. Please forgive me. I've been such a fool, wasted so much time we could have been together."

Taking a moment to steady her nerves, she put the house back into its box, took a deep breath. "Tell me again."

"I've been a fool—"

"Not that part," she interrupted, meeting his gaze, amazed at the emotion reflected there. "Tell me you love me again, Dirk. Please."

Eyes shining with everything Abby had ever hoped to see in a man's gaze, he took her hand into his, lifted it to his lips. "I love you, Abby. Completely. Always. For ever."

"I love you, too." She wrapped her arms around him, leaned in to kiss him, to show him everything in her heart.

But rather than take her into his arms and kiss her, he held her hands and stared into her eyes, looking almost nervous as he slid his hands into a jeans pocket and pulled out a small box, snapped it open. "Marry me, Abby."

"What?" An earthquake hit right in the pit of Abby's stomach. One whose aftershocks caused wave after wave of emotion to crash through her.

She stared in awe at the marquis-cut diamond reflecting the multicolored lights from the tree.

"Agree to be my wife. To share your life with me. To share all your Christmases with me. Always."

Abby couldn't believe her ears but, looking into his sincere eyes, she knew he was serious, knew he really did love her. No way would Dirk Kelley be pulling that ring free of its box and slipping it onto the third finger of her left hand otherwise.

She stared down at the ring, at where he held her hand. Could this really be happening?

"What about Sandra? Shelby?" she asked, not quite able to accept that her dreams might be coming true.

"They'll always be a part of my past, a part of who I am. But you are my future, Abby. You and our baby."

"I would never ask you to forget them, Dirk."

"I know you wouldn't, Abby. That's just one of the many reasons I love you. That and how you see the good in everything, including a man who'd lost track that there was anything good left in him."

"There's so much good in you, Dirk. Anyone who'd ever seen you with a patient would know that." She brushed her fingers across his cheek.

"But only you saw. Only you believed in me when I didn't believe in myself. All I knew was that from the moment we met I felt different, alive for the first time in years. You put breath back into my dying body, Abby. Say you'll let me love you always."

"Yes," she whispered, tears brimming in her eyes. "Oh, yes, Dirk."

This time Dirk took her into his arms, kissed her so thoroughly she'd have sworn she must be wearing that halo made of mistletoe, made love to her so thoroughly she'd swear they rocked the Christmas tree.

"Hey, Abs?" Dirk said much later, holding her against him.

"Hmm?"

A sheepish look shone on his face. "Your house wasn't the only place on Santa's list."

Realization hit her and Abby's heart swelled with love and pride of this wonderful man who'd truly opened his heart. "We're going to your family's for Christmas?"

He nodded. "I've got some making up for the past to do. Especially to my mother."

"What time are we supposed to be there?"

He brushed her hair away from her face, pressed a kiss against her temple. "They don't know we're coming, so whenever we arrive will be okay."

She wrapped her arms around him, kissed the corner of his mouth, excited at the magic filling the day. "Your mother is going to be so happy when you walk through that door, Dirk."

"She's going to be even happier when I tell her our news."

"That we're getting married?"

"That she's getting a new grandbaby for Christmas." He smiled wryly then shrugged. "And that she's getting her son back, along with a daughter-in-law who he loves more than life itself."

She hugged him, so proud of how far Dirk had come. "Your family is going to be so excited to see you."

All her dreams were coming true. She was getting a family. Dirk's family. And most importantly, she was getting the man she loved and who loved her. Dirk.

He grinned. "Yeah, and you know what? I'm going to be excited to see them, too, and to see their faces when I hand out their gifts."

"Gifts?" Abby raised her brow in question. "What did you get them?"

"Bought each one of them a *Dummies Guide to Holding an Intervention* and wrote a message, letting them know how much I appreciate them and that they have my permission to intervene anytime deemed necessary."

Abby laughed. "Oh, Dirk, you really are serious about this, aren't you?"

His brow lifted. "Did you doubt me?"

Had she? No, she trusted him with her heart, with their baby's heart. He loved them. She could see that truth in his eyes, feel it in his touch, in the way he'd cherished her while they'd made love. "Not in the slightest. You're a good man."

"I'm your man, Abby." He smiled in a way that reached in and touched her very being. "I'll always be your man. Merry Christmas, sweetheart."

"The best." But she suspected only the beginning of even happier times when she and Dirk celebrated the holidays with their baby, with his family—their family. "Merry Christmas to you, too. You've given me so much."

"Not nearly as much as you've given me. You gave me back my life, my heart, my family, my belief in Christmas." He placed his palm over her belly, caressing her there. "I love you and our baby."

Knowing Dirk had made her Christmas dreams come true, would continue to make them come true every day for the rest of their lives, Abby rolled over to kiss her very own Santa all over again.

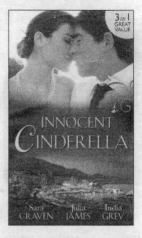
4_ST_6